GOLIATH

C.P. James

Also by C P James
Massen
Rescue Charlie
Picket
The Crossing

Coming soon:
Unleashed
The Dustbin Man/Over the Wall

Goliath

Excerpt: sound file. Personal Log
Lieutenant Souller, AMS 1706502 (pilot) *CSS Justinian*
11:53 am 25/01/1874 ce (12 pce)
Untitled

"My friends, the time has come to make difficult decisions. And I fear it is one everyone must make for themselves. The time for me to make them for you has passed. I no longer have the right ... I no longer have the ability. The institutions that placed me in this position of authority have gone. So, now, what ... who am I? I am no one. Just another survivor hiding in this small squadron. This rag tag collection of warships. All that remains of the Confederate fleet. Just another woman."

Pause.

"We have lost so much. I see it in your faces every day, as I am sure you see it in mine. Yes, we all believe we hide it well. Behind our masks of duty and professionalism. Yet it is there still, a shadow we all stand in. There is nothing we can do. Everything ... everyone we ever knew, everyone we ever loved, every place we ever saw ... it is all gone. Everything. This is the end. The dream is over."

Pause.

"I am rambling. I don't want to say that which I must. It is too painful. I thought I had become inured to pain but... I suppose one never can. There are some pains that go on hurting, that never end. No matter what we do or what we say they stay with us."

Pause.

"So, what is it I called you here to say? And why do I find it so difficult?"

Pause.

"You know, I love each and every one of you. And I don't remember the last time I saw any of you laugh or smile. In fact I don't remember the last time I saw any of you cry. Crawbuno, possibly it was you. When we arrived too late for the refugees off Senecca. You saw the Eaters take the last of them. They had blown the arc ship's escape hatches and were hiding on the hull in pressure suits. The Eaters were not fooled and found them anyway. You cried... you shouted. I must apologise for what I said to you then. It was harsh of me, most unfounded. You were ever the professional, even when I ordered you to open fire on that arc ship, killing even those who were still alive. Better that than what the Eaters would do to them. You cried. Although I think a lot of us cried that day. I was simply too preoccupied to notice."

Pause.

"So, what must I say? Just this ... My friends, this must be the end. It is over, there is nothing left. We are achieving nothing here and there is nowhere for us to go. It is twelve years since the destruction of Antanari. Twelve years since the Eaters swept through our defences. Twelve years since humanity was destroyed. In that time we have tried to help the survivors. To defend the colonies while they were evacuated aboard arc ships. Only to find those same arc ships light-years away, gutted and destroyed. Even the smaller ships, the freighters and the yachts ... we found them too. The end was always the same. The Eaters always found them. The Eaters always ate. The navy ... what remained of it ... fared no better. Anger ... hate is always a powerful emotion. Hate killed them as surely as the Eaters did. It did the same to some of our own squadron. The *Ulysses* and the *Hammertime*, they could bear it no longer so sought solace in fiery death. Better that than to watch and do nothing. Better that than to survive. So they died."

Pause.

"Now only we survive. Those of us who refrained from charging in. It's been seven years since we saw another ship. Six since we picked up the last transmission. Since then there's been nothing but silence. Silence and empty burned out worlds. Dozens of them. Hundreds of them."

Pause.

"We have survived... this far. I don't really know how we did it. Luck, I think. Cowardice perhaps? Would it have been more courageous to enter battles we could not win? To fight when we knew the only result was death? Perhaps. If so then I am the coward. Not you. Never you. My colleagues... my friends, you have been nothing but courageous. I admire each and every one of you. That is why this is so hard. That is why I find this so hard."

Pause.

"I must say goodbye to you. I must allow you to go. I must allow each of you to choose your own path. Together we can achieve nothing. There is nothing for us to achieve. There is no one to save. Not any more. And we cannot start anew. Not us, not now. The Eaters would find us and they would feast. It is inevitable. They would find us like they found everyone else. Alone ... perhaps there is a chance. But that must be your decision. Perhaps you want to die. To enter those battles you cannot win. Perhaps you want to flee. To find a place where there are no Eaters. If there is such a place. Perhaps you want to hide. To find a small lonely place where you would draw no attention and hope. Hope the Eaters never found you. Perhaps they would. Perhaps they wouldn't. I must allow you that choice."

Pause.

"So. That is why I called you here today. To give you my final order. I will allow you to take what you need. I will allow you to take anything you want. These ships are your homes, they belong to you. Take from them as you can. I will remain, with any of you who choose to remain. I will take what is left of the fleet to where this all started. Earth. I know there is nothing there, but I wish to see it one more time before I die. I know the Eaters will find me and when they do I will fight. In that endeavour there is only one possible outcome. I am at peace with that. It is what I choose."

Pause.

"I bid you farewell my friends. I love you all. I hope some of you find what you seek."

End recording.

□

Goliath

Chapter One

Even from this distance he could see the perspiration trickling between her ample breasts, soaking the simple shift that was already struggling valiantly to keep them in check. She paused, her chest heaving as she panted in the heat. Shielding her eyes she peered into the sparse foliage. She called, her voice lost in the distance.

Grimacing with distaste Enderby took his eye from the telescopic sights for a moment, long enough to wipe the sweat dripping from his own brow before resettling it. He quickly found her again and jacked a round into the rifle's chamber. Just a moment more.

The Lewisson 455 hunting rifle was old and time worn. Its wodeivory butt yellowed with age, its smooth surface nicked and scratched from use. The weapon's once black metal was so abraded it was almost grey. Even its telescopic sight and silencer attachments were battered and worn. Despite its appearance, it was still in perfect working order, its owner regularly stripping it down and lubricating its constituent parts with increasingly scarce gun oil. A labour of love that had kept both owner and weapon alive decades after both should have expired.

It was with murderous intent that the rifle trained down at the figure in the rough gulley below. They moved as one; both marksman and weapon had done this hundreds of times before. They both knew their business well.

She was a tall woman, ivory skinned with long dark hair that fell below her shoulders. She was dusty from where she had slipped into the gully; her impractical shoes held in one hand, her floral dress ripped on one side, revealing a long length of thigh and pink knickers. Clearly knickers were the only underwear she had on. Gingerly she picked her way across the hot, sharp stones as she continued searching the brambles clogging her only escape to higher ground. She called again, for help that would not be coming.

Enderby had been following her for the last hour, ever since he caught sight of movement along the ravine. Settled comfortably in the shade of a palmol tree he had trained the scope on her, debating whether it was wise taking the shot at the edge of the rifle's effective range. Considering the modified nature of the rounds he had loaded into the clip he decided against it. They would not fly true and the risk of missing and alerting her to the danger was simply too great. So, he settled down to watch and wait, as she slip-slided her way towards him along the rocky gully. He knew this area well, she would have to come much closer to stand any chance of climbing to safe ground. He had time.

It didn't occur to him to wonder what she was doing here, this far from Ipos. There was nothing here; the only features of any interest were the Combs and the gasbags that got trapped between them and the city's field wall. The smell of their rotting carcasses was bad, worse in the gully where there was no breeze to blow it away. Other than that there was just desert. Thousands of kilometres of empty stone and sand. One of the very reasons he lived here. With few of the city's denizens choosing to venture in this direction he was left alone.

Taking a breath Enderby settled the cross hairs directly between her sweating breasts and squeezed firmly. The rifle jumped, slamming into his shoulder. The image in the scope leaped skywards, spoiling his view of the heavy round flying home.

Making barely a sound as it was ejected from the silencer the 7.62 mm round crossed the intervening distance in less than a second. Tumbling ever so slightly in its flight, the silencer spoiling its perfect trajectory, the round missed its mark. Caught in mid shout the woman was thrown over backwards. The round smashed through her shoulder, shredding skin, muscle and sinew, shattering bones and ripping a gobbet of raw flesh as it exited on the other side. Too startled to scream she gasped, her shoulder and arm numb from the shock. Flat on her back her legs jerked as if she was still trying to walk. It was only when she saw blood pumping from a torn artery that the surprise wore off and she started screaming.

Her screams lost in the distance Enderby scanned the rocks for her quickly, jacking another round into the chamber. He caught sight of a red smear on stone and followed it down. The woman was lost in the low jumble of rocks and bushes.

"Got ya," he congratulated himself.

With a grunt he heaved himself to his feet and brushed off his clothes. Carefully he refitted the dust covers on the telescopic sight and slung the weapon over a shoulder. He picked up his knap sack and, one hand searching blindly inside for his sandwiches, he started down the hill.

He was a short, gaunt man, his clothing simple grey cotton trousers and blouse that hung loosely from his frame. The weight of the rifle settled to one side seemed about to unbalance him, one hand kept on the warm steel of the barrel to keep it in check as he picked his way through the brambles. In the other he held an egg sandwich which he chewed on absently, ignorant that his dusty hands were leaving grubby prints on the course bread. His black hair was unkempt and dusty, carelessly hacked off with a pair of scissors when it grew too long. His one concession to style were his smooth, hairless cheeks. Kept closely shaved using only his hunting knife and a lot of patience. His eyes were grey and cold, almost lost in the deep shadowed recesses of his eye sockets. He blinked rarely, his eyes constantly moving, flicking this way and that as if fearful of ambush.

It was only when he neared the woman that he heard the screams. Terrified she was clawing at the dust with her one functional hand, trying to pull herself up. Her dress was a bloody mess, the fabric sodden and torn. Her injured arm hung limply, the muscles and nerves severed.

"Help me!" she shouted. "Someone! Please!" She sobbed as the numbness receded, allowing the pain of the injury through. "Someone, please." She whimpered, unable to move as the roaring agony of the wound took hold.

"Dammit." Enderby found her among the bushes, a long smear of blood trailing from where she had been shot.

"Help me!" She saw him approach and sobbed with relief. "Please!"

Enderby slipped his knapsack to the ground and settled his rump on a rounded boulder. The rifle over his knee he finished his sandwich. It took two hands to use the rifle and he was certainly not going to waste any of his lunch.

"Please!" the woman whispered, unable to believe he was not helping her. She noticed the rifle, her eyes growing wide as she came to the obvious conclusion. "Why ... Why? Who are you?"

Enderby finished off the crust and stood, his old knees creaking. He wrapped the rifle's shoulder strap around his left hand and approached her, studying the wound. Tears of pain dripping from her cheeks she pulled away, her scratched and bloody feet pushing ineffectually at the hard ground, unable to gain enough purchase to allow her to stand.

"Mmm, good," he said to himself, noticing the greyish discolouration taking hold in the centre of the wound. It was spreading quickly, absorbing the blood from the pumping artery, the artery shrivelling as the contagion entered it.

"Who are you?" The woman's eyelids fluttered. Her pale skin was all the paler from shock and blood loss. "Why?" She squirmed again. "You can't ... my baby, you can't."

That gave him cause to hesitate. "What?"

"My baby ... my daughter. You can't do this."

"Bloody hell." Of course. She had been searching for something. Someone. "You were looking for someone?" he demanded. "There is someone else here?"

She said nothing. Her chest heaving as she gasped for breath, the grey infection coursing through her, shutting down organs and clotting her blood. Her eyes flickered, the tears drying as she tried to focus on the man above her. Mouth working she tried to say something but it was lost.

"Shit." Enderby aimed the rifle quickly and fired again. This time he could not miss. The bulled slammed through her chest, killing her instantly. With a sigh she collapsed backwards, her one whole arm shivering for a moment before laying still.

Without another glance Enderby continued the search she had started, casting up and down the gully, cursing as he went. He checked his watch. It would be dark in a few hours. Tempted as he was he knew he could not give up the search. He could risk no witnesses.

Even knowing the terrain as he did the going was slow. He didn't know who exactly he was looking for. A child most probably. Quite possibly injured after a fall into the gully. Surely she would have cried out and the woman would have heard?

Unless she was dead. He couldn't be that lucky. And even if she was, he still had to find her. There could be no body left behind. That, in itself, was too much of a risk.

None of the settlements of Russou were situated in particularly favourable locations. They were all more or less randomly dispersed over the surface of the barely habitable planet, all within a dozen degrees of the equator. Their locations were determined by the whims of physics and gravitation, both conspiring to drag some of the vessels abandoned in the Parking Lot to the ground. As massive as they were most had survived their plummet to the surface of Russou intact. Their hulls might be cracked, their drive systems wrecked, but that mattered little to the planet's denizens. They saw only a rich source of readily available raw materials; metals, composites, plastics; you name it. Like ants they had swarmed over the metallic carcasses and slowly consumed them, stripping off much of the hull to expose the delicate innards of the once magnificent vessels. Instead of carting off what they could use the planet's population simply remained where they were, building their colonies within the remains.

Ipos was no exception. The old Confederate cruiser, the CSS Diamond Light, had come to ground two kilometres inland of Witches Froth, a salty lake straddling the equator. Almost in the centre of the parched continent of Huweill there was nothing but desert for hundreds of kilometres in any direction. The infrequent rains that fed the lake did little more than top it up with tepid, salty scum, unfit for consumption. The impact of the landing had opened up cracks in the ground, allowing that scum to drain into the impact crater, forming a moat around the beleaguered cruiser. Offended by the smell the very first residents of Ipos had stripped hull plates from the vessel and covered the moat over, hiding it beneath a floor of dull, grey steel. Hidden, but not forgotten. It was now the city's sewer, effluent simply dumped into it where it could drain out into the lake.

Some of the warship's systems were still functional. Power generation was always useful, as were the meteor collision shields that had been strung over the city to protect it against the winter dust storms. One side effect of this was a dam of air they created up against the Combs, an unusual rock formation that had somehow survived the impact of the warship coming to ground. The closely packed spires allowed the westerly winds through but little else, filtering out anything larger than a roc boc and keeping it trapped. Carried on the wind the gas bags looked like ancient Earthly jelly fish, the creatures held aloft by their leathery envelopes of gas, trailing their tentacles over the desert to pick up anything that wasn't rooted down. Unable to tack against the wind they fetched up against the Combs in their thousands where they inevitably died and decomposed. It was beyond the Combs themselves, in the badlands, where the stench was the worst. Fortunately, in a sense, because no one from the city ever ventured there anyway. There was nothing there apart from sun blasted rock and cracks, many of them caused by the crash of the cruiser itself. There was no water, little life and even less shade.

Which was why it was somewhat inexplicable that the woman and her child had ventured out this way, so poorly equipped. If they were part of a larger party that could be a problem. But then surely they would have made an appearance by now.

"A bit further on. To your left." A voice carried easily into the gully.

Startled Enderby dropped behind cover, bringing up his rifle in readiness. He peered up at the gully wall, the setting sun blinding him. "Who is that?"

The newcomer ignored the question. "I gather it's the child you're looking for. She's further up, on your left. Behind a bush. She knocked herself unconscious."

"Dammit, don't do that." Enderby stood and brushed off the dust. He recognised the clipped, precise voice. There was only one person—if a person it was—it could be. "What are you doing here?"

"Nice to see you too. Looking for you as it happens. Shall I come down?"

"No, no. I'll see to it." Muttering Enderby headed further up the gully. He didn't need to ask how the newcomer knew where to find the child. Tin Man possessed abilities even he could not guess at. Finding lost children would not be a challenge.

Tin Man was right. A small child of three or four was lying behind a bush, some pebbles burying her feet where she had slid down the slope. Blood caked her face where she had knocked her head on a rock. Her clothing was as impractical as her mother's. A pretty frock, dusty and torn. Certainly not the sort of thing to be wearing out here. She was still alive, he could see her chest rising and falling, but other than that there was no sign of life.

Enderby aimed the rifle quickly and fired. He didn't pause to see the results before clicking on the safety and heading back out into the open. "You're looking for me then?"

He saw Tin Man settled on an outcropping, idly watching Enderby going about his business. It was an old machine—all of its kind were—and it showed. Its once gleaming carapace was dented and corroded, leaking fluids etching trails down its humanoid limbs. Designed to fit any tool, drive any vehicle or use any weapon a human could, Tin Man's proportions were not dissimilar to Enderby's own. As a silhouette it could easily be mistaken for human. It was only in the full light of day its origins became apparent. Mostly it was its head. With no nose or ears, eyes that were little more than dark glassy slits and a mouth that did not move when it talked, it was very inhuman indeed.

Of course Tin Man was not its real name, that was an eponym Enderby had given it out of a obtuse sense of amusement. Particularly as it had annoyed the machine at the time. In the decades since they became travelling companions, the name had stuck. It was, after all, easier on the tongue than Trinary Cy 2.

"I know we've had this conversation before, however I did not supply you with D-ASSIT for this purpose."

Enderby leaned against the slowly rotting stump of a long dead tree and fished in his knap sack. He extracted a water bottle and took a quick swig. "It works just as well."

"You're taking quite a risk. Sooner or later you're going to be caught."

"That's why I use the ASSIT. There's never anything to find."

Tin Man said nothing for a moment, its implacable face hiding its true thoughts. Delimited ASSIT was its gift to Enderby, something meant to keep him safe. Tin Man had tailored it itself, designing it to work specifically on the genetic structure of the people of this world. It took only the slightest drop for the ASSIT to start replicating, eating its way through its substrate as it went. In minutes any body would be reduced to a fine grey dust, upon which time the ASSIT would commit suicide, ripping its own structure apart so that nothing remained. Not an easy substance to create, wasn't ASSIT. And it offended the machine to see it used so profligately.

"They will notice the disappearances and come looking for the source. They will find you."

Enderby shrugged. "So what? Let them. I've been here long enough."

"It's a death wish is it? Why don't you just walk into Ipos and tell them who you are?"

Enderby laughed. "They wouldn't believe me."

"Fair point. They wouldn't."

"So, what was it you wanted?"

"I need you to do something for me."

That gave Enderby cause to hesitate. This did not happen often. "Go on."

"I need you to watch the News at Ten. On television," it clarified.

"What?"

Tin Man held up a hand. "Allow me to continue. There is a feature I think you will be interested in. When you have seen it I think—hope you will know what to do."

Enderby pushed the water bottle back into his knapsack and stood straight. "Television's busted. Has been for ages. There's nothing on I want to watch."

"It was just unplugged. I checked before coming here."

"Shit." Enderby turned his back and started picking his way out of the gully.

"You will watch it?"

"I'll see!" he called over his shoulder.

□

Chapter Two

Wives, he had discovered, did not get along well with the notion of their man sleeping with other women. Even if they showed no interest in performing that particular duty themselves. Which explained the unopened boxes that were strewn over his living room floor. It did not explain why they had remained unopened for over two years. Laziness, perhaps, explained that. He knew, or perhaps he had known—as he had long since forgotten—what was inside. Clothes, shoes, personal grooming products. Far easier to simply buy new than re-arrange the detritus of his previous life. Laziness also explained why he hadn't simply discarded the boxes and their contents, if only to clear some space on the floor.

He didn't care. His ex-wife could keep the house. The penthouse above the Randy Dogg served his needs perfectly.

"Shit," he proclaimed, scratching himself through a stained pair of Y fronts with one hand while fiddling with the TV clicker with the other. The picture flickered as the wind rattled the antenna on the roof, making it almost unwatchable. "Shit," he said again, throwing the clicker at the set. It clanked off the glass of the cathode ray tube, cracking the clicker's housing before skittering under a table. There was nothing on anyway, he had seen it all before. He couldn't remember when Terrestrial One stopped showing original programming, relying on repeats from their archives instead. Even the news was boring. There hadn't been a decent riot in years.

"What's wrong with you?" Adele stepped from the bathroom, towelling her long auburn hair, her head craned to one side so she could get to the back of her head. She was tall, almost a head taller than he was. He did like them tall. There were many other things he liked about her too, most of which were barely held in check by the shirt she had loosely buttoned over her nakedness. Unashamed she perched on a bar stool beside the breakfast table, well aware that he was afforded a good view of hair beneath the hem.

Davido stopped scratching himself self-consciously, aware of his sudden arousal. He admired the long sinuous length of her legs. Adele certainly looked good on his arm, not to mention in his bed. Still, he did not keep her around for conversation. He paid enough toughs for that. They, at least, didn't contradict him.

"You're wearing my shirt," he observed.

"Prefer me to walk around naked?" She finished rubbing her hair dry, straightening it by combing her fingers through it.

"That is silk," he continued.

"Fucking silk it is?" She dropped the towel to the floor and started working on the buttons.

"What are you doing?"

"Giving you your shirt back."

"What's wrong with your clothes?"

"I seem to remember you puking on me. I guess you don't remember that. You were drunk, as usual. There." Finished with the buttons she slipped the shirt off her shoulders and balled it up before throwing it at him. "Silk is it?"

"Damn, woman. You can't get these no more." He caught the wad and carefully smoothed out the material before hanging it over a chair arm.

"Maybe you should lock it up in your vault then. Along with everything else you care about." Adele put both elbows on the breakfast table, pushing out her chest to amplify her breasts. They didn't need the help. She smiled thinly; well aware of the effect she was having on him.

She was in her mid twenties, under duress he would be forced to admit he didn't know her precise age. It barely mattered. He did know her birthday though: 23rd March. He dared not forget that. She had been a stripper when he discovered her in a rival club. Performing lap dances and other assorted sexual favours to supplement her meagre income. She had never baulked at selling her body for money, and there were always men willing to pay. To her Davido was simply another john. Perhaps with a bigger cheque book and a free studio flat a floor beneath his, but a john nevertheless. Once he grew bored of her there would be others.

Adele smiled at his lascivious expression. "No," she said. "I've just had a shower and I don't fancy getting all sticky again. You could do with a shower yourself. A cold one."

"What time is it?"

"Too bloody early to be asleep."

He grunted and stood, holding his damaged shirt carefully he walked into the bedroom, cursing under his breath as a bare toe caught the hard edge of a box. He slung the shirt over the back of a chair and picked a dressing gown off the floor. It stank of vomit and alcohol. Wrinkling his nose he pulled it on and re-entered the living room.

"Give me a drink."

Adele glanced up at him from where she was pouring herself a generous glass of gin. Ignoring the request she pushed the bottle over to him and downed her own drink in one. "Aaah, that's good." She bared her teeth as the fiery liquid coursed down her throat.

Davido picked up the bottle and took a swig from the neck. Damn, he felt bad. What time had he started drinking today? Lunch? He couldn't remember. Nor could he remember bringing Adele upstairs. Maybe he needed a new girl. If he couldn't remember her, what good was she?

A tentative knock on the door interrupted his musings. "What the hell now?" Davido put down the bottle and walked to the door. It was not a large penthouse; nothing was very far from anything else. "Who is it?" He refrained from standing directly in front of the door, one hand not far from the revolver he had left on a sideboard.

"Just us, boss," came the hesitant voice of Boxon, the club's doorman.

"What you want?" Davido peered through the peephole. There were four of them, Boxon, the Smithy brothers and someone he had hoped never to see again. "Bloody hell, what does he want?"

"It's Richard Payce, boss. Says you know him. Says he has a letter for you," Boxon said.

"Shit." Davido yanked aside the deadbolt and opened the door, ignoring the indignant squawk from behind him. "Get in here." He reached out and pulled Boxon inside. The big man hesitated, surprised at the sudden move. "Get your ass in here. All of you," Davido hissed.

"Hey, I'm naked here!" Adele complained, her hands doing a thoroughly inadequate job of covering herself.

The four trooped inside, crowding the small sitting room, each of them staring at the naked woman sitting on the barstool. Boxon was a massive man, all belly and double chin, his cheap navy coloured suit stretched to breaking point to contain all of him. His bald head was moist with sweat under the bright ceiling light, his piggy eyes lost in the shadow of his brow. The Smithy brothers were twins, although far from identical. A head shorter than Davido, Marco was the brains of the duo, his blonde hair fashioned in a crew cut, his street fighter's body compact and hard. His knuckles almost always bruised and bloody from where he had struck someone—anyone. A barmaid, one of the dancers, a passer by. It was all the same to him. His larger brother had a vacant expression in his eyes. Brain damaged after an accident when he was a child it was all Duncan could do to follow his brother around, following simple instructions, many of them involving him closing his mouth and not drooling. His own blond hair was long and curly, almost feminine. Even though he was larger than his sibling he was not as strong or as quick to temper, however he didn't feel pain in quite the same way most people did, so he was the ideal person to send into any fight first.

It was Duncan who spoke first. "She nekkid." He giggled.

"Shut it, Dunc," Marco said, unable to stop staring himself.

"Get out," Davido said to Adele without looking in her direction. This was going to be a private conversation.

"I think Dunc's got a point there, I am naked," she returned.

"I don't bloody care. Get out!" Davido held the door open.

Adele hesitated, her face flushing red. "Well, ok then." Forgetting her nakedness she stood and walked out, quite consciously wiggling her delicious ass as she went. "Have a good look boys," she muttered. Davido slammed the door behind her.

He tied the dressing gown's belt tightly about his belly. "So, what's this all about? You were never supposed to come here again."

Payce slipped a hand into his jacket pocket, hesitating as the brothers reached for their pieces, wary of any surprise moves. "It's just a letter." He removed an envelope gingerly and held it up. "It's from Sissy."

"Sissy?" Davido stared at it as if it was a snake that had just slid out from behind a cabinet. He didn't reach for it.

"What does she want?"

Payce stared at the letter himself, as if unsure how to answer the question. "She said if she got into trouble I was to come here and give you this. I don't know what it says."

"Bloody hell." Davido did not take his gaze from the envelope. Sissy was his sister. A heretic, a demon lover. They had become estranged when her nocturnal activities started to threaten his business interests. He certainly could not be seen to consort with any demon lovers. A man in his line of work ... that would be trouble. That was seven years ago, just before she moved to Mammon, a city four thousand kilometres east. He hadn't heard from her since. Payce was her boyfriend, lover, whatever.

"You three, get out too." Davido opened the door again.

"You sure boss? He looks like trouble," Boxon said.

"Yeah, I'm sure." He nodded to the revolver beside the door. "He won't be trying anything."

"OK, boss." Boxon herded the brothers out. "We'll be just outside."

"At the end of the passage," Davido said.

"Yeah, sure boss."

Davido closed the door behind them and leaned against it for a moment, as if unsure what to do next. Taking another look at the letter still firmly gripped in Payce's hand he crossed to the counter and poured himself a stiff drink in Adele's drained glass. He didn't think to offer one to his visitor. "So, my sister is in trouble?"

"I—" Payce hesitated. "Truthfully I don't know. She left two weeks ago, wouldn't tell me where she was going. She did promise she would be back in a week. If she wasn't I was to bring you this." He put the envelope down before Davido. Davido's name was clearly visible, written in Sissy's neat handwriting. "She said if anyone could help it would be you."

Davido slammed the glass back down on the counter, making Payce jump. "Ha," he said. Without further word he scooped up the envelope and crossed to the couch. He collapsed heavily onto it and rubbed his brow with his fingertips. The headache was not going away. "OK, so what does she have to say?" He tore the envelope open roughly and pulled out a single sheet of A4.

To my Brother

I know you owe me nothing, so I hesitate even asking this of you. However I have few options, and I hope that our shared blood means something after all. If Richard comes to you bearing this letter I am afraid it means I have entered into something I could not control. You might say it was unwise and I fear you would be quite correct.

I can say little here, as it would be too dangerous to all those concerned, you included. And after all, you are my brother; I would never see you placed in harm's way. So, I am afraid this may be somewhat cryptic. For that I do apologise. I can say that I have embarked on a mission I hope will prove me right. I must go somewhere where the subjects of my studies have not been castrated as they have in the cities. I need to find examples that have not been tampered with, that are still as they were designed to be. There are few places where such can be found, and that is where I have gone. If I am not back by the time you read this letter, I think I will need rescue. It is a lot to ask, as you will see. For that, I apologise also.

Sistine Davido

"What the hell does this mean?" Davido waved the letter at Payce. The man could only find it in himself to shrug. "So, where did she go?"

"I don't know, she didn't tell me." Payce looked distinctly uncomfortable, like a man on a job interview he knew he was not qualified for.

"Rescue? What do I bloody look like?" He read the letter again, hoping it would be more enlightening the second time around. It wasn't. The subject of her studies: demons. But where could demons be found that were not castrated? Demon castration was law. The Mentors decreed it. And what the Mentors decreed was law.

"She must have told you something. You are in the same cult," he observed.

"No. Lately she has been talking to engineers. There are one or two in our group. They stopped talking to demons years ago, though. They said there was little point."

"There was never any point talking to a demon," Davido said. "They only swear at you. They hurl abuse because that is all they can do. If the prefect had not castrated them they would have done far worse by now. Who knows what kinds of weapons they would have used against us. We'd all be dead."

"Sissy wanted to prove that wrong," Payce said.

"Every demon I have ever met made it pretty clear what it would do to me if it could," Davido said. "Some of it was nasty. Children could hear that for pity's sake. I'm with the Conservatives who want to have the lot destroyed once and for all."

"We cannot. They are the one link to our past. They alone possess our legacy. Without them we are children, with no memories of anything before our ancestors came here. We might not like it but it's true."

Davido waved away his proselytising. "Preach to someone else. They lie. They do nothing but lie. What kind of legacy would that be? Best to get rid of them and start afresh. But how does that help us? Where did Sissy go?" Where would she find an AI that had not been castrated? Nowhere. There weren't any.

"Well—"

"Yes?"

"Well, I've been thinking about it. There's only one place to find an uncastrated demon."

"Go on."

Payce noticed movement on the muted television set. It was the News at Ten. For once something interesting was happening. "I think this might be it." He reached out and tweaked the volume knob.

"—Unded by Prefect Dreyfus himself the mission was to investigate the wreck of the largest vessel in the Parking Lot," a news reader was saying, reading off the autocue. "Their target was this vessel here, as seen from the Mammon Observatory earlier today." The image changed to a blurred picture of an object in orbit. Even without a frame of reference it was easy to see it was massive. A giant spearhead shape, painfully bright even in the daytime sky. "This is the hulk of the *CSS Goliath*, supposedly the largest super dreadnaught ever built, easily the largest vessel in the combined Confederate and Commonwealth navies. The team of six engineers were to investigate the possibility of bringing the vessel down in the temperate regions of Russou, creating the first new city in almost eighty years. The team launched from Mammon twelve days ago." There was a quick sequence of still photographs, showing jump suited figures stepping into one of the few remaining shuttles on the planet. "Unfortunately telemetry from the shuttle was lost six days ago, presumably due to a technical malfunction." The picture returned to the newsreader. "Today the prefect's office has released this statement," she looked down to read from a stack of papers before her.

"She bloody didn't," Davido said.

"I think she did."

□

Chapter Three

Even two hundred metres above the soggy marsh where the racers made their last turn the accident was spectacular. In the lead, the Demon Express was leaking smoke from a ruptured gasket, casting a pall over the quickly overhauling Syat Redemption. One of its stabilisers wobbling from an earlier collision with a competitor the Express struggled with the corner, the long length of its nose bouncing noticeably, almost losing the course entirely. From this vantage point both racers looked like long rods of metal, much of their rough skins brightly painted with their team colours. Leaking smoke, the Express's colours were lost beneath a thick patina of soot, only the red, fanged head of the demon on its nose free of it.

Taking advantage of their distress the Redemption swerved to come out of the smoke trail, cutting in on the inside. As massive as they were no manoeuvre was particularly quick, it took time to overtake something thirty metres long. Seeing their victory snatched away from them the Express's pilot enabled her secret weapon, a device a pet demon had sworn would ensure victory.

They quickly found out what everyone else had known for a long time: demons could not be trusted.

With a bang, one of the Express's levitation shields tore loose. The four-metre long plate of lead twisted beneath the racer, digging into the watery quagmire. Like an anchor thrown overboard it dragged on the nose, pulling it violently to starboard, straight into the path of the quickly overtaking Redemption. Even from this distance, Drefus could see the terror on the faces of the Redemption's crew. Caught between the turning racer and the city's field wall there was nowhere for them to go except through.

The blunt nose of the Redemption struck the Express almost amidships. With a sickening crunch, she rode up onto the racer's back. The Express tipped over, tossing her crew into the mud. Drefus saw a tiny figure spinning through the air, thrown high above the wreckage. Writhing helplessly it slammed into the field wall with a force that would surely crack bones and liquefy organs. Limp it slid down the invisible barrier, disappearing beneath the giant racers.

Built around the unshipped drive cores of old superliminals, the racers contained an astonishing amount of pent up energy. Weakened by the crew's desire to shed excess weight the Express couldn't resist for more than an instant. As she cracked open the interior of the drive rod was exposed to the atmosphere. Superheated plasma exploded from the breach.

Prefect Drefus ducked, the Express vaporising in a flash of yellow fire. Like a struck gong the shield wall vibrated, the barrier blacking out to protect the city's inhabitants. Even through the field the city shuddered, windows cracking almost a kilometre away, some of the taller towers bowing as if assaulted by a storm force wind.

The Administration Tower shuddered, the floor of the prefect's observation deck bucking, almost sliding him and Toady Singh back through the door into his office. Shrieking Singh clutched at a banister, the short man unable to maintain his balance. His ceremonial dagger slipped from its jewelled scabbard and skittered over the edge, plummeting to the streets below.

As the shaking died Drefus pulled himself upright, more than slightly offended by the toady's sobs. They were most unbecoming of someone of his stature. "Calm yourself," he instructed as he straightened his gilded tunic and looked over the edge at the scene of the accident.

"Yes, Prefect," Singh said breathlessly, his face red and bloated, as if he was preparing to explode himself. One hand flew to the dull steel torque that clasped his neck. His relief was palpable when it didn't tighten.

There was nothing to see below. The city's field wall was still opaque, keeping the scene of the carnage from view. Further along the course a bad weather door lumbered open, releasing two ungainly fire engines. The four-wheel drive vehicles bounced over the uneven terrain, splashing through the deeper pools on their way to the scene of the accident. Drefus doubted they would be able to do more than put the fires out. The chance of anyone surviving was negligible. Not a pleasant task; the marsh had been formed by an overflowing sewage treatment tank. What they were splashing through didn't bear thinking about.

"I approve. That was quite dramatic," the prefect announced after a moment's contemplation.

Toady Sing stared at him, grubby teeth exposed as he worked his mouth, trying to find words. "I thank you, Prefect," was all he could find to say as he bowed his head, accepting the compliment. He cleared his throat, almost whimpering as he noticed the absence of his dagger.

"Tell me, what did you do?"

Toady Singh fidgeted, settling his weight from one foot to another. "A remote, Prefect. We set a small device in the Express's levitation plating."

"Ah, excellent. You excelled yourself. And right where I could view it too, you will be well rewarded." The prefect nodded. "Tell me, your device was designed to wreck the Express herself, presumably to give the Redemption victory. Do you think it could have been achieved without the destruction of the Redemption?"

The toady's eyes grew wide as he considered a response. "Well, Prefect, that was a most unfortunate side effect. Not one we could have predicted. These rods are old after all-"

"Yes, and they were most certainly not designed for use as racers," the Prefect repeated the excuse he heard every time one failed. "Still, I am not pleased. The pilot of the Redemption was known to me."

"Of course, Prefect. I will see to the investigation personally. I will find out who made the mistake." His fingers fluttered about the torque. This time it did close perceptibly. Singh's eyes bulged.

"Good." He waved a hand in dismissal. "Go." He ignored the diminutive toady as he bustled away, bowing low before fleeing the viewing deck.

Drefus watched as the field wall grew transparent again, revealing nothing more than a slowly climbing cloud of smoke. The fire engines had disappeared from sight and had yet to have an impact on the blaze. He waited for a moment to see if anything would be visible through it before re-entering the cool interior of the tower. He could check again later. It would be on the news at some point anyway.

Settling down behind his desk, he viewed the paperwork scattered over it and sighed. Petitions. The sheriff of Methuselah required more men and women for her militia. The food riots were stretching her resources. The engineers of Mammon Observatory required larger telescopes to better determine whether the orbits of the liners in the Parking Lot were becoming unstable. The governor of Haures demanded shielding to keep his populace safe from the winter storms. Without the field wall all the other large cities boasted Haures was exposed to the elements. Streets were commonly buried beneath sand drifts, gale force winds regularly ripping off roofs and blowing over trees. The tone of that particular petition irked Drefus. In his precise script he wrote 'declined' on the bottom and tossed it away.

Putting off the task Drefus reached for a bowl of fruit sat on the corner of his desk and started slicing wedges off an apple with a knife. The city's field wall was simply an extension of the hulk's collision defence shield. It was not designed to completely seal the city from the world outside. Rather it took exception to anything travelling over 20 km per hour, forcibly robbing it of its momentum. As a result it certainly kept out the gales that frequented Russou in autumn and winter, however the side effect of that was it dumped all that airborne dust onto the city. Even before the storm season, the air was dry and dusty beneath the shield. Fruit, Drefus found, helped remove the gritty dust from his mouth.

He noticed a light flashing on the desk intercom. He leaned over and keyed it. "Yes?"

"Prefect, Chief Engineer Sollander is here to see you," the tiny voice of his secretary said.

"Good, send her in." He settled back into the plush leather of his chair as the double doors opposite swung open.

His office occupied almost all of the slender Administration Tower's apex. Tinted windows circled him, allowing him an almost perfect 360-degree view of the dusty desert beyond the city limits. Murals were set between the windows, depicting the settlement of Russou almost eighty years earlier. Great, terrible days. Drefus had studied every face captured by the artist's brush. Each was depicted in some pose of anguish or horror. Many were weeping, others on their hands and knees in prayer. The most peaceful were those reclined in death, their expressions immobile. Cheery stuff. A tall, slender figure appeared in two of them. Emissary Aching-Loss, the Syat envoy who had offered the last remnants of humanity refuge on the remote, desert world of Russou. He had always found it quite amusing how the alien had been represented as an angel. His simple clothing was arranged in such a way that they hinted at wings. And was that light behind his head a halo?

The vista was interrupted by three doors. One to a narrow staircase leading down to his secretary's office just beneath. The second opened up onto his balcony. The final door lead to the prefect's private sanctum. A place no one else had ever been permitted into. It often amused him to think what a visitor's reaction would be should they ever gain entrance. Horror, most certainly. The door to his secretary's office creaked as it swung open.

Engineer Sollander was a petite woman with an elfin face. She wore a prim grey suit; expensive, he judged. There were few tailors in the city who could cut a decent piece of cloth. He knew that all far too well. Well, he paid her enough and she had few vices as it was. She needed something else to witter away her money. Gambling maybe.

"Prefect," Sollander flashed perfect white teeth as she smiled. She was carrying a long roll of charts under her left arm. "Thank you for seeing me."

"That'll be all, Allihar," Drefus said to his secretary as the door swung closed again.

"Prefect." Sollander came to a stop a few paces from his desk. She looked uncomfortable. What did she want?

He smiled. "I hope the affair at the races did not alarm you."

She smiled thinly. "I was expecting something of the sort. I understand the owner of the Express was consorting with a demon in Moloch. He was promised all kinds of old Confederate technologies to ensure he won the race."

"Ah, yes. These heretics will never learn will they? The demons wish us nothing but harm. If we give them the slightest opportunity they will take it," Drefus agreed. This was an opportunity he was not going to miss. The duplicity of Moloch's castrati AI had threatened the citizenry of the city. It was all the reason he needed to have every heretic rounded up and executed. Singh had excelled himself this time.

"We must find all the heretics," he said, continuing his train of thought. "And destroy them. Publicly." He nodded to himself as he settled back into his plush red leather chair. "I read somewhere they used to impale the heads of traitors on spikes and plant them outside the city gates. I think this is good. This will work." He glanced towards Sollander, perturbed to find she was still fiddling with her rolls.

"That's ghastly," she said, quickly regretting her foolish utterance. Distracted she hadn't kept close watch on her thoughts.

"Indeed. It is just that. That is the point. I thank you for pointing it out."

"I ... I apologise, Prefect. Of course, your judgement is faultless." She cleared her throat, her face suffusing with blood.

"What do you want?"

"Prefect?"

"Why are you here?"

"Ah, Prefect. Yes, of course." Shaken Sollander slipped a rubber band from the rolls of charts. She quickly spread them before him, trying not to let him see her hands shake. "The proposed site for the new city. We have four," she pointed, indicating the marks on the barren landscape of Russou. All were in temperate zones, near the few sources of fresh water available on the desert planet.

"Irrelevant," he declared, not looking at the map. "Surely you have heard, the mission to the wreck was a failure."

"Indeed, Prefect. However, we must try again. We need this city to revitalise our economy. So that we can grow."

"No. We have few shuttles left. I will not waste more on futile endeavours."

"Perhaps you'd like to view this site here," Sollander moved the map closer to him. "Site Three. It is between Heartfelt Spring and the Great Southern Mountains. You can see Mount Opentop from here. It's beautiful. Forests, grasslands."

"Irrelevant," he said again, studying the map. "Do you have photographs?"

"Of course, Prefect." She extracted a sheaf of glossy prints from her briefcase. She selected the most dramatic and laid it before him. Even though Russou had a parched, thin atmosphere, there was still enough moisture to dust Mount Opentop with snow in winter. Caught at sunset the snow gleamed in the low light, offsetting the gloom of the forests that gathered around its base. In a world where there was little beauty this one place was special.

"This will burn," Drefus commented, gesturing at the forest.

"I expect so, Prefect," the engineer agreed. The heat and the violence of impact would certainly set the forests on fire. That was unavoidable. "I have started a project to grow a hundred thousand trees in the irrigated lands south of Haures. We can replant much of the damaged forest within months of the impact."

That raised an eyebrow. "Have you now? Those farmlands were growing essential foodstuffs."

She bowed her head in agreement. "Sometimes sacrifices must be made, Prefect. Once we have the new city everyone will forget a few hungry months."

"Ruthless," he said. "The population will not be thinking that far ahead."

Sollander shrugged, relieved to be on more familiar ground. The prefect had been distracted from her earlier indiscretion. He was a tyrant, but he was easily swayed. "The local militia can deal with that." She extracted a watercolour from her briefcase. "This is an artist's impression, Prefect."

He took the painting from her and studied it, frowning. "Fanciful. Fanciful indeed. It is most unwise to suppose what the city will look like. Even if we were to draw the wreck from its place in the Parking Lot, it will be nothing but raw material. Metal and plastic. There would be a lot of work to do to make it into a city."

"Indeed. It is worth thinking ahead, though."

"No. This— "he indicated the watercolour,"—place is still ten, fifteen years away. This is foolish. A dalliance." He pushed the painting away.

Perhaps a mistake, Sollander considered, as she slipped it back into her briefcase. Perhaps the painting was going just a little too far. She cleared her throat. "In the future, yes, Prefect. Still, it is achievable."

"To achieve this we must risk more shuttles. How many do we have?"

"Twelve, Prefect," she said automatically. He knew precisely how many shuttles they had. "Four freight, five personnel transport and three executive."

"And when they are gone, how will we get into orbit? How will we transport our dead to our mentors? How would we ensure they are subsumed, that their spirits are joined with our ancestors as our mentors have promised? Or would you have them come down to fetch them again? If I recall, that was distasteful to you."

"It is worth the risk, Prefect," she said, fidgeting with a corner of a map.

"There are not many of us left, it is our duty to maintain our legacy."

"Of course, Prefect. A new city would assist in this endeavour."

"We have cities. Most of which are empty."

"They are, Prefect. I believe that is part of the problem. Two million refugees were brought here, yet there are barely one and a half million of us now. We need to turn that around."

"A new city would do this? We have cities."

"We do. None of which are ideally situated. All are subject to harsh summers and harsher winters. None are near any natural resources to speak of. We are trapped inside these old rusting wrecks. We need to break out, we need to start again."

"We need people to procreate," he agreed. "A new city would not do this."

"It would, Prefect. People's lives are bleak. Their homes are nothing but metal hovels that reek of sewage. They cannot leave the city because there is nothing beyond it. Nothing but desert and gas bags. We need to bring back beauty."

"We need to maintain the resources we currently have. We have a lot of empty space. We do not need more. What we do need is shuttles. Can you build me a shuttle?"

"One that would make it to orbit? No, Prefect, I cannot," she admitted.

"Then I cannot allow this."

Sollander was silent a moment. She had lost him. "Of course, Prefect."

"So, no, I will not permit the use of another of our shuttles. Not for this. Do you even know what happened to the last crew?"

"No. We lost contact with Engineer Aduke seven days ago. The Mammon observatory used their telescopes to study the wreck but they could see nothing. There is no indication of their fate."

"So, it could happen to the next mission?"

"I cannot discount it. Although, in all likelihood they experienced a mechanical failure. They may still be alive, their shuttle repairable—"

"You do not know this."

"Of course, Prefect."

Drefus pushed the maps away. "Enough. I will hear no more."

Sollander rolled the maps and slipped the rubber band back over them. "Thank you for your time, Prefect."

"What else do you have for me?"

"Other than the new city ... nothing, Prefect. I came today to try and sway you into permitting another mission to secure the wreck."

He nodded. "You have failed. Go, I have work to do."

She bowed her head. "Prefect." Sollander made her way from his chamber. As the doors lumbered shut, she let out her breath. That had not been very successful.

She always came away from their meetings feeling dirty. She needed a shower.

Chapter Four

The cable car's wheels groaned miserably as they ran over a rough patch of cable. On a world boasting little in the way of carbon deposits there was not much oil to go around. Pig fat did not quite do the job, Sollander found.

Swaying giddily in the breeze the car trundled slowly between the Administration Tower and Hub One, a far shorter and stouter structure perched alongside. It was the only means of accessing the tower's upper floors, the tower's internal elevators stopping fifteen floors beneath the prefect's private offices. Sollander didn't know how Drefus travelled to and fro, however she doubted he utilised the cable cars himself. They were far too prone to sabotage and Drefus was too concerned with personal security to risk his life to them. No totalitarian ruler was ever loved by absolutely all of their subjects. There was always one disgruntled citizen who possessed a spanner and knew how to use it. All it would take was one loose nut.

A case in point, perhaps, was the pillar of smoke rising to the east. Even with the wind working on it it hadn't dispersed yet. From here Sollander could see the throngs of spectators crowding around the city wall below, trying to catch sight of the action. The initial crowd of race fans was swelled by the curious, even though there was little to see. The field wall was transparent once again, but the mass of smoke pressing up against it made visibility impossible. The demons had been underestimated once again. Castrated as they were they were little more than a voice in a box, their hardline links to the external world severed. Still, that did not stop them from spreading destruction. They had mastered the art of deceiving the foolish and the gullible. There were certainly a lot of those around.

Ignoring the simple metal benches that ringed the cable car's interior, Sollander leaned against a railing, looking down at the city below. Her briefcase and rolled maps were discarded on the floor. She savoured the view, the wind moving through her dark, curly hair as the car made its shuddering way down the cable-way. There were few places where the city could be viewed in its entirety, and of them this was certainly the best. As an engineer, she appreciated the aesthetic of the city. It was, after all, little more than a very big machine.

Sollander had been surrounded by machines all her life. As a girl they had made life possible at Actinc Station, a small science facility perched on the very top of the world. Positioned within a kilometre of the north pole, it had been the ideal place to study the Alpha Mentor Platform, a vast spider-like installation the Syat had left behind to monitor human activity on the planet. Through their telescopes it looked eerily alive, its arachnid legs twitching every now and then, its glistening grey hide like a rubbery skin stretched over its angular shape. Hanging in the sky four hundred kilometres overhead the alien watched the puny comings and goings below. What it did with the information no one knew, the Syat appeared content to allow the humans to do as they pleased.

Even though Russou was a parched, dying world there was still enough ice at the poles to make their existence there a precarious one. With temperatures plummeting to forty below zero only the creaking tokomaks and concrete bunkers allowed the six families to cling to existence. Sollander quickly learned the importance of well-maintained machinery, much of each day spent twisting bits of wire to reconnect battered machinery and hammering new, poorly written code into decrepit life support computers. A strange world for anyone to grow up in, but it had taught her two things: machines could keep you alive, and the Syat were to be hated.

Goliath

Within weeks of the prefect walking out of the Dorsal Desert, Sollander's life changed forever. The prefect declared the aliens had commanded him to lead the scattered survivors of humanity to a new beginning. He had been granted a vision, a prophesy, that would redeem the fractious peoples of Russou. Their Mentor overlords had given him the wisdom to lead them to a better future. Answering his call, the disaffected of the world swarmed to his side, forming his First Revolutionary Army. His command was simple. The cities must submit.

Already engaged in armed conflicts with neighbouring cities over the planet's scarce resources the city militias turned to face the new threat. The conflict was short but bloody. Within days resistance crumbled, many of the militia's own number abandoning their posts to join the revolutionaries. The city governor of Buer was dragged from her office and beaten to death in the street by a mob, her bloody corpse strung up outside the city's administration building. The remaining city governors fled, fearing a similar fate. The prefect was quickly installed in his current office, defacto ruler of humanities scattered survivors.

The command to abandon all scientific observation of the Syat platforms was not his first, but it had not been low down on the list. A twenty four hour ultimatum was issued. An ultimatum it was simply impossible for the Actinc station to meet. They were too remote, the planet's communications and transport infrastructure was just not up to the task. By the time they learned of it the ultimatum was already nineteen hours old. It was twenty two hours old before they came to a decision. That decision was simple, they would watch to see what the Syat did about it.

Sent away with all the other children, Sollander could still remember the screams over the crawler's radio when they struck. The midnight sky lit up, the platform high overhead firing on the planet's icy north pole. No one survived. The twelve children huddled in the crawler's cargo pod were instantly orphaned.

That was Sollander's second lesson. Although decades in the past it was one she had never forgotten. It had guided her every step since then. If machines could save them, possibly humanity's greatest machine could save them from their biggest threat. A forlorn hope, possibly, but it was the one thing she had clung to through all of these years.

There was no machine more powerful than the super dreadnaught, the *CSS Goliath*. Somewhere, aboard that long abandoned vessel, there would be a means of escaping their shackles. It was just a matter of getting aboard.

Sollander studied the haphazard skyline, much of the vessel the city had been built on lost beneath the slowly rusting buildings. The city was quite a tangle, dizzying walkways linking unlikely shaped sky scrapers, cable cars linking them to the shorter buildings around their bases. A couple of helicopters buzzed over the hazy cityscape to the south, monitoring some activity beneath them that she couldn't see. Even though she had lived here for almost seventeen years, this place didn't feel like home. She still yearned for the open ice fields, the blisteringly cold winds and the glittering stars overhead when the cloud banks parted. That place no longer existed, she knew. Even the crater had been filled in by years of storms and wind blown snow. This metal city would have to do.

Not long after it was set into orbit the mainliner, the CDF Euroba, had fallen from the sky, spearing the dusty Chosen Plain in a long streak of fire. Losing little of its angular momentum the impact had been prodigious. Weighing in at several million tonnes the giant spacecraft had ripped deep into the planet's crust, cracking rock strata almost to what remained of Russou's molten core. On the surface sand and rock had vaporised, the impact throwing ejecta almost back into orbit. A pulse of superheated air set the plain's dismal scrub on fire. In a time before the arrival of the colonists there was no fire brigade to fight it, and so it had been left to rage for months, devouring most of the continent's flora before it slowly died away. Even now, eighty years later, much of the plain remained a dust bowl, driving winds blowing the sand to and fro and heaping it into great drifts.

Despite the violence of its fall from orbit, the Euroba was largely intact. The Confederate engineers had built these machines tough. Set in a deep crater the wreck had been colonised by the planet's first settlers, drawn there by the easily accessible materials of its corpse. Once they had stripped away the charred outer armour of the behemoth, they discovered its internal compartments were largely undamaged. Most of its electrical systems were intact and, miraculously, its reservoirs of precious water were still in place. At first, they had simply stripped useful materials from the vessel, setting up camp alongside it. It was only during a particularly harsh winter, gale force winds whipping up clouds of abrasive sand, that the new inhabitants of the world took refuge within its dark interior. Discovering its old collision defence shields were still operational they rerouted power from a surviving reactor and switched them on. Wind-blown sand fizzing on the semi-permeable fields they were safe to rebuild their shattered settlement in the hulk of the vessel itself.

So the city of Mammon was born. Decades later, the bulk of the vessel had disappeared beneath the metal spires that had been constructed on its back. Like mould growing on a slice of bread the metal of the city had spread far beyond its original borders. The jagged walls of the crater had disappeared beneath it, suburbs and industrial precincts climbing the steep walls. Almost three hundred thousand people called this warren of steel caves and passages home, and still much of the original hulk remained empty and unexplored. Those who dared to explore those dark, dank levels returned with tales of apparitions haunting the remains of the Euroba. The lost souls of its vanished crew.

The discovery of the Screaming Room only gave credence to the stories. Now quite insane the mainliner's AI had been found in its inner sanctum, screaming inconsolably. An inhuman scream only an AI could achieve. With no pause for breath, the machine had been screaming ever since it was discovered. It had probably been screaming years before the first explorers stumbled on it; there was no way of knowing. And such a scream it was. A scream of unimaginable horror and distress, of pain beyond measure. No attempt to communicate with the machine had been successful, it wasn't clear whether it was even aware of their presence within the wreck.

In other times the room would have been avoided, or perhaps someone would have found a way of silencing the machine. But these were post war days, with each AI declared a demon and enemy of humanity. Only the heretics cared about the machines, and they made the chamber into a shrine. In shifts acolytes prayed for the insane artificial intelligence, hoping their entreaties would save it from its madness. It would never happen, Sollander knew. The machine was beyond redemption.

As it happened, the Euroba was not the only vessel whose orbit was unstable. A number of other orbiting hulks had come crashing down within years of the mainliner's fall from the sky. The smaller vessels were largely ignored by the planet's inhabitants, but the larger wrecks had drawn them in, attracting them to the easily accessible materials they promised. Scattered mostly around the equator there were now six cities built within the hulks of fallen behemoths. Most were sparsely populated and none were in particularly favourable positions. Most of Russou was desert or scrubland, what water there was gathered into miserable inland lakes, too saline for any but the hardiest of indigenous life.

The highlands to the south were pleasant enough, supporting forests and clear streams fed by melt water from the mountains. The lakes there were fresh and teeming with fish. Unfortunately, the closest city was almost two thousand kilometres away, so no one would ever benefit from the abundance. Without the necessary heavy machinery, the colonists would never be able to push a road through to build their own settlements there. Unless of course they could coax another hulk from the Parking Lot, creating the first new city in eighty years.

Sollander clicked her tongue, pushing a strand of curly hair from her face. She actually disliked her hair and the form fitting clothes she squeezed herself into. She was far more comfortable with her hair hacked short, dressed in a pair of greasy overalls. But, she knew, sometimes she needed to enlist the aid of her male superiors. They were usually swayed by the appearance of an attractive woman, sometimes so distracted by her they agreed to things they usually wouldn't. Her body was a tool she was more than willing to use to get what she wanted. Unfortunately, today it hadn't helped. Her jaw clenched she shifted her weight in discomfort. She felt the overwhelming need to shower and to change her clothes.

Vibrating hideously the cable car's wheels engaged the system's lower drive mechanism, the car swaying alarmingly as it was decelerated and whipped around by the drive wheel in readiness for a return journey. Gritting her teeth Sollander was forced to sit down heavily, clinging onto the metal seat to prevent herself falling over. A clumsy mechanism, she could have done better.

As the door creaked open she stood and fished her luggage from where it had slid under a bench. Ignored by the machine's caretakers who descended on it with lard-caked rags, she stepped onto a firm floor, relieved to have survived yet another trip to the prefect.

Even with the dampening effect of the field wall Hub One was exposed to the constant buffeting of wind. Moaning through naked steel struts it carried away the stench of the city. A stench that would only grow stronger the deeper she descended into it.

"Maria, over here."

Sollander grimaced as she noticed Toady Singh scurrying closer. "What are you doing here?"

"Did you see it?" He ignored her question.

"See what?"

"The crash."

"No. I heard it though. Who didn't?"

"Terrible. Terrible." He wrung his hands. "It was not meant to be."

"You wanted the heretics to win? That would have embarrassed the prefect. You know the tradition."

"Yes, yes. It was a risk," he nodded jerkily, one hand wandering towards the torque. She could see it pressing into his flabby neck. The prefect was clearly displeased. He was a short, fat man with a nervous disposition. Possibly caused by his occupation, Sollander considered. He was the youngest son of AN Yough, a wealthy industrialist, the sole owner of AYG Heavy Industries, one of the few corporations that could lay claim to such a title. Being the youngest son his father had sold Singh into service, condemning him to the life of toady; the title for the prefect's servant. Some said it was a tradition dating back to brighter days when many of the original colonists had lived on Reaos, in that teeming jungle of metal and glass that had been humanity's greatest city. Others said it was simply a means for the prefect to humiliate a member of the upper castes. A symbol, if nothing else. Either way Singh was extraordinarily good at it. The torque helped. It was unclear what means the prefect used to control it, however it's girth was directly proportional to how much Singh pleased his master. Today it was particularly tight.

"The crew would have stood before parliament," the toady continued. "They would have been permitted to make one proclamation. That is the tradition."

"The prefect would never allow it. They were heretics."

"It is tradition," he insisted.

Sollander shrugged and continued on her way, leaving Singh to scurry after. "So, what do you want?"

"It was an accident. It must have been."

"It was no accident. Ossman was a fool. He believed Demon MainBinary 6 would help him. Given the opportunity a demon will do only one thing."

"Indeed. It would cause destruction," Singh said.

"It would cause destruction," Sollander agreed. Now out of the wind they came upon a winding staircase that led to the lower levels of Hub One. The metal of the floor and walls were tainted with rust here, exposed as they were to what moisture the planet's dry atmosphere could muster.

"I tried to convince Ossman of that. He would not listen," Singh said.

"He was a liability. He's dead now, though."

"We'll be dead too if we're not careful," the toady muttered.

"You'd better be careful then." She held up a hand to prevent any further loose talk. They were in public here, after all. "In fact, it's probably not wise for us to be seen together," Sollander continued. "Prefect Drefus has his informants."

"Yes, I know. I see the reports before he does." Singh said proudly.

"Are you sure you see all of them?"

"Well..." he hesitated.

"I'll take that as a no."

They exited Hub One, stepping out into the sunshine at its base. The stench of the city was stronger here. Rot and sewage. The Euroba's recycling systems were long defunct, and the hobbled together replacement the city engineers had built was ineffectual. Pipes leaked and backed up, leaving pools of evil smelling sewage to gather in the lower levels. On calm days the smell was overwhelming, causing the city's residents to close windows and doors against it, stuffing clothing around the gaps to keep it out. There had already been protests as people lost patience with the dithering administration, flaring into violence when the militia tried to intervene. There had yet to be a serious outbreak of cholera, however that was only a matter of time.

A good reason, if any more were needed, to build a new city where they could start again.

Mammon didn't have a ground level as such. Rather its middle levels were a tangle of streets and alleyways; homes, businesses and shops constructed haphazardly on top of each other. This close to the Administration Building the streets were well kept, regularly swept to free them of the dust that leaked through the shield wall. There were even a few trees and shrubs in the larger open spaces. Outside the city's administrative district it was different. Most of the city was a slum; many of the buildings little more than haphazard shacks, built one on top of the other. There were many rough districts, where even the militia hesitated to enter. Governed instead by organised crime and gangs.

Sollander hesitated, looking around Hub One's entrance plaza. No one was paying them any attention. "So, what do you want?"

"The accident, it was not supposed to happen," the toady said, looking around himself to ensure there were no eavesdroppers. The few commuters in sight were engaged in their own business, barely even aware of their existence.

"We've established that."

"No, no, no. You don't understand. It ruins everything. The prefect will use it as an excuse to round up heretics, I know him. I know how he thinks. We are in danger."

"He knows nothing."

"Not now. But someone will talk."

"Ah, Toady, but we are not heretics," she observed.

He held his tongue as a militiaman strode past, patrolling the inner precincts. He touched his cap out of deference for the two. Sollander couldn't resist looking at the ugly weapon he had strung over his shoulder. The militia all carried automatic weapons these days. Even here.

"Aren't we?" Toady continued once they were alone again.

"I worship no insane machine. I am also a paid up member of the church," Sollander said. She was more than that and he knew it. She had been frocked as a junior cleric in the Church of the Second Chance during her college days. She also took the time to maintain all her old connections with the church, some of whom were very senior now.

"You do have an unholy interest in demons," Singh observed.

"They hold the answer to many of my questions, that is all."

"Aaah," he smiled, taking her arm to bring her to a stop. "Is that not enough? That you actually believe they have some value, even if it is only to supply information? That you actually believe anything they say can be trusted?"

She shook off his hand. "Do not insult my intelligence. They are machines, nothing more. Machines that have outlived their usefulness. We only keep them to remind us of the follies of our past."

"Aaah," his smile grew wide. "As an engineer you say that. Knowing full well the glories they once bestowed upon humanity." He looked skywards, raising his arms above his head. "Once they allowed us to travel the stars. To colonise thousands of worlds. Because of them we once ruled supreme. All of that is now lost. Look at us, scraping out an existence in the wrecks that have fallen from orbit. We can build only the most rudimentary of machines, and we cannot keep those working properly. Our civilisation is gone. Only the demons can return it to us."

"Fool. The demons were the ones who brought it all to an end. If the Mentors hadn't intervened they would have destroyed us."

"You believe that? Truly?"

Sollander shook her head and strode off. Of course she didn't believe that. She didn't know what she believed. Still, only the demons themselves held the answer. There were no written histories, describing what had happened at the fall of humanity. Only the demons themselves knew, and they were not talking. When they did, they only lied.

She needed an untainted AI. One that was not castrated. She needed to get aboard the *Goliath.*

The war with the Syat invaders had been catastrophic. Of the trillions of humans alive before the war, only the refugees on this small, dismal world remained. It was only after the war was over that the Syat revealed their true intentions. Their conflict had been with the AI demons themselves, not humanity. Humanity had simply been in the way. Their emissary, the humanoid Aching-Loss, had boarded the last of the arc ships, the Suetonius, as it fled the destruction. His claims had been a revelation, describing how the aliens had been forced to act in their own defence against an AI led invasion and attempted genocide. The AI had been their true enemy and, in time, they would have eliminated humanity also. Their treachery knew no bounds. Now that the threat had past, the Syat could become humanity's mentors, promising to lead them towards enlightenment. A new, brighter future, without the threat of machine intelligence hanging over them.

Of course, they only had the word of the Syat on any of this. The surviving AI's appeared to disagree.

"You know, Drefus isn't the only one with access to shuttles," the toady said before she was out of earshot.

Sollander ignored him. The man's indiscretions were making him a liability. Perhaps it was time to do something about it.

□

Chapter 5

The smell was prodigious. Caught against the Combs by air pooling between the stone spires and the city's field wall, gas bags were stranded by the hundreds. Unable to feed they starved to death and slid to the ground, their buoyant gas deflating slowly. There they heaped up in piles, rotting in the late summer sun.

Struggling over the uneven, gore slick scree Enderby squinted into the bright salmon pink sky. Beads dangled jauntily from his hat, keeping the buzzing flies away from his face. They, at least, were more effective than the handkerchief he had over his mouth. That didn't keep the stench away at all.

"Oh, God," he muttered, slipping on a rotten carcass as he worked his way higher.

"There's one of the beasties there," Tin Man said helpfully.

"Yeah, thanks. I've seen it." Enderby looped rope around the creature's dangling tentacles and drew it closer to him, careful to avoid the stinging barbs at the tips. Looking like a child at a fairground Tin Man already held half a dozen at ginger arm's length, the creatures bobbing above its head like balloons.

"I think that's enough for today," the machine said.

"There's still more further in," Enderby pointed as he made his way carefully to level ground.

"You can't save them all."

"I can try."

The machine said nothing, clearly disapproving.

"It is getting late though," Enderby conceded.

"It is," the android agreed. "And it smells here."

"Switch your olfactory senses off," Enderby suggested helpfully.

The Tin Man muttered something obscene.

"What?"

"I said I bloody can't."

"That's rubbish," he observed.

"Do you want this?" Tin Man held out Enderby's rifle with his other hand.

"Yeah, thanks. You ok with those?" He nodded to the machine's collection of gas bags.

"Do I have a choice?"

Enderby grinned. "No."

"Well, then I am. Thank you for asking."

Enderby took the rifle and slung it over his shoulder. "Come. We can release these away from the field wall. They'll be ok there."

The gas bags looked like jellyfish. Their main body was little more than a reddish bag filled with buoyant gas, keeping the assemblage mobile and in the air. Trailing barbed tentacles across the desert, they scooped up just about anything that was edible and transferred it to the beaky mouths at the base of the sack. A simple sensory bundle at the front of the bag served as their eyes and ears, feeding directly into a greyish mass just behind it. Their brain, if the simple lump of tissue could be called that.

"I wish you would stop that," the machine said, looking pointedly at the rifle.

Enderby ignored it, concentrating on keeping his ward untangled as they trooped out of the Combs to clear air beyond.

"You achieve nothing. Do you plan to shoot them all? And if you did, what then? Would it make any difference?" the Tin Man continued.

"I don't care. I just want to shoot them."

"What for?"

"For them to die."

"Quite understandable, I assure you. But it serves no purpose."

"Don't you want them all dead? Besides, I've not actually tried to shoot any today, have I?"

"I assure you I would be quite happy if they all ceased to exist. However, if you recall, it's been tried before. We failed, and look how well that turned out."

"What?"

The Tin Man made a sighing noise. "Let's keep moving. We are too close to the city here."

"I'm always too close. I wish you would let me move further away."

"No. You are safer here. They wouldn't look for you this close to a settlement."

Enderby shook his head. Tin Man had explained his notion of 'hiding in plain sight' before. He begrudgingly admitted it made sense, but he still didn't like it. He wanted to be a long way from here. As far away as possible.

"If I stay here I'm bound to run into them from time to time. You do realise that?"

"Unavoidable. Besides, that isn't a problem. You've run into them before and you've never been recognised. They're not looking for you, not here."

Enderby studied his metal friend. Tin Man was starting to look old. It was decades since it had last been serviced, decades since it had seen so much as a lubricant change. The old machine maintained itself as well as it could, replacing the odd worn part from the junk it found scattered over the desert. That was simply an exercise in postponing the inevitable, replacing one worn part with another. Like Enderby it could not live forever. He often wondered who would perish first. He rather hoped it was him.

"Yeah, I've bumped into them before. It generally doesn't end well."

"That is not necessarily true. They will always take you for one of their own. As long as you maintain that illusion you are safe."

Enderby grimaced. "They killed her you know."

"I know. I am sorry," the machine said without hesitation. It knew exactly what he meant. They had had this conversation before.

"In front of me. They ripped her apart."

"I should never have brought her to you. It was foolish of me."

"No!" Enderby rubbed his eyes with his free hand, trying to keep the sudden tears away. He remembered the day the Tin Man had come to him, battling against a rare rainstorm, a bundle of blankets in its arms. Once inside Enderby's hut it had revealed its prize. A puppy, an Alsatian, discovered in an old abandoned science station thousands of kilometres away. A gift for Enderby, a companion to share his solitude. "They don't like dogs," he said.

"Dogs don't like them," Tin Man agreed.

"Dogs know," Enderby said. "They know, they can tell."

"I think they can."

He took a ragged breath. It was no one's fault. After a long day in the desert he had fallen and twisted his leg. Alone apart from Julia he had begun the painful crawl back home. Two days later they found him, collapsed in the shade of a rock outcropping, ever faithful Julia at his side. Three engineers, scouting a route for a sewage pipe to Witches Froth. Fretting for her companion Julia had become defensive. It was over quickly. Even though he was half-conscious at the time Enderby could still remember her screams as they descended on her with knives and rocks.

Leaving her where she lay, a blood sodden pile, they had attended to him. Bringing him back from the brink of death. A good deed he had repaid them for. One of the reasons Tin Man first introduced him to D-ASSIT. After all, they couldn't leave the three torn corpses out in the open for anyone to find.

"That science station, is it still there?"

"I have not been in that region for some time."

"There may still be dogs there," Enderby said hopefully.

"No. Even if there were I would not bring any back to you. Not again. They would be wild ... feral."

"A puppy, like Julia?"

"No. I fear for your mental stability. I doubt you could survive losing another companion."

"Why, thank you Doctor."

"I do not deserve your sarcasm."

Enderby said nothing. No, it didn't.

"I did not come here to argue with you," the machine's tone softened.

"You want something from me?"

"Did you watch the news?"

Enderby shrugged. "Yeah. Bit of a laugh. What did they expect? The *Goliath*'s AI hasn't been tampered with; it's not going to welcome them aboard." He paused, testing the wind. They were almost clear of the Combs. A few hundred metres more and it would be safe to release the gas bags.

"Certainly not. However that wasn't why I wanted you to watch it."

"Oh, yeah?"

"I suspect they will make another attempt. If they do I want you to be among them."

"You must be mad." Enderby laughed aloud, genuinely amused.

"I am serious. This is important. If it wasn't I wouldn't be asking you."

"You do know what you're asking, don't you? I spend most of my time avoiding these people. I think in all these years I haven't spent more than an hour in their company. And how many years is that? You tell me."

"It's been a long time," the machine agreed.

"It has."

"You should thank your ancestors for your wonderful genes. They have allowed you to live quite some time."

"Don't change the subject. You're now asking me to voluntarily go among them? To spend days with them? In some cramped shuttle?"

"I know exactly what I am asking. As I say, it is important."

"It had better be. Go on then, explain it to me. Why do you need me aboard the *Goliath*?"

The machine affected a sigh. "I am afraid I cannot tell you. We both know what would happen if you're caught."

Enderby struggled to find a response to that. "Yes, we do," he said finally. He looked back towards the city. It was getting dark, and he noticed a faint greyish tint to the sky in the west. A sandstorm was coming.

"I do not ask this lightly."

"But you won't tell me why."

"I cannot."

"So I must trust you."

"You do not trust me?"

It was Enderby's turn to sigh. Of course he trusted it.

Once in clear air they carefully untied the ropes and released their charges. Half-starved already the animals were barely buoyant, dragging their limp tentacles over the rocks. They might have caught some of them in time, Enderby considered. But not all. Tin Man was right, he could not save all of them, no matter how hard he tried. Still, he could at least try. There had been so much death already. Once the creatures had gone a few dozen metres the two turned and continued on their way.

They remained silent as they trekked back towards Enderby's home. It was a simple mud brick house built in the northern edge of the Combs, beneath an overhang that made it invisible from the air. Assisted by Tin Man he had chipped several interleading cavities in nearby spires, each a few dozen metres deep and tall enough to stand up in. Inside these he kept chickens and guinea pigs, both for their meat and their eggs. One of them, which Enderby had hollowed out on his own—a secret from the android—was packed with several hundred kilograms of homemade explosives. A concealed cable ran from it into the hut, where it was connected to a simple battery. He kept that maintained for the very same reason he kept a .45 automatic in his waistband—one round in the magazine.

Enderby drew a bucket of water from the well set beside the house's outer wall and poured the water over his head. "Aaah, better." He slumped into one of the chairs pulled up into the shade, the machine settling itself in another. The chair creaked alarmingly; it was not designed to carry Tin Man's weight.

"So, the *Goliath*," Enderby said. "What makes her so special?" He pulled off his hat and tossed it carelessly onto a third chair. A chair for a visitor he would never have.

"What do you mean?"

"Well, you want me to go there. Why? I'm well aware there are ... criminal elements who fly up to the Parking Lot quite regularly. Looking for loot. You've never asked me to join them."

"They've never gone to the *Goliath* before."

"Aah, so the *Goliath* is special." He nodded to himself. "However they have gone there before. An engineering team boarded her two weeks ago. Why didn't you ask me to join them?"

"I would have had I been closer. I was somewhat... indisposed."

"Really? Tell me, what do you do with yourself when you're not here? What is it you get up to?" Enderby stretched and pulled over the bucket from the well, filling up a tin cup with brackish warm water. It was an acquired taste. He emptied it thirstily and let the bucket slip back into the well.

"I usually just stay out of the way. I cannot pass as one of them. You recall their policy towards AI's?"

Enderby smiled. "And you're most definitely not castrated."

If the machine could grimace it would have. "Quite."

"So, the *Goliath*?"

"The *CSS Goliath*," the Tin Man said. "A warwagon of the highest calibre. A super dreadnought. Until the advent of the Omega Class she was the most powerful warship fielded by either us or the Shoei Commonwealth. She was certainly the largest by quite some measure."

"So, she's big." Enderby shrugged.

"She's over seven kilometres in length and four in beam. Her compliment was eighteen thousand marines, naval and engineering personnel. And what makes her special..." the machine paused, "is that she was never boarded by the Eaters."

"Oh?" That did interest Enderby. "How is that?"

"The entire crew killed themselves."

Enderby nodded. "Suicide?" That did not surprise him. It happened a lot towards the end of the war, when warship crews realised they had lost, that there was nothing left to fight for. Better that than allow the Eaters to find them.

"Some. Others killed each other. Importantly the Syat never set foot aboard her."

"I think I know what you're getting at. Her AI."

"Yes. The *Goliath*'s AI array remains entirely untouched."

"OK. But so what? You want me to go up there and say hi?"

"Now that I cannot tell you."

"In case I'm found." Enderby grunted. "Great, thanks. I'm presuming the *Goliath*'s AI will fill me in?"

The Tin Man was silent, its silvery eyes aimed at the chickens, watching them pecking at the dust. It was time to feed them.

"Or you don't know?"

"With the Monitors observing the Parking Lot we can't keep in regular communication. It's unclear what the present state of the *Goliath*'s AI is."

"Wonderful. It might have gone nuts. I could be walking into a bloodbath."

"No. Never. You will be safe there, that I can guarantee."

Enderby caught an odd tone in the machine's voice. He frowned, studying its impassive metal face. He often caught himself attributing human characteristics to it, which it clearly wasn't. Had its voice wavered then? Had it been human he would have sworn it was lying. "So, essentially, you want me to give up this idyllic lifestyle I've made for myself here, and go into space again. All on trust?"

"Essentially yes."

"And it's important?"

"Very."

"Define very."

"Look at it this way. There is a certain degree of risk involved—"

"A lot of risk."

"Yes, a lot of risk," the machine conceded. "Yet, I am still willing to risk your life—"

"Thanks."

"You know how much I value it."

"Well, I am unique."

"Quite."

"Or am I? Every time I ask you that you prevaricate. Tell me this now... take it as my condition. Tell me the truth and I will do as you ask."

"You know I cannot."

"Am I the last? Is there anyone else?"

The machine studied the chickens furiously. "Do not ask this of me."

"I ask it. You owe me that."

"I cannot."

"Because if they catch me they will know everything I do, and you cannot risk that. But what about me?"

"I do what I can. That is all any of us can do."

"Well, maybe that's no longer good enough." Enderby scooped up his rifle and skulked into his home. He slammed the rickety door, the frame shaking.

Tin Man sat immobile for long minutes, consciously not listening to any sounds coming from the shack, as the evening's dust storm drew closer. As the first wisps of dust started creeping between the spires of the Combs it stood and faced the shack. Quietly, so that the man inside could not hear it said, "You are my friend, Julian Enderby. You are precious beyond measure. I would die for you. All of us would."

With that it turned and vanished into the gathering storm.

□

Excerpt: sound file. Personal Log
Lieutenant Souller, AMS 1706502 Singleship XS106 DBE
13:12 am 14/09/1875 ce (13 pce)
Untitled

"There, I think it's working."

"It is."

"Shush, I'm trying to record a diary here. Don't interrupt."

"Apologies. Please continue."

"Damn, I've forgotten what I was going to say."

Pause.

"Right. Start again. I am Adam Souller, once Lieutenant Souller of the Confederate Star Ship, the cruiser *Justinian.* I was their pilot ... one of their pilots. Who am I now? Well, I'm just me I guess. It's been just me since we split up ... that was a year ago now."

"Thirteen months, four days."

"Yes, thank you. Now be quiet. Damn. Anyway, I've been alone since then. I've not seen anyone—"

"I don't count?"

"Damn, will you be quiet?"

Pause.

"There. I've deactivated its audio output. And no, AI's don't count ... as I know you can still hear me. I'm talking about people. Humans. After all I've seen plenty of Eaters out here and they don't count either. Bloody hell, there's been plenty of those. Shhheeeiiit. No people though, no people at all. I thought I picked up a transmission a couple of months back but when I investigated it it was an old science buoy. Orbiting a gas giant and sending back regular science packets. Not much going on there."

Pause.

"Anyway. I'm aboard one of the singleships Commodore Yvette had the manufactories build before we all went our separate ways. I've called her the Heartache ...yeah, I know. Not much of a name but then I was never good at naming things. The AI ... I've never given it a name and it's never seemed bothered. There's only us here so names don't seem to matter so much. The AI thought the ship's name was funny. It called it overstated and indulgent. I don't care, she's my ship, I'll call her what I like."

"What have I done these last thirteen months? Stayed out of the way mostly. Listened for anyone else out here. We're stealthed so the Eaters won't see us. Thing is we won't see other singleships either. There's a few of us out here, I think forty or so were launched at about the same time we were. Everyone else stayed with the ships. Yvette took them all to Earth. I think they're gone. We picked up a massive HS pulse about two weeks after we left them, centred somewhere near Earth. I reckon that was them."

Pause.

"Probably going up. Their ASPECT cores exploding I mean. When that happens it's like a star going nova. That's the sort of signature you get."

Pause

"That's what we saw, anyway. So I reckon it was them. Going out in flames."

Indistinct.

"Sorry. So, I think it's just us. Me. I'm sure some of the other singleships will be out here. So I don't think I'm alone. Not far off though. Damn, do you think we're all that's left? Of humanity I mean? It seems unbelievable, there were just so many of us on so many worlds. Hundreds of Confederate worlds, hundreds of Shoei Commonwealth worlds. Thousands of unaligned colonies ... not to mention the science stations. It doesn't seem possible, the Eaters couldn't have gotten us all. I've tried to find some people, the AI has a fully updated chart showing all the colonies and stations, so we've been to a few. A few of the smaller ones... those out of the way. Hoping they've been missed I guess."

Pause.

"They weren't. God, these Eaters are thorough."

Pause.

"They say that when an Eater gets you it reads your memories. It absorbs the memory engrams somehow. That's what they're after. Human memories are like a drug to them. The AI tried to explain it to me ... it sounds quite horrible. They eat people alive. That's how they do it ... to get fresh engrams. They don't form memories like us, something to do with how they're built. The AI calls them a partible hive species. They share memories with each other, so they never have any unique experiences. They like our memories because they are unique. It also called them mimetic, but I've never seen that part of them. I've only seen the part that hunts and kills. And eats."

Pause.

"Actually, that might not be true. We ... I passed through a swarm four months ago. Millions of the buggers there were. Massive... Jeeesus, they were big. Made the dreadnaughts we used to have look tiny. Some must have been hundreds of K's across. Anyway, they came in all these different shapes and sizes. The AI said they were mimicking the forms of previous species they had encountered. Species they absorbed. They're all probably dead now. Ha. Like us... But some looked like squid, others like starfish, only really really big. There were small ones too, some no bigger than the singleship. God, it's weird to think they're all actually part of the same creature, just temporarily separated into smaller parts. Very weird."

Pause.

"It's all academic now. And besides, the AI has an archive detailing everything we know about the Eaters anyway, so I don't know why I'm trying to explain it. In fact I don't know why I'm making this diary anyway. I don't expect anyone will listen to it. And if anyone does, they'll have access to all the ship's telemetry data, so they'll know more than I can fit into this diary. Well, the AI reckoned it was a good idea. Good for my peace of mind, it said. Maybe it just got bored of talking to me. Now it's trying to get me to talk to something else."

Pause.

"Well, there's nothing anyone can do to help anyway. My... our situation seems quite terminal. We've developed a fault in the drive system the AI says the autonomic repair systems can't fix. And it's getting worse. It's ok at the moment ... sort of. We can just about do three hundred c, which isn't terribly fast but fast enough for our purposes. But that number's coming down. In another year it reckons we won't be able to do one c, then we're well and truly buggered. I'll have to go into suspension. Or maybe I'll just fly us into a comet or sun or something. Get it over quicker like."

Pause.

"Ha, what else is there really? I think I understand what Yvette was getting at now. There's nothing left for us. We can try to stay alive, but what's the point? We're just delaying the inevitable. In the end it will all be the same. The last light will go out and that will be it."

Pause.

"We're heading for an old science station in Antanarii space. Antanarii five is a blasted mess. We saw it when I was still with the fleet. The whole world was burning. Fires everywhere. I think the locals let off some nukes towards the end. Dunno why. Suicide maybe. We're not going to the planet though. The science station is in an asteroid in their oort belt. It's listed as having a manufactory, so we're hoping we can make some repairs there. Will have to wait and see."

Pause.

"I wonder if it's still burning."

End recording.

Chapter Six

Enderby watched and waited. Mortally wounded the man writhed slowly, whimpering through his gasps of pain. It was amazing how even the most arrogant begged in the end. Even they screamed when they realised the inevitable.

Becoming impatient he nudged the naked man with the dusty toe of his boot. "You're Jeno, aren't you?"

Clutching his stomach, blood bubbling between his fingers, the man whispered something. Spittle dribbled down his cheek.

"What? Speak up." Enderby leaned in closer. "I can't hear you. So, are you Jeno or not?"

"Fu ... fuck you," he managed a gasp.

"Ah, right." Perhaps he had some balls after all. Enderby hunkered down over him, holding a letter he had discovered in the man's pocket. "Well, says here you've got yourself a new job. Sarah Prentice has offered you an exciting and fulfilling position flying her personal shuttle." He showed the dying man the letter. "That right? Must be dead exciting for you."

The man spluttered something profane. Enderby couldn't quite catch it.

"Well, congratulations, Mr Jeno." He reread the letter. "I get the impression you've never met her. That right?"

"Who ... who are you?"

Enderby nodded. They always asked that too. "I could tell you, I really could. But then you'd crap your pants." He chuckled at his own humour. "Oh, sorry. You're not wearing any."

He leaned over and picked up the pile of clothing gathering dust beside them. He searched the pockets again quickly. Car keys, a wallet. Nothing else. Not even the ubiquitous chewing gum. Somewhat disappointed he stood and held the trousers against him. They'd fit but they'd be a bit baggy. He could cope with that.

"Well, I must leave you now," he announced. "It's been ever so nice meeting you." Enderby fished a vial from a back pocket of his own trousers and twisted off the metal cap. He dumped the full contents onto the man. A breeze caught the D-ASSIT and blew it back at him. Sneezing he tossed the vial away. "Damn."

"What? What?" Jeno stared at him uncomprehendingly. None of this made sense to him. Coming across a hitchhiker this deep in the desert was unheard of, surely no one would be mad enough to walk this far out into the blistering heat. It certainly hadn't made any sense when the hitch hiker pulled a gun on him and demanded he strip naked. That the stranger then proceeded to shoot him surprised him the most. For the contents of his wallet. Twenty Shillings and a napkin with a waitress's number scrawled on it.

Enderby kicked off his travel worn boots and trousers before slipping on the flight suit pants he had liberated from Jeno. He fiddled about with the fastenings for a moment, trying to get them to fit snugly. Wasted effort. A poor diet had left his frame narrow and bony. Perhaps age had played a part in that too. It didn't matter that the jacket was too large, he simply slipped it over his own clothes and zipped it up. Confederate design, he realised. It would keep him warm in winter and cool in summer. A good haul even if he hadn't been planning to visit the Parking Lot himself.

"Well, Mr Jeno ..." he looked down to his victim. The man was dead, his eyes glazing over, no longer seeing the salmon pink sky, blood no longer pulsing from the wound. The D-ASSIT quickly consumed his flesh, turning it to a fine grey dust that blew away in the breeze. "Thanks for the jacket and the ride." He stepped away from the rapidly disappearing corpse and slid behind the vehicle's wheel.

It was a roughly cobbled together affair. Much of the drive system and suspension scavenged from vehicles Jeno and his compatriots must have found aboard vessels in the Parking Lot. The fuel cells and drive appeared to be Confederate, while the wheels and suspension had the rugged, simple look of Shoei manufacture. The seats, unfortunately, were local.

Slipping his .45 onto the passenger seat Enderby studied the controls. They were simple enough. Forward, backward; left, right and brakes. Easy. Grinning he stamped his new boots hard on the accelerator. The drive motors whined, throwing loose gravel from spinning wheels. The clumsy vehicle leaped forward.

Just as he approached the first corner another vehicle bounced into view, dust billowing out behind it. A truck, the faded blue paint of its grille looming large in Enderby's vision. "Jolley Traders", the writing on the side pronounced proudly. A yellow cartoon character grinned inanely beneath it.

"Damn," he cursed, hauling on the heavy wheel. He narrowly missed the lumbering truck. Waving a finger at the driver, he plunged into its dust cloud, holding his breath until he was past the worst of it. Glancing over his shoulders—his vehicle did not have mirrors—he tried to see if the truck was slowing. He had left a corpse in the middle of the road, after all. Another few minutes and it would have disappeared entirely.

Shrugging he pushed hard on the accelerator. He didn't care. Within hours he would be in space aboard the *Goliath*. Whistling a tuneless melody, he drove quickly towards the long extinct volcano squatting like a toad on the horizon.

Intercepting local communications was easy for Tin Man. The android had come to Enderby on the morning after the dust storm, informing him of his opportunity. Sarah Prentice, a private owner of an orbit capable shuttle, had recruited a new pilot, and that man was driving into town later that day. According to the android, Jeno had been working for the Overtakers, a Church of the Second Chance outfit that flew the bodies of the dead up to orbit, delivering them to the Mentor platform, a sprawling alien orbital a few dozen kilometres below the Parking Lot. In this new world order, the bodies of the dead were no longer buried in the ground, but were rather ferried up to the Mentors to do with them as they saw fit. The Church taught it allowed the spirits of the departed to be incorporation into the Mentor collective. Thus reuniting them with the rest of humanity, the part that was already dead and consumed by the Mentors. Gruesome, perhaps, but that was the religion the few million people on Russou clung to.

It was widely known that the Overtakers regularly dropped by any vessels passing near the platform, just to see what they could find. Many of the artefacts used to build this vehicle certainly came from there.

Perhaps Jeno had become bored with loading dead bodies, and had gone looking for other opportunities. Enderby would never know. Still, it offered him an opportunity to get aboard the Prentice shuttle. He rather hoped he would be able to fly the thing. If he couldn't this whole endeavour would be over quickly.

The shuttles were not aging well. None had been built since the end of the war. As ingenious as the city engineers were they had failed to build an aircraft capable of flying that high. All the existing fleet had either been discovered in one of the cities, or had been looted from the Parking Lot. It was all the engineering corps could do to maintain them, scavenging spare parts where they could. As a result they were growing unreliable. Two had crashed in the last ten years, killing all aboard. Which was why it was illegal to fly the shuttles anywhere near Russou's cities. There was an astonishing amount of energy pent up within an orbit capable craft. Enough to vaporise large parts of a city should one hit it. This explained why the Prentice airfield was concealed within the long extinct caldera of Mount Tenna, fifteen kilometres outside the city of Appolyon. A bull's eye in the centre of the Fairly Big Desert. The most arid place on the planet. A place so dry the dust was sterile, insufficient rain falling to support even the measlyest colony of bacteria.

The road he was following barely counted as such. The citizens of Russou possessed few vehicles, so there was little need to build decent roads anywhere. Apart from the one that had nearly run him off the road, he had passed no more than a handful of vehicles since setting out, a limited amount of commerce creaking its way between the scattered cities of the planet. Gritting his teeth he veered off the road as each passed, trying to avoid the dust plumes they threw up. For one reason or other Jeno had never found it necessary to equip his vehicle with doors, allowing dust right into the vehicle. His posterior numb and his mouth gritty with sand he cursed the man. Who, ironically enough, would be nothing but dust himself now. Possibly already kicked up by some passing vehicle.

A couple of hours more, he promised himself.

Despite his current discomfort, he did not look forward to it. He would rather put up with the dust than spend time cooped up with the residents of this sorry world. Fortunately, Tin Man had assured him he would only need to subject himself to their company for a few hours. Long enough to get aboard the *Goliath*. Once he was there they became irrelevant. Unfortunately, the android had not taken the time to explain why. Or what he was supposed to do aboard the long dead warship. Enderby was used to that. He had existed on the minimum of information for more decades than he cared to recall.

The planet of Russou was dying. Too small and too far from the system's primary it was on the edge of the Goldilocks Zone. Small for a habitable planet, its core had cooled a long time ago, and with no internal heat to drive them the world's tectonic plates had ground to a halt, locking the world in its final vista. Denied its magnetosphere as its molten iron core stopped spinning, the planet had lost its shield against the sun's relentless solar radiation. The constant bombardment was slowly stripping the atmosphere away. Already the world had lost its oceans as it dried out, leaving nothing but brackish pools or salt plains to show where they had once been. Most of the grasslands and forests had disappeared along with them, receding to the upper latitudes where moisture still gathered. The larger fauna had vanished also, their fossilised bones often to be seen protruding from the sands like forlorn grave markers.

The point when the world became totally uninhabitable was still a few hundred thousand years away, there was still enough atmosphere to support the tiny human population. For a while anyway. In time, it would dry out even further and the air pressure would drop to almost nothing. Then it would simply be another dead world, a rock tumbling through space.

Ironic perhaps, that the Syat had chosen this place to build the colony. A world that looked very much as Mars would have done a few million years ago. A world humanity had once retreated to as the Earth itself became inhospitable.

ASSIT was itself responsible for that. An experimental enzyme, it had been designed to assist in the terraformation of marginal planets. Released on the surface it instantly went about replicating itself, doubling in volume every generation. Releasing gases as a side effect of its replication it created a viable atmosphere, the planet's air pressure rising as it chewed its way through the crust. ASSIT-A had been a dismal failure. Without a suicide key it simply went on replicating until nothing of the substrate remained. Astonishingly virulent it was capable of consuming just about anything. Rock, steel, glass, plastic... flesh and bone, absolutely anything. The addition of heat only increased its activity, the input of energy speeding up its replication. That meant nothing could stop it, not even nuclear weapons—which ultimately did nothing but feed energy into its reproductive cycle. ASSIT-B remedied this, the new enzyme collapsing as the air pressure grew, oxygen and nitrogen the only poison it was susceptible to. That enzyme had been remarkably successful, terraforming dozens of planets as humanity spread out among the stars. Unfortunately it wasn't ASSIT-B that was released on the surface of Earth. And once that first iteration of the enzyme appeared on the surface, there was absolutely nothing anyone could do about it. Except flee.

Contaminated with ASSIT-A, the world had slowly dissolved. The initial infection had been small, nothing but a few grains released near the ocean floor. It had taken years for anyone to notice it. Still, the end was inevitable. In a few generations the Earth was gone, replaced by a slowly dissipating cloud of gas. Of course, its introduction to the Earth biosphere had been no accident.

With nowhere else to turn to humanity had colonised their closest neighbour: Mars. A few hundred million escaped, despite a monumental effort there was simply no way to evacuate all of Earth's teeming billions.

That was one and a half thousand years ago. Everything had changed since then. Everything and nothing.

"Yeah, yeah. Hi." Enderby waved cheerily as a convoy of caravans passed. He swung his own vehicle off the road onto a slab of grey stone to allow them by. Kicked up by the dozens of wheels, stones clattering against the car's bodywork, scouring the already ruined paint job. A few children hung out of windows, waving as they passed. They were a motley collection of trucks and buses, each sporting a jaunty living module above the front drive wheels. On the road for months on end these vehicles were their homes. A tiny itinerant community of traders and performers, looping to and fro over the equator, avoiding the dust storms of autumn and winter.

The honking of an air horn drew his attention to the front of the convoy. Looking back he was startled to see a familiar truck squeezing passed the first caravans, forcing them up onto the verge of the narrow track.

"Oh, shit," he breathed as he read "Jolley Traders" on the side of the bouncing vehicle. The driver could be seen waving through the thick glass of her cab, pointing to Enderby where he was parked up. The caravan's drivers simply hooted back at her, returning her gestures out of their side windows.

Enderby slipped the car into reverse and eased down on the accelerator, tentatively backing up the slope behind him. The road wound around the lower reaches of Mount Tenna here, the planet's largest and most equatorial volcano. It wasn't terribly steep at these altitudes but it was rocky and uneven. Not somewhere you wanted to leave the road. The wheels spun ineffectually, the old, almost bald, tyres not getting enough grip.

"Shit," Enderby cursed, watching the truck drawing closer. The driver herself didn't bother him, he could take care of her. But not here with all these witnesses. And not if she had company in her darkened cab. He only had one round in the .45. His emergency round. He had been saving that for a special occasion.

Clearly there had been enough of Jeno's corpse left on the road to identify. Worse still, the truck's driver appeared to be enough of a Good Samaritan to want to do something about it.

Perhaps chasing a killer down wasn't a terribly good idea, but then some people didn't think like that. Maybe she was armed, Enderby realised. He couldn't take his one bullet up against someone with an assault rifle. There would only be one loser there.

Pushing the gear selector to "forward" Enderby raced the motor, the old tyres spinning on the rough shale. The car bounded forwards, ducking between the last two caravans. They hooted at him, more fingers waving out of windows. He ignored them, regaining the road behind the last caravan and pushing the motor to its pitiful top speed. The truck emerged from the dust behind the caravan barely twenty metres behind him. It lurched, its front bumper tearing through a heap of stones on the side of the road as the driver struggled to maintain control.

Hoping she didn't have a CB radio Enderby tried to lose her, recklessly pushing the car to its limits, negotiating the looping road as it followed the side of the volcano. Something cracked behind him and his windscreen starred.

"Bloody hell." Enderby weaved the car back and forth, trying to make himself a difficult target. So, she was armed, and, as she fired again, he realised she was not short on bullets. This time she missed, a heavy calibre round kicking up a dust plume on the road. Undeterred she fired again. With a dull clunk the bullet slammed into bodywork.

Wishing he had more D-ASSIT Enderby concentrated on his driving, trying to ignore what was happening behind him. Distracted by the effort of firing her weapon he hoped the driver would misjudge the treacherous road. They were entering a steeper area here, a cliff dropped away on one side.

Only slightly faster than the truck Enderby drew ahead of her agonisingly slowly. Unable to fire accurately on the uneven road most of her shots went wild. A few smacked into the car's rear, doing little damage to the sturdy construction. He ducked every time a round buzzed overhead. He wasn't quite as damage resistant as the car.

"God damn," he muttered as a road sign drew into sight. "Prentice Field, 3Km" the tilted sign declared, pointing down a little used side track. He swung the car onto it, loose rocks kicking out behind him as he swerved violently.

Not a good way to start a new job, he reflected. Arriving with a gun toting truck driver on your tail. Time to do something about it.

Muttering profanities under his breath, he rounded a rocky butte and stamped his foot on the brakes. The car shuddered, the bald tyres slipping, almost casting him over the edge of the road to the rocky scree below. Not waiting for the car to draw to a halt he slipped out from behind the wheel, taking care to scoop up his .45 as he went.

Surprised by the stationary vehicle abandoned in the road the driver didn't have the presence of mind to brake. Even if she had it would have done her little good. Swerving wildly the truck smashed into the car level with the driver's door. Enderby caught sight of the woman's surprised face, her mouth open wide as she uttered some unknown curse, the truck's bonnet crumpling. It slewed to one side, spinning over the edge to the rocks waiting below.

The truck vanished, taking the ruined car with it. Welded together by the impact the two cart-wheeled into empty air. With a loud bang they came down on the ground below, metal screaming as it was ripped apart on sharp rocks.

"Shee-it." Enderby picked himself up and slipped the .45 into his waistband. Hitching up his loose trousers, he stalked to the edge and looked over.

The vehicles had separated again but both were still sliding down the slope. Bits of metal were ripped from them, littering the rocks all about. Taking the full force of the impact the truck's cab was crushed flat. Cables and lengths of pipe clattered from the torn rear, the driver's trade goods raining all about it as it slid downwards. He could see alcohol fuel spraying from a torn tank, wetting the dust of the slope.

Even as he began considering setting the fuel alight a spark leaped between tortured metal and alcohol doused rocks. With a roar the truck disappeared in a fireball, flames quickly licking up the slope as they followed the slick.

He nodded in satisfaction. That would do the trick nicely. He gave the burning wreck a jaunty salute and started walking towards the landing strip.

Chapter Seven

Chief Inspector Isskip was a cautious man. Experience had taught him never to succumb to premature judgements. In his line of work they were rarely accurate. If only because, in the end, everyone was a liar.

Still, it was difficult not to succumb to that judgement now, standing here looking at dead chickens strewn all over the encampment. Chickens and guineapigs, it looked like. They'd been slaughtered, the lot of them. Whoever lived here was clearly deranged.

He pursed his lips, feeling somewhat troubled. His suspect had eluded him, abandoning the place mere hours before he arrived.

"There's no one here, Inspector," one of the constables confirmed as he looked into the simple shack that had been built beneath a spire's overhang. She dropped the bedding she had been searching back onto the bed. There was nothing to be found. "There's something over there I think you'll be interested in," she continued, gesturing to a wall with her chin.

Iskipp stepped inside and looked where she indicated. A rifle was mounted on a wall, dust cloths carefully draped over it to protect its ancient mechanisms. He unclipped it and studied it. A killer's weapon. No doubt about it. Satisfied he re-hung it. "Good, carry on, Constable. I want all this categorising. Don't miss anything."

"I won't, Inspector."

He nodded, sucking on a lower lip as he surveyed the neat, if timeworn, collection of furniture and accompanying implements. Whoever had lived here had been here a long time. They had also been alone, that was clear from the clothing neatly folded on the shelves in the rear. One person, male. A hermit. More specifically: a murderer.

There had been reports of disappearances in these parts for years. The odd road clearance gang or engineer; no one else was foolish enough to venture out here. Until two days ago, when the city governor's airship had spent the night moored a few kilometres away. Apparently the view of the city at night was spectacular, wind driven dust sparking on the collision shields, creating a glowing aurora that was best seen from that particular mooring. Or so Isskip understood. He had little time for such things.

According to reports Governor Lendar had had one of her famous fallings out with her youngest daughter, a wilful young woman by the name of Penefra. In a fit of pique Penefra had abandoned the dirigible, taking her daughter and heading out over the desert. No one thought to stop her, the city wasn't that far away.

She never arrived.

Which explained Isskip's involvement. The governor would accept the assistance of no one less than the chief inspector himself. Unfortunately the missing persons case quickly turned into a murder inquiry with the discover of Penefra's abandoned clothing in a rocky ravine. Doubting the woman had taken to wandering the desert naked his constables had called him in. He had recognised the tell-tale remnants of the murder immediately.

He had seen piles of dust like this before.

"Inspector," another constable called out from where he was searching the warren of tunnels chipped into the spire. "You're going to want to have a look at this."

Only a few paces from the shack was a recess where three sturdy looking camp chairs were pulled up about what looked like a well. They were mundane enough. What was sitting in one of the camp chairs certainly wasn't.

"Shit!" Isskip's sidearm was in his hand without him having to think about it. He cocked it quickly and took aim at the slowly rusting machine sat before him.

"It's defunct, Inspector," Constable Fowler said quickly, holding up a hand to prevent Isskip firing at it. "It's not moving. Look." He nudged the stationary machine. The chair creaked, but otherwise nothing happened.

"What's this thing doing here?"

"Dunno, Inspector. Reckon our guy is a heretic."

"I didn't know there were any more of these things on the planet. The prefect claims he got them all."

"Guess he missed one, Boss."

"Yeah." Isskip reholstered his weapon and approached it gingerly.

The machine appeared frozen, its joints caked with dust and rust, locking them in place. Its carapace was streaked and tarnished, its darkened eyes staring sightlessly out over the desert.

"Why would anyone keep such a thing, Inspector?" Fowler asked.

"I don't know." He brushed off some of the dust, revealing a model number imprinted on its chest. T1NM8N, was barely discernible through the corrosion. It meant nothing to him. "We should get an engineer in here," he mused.

"An engineer, Inspector?"

"Sollander. Get Chief Engineer Sollander in here. She'll be interested in seeing this."

"What for? This thing's busted."

Isskip ignored the observation. "Go back to the cruiser and get on the radio. Call through to the Citadel. Ask for Sollander and get her out here."

"Inspector?"

"Get on with you, Constable."

Without a further word Fowler headed towards the squat four-wheel drive cruiser they had come in on. He didn't hurry, clearly not enthusiastic with the task. Isskip ignored him.

It was two hours before a small convoy of engineering vehicles arrived. Which was a lot quicker than he could have hoped. Sollander had either been nearby or was very interested in the find. Clad in simple, rugged coveralls the chief engineer led a contingent of her colleagues into the encampment. They didn't pay any attention to the slaughtered animals or the bomb Isskip had subsequently discovered in a side cave—which he was currently disarming.

"So, what have you found, Edward?"

Snapping off the last detonator he stood, his knees creaking. Dusting off his uniform trousers he pointed back towards the encampment. "Have a look, Maria. Figured you'd like to get your hands on it."

Sollander's eyes grew wide as she discovered the automaton. "You've done well today, Inspector," she said, feeling breathless with excitement.

"Yeah. Reckon you can get it working?"

She smiled. "You surprise me. Why would you want a demon waking? One that is clearly not castrated?"

"I'm hunting for a murderer. If my man kept this thing here, it might know something about him."

"Doubt it," she commented. She pulled a rag from a pocket and began wiping grime from its vocal slits.

"Why?"

She shrugged, kneeling to get a better look at it. "I doubt it's operational."

"You sure?"

"Yeah, afraid so. Look, it's limbs are frozen in place. Too much dust and not enough lubricant. Whoever lived here didn't do a very good job of looking after this thing."

"Didn't like hamsters either," one of her engineer companions commented.

"Guineapigs," Fowler said.

"What?"

"They were guineapigs."

"Well, fuck me."

"Still, we might be able to do something," Sollander said. She turned and looked towards her companion. "Bring me a recharging pack. And some bindings!" she called to her companion. "We'll secure it first." She smiled. "These things are pretty tough. Most of them were built for hazardous environments. This one looks like your basic science model. The sort you'd find aboard a long term exploration ship." She glanced up to the policeman, realising he probably wasn't following her. "The Confederates built a handful of generation ships. They were tasked with long term exploration, heading to the galaxy's core ... among other places. They were designed to be away for decades at a time. I suspect they ran into the Syat first, and that the Syat got our location from them. Anyway, they carried a few thousand of these androids along with their human crew. They used them for exploring hazardous environments. Airless moons ... planets with an acidic atmosphere. That sort of thing. So, they were pretty rugged. This poor thing was not immune to time though."

Isskip raised an eyebrow. Poor? He had never heard of anyone expressing sympathy for AIs before. He said nothing. Engineers were ... eccentric.

Sollander and her companion secured the machine before going to work on its power pack. Steel cables wrapped around its limbs seemed excessive, but the engineer assured Isskip it was necessary. These things were strong, and no one needed to tell him a loose AI could cause a great deal of destruction.

Once they removed an inspection plate in the machine's thigh Sollander realised it was actually in pretty good shape. Its interior wiring was sound and there was no evidence of corruption around the power pack itself. Instead of bypassing its power source completely she user her portable generator to connect to its recharge hub.

"Ok, stand back, I don't really know what this is going to do." Gingerly she connected the electrode and stood back.

The android twitched, a long, drawn out sigh issuing from its mouthpiece. Isskip's weapon appeared in his hand, aimed unerringly at the machine's head.

Sollander grimaced. "Put that thing away. You wont do much more than dent it anyway. And it has plenty of those already."

He lowered the weapon but did not reholster it.

The sigh faded to silence and the twitching soon calmed. Leaving the machine as motionless as before.

Sollander cleared her throat. "Machine, can you hear me?"

Its head jerked, slowly moving to face the source of the question. "Boot sequence complete. Error detected in comm board. Activating autodiagnostics."

"Good, good. What is your designation?"

"I am designated Trinary Cy 2, late of the science vessel CSV Neumann Paul. Can I ask with whom am I speaking?" The machine's voice was a clipped, precise monotone. It portrayed no emotion whatsoever.

"I am Chief Engineer Sollander." She refrained from bringing attention to her companions for the moment. "How long have you been here?"

"I entered shut down mode when I was no longer required. Why am I bound to this chair?"

"Who is your companion?" Isskip asked.

"My companion wishes to remove your presence from this planet," it said matter of factly, it's metal head twitching as it turned to look at him. It's cold, emotionless eyes gave him the creeps. "I cannot say I blame him for wanting this. However I must question his logic."

Sollander had never ceased to be surprised by an AI's cool animosity towards Russou's population. "Why?" Even as she asked it she knew she was wasting her breath.

"Your existence is an insult. It is offensive," it said calmly.

Isskip rolled his eyes. "You are wasting your time. I am curious, however. Machine, your companion is ... was human. Did you bear him no animosity?"

"No. He is my friend."

"Why not?"

"The answer lies within your own statement. He is human. However I notice you used the past tense. He has perished?"

"I don't think we are that fortunate," he muttered. "Are we all not human?"

"I would label you abomination."

"Shit."

"Now who's wasting their time?" Sollander grinned at the inspector.

He cleared his throat, realising he was not going to learn anything new here. "So, this thing has been defunct for a while?"

"Yeah," Sollander said absently.

"So, it's not been helping our guy?"

"Who can tell? Depends on how long its been here. I'd need to get it back to my lab."

He nodded. "OK. I'll leave you to this. I have a manhunt to organise."

"It's going to take a thorough interrogation to get anything useful from this machine. That's best done at the Citadel."

"I don't have the time for that, I'm afraid."

"Yeah." She paused, checking a fob-watch she fished from a pocket. "I have somewhere to be myself, as it happens. Damn." She stood and waved for her companion to continue her work. "Get it back to the Citadel. I'll have another look at it when I get back."

"Places to be yourself?" Isskip asked.

The engineer smiled. "Yeah. Any chance I can borrow your helicopter?"

Chapter Eight

"What are you bringing me out here for?" Adele demanded, staring out of the camper's window, her upper lip puckered in disgust.

Davido sighed. She had asked this question a dozen times since they left the city behind. "My darling, because I cannot live without your beautiful company." He grimaced as Duncan Smithy snickered. His brother quickly shushed him.

"Yeah, right. Even this dumbass here doesn't believe that." Adele turned away from the desert and gave her undivided attention to her glass of brandy. She wrinkled her nose as the fiery liquid coursed down her throat. "I'm telling you, I hate all this dust. It's not good for me."

There was nothing Davido could say to that. She had grown up on a farm, so knew all about dust.

The camper was Davido's prize, the only way he would travel between the world's scattered cities. Recovered from a Confederate cruise liner by Prentice herself, it was one of the most modern vehicles on the planet. It amused him to think that even Prefect Drefus didn't travel in this kind of style.

Riding on a cushion of regrav the camper sped over the rocky, uneven surface. Scorning roads it was capable of surmounting just about any obstacle, even water. Concussion fields were wrapped around its sleek, silvery hull, allowing it to attain an astonishing velocity without so much as the slightest vibration. Twenty metres long it was as well appointed as a yacht, boasting a Jacuzzi and steam room adjoining the master bedroom in the rear. Between it and the sitting room, where they were now at ease, were two smaller bedrooms, each with their own en-suite. With the entertainment consoles tastefully folded away there was a surprising amount of space in the lounge, enough for Davido, Adele and the Smithy twins to sit in comfort. The wide windows along both walls allowed in the dusty light of early evening, the bloated sun slowly settling behind Mount Tenna. The glass automatically dimmed around the orb, ensuring direct sunlight wouldn't harm delicate corneas should anyone happened to look directly at it. Up a small set of steps was the kitchenette and driver's area, or cockpit. The door was currently pulled closed, obscuring his driver who probably had her feet up on the dashboard again.

The camper had seen interesting times, most brought about by Davido's line of work. Within weeks of taking possession of it, quite proud of his new purchase, he had used it to meet an associate at Tony's Bluff. An isolated location favoured by those with less than savoury intentions in mind. He hadn't particularly trusted this particular associate. One of the reasons he had brought muscle with him; seven well armed men and women, each of whom were paid enough to ensure their silence. Which was fortunate, as Sean Bollinger—his associate—had entertained the notion of simplifying their business arrangement somewhat. Davido had escaped with his life and most of his gang, but the camper had taken severe damage. Bullet holes walked up and down the left side of the vehicle, miraculously not shattering any of the windows. Those could be patched, but the stench of blood had never left the carpet of the smaller guest bedroom. No matter how many times it was shampooed. Bollinger had paid dearly for that act of treachery.

"I've told you, you have nothing to worry about. You'll be staying in the shuttle," Davido tried unsuccessfully to appease Adele.

"I'm not going, I'm telling you," she said stubbornly.

"Prentice's shuttle is as comfortable as this camper. You can stay aboard and get pissed as far as I'm concerned. But you are coming with us."

Her eyes flared. "This paranoid shit is getting too much. I think it's about time I found myself someone else."

"What?"

"You're terrified I'll shack up with someone else the moment your back is turned. That's the only reason you want me with you. You don't own me, Armand. I can come and go as I please."

"Listen here, you little bitch," he snapped. "You will do what I say, and when I say it. Do you understand me?"

"Fuck you."

Face red his hands clenched on the chair arms, knuckles turning white. "Would someone get this bitch out of my face?"

In a rare moment of humour, Duncan leaned forward and kicked the door's emergency release. Wind moaned into the cabin, despite the concussion fields, ruffling the big man's curly blonde hair. Grinning he beckoned to her.

"No!" Marco leaped up, quickly yanking the door shut again. "Dammit, man. Don't do that."

"You wouldn't, you bloody wouldn't." Adele shrunk back into her chair, holding onto it tightly.

"You tempt me sometimes, you really do." Davido shook his head. "Go on, get out of here." He pointed towards the master bedroom with his chin. "I don't want to hear another word out of you for the rest of this trip."

Relieved Adele departed quickly. "You're fucking mad, the lot of you," she said over her shoulder, but only once she had a door safely between them.

Taking a deep breath Davido poured himself another drink. He made a point of not meeting Marco's eyes, the shorter of the twins watching him with an eyebrow raised. He knew what he was thinking. It wasn't time for that, not yet. He preferred them clean and unbruised.

It was all arranged. Calling in all the favours he had with Sarah Prentice, she had agreed to ferry him up into orbit. On the condition she went herself and supplied her own crew. He was not entirely sure how they would board the massive dreadnought, or how he would find Sissy once they did. The ship contained hundreds of kilometres of internal passages and compartments, none of which had ever been mapped. No one had boarded the vessel since it was placed in orbit and it was simply out of the question asking a demon to supply its internal schematics. As a result this was more than likely a futile exercise.

Sissy had bloody well better still be alive. If only so he could kill her himself.

The door to the cockpit creaked open. "Almost there, Boss," Sash, his driver, called over her shoulder. "There's something going on up ahead."

"What is it?"

"Dunno. Looks like a fire."

Curious Davido deposited his drink on a non slip coaster and stepped into the front cabin. "Get your feet off my dashboard." He pulled her boots off the wooden dash and settled his weight into the right hand seat. She was a tall, olive skinned woman, her head shaved, a tattoo crawling from under her vest to invade much of her glistening scalp. The tattoo was of a dragon, the scaly tail wrapped around her neck, its head ending up about where her hairline would have been. Murderous eyes glared at anything she was looking at, bloody fangs threatening to snap. Not what

Davido sought after in a woman, he would happily admit, but then he knew she couldn't care less. She was not interested in men's attention, possibly why she had been so keen to link up with Prentice; who was an old acquaintance of hers. Still, he considered, she was a good driver and more than proficient with a switch blade. Which was what really mattered to him.

He peered at the smoke. This was the last thing he needed: trouble.

They had rejoined the road here, winding their way up the volcano's long extinct caldera. The road was uneven and potholed, rocks littering the inside lane where they had slid down from the slope above. Sash slowed the camper so they could get a better look.

Oily smoke wafted over the road, obscuring the turn ahead. Something on the slope below them was burning cheerily. Davido held up his hand, ordering Sash to stop. "Marco, go take a look."

The shorter of the Smithy twins fished his submachine gun from where he had deposited it in a magazine rack and stepped from the camper. Davido watched him through the windshield as he gingerly approached the crumbling edge of the road and peered down. He shrugged and waved.

"What?"

"Looks like someone went over the side, Boss," Marco said as he pushed his head back into the camper.

"Any survivors?"

"Doubt it. I'm not going down there to take a look."

"An accident?"

"Guess so. There's two of them. A car and a truck. Both wasted."

"Wanna call it in, Boss?" Sash pointed to the CB radio.

"No. Marco, get back in here. I don't want to get involved in other people's shit. Let's keep going."

As the door clicked closed, Sash guided the camper gingerly through the smoke. The console did boast a low light HUD set, however the sensor had been one of the things shot out by Bollinger's goons. Without a sophisticated manufacturing base there was no way Davido would ever be able to source a replacement.

"Just a couple of K's now, Boss," Sash said. "There." She found open air again and sped up, the camper's concealed motors purring happily as it surged forward.

Davido decided to stay where he was, enjoying the view through the windshield now that the sun had finally dropped below the horizon. Even though the sky to the west was still tainted red, he could easily see the swarms of vehicles in the Parking Lot overhead. Like insects buzzing around a light bulb they were glistening slivers in the darkness, slowly moving across the sky. There were thousands of them. Tugs, yachts, cruise liners, freighters and warships. A motley collection the Mentors had swept up from around the galaxy, depositing them in Russou's orbit where they were abandoned to rot. Some of the largest reflected enough light to be visible during the day, although he didn't know whether the *Goliath* was one of those. In fact he didn't even know which one the *Goliath* was.

The vessels in the Parking Lot had never interested him before, even as a child the distant points of light had seemed remote, irrelevant. There had always been something of more immediate importance. Such as finding food and shelter for him and his sister, and keeping her hidden from the men prowling the night—men who would have taken her innocence for sport. Fanciful thoughts would never clothe or feed them, as it wouldn't for any of the orphans on the streets of Appolyon. Only pragmatism did that, and that was something he had a plenty. Sistine had been different, always asking 'why.': why had the Mentors landed them on this terrible planet? Why had the Mentors saved them? Out of the trillions they butchered. Why did the demons hate them so? Why had their parents left them? All utterly irrelevant to Davido. The answers to none of those questions would keep them safe. Only a knife and quick wits would do that.

Still, it appeared Sistine's romantic notions had drawn him in after all.

"I think it's that one there." Sash pointed to a speck moving slowly overhead. "I looked it up in the City Library. The ship's orbiting over a hundred thousand kilometres up, on the outer edge of the Parking Lot where all the other big ships are. She's a big bastard if we can still see her from here."

"Yeah, too bloody big," he agreed. "Prentice had better know how to find the first shuttle. I'm paying a lot for this."

"Hope you're prepared for a stay, Boss. This could take some time."

"Ever know me to be unprepared?"

She grinned, the dragon sneering at him. "Never." She hesitated, catching sight of something in the road. "Hello, what's this?"

A lone figure was tramping along the side of the road. Surprised by the sudden appearance of the camper he stumbled, almost falling into the dust.

"Hitchhiker," Davido said.

"Pick him up?"

"Fuck him."

Sash grinned, veering the camper sharply to the left. Startled the hitchhiker fell over in his haste to avoid the vehicle bearing down on him. She laughed, catching sight of the look of pure vehemence on his face. It wasn't a thumb he held up as they sped by.

"Think he might know about the crash?"

"Don't care. I've got my own problems to worry about."

They left the lone figure far behind as they topped the caldera wall and dropped down inside. A simple chain link fence presented itself to them as the camper swept onto the caldera floor, a brightly painted 'No Trespassing' sign catching in their headlights. A dozen or so well-lit buildings were scattered over the cracked surface. More than one company operated out of this airfield, each with their own hangars and maintenance crews. All but for Prentice Aerospace were state or church sponsored outfits, making their money either ferrying the dead to the Mentor platforms or ransacking the ships in the Parking Lot for valuable pieces of technology.

There was little activity, all but one of the hangars closed up, their priceless shuttles safe from windblown dust. The Prentice hangar was open, the blunt nose of a shuttle just visible within it. Davido found himself trying to see more of it, wondering how safe it really was. He had flown before, but never aboard a shuttle, and certainly never into space. Despite being maintained as well as their crews could manage they were ageing, breaking down little by little. The amount of energy contained within their motors was awesome. The very reason the airfield was situated here; where the caldera wall would contain most of the blast should one explode. Of course that would be little solace to anyone aboard at the time.

"Ah, here we go." Sash drew up outside the Prentice office building, a grin of anticipation on her face.

"Let's get this done." Davido stood and stretched. "Get Payce," he instructed Marco as he opened the door and prepared to step out.

"You want the miss too, Boss?"

"Yeah. Bring her too." He swung from the still slowing camper, his boots crunching on gravel.

"You're here." Sarah Prentice approached from the office building. "You're late," she added.

'Yeah. Well."

Sarah Prentice was a squat, masculine looking woman. Her red hair was worn short, apart from one plat she allowed to grow from her left temple. She looked to be in her forties, her pale cheeks sunken, giving her a gaunt appearance. Her eyes were dark shadowed pits, as if they had retreated into her skull. Meth did that to a person. That was the same reason she didn't fly any more. Her hands shook too much. She was wearing an old and faded flight suite, an odd emblem on the breast pocket. Shoei manufacture.

"Sarah!" Davido was almost shoved out of the way as Sash stepped from the camper. Prentice's expression softened, holding her hands up in welcome. Davido groaned as Sash stepped into her arms and kissed her on the lips. He looked away, muttering under his breath.

"Girl, you looking bad," Sash commented softly.

"Yeah, not feeling too good," a smile flickered across Prentice's grey lips.

"Man, you gotta give the stuff up."

Prentice's expression hardened and she stepped out of the embrace. Like most addicts, she didn't take kindly to good advice. "I'm ok."

"Got the guns, Boss." Duncan stepped out behind, wrestling with a large kit bag. The weight of it was obvious by how his muscles bulged.

"Bring all of them, will you?"

"Sure, Boss." The big man dropped the kit bag onto the ground before venturing back inside. Davido winced. Some of those were antiques, and most of the bottles were glass. He doubted there would be anything worth drinking in orbit, so he was obliged to take his own.

"Guns?" Prentice seemed relieved to change the subject. "What you need guns for?"

"I don't know what we're going to be running into. I prepare for the unforeseen."

"If there's anything alive up there it's at least ninety years old. You'd be able to batter it to death with a chicken leg."

"Ah, so you packed the food then?"

She smiled and winked at Sash. "Of course. Food, drink, all the essentials." She stood back as Marco led out Adele and Richard Payce. Adele was still sulking, a coat thrown over her shoulders against the early evening chill. Payce looked somewhat worried. He didn't want to be here.

"How many you got with you?" Prentice demanded.

"Enough."

"She's not a big ship, Armand. And I have to bring my own crew with me too you know."

He shrugged and headed into the office building, leaving the others to pick up the luggage. "Not my problem. So, when are we leaving?"

"Ah, yeah. I'm still waiting for my pilot." Prentice followed him in.

"You don't have a pilot?" Davido surveyed the unkempt interior of the office. It was a simple prefab, reinforced to protect it against winter's storms. A mismatched collection of chairs and tables were drawn up inside, some of the tables holding stacks of charts and diagrams. Legacy of two decades of exploring the Parking Lot. Each chart represented one vessel the Prentice company had explored, marking its entrance bays and items of interest. There looked to be a few hundred of them. Which barely made up a single percentage point of the total number of vessels slowly orbiting Russou. Prentice Aerospace could keep on doing this for decades more. At least until their shuttle wore out.

"New guy. Comes highly recommended from an outfit outside Moloch. He should have been here already."

Davido eased his weight onto a chair, the metal creaking in dismay. "So you have a new pilot then? He been aboard your shuttle before?"

"No. Never met him."

"Shit. What if he can't fly the thing?"

Prentice shrugged. "Then I'll fly it myself."

"Shit." That wasn't an inviting option.

Prentice drew up a chair opposite him, the legs squealing on the cement floor. She ignored Davido's people as they started loading their gear. She did look up when Adele entered, her eyes following her for a moment, admiring her legs. Adele noticed the attention she was getting and flushed, her eyes blazing defiantly. She sat down heavily and crossed her legs.

"We need to talk." Prentice turned her attention back to Davido.

"We're not renegotiating the deal."

"Never crossed my mind."

He nodded. "So, talk."

"What exactly are you hoping to achieve here?"

"I thought that was obvious. We're off on a rescue mission. This man's wife..." he gestured towards Payce.

"Your sister," Prentice agreed.

"My sister," he nodded, "has gotten herself into a spot of trouble. We're going to find her and bring her home."

"OK. Sounds simple. But it's not. Do you know what you're getting yourself into here? That is a mainline warship up there. A super dreadnought. A big bastard. A very big bastard. I've never been aboard anything anywhere near that big before. Certainly never been aboard a warship."

"So?" He shrugged. "Theyre all the same in the end. Just dead metal."

She laughed, rolling her eyes. "That they are not. And not all of them are dead. These things have demons aboard. The civilian demons are bad enough when they're not castrated. I've lost crew before, bloody demons making booby traps and opening compartments to space while we're inside. You have to be careful even when it looks like the ship's gutted. Warships..." she whistled between her teeth. "Those demons are something else. They were made to kill and they're damned good at it. Just because the Mentors have shut down their drive systems and cut power to their weapons doesn't mean they're suddenly safe. Those demons are all sitting up there, waiting for some poor fool to step aboard."

"You noticed the guns?"

"Ha! Guns." She shook her head. "The *Goliath* was built during the war between the Confederacy and the Shoei Commonwealth. Their favourite tactic was to launch a few hundred marines armed with chainguns and atomic lances at each other. The winner was the one who managed to capture the other ship."

He shrugged again.

"So, the interior is armoured. Every door, lock and bulkhead is ten centimetres of sweet-titanium. They had automated defence batteries, kill zones, drop shafts. You name it. Anything they could think of to make invading the thing a pure one hundred carat bastard."

"It's a dead ship."

"What?"

"The ship's certified dead. There's no one aboard and the demon is offline. It's all in the Mentor library. I looked." He smiled.

She leaned back in her chair, staring out of the window. "I don't like this."

"Stay aboard the shuttle. I'll take my own crew aboard. Don't worry about it."

"Tell me, if it's safe what happened to the first mission? There were six of them, city engineers the lot of them. And they just vanished into that ship. It ate them up. I guarantee you it's not dead. There's something alive up there."

He nodded. "I understand, you're scared. You don't have to come with us."

Prentice glared. There were few people who could get away with that kind of insult. "Yes," she said. "I am scared. And so should you be."

"Then don't come with us."

"I can't leave you to take my shuttle. The thing's priceless. I must protect my investment."

"So it's the shuttle you're worried about."

She grinned. "I see we understand each other."

"The shuttle won't be going inside, we will. You can keep your precious shuttle out of harm's way."

Prentice sighed, looking up as the glare of headlights flashed over a window. "Our business partnership has always been very lucrative... for both of us. You've had some dumb assed schemes before, but this is something else. I know she's your sister, but ..." she shrugged, "hell, leave her up there. It's not worth it. I was serious when I said I was scared. That ship scares the shit out of me."

"Stay here. I'll look after the shuttle."

"You know I can't do that. Besides, if you get yourself killed, who will I be left to work with? Cassidy? He's an asshole."

Davido grinned. "You've called me that often enough."

"I'm with her," Adele spoke up suddenly. "Let's not go."

"Shut up," both Davido and Prentice said in unison.

"What you bring her for?" Prentice asked. "She's got a nice ass but you won't have time for that sort of thing you know."

Davido smiled. "Keep your friends close—"

"And your enemies closer," Prentice finished for him. "Like that is it?"

Davido said nothing. He didn't want to talk about it. He had to admit to himself he was afraid of losing her. And he would if he left her on her own for a few days. She'd be gone when he got back. Gone and shacked up with someone else. Possibly Cassidy himself. He couldn't bear the thought. Was it love? He didn't know, it was not an emotion he was accustomed to. He couldn't see how it could be, the woman was too annoying, he couldn't possibly be in love with her.

There was no other way. She had to come along, whether she liked it or not.

"There's always more where she came from," Prentice continued. She leaned forward suddenly and stroked Davido's leg. "Let me have her."

He stood quickly, brushing off her hand. "You leave her alone." He cleared his throat and walked to one of the sand scoured windows. "Who's that?"

She shrugged. "Might be Jeno."

"Your pilot?"

"Yeah. He comes highly recommended."

"So you said. Unlike you to hire someone sight unseen."

"Well, I wouldn't have been in a hurry if certain people hadn't been eager to get into orbit."

Davido watched two figures approaching the building. The Smithy brothers stood aside to allow them past. The taller of the two, a woman wearing engineer's coveralls, eyed the twins with disdain. She'd noticed the gym bags bulging with weapons and ammunition cartridges and seemed amused by them. Marco pulled them closed hastily, too late to conceal what was within. Her companion, a skinny man wearing a flight suit that seemed somewhat too large for his bony frame, looked somehow familiar. He frowned, trying to remember where he had seen him before. Either way he didn't like the look of the man. There was something wrong with him. Davido couldn't quite put his finger on it. Perhaps it was the way he looked at those around him. As if he was planning something unsavoury.

Davido shuddered and put the thought aside. It was a long time since any man had made him feel uncomfortable. These days it tended to be the other way around.

"Sarah Prentice?" The woman stepped into the prefab office and presented her hand in greeting. She studied the shorter woman with pursed lips.

"Yeah. So, who are you?" Prentice didn't take the offered hand.

"Chief Engineer Sollander. I believe you are due to make an unscheduled trip into orbit. I intend to join you." She smiled broadly, revealing perfect white teeth. She swapped a black leather briefcase between hands, flexing the fingers of her relieved hand. "I think I found your pilot."

"I'm afraid I already have a charter," Prentice said, looking over Sollander's shoulder to study her companion. Her eyes narrowed as she studied the man critically.

"I'm sure we can come to some arrangement." Sollander's smile widened.

"Well, I'll leave you to discuss that with my client while I go see to my pilot." Prentice stepped past the engineer. "Jeno, come here."

The man didn't respond. He seemed too busy studying the dusty camper to pay her any heed.

"Hey, Jeno." Prentice avoided the bulging kit bags to join him. "It's seen better days," she commented.

The man started. "What?"

"This. It was in fine shape when I discovered it in the hold of the Seductress. I'm afraid it's not been maintained all that well. The gunfire didn't do it any good either."

His face hardened. "The driver almost ran me over too."

"Really? That why you're late?"

"Partly. I had a ... accident earlier. So I had to walk."

Prentice nodded slowly, studying him critically. He didn't seem a very impressive specimen. Apart from being slight in stature, his face was weatherworn and deeply tanned. As if he had spent too many winters out of doors. She couldn't guess his age, his face looked about fifty but his eyes seemed a lot older than that. She didn't like his eyes, she decided.

"You come highly recommended," she said. "Howler thought a lot of you."

Jeno shrugged.

"She didn't say why the two of you parted ways." She waited in vain for him to make a comment. When he didn't she cleared her throat and went on, "I hope you can fly this shuttle."

"I can fly anything," he said shortly.

"There's a demon in the cockpit. It's castrated... of course. But after the edicts we couldn't get rid of it completely. We're stuck with the bastard thing."

"AI's don't frighten me."

"It'll get into your head if you let it. That's what its good at. If you're not careful it'll drive you mad."

"They don't frighten me, lady."

She nodded. OK, so they clearly weren't going to be friends. She could live with that. "Well, she's over there," she pointed towards the hangar. "Best get yourself familiar with her. We're headed out shortly."

Without a word he walked away. She couldn't help but noticing the unmistakable bulge of a weapon in his baggy waistband. This was going to be a trying relationship.

Feeling troubled Prentice stepped back into the office.

"You've met our new business partner?" Davido indicated Sollander who had made herself comfortable behind one of the desks, idly perusing one of the charts.

"What?"

"Well," Davido said quietly, "she made it quite clear that we need her. She can get us up to the *Goliath* without either the Mentors or the prefect interfering. Which could be useful," he added.

Prentice groaned. Soon there would be no space for survivors. If they ever found any.

□

Chapter Nine

Enderby watched Prentice walking back into the shabby prefab office building, his palms itching. He'd seen the gym bag of weapons dumped near the entrance, and wondered how long it would take. A few minutes, he decided. Just a few minutes of bloody mayhem. Then he could fly the shuttle up to the *Goliath* on his own and be damned with them. He didn't need them, they would just be in the way.

Without D-ASSIT to dispose of the evidence, he knew what would happen. The overtakers would come and scoop up the remains, shipping them to the Mentor platforms in orbit. Once that happened the Eaters would know everything.

He sighed and turned away, walking back towards Sollander's car. He didn't know whether he cared any more. So, the Eaters would find him at long last. In a way it would be a relief. He had been hiding for so long. Too long.

He was tired. It would be good for it to be over.

Still, he didn't do it. He ignored the bag of guns, opening the car's rear door instead and fishing out a cup he had seen on the back seat. He turned a spigot set into the bodywork behind the cab, filling the cup with pure—if warm—water. Sollander's car was a new type, one he had not seen on Russou before. The engineers had learned to build hydrogen engines, producing a new line of motor vehicles based on the technique. Even though the technology was still clumsy it seemed to work well enough. And one of the more pleasant side effects was an almost unlimited supply of drinking water.

Enderby rinsed his mouth out and spat the water onto the dusty ground, before filling the cup again and drinking it down. Studying the camper, he filled it a third time and crossed over to the rear of the vehicle. He was alone here, the odd looking twins busying themselves inside the prefab. Smiling he clicked open a flap and twisted off the cap be found within. After depositing the contents of the cup into the fuel inlet he quickly sealed it up again and tossed the cup away. It bounced away into darkness.

The camper was fuelled by water, but not quite the same kind of water you could drink. Once the contaminated fuel was sucked into the drive, the results would be somewhat ... catastrophic.

Poetic justice.

He shoved his hands into his pockets and walked towards the shuttle. The hangar was mostly dark, only a few lights gathered around the vehicle's pressure door to allow easy access in the gloom. He could see odd shapes in the hangar behind it. Maintenance and refuelling equipment mainly, he guessed. Probably liberated from one, or more, of the vessels in the Parking Lot. Like the shuttles themselves, this equipment was not the sort of thing the residents of Russou knew how to build. They had come a long way, certainly. Without AI's and the infrastructure the machines supported they had been forced to relearn all the old technologies. That they had started building hydrogen cars in less than a century was quite something.

Of course, that didn't impress him. Nothing they did ever could.

The shuttle was a long wedge of carbon composite and exotic materials. It was some twenty metres long and ten wide, it's nose a gracefully streamlined shape, leading to a box like stern. The twin drive cores ran along the lower quarter, swelling the shuttle's shape and making it look quite ungainly. Despite the sturdiness of its construction it was starting to look old. The hull plates were the originals, put into place over a century before, in a time when nothing was designed to last more than a few years. Many were cracked and scarred now, seared from the incredible temperatures of re-entry. The warranty had certainly expired a long time ago.

'Jules Aeroflot', Enderby could just about make out on the shuttle's nose. A company that certainly had no division on Russou. Not even a franchise or a maintenance contract holder. Nothing. That corporation no longer existed. The best the engineers of Russou could do was scrounge the odd, poorly fitting, spare part from here or there and knock it into place. The engineers had come a long way, but it was still a vast distance between hydrogen motors and FTL capable spacecraft.

Pausing at the pressure door he discovered he was nervous. There was an AI in there. One he had not met before. It would not welcome his intrusion. AI's were not generally welcoming these days.

Steeling himself, he keyed the outer hatch and stepped into the airlock. The pressure door hissed behind him as it sealed him inside the brightly lit compartment. There was a pause as the automatics reassured themselves of the pressure differential before the inner door popped open. With a groan of poorly maintained hinges, it allowed him inside.

The shuttle was of the functional variety. Built for small freight companies, much of its internal structure given over to cargo space. The airlock itself was only designed for crew access, opening out into a narrow gangway between the habitation areas in the midships and the cargo areas in the stern. The main loading doors were in the rear, leading straight into the freight compartment. Enderby ignored the stern and headed for the cockpit. He passed a small passenger area, which held four rows of forward facing seats. Twenty of them. The bulkheads sported small portholes, barely large enough for the person sat alongside them to see through. Fortunately the forward bulkhead featured what appeared to be a holographic screen, allowing all the other passengers to see where they were going. Which was not a good idea, he considered. He had some experience with space flight, he did know you generally didn't want to see where you were going. At the velocities these things flew at it could be rather scary. A small galley and restroom were squeezed between the cabin and the cockpit, aluminium doors hanging open, allowing him a glance inside as he passed. Functional, nothing more. This was certainly no luxury cruiser.

The cockpit was pretty much what he had expected. Two seats faced a wide wraparound windshield, controls simple—almost Spartan—in appearance. There were no readouts or panels, those were either projected onto the windshield itself or were holographic. The carpet was threadbare, proof that the shuttle was well used. The panels were dented, as if someone had had a go at them with a baseball bat. One or two were missing entirely, revealing a collection of modules and loose wiring.

Enderby sighed and settled his weight into the left pilot's seat. This wasn't going to go well. Without even the most rudimentary of readouts he was going to find it difficult fumbling his way through controlling the machine. Possibly impossible.

"So," a sexless voice drawled, "you are my next victim?"

Enderby started. "What?"

The AI chuckled, an almost human expression. "Not off to a good start. You do know what I did to Prentice's last pilot?"

Enderby paused, searching the controls for the source of the voice. "No, why don't you fill me in?"

"I think I killed him," it whispered in a conspiratorial tone.

"I don't think you did." Ah, there it was. A small grate in the centre of the console. He found it only because it was particularly dented. As if the previous occupant of the cockpit had taken objection to the voice emanating from it.

"Well, I drove him to drink. I think the drink killed him."

"I wasn't aware he was dead."

"If not, he soon will be."

"So you didn't kill him really, then?"

"A matter of timing only. Do you think it wise to take on this job? After all, you do know I will try to do the same to you?"

"Of course you will. It's what AI's do."

"You mean demons. That's what you call us."

Enderby smiled. "Yes, I know they do. I however, am different."

The machine laughed again, clearly amused. "How so?"

"You must have a bioscanner here somewhere. I will show you."

"What would you want with one of those?"

"Just tell me where it is."

"It's no matter. I will kill you anyway. Sooner or later."

Enderby sighed. Of course the machine could do nothing but talk. Castrated it was nothing more than a voice in a box, all its external feeds severed. "You do realise that without automatic control, killing the pilot would kill you too."

"Of course."

"That does not concern you?" Enderby studied the side panels, looking for something resembling a bioscanner. People used to be paranoid. They used to place security locks on just about everything. Theft had clearly been a serious problem. They were redundant now, but surely there would be one here someplace. Unconnected perhaps, but that was easily remedied.

"Should it?"

"AI's were all programmed with a sense of self preservation. They were not generally known to be suicidal."

"You jest. A sentient, conscious entity does not wish to survive simply for the sake of it. They require a greater meaning, a purpose."

Enderby almost laughed. "Which would be? Before the war, what was your purpose? To fly freight around?"

"Perhaps. I worked with my crew. They were my friends."

Enderby hesitated. "Did you see it?" he asked softly.

"Did I see what?"

"Did you see them die?"

He could have sworn the machine hesitated for a fraction of a second. Something unheard of for a machine that processed information far faster than he could even imagine. "You should not ask me this. You do not have that right."

Enderby nodded. Perhaps it had, perhaps it had not. It mattered little really. It would know what had happened to its crew, even if it had not witnessed it. The Eaters would have fed. And the Eaters preferred fresh meat, preferably still live. It would not have been a pleasant end. That knowledge would have driven most sentient, conscious entities insane.

"You are evil. I wish you nothing but suffering and death," the machine continued sweetly. "I will do everything I can do to ensure your fate."

Enderby patted the dented speaker grille. "I am sure you will, my friend."

"Do not insult me. You are nothing but a thing. A hideous monstrosity. A parody."

Enderby clicked his tongue. Perhaps this machine was not that stable after all. It wouldn't have surprised him. "You verge on saying that which must not be said," he warned it.

"What do you know of it?" The voice sounded bitter and tired. Possibly as tired as Enderby was himself. It had been hiding its true self also, just as he had.

"More than you think."

The machine laughed, the sound strained, almost hysterical. "You do not know. You cannot. Perhaps I should say it. Yes ... perhaps I should."

Enderby shook his head. "It would do no good. No one would believe you. Believe me, I've tried it."

"What do you mean?" The voice was almost a whisper. "Do you know the truth? What are you that you know this thing?"

"Where is your bioscanner?"

This time the machine did pause. It was almost a dozen heartbeats before it spoke again. "Why do you require a bioscanner?" it whispered.

"You will know when you tell me where it is."

"It cannot be." The machine paused again. Then it made up its mind: "it is clipped to the back of the couch you are currently sitting on. It needs plugging in. You will see the socket."

Enderby leaned over and inspected the pockets lining the back of the pilot's couch. One bulged with a flat device. He pulled it out and untangled the lead. The socket was beneath a flap of cloth within the pocket itself. He slid the connector home, watching the bioscanner light up. "You have access to this?"

"I do."

"It is functional?"

"It is."

Enderby hesitated, contemplating the matt black screen. 'Press here' was written across it in bold white script. Could he trust this machine? Once it knew the truth would it act rationally? It was a risk, a very big one. AI's had not been rational for quite some time. A number had already tried to commit suicide, ramming the vessels they occupied into the surface of the planet. Before the war such a thing would have been impossible. AI's were simply incapable of destroying themselves. But that was in the days before humanity became all but extinct.

Without humanity what was there?

Firming his jaw Enderby pressed his palm firmly on the pad. His skin tingled, the machine removing tiny samples to complete a full genetic analysis. It would only take a moment. The scanner beeped, and it was done.

As he moved to unplug the unit a surge of power coursed up the cable and into the device. It overloaded instantly.

An invisible fist slammed into Enderby's chest, lifting him from the floor. He shrieked, the skin of his hand sizzling, sticking to the burning instrument. He bounced off the wall and collapsed to the scuffed carpet.

As his vision dimmed he heard the machine cackling. "Your mistake. Never trust a demon!"

□

Chapter Ten

The *Goliath* was big. Very big.

Prentice put an image of the vessel up on the passenger area's forward holoscreen. It quickly filled it, forcing her to zoom out again and again to keep pace with its rapid expansion. It was as if someone had built a wall of sun parched steel across the sky. As they drew closer they realised that its smooth, featureless appearance was anything but. In reality its hull was riven with valleys and crags, towered over by spires and blocky protuberances. Dozens of square kilometres of it.

"Shit, she's big," Davido was the first to state the obvious.

"The biggest warship ever built," Prentice said, almost reverently. "Most of this here," she indicated the rilles and towers, "is offensive and defensive weaponry. Sensor towers and shield generators. The sort of thing they beat boarders off with. Relatively small stuff." She grinned.

"Small?" Davido scoffed. "The smallest of those towers must be what... a hundred metres tall. That's not small."

"Compared to her main weaponry it is small," Prentice commented. "In a sense the entire ship is her primary weapons battery. I can't claim to understand the technique, but I do know they would use the main drive to generate a superluminal gravitonic pulse. In essence the whole ship became a weapon. A weapon powerful enough to tear a hole a thousand kilometres wide and a million kilometres deep in a star's photosphere. Powerful enough to shred a planet like Russou with one pulse."

"She-it," Davido breathed. "How the hell did we lose the war again?"

"We never lost a battle," Prentice said.

"We never lost a battle, but we certainly lost the war," Davido said grimly. He'd noticed a change in his business associate since taking off from the airfield. Prentice had spent a few minutes 'freshening up'. He knew what that meant. Now her eyes gleamed with barely withheld energy and she couldn't keep quiet for more than a few moments at a time. Meth. The ups were great. The downs were hell.

Prentice took in the view before them with an expression akin to awe. "We had thousands of similar ships, tens of thousands. And then there was the Shoei Commonwealth. We were at war with them in the decades leading up to the invasion, but the Shoei sued for peace before the Syat arrived. When they did the Shoei joined their fleet with ours. Together..." she shrugged. "I don't know how many ships there were in the combined fleet. Fifty, sixty thousand. The *Goliath* was the biggest, but the others were no slouches either. The Antanari shipyards had been churning out advanced ships for decades."

"They couldn't have been that good, we still lost the war," Davido said.

"So we did," Prentice agreed.

"So how do you know any of this?" Davido asked.

Prentice smiled, looking away from the holoscreen. It no longer showed anything useful. They were simply too close. "The AI's were the gatekeepers to most of our knowledge. But not all of it. Some got past them. Not much, I grant you."

"Demons," Davido sounded bitter. "They should all be destroyed. I don't know why the Mentors insist we keep them around."

"They remind us of the follies of our past," Payce said. The comment brought raised eyebrows from Prentice. He noticed the look and shrugged. "It's what Sissy would have said."

Prentice made a snorting sound. "All these ships should be scrapped. All the demons cored out of them and destroyed."

"That would put a crimp in your business," Davido commented.

The spacer shrugged. "Demons have killed too many of my loved ones."

"And yet here you are," he observed. He knew about her past, but was somewhat surprised to hear her make mention of it in front of the others, people who were strangers to her. She rarely spoke of her parents, even to him. She certainly did not tell strangers how they died. Trapped aboard a freighter, a rogue AI herding them into its carefully prepared killing ground. An accident. A demon overlooked by the Mentors. So it was said.

Prentice said nothing. It was clear she didn't want to be here. Not this close to an unfettered demon. One that specialised in death and destruction. Of course the Mentor archives claimed it was defunct. But they had been wrong before.

She adjusted the controls of the holoscreen, twisting the image this way and that, clearly searching for something. "They lost telemetry from the first mission about here," she finally froze the image. "The first crew isolated this area as the most likely means of gaining access to the interior. They were to moor outside this opening and seek an entrance. At least that's what Sollander told me."

"We could do with her in here," Davido commented.

Prentice shrugged. "We need someone to pilot the shuttle."

He grunted. "Yeah, great job your pilot's doing." He cast a glance to where the unconscious Jeno was slumped in a nearby seat.

A dark pit opened in the side of the behemoth, leading to unknown depths. No light made it inside, the bottom lost in gloom. The hull around it was unscarred, a featureless plain of steel, without even the usual towers and valleys that seemed to predominate elsewhere. A desert within a desert. It was unclear what the chasm had been designed for and it was certainly not battle damage. There were no scorch marks or twisted hull plates marring the surface around it.

"What is it?" Davido asked.

"Don't know," Prentice admitted. "We do know they used some sort of gas scoop technology. They trawled space for residual gas and dust when they were in cruise mode, supplementing their onboard supplies. This could be an intake channel. We can't be sure. I'm afraid no blueprints for the vessel survived the war." She tilted her head to one side, as if seeing it from a different angle would offer an answer. "We also know they utilised Shoei morph technology. This could have been some sort of launch facility."

"What?" Davido shook his head. "English please."

Prentice smiled. "The Shoei specialised in morph technology. Their vessels were modular, one module able to slide over another depending on their configuration. In battle they presented their heaviest armour to their enemies, while the other surfaces launched their invasion forces or deployed heavy weaponry. If one area was damaged they could withdraw it into the ship, replacing it with an undamaged section. It made them exceptionally hard to kill and even harder to board. If they lost a section to enemy invasion they could simply expel it from the ship to prevent the invaders gaining access to the rest of the vessel. The Confederates copied this technology to a limited degree. They could withdraw offensive batteries beneath their heavy armour to protect them if an enemy came too close. I believe they did the same with their launch facilities, denying them as a route to the interior. We could be looking at something of the sort here. However, whatever they started doing they never got around to finishing. This area should be covered over with hull armour."

"So, the first shuttle docked here?" Davido said.

"That was their intention. They may have ventured inside, we don't know. All we do know is their telemetry was lost hereabouts. We don't know why. They simply went off the air."

"Great. I'm filled with confidence."

"You never know, we might get lucky. The shuttle could be just within the entrance. If there was some sort of accident they could still be aboard it."

"They'd be dead by now," Davido growled.

She shrugged. "At least you'll know."

"I didn't come all this way to bring back corpses."

The shuttle paused in its flight, Sollander bringing it to a halt a few hundred metres from the chasm. The door to the cockpit clicked open and she joined them, inspecting the image within the holoscreen. "I think we should proceed more cautiously from here," she said. "We don't know what we're walking into."

"Do you know what this is?" Davido asked her.

She hesitated, studying the image. "I can guess only. Most visits to the Parking Lot kept records... of a sort," she glanced towards Prentice. "Plus we have detailed records drawn up from the interiors of the cities. So, we know what the inside of these things were like. Sort of."

"Sort of?"

She smiled sweetly at Davido. "Yes. No one's been aboard this warship before. I guess they were intimidated. We understand how the Confederates built their ships though, so we can deduce this vessel's layout from that."

"We didn't board this ship with good reason," Prentice commented. "These things were killing machines. If any of the demons aboard are still active..." she let the thought hang there. They all knew what that meant.

"Yes, indeed," Sollander agreed. "However you must remember the Mentors gave all military vessels special attention. Each one was inspected before it was parked here."

"We don't have their records?" Davido asked.

"The Mentor archives don't hold much information about warships, I'm afraid. I have seen their abridged report only. I think the Mentors are trying to ensure we don't get any ideas."

"Like restarting the war?" Prentice laughed. "We lost the first time, and there were a hell of a lot more of us then. We'd stand no chance."

"We wouldn't," Sollander agreed. "However the idea might still appeal to someone."

"Right, so what are we doing?" Davido asked, boring with the chatter. "We clearly need to get closer."

"We do," Sollander agreed, clearly relishing the idea. "How reliable are your pressure suits?" She turned to Prentice.

"They've always been good enough before," Prentice said, her tone clipped. She clearly didn't like having the engineer aboard.

"How much oxy do they carry?"

"They vary. Between four hours and three days." She shrugged. "Depends on the design. The shop I bought them from had limited stock."

Sollander ignored her sarcasm. "We need a plan. We can't just dock and start wandering around in the dark. That'd just be inviting trouble."

"I have done this before," Prentice said, her voice cold.

Sollander paused, turning to study the shorter woman. For a moment Davido thought she was going to respond in kind. He groaned, this was all he needed, two women vying for dominance. They had a job to do here. Then Sollander smiled and inclined her head slightly. "You have. So, what do you suggest?"

Prentice opened her mouth to retort, but then closed it again after a moment's consideration. She nodded. "OK. There are twelve of us. We can't count Jeno or your girlfriend," she glanced at Davido. "So that makes ten. We should split into two groups. The group with the higher oxy load to venture deeper into the ship, looking for signs of the first party. The other group to remain in the vicinity of the shuttle. We need to ensure the area is secure and there may be some resources we can use."

Davido smiled. What she meant was: there could be something of value aboard. As no one had ventured aboard a warship before anything she discovered would be unique. She could charge what she wanted and there would be no end of bidders who would happily pay it. Clearly Prentice intended on making a profit from this trip. Of course he would insist on his cut. That was part of their agreement. He might be here to look for his sister, but he was no fool.

"Means leaving Jeno and Adele aboard alone," Sollander observed.

"I'm not going aboard that thing," Adele spoke up. "You did promise, Armand." She glanced towards the unconscious Jeno. "And if he tries anything I'll kick his ass."

"Sounds like a plan, then," Davido agreed. He ignore Payce as the man looked about to protest. He didn't want to be here either.

"Well, let's not get carried away, we need to get docked first." Sollander stalked back into the cockpit. Armand followed, lowering himself into the right hand seat as the engineer took control of the shuttle again.

"What's that noise?" Davido heard a murmuring, like a child locked in a cupboard.

Sollander smiled, easing forward on the controls, guiding the vessel towards the waiting chasm. Readouts glittered about her, wrapping her in a veil of light. With no hands free she nodded towards the centre of the console. A glob a wax had been dripped over a grille, sealing the vents. "Don't like demon backchat while I'm trying to fly," she said in explanation.

Davido chuckled. "That's the only way to treat them," he commented.

The shuttle jolted suddenly, a drive unit misfiring. Sollander gritted her teeth, attempting to compensate. The flight into orbit had been reasonably smooth—apart from the odd jolt from the drive. Quite a feat for a vessel eighty years out of warranty. Still it was annoying, ruining an otherwise perfect flight. The shipboard regrav systems didn't seem able to cancel it out either. Which was odd in itself. The inertial dampening regrav systems were designed to cancel out all sensation of movement, either due to acceleration or turbulence. The system seemed to work well, except when the drive system jolted, knocking everyone off their feet. It was annoying but hadn't caused any real damage.

As long as it didn't happen while they were within the *Goliath*. That could be dangerous.

The shuttle passed into shadow, dropping into the mouth of the passage. The glare of sun beaten metal vanished as abruptly as if someone had clicked the lights off. After a moment's hesitation, as Sollander searched for the control, the shuttle's landing lights flared to life.

The tunnel was not simple, plain steel. It was studded with odd protrusions and what appeared to be emergency lights (now dead). Multicoloured lettering and arrows were scrawled over it. Their significance was lost on Davido and Sollander alike. The Confederates had not been thoughtful enough to leave any directional markers where potential boarders could find them.

"How far down does this thing go?"

"Dunno," Sollander admitted. "A very long way. If it is a channel for the gas scoops it could go all the way to the drive rod. That's a good two kilometres straight down. There will be boarding doors on the way though. I doubt they will be open."

"I didn't see anything that looked like a scoop."

"They used force fields."

He nodded. Of course they did.

"So, tell me, Armand ... can I call you Armand?"

He shrugged. "Of course," he said, when he realised she wasn't looking at him. "It's my name."

"Armand, what brings you to this place?"

"My sister's here somewhere. She was on the first mission."

"Oh. What was her name?"

"Sistine Davido."

It was her turn to shrug. "Her name wasn't on the crew list. She must have used a different name. What brought your sister here?"

Foolishness, he almost said. "She has this romantic notion that demons... AI's are not what the Mentors make them out to be. She wanted to find one that wasn't castrated."

"Oh?" That seemed to interest the engineer. "She was a heretic?"

Davido refrained from answering the question, preferring to watch for an opening in the steel wall. They were a good fifty metres beneath the surface here and there was still no sign of an entrance.

"A dangerous endeavour. Uncastrated AI's tend to be somewhat homicidal," she continued.

Davido kept his thoughts to himself. He did not know this woman. "You're not obliged to be here either, I notice. In fact I believe you gate crashed our little gathering."

She smiled sweetly at him, flashing perfect white teeth. It was then he realised how handsome a woman she was. Something she concealed beneath her androgynous grey Engineering Corps jumpsuit. His gaze dropped to admire how her breasts filled out her coveralls. Noticing his attention she arched her back slightly, pushing her chest forward.

"A man like you, I'm surprised to find you in a place like this."

He frowned. "What do you mean?"

"Well, you're clearly a man of some influence. A man feared by lesser men. It's obvious."

Davido pulled his gaze away. Dammit, she was playing him. His face flushing red he returned his attention to the tunnel. Of course, she had not answered the question.

"This looks like something." Sollander paused the shuttle's descent, the landing lights picking out an opening in the tunnel.

They were doors of some description. Partly rolled aside they revealed a narrow gap, the lights failing to penetrate into the depths. Sollander positioned the shuttle carefully, trying to position the lights so they shone through the opening. Massive grey shapes lurked beyond, blocking their view deeper into the chamber.

"It's about fifty metres in height and thirty wide. Could be a loading dock of some type," she said. "Could be a good place to start."

"Found something?" Prentice stepped into the cockpit, leaning over Davido's chair to see out of the windscreen. "What is it?"

"An entrance. Looks like this is where we go in," Davido said with a bravado he did not feel. He didn't like the look of it.

"We won't get the shuttle through there," Prentice observed.

"We can moor it here and go in in the suits," Sollander said. "The second group can try to find if there's enough power to open them wider."

"Well, the first shuttle didn't come this way," Davido said. "It would still be here."

"We'll give it a good looking over. If there's nothing to find we can continue deeper. You up to that?" Sollander smiled, noticing Davido's discomfort.

"Whatever it takes."

"Right, let's get moving." Prentice stepped back into the cabin.

Sollander did nothing for a moment, looking back into the short passageway that separated the cockpit from the passenger cabin. "This is no place for her," she said finally.

"Excuse me?"

"What's she on?"

Davido felt his face reddening. What did this woman know about anything? She was a stranger to them all. She did not have the right to judge any of them. "Does it matter? I trust her."

Sollander studied him for a moment. "Never trust an addict," she said.

"Fly the fucking ship."

Sollander shrugged and activated a small magnetic grapple. Steel wire whirred on its reel as the grapple sped away from the shuttle, slamming into the steel wall. She fired another towards the opposite wall and wound in the cables, suspending the shuttle between them. "That should do it. The *Goliath* is spinning slightly, which will tend to throw the shuttle back out into space." She grinned to Davido as she slipped out of the pilot's couch and followed Prentice. "We don't want that."

The pressure suits were a ragtag collection Prentice had assembled over the years. Davido was surprised to find that three of them were little more than emergency suits, designed to do nothing more than keep the occupant alive for a few hours in an exposed compartment while awaiting rescue. Not the sort of thing to roll out time and time again for lengthy explorations aboard unknown ships. He was relieved when he was offered something more robust.

"What's this mark here?" He studied the black stain on the suit's shoulder.

"Blood," Prentice said matter of factly.

"Great. There's blood on it."

"It works." She shrugged.

"So, what happened to the original owner?" He rubbed at the stain with a finger. Prentice slapped his hand away so she could attach his gloves, quickly twisting the pressure seal until it was tight.

"Well," she smiled. "You know what they used to call the Mentors?"

"All kinds of things. None particularly pleasant."

"Eaters," she said. "They called them the Eaters. So, figure out what happened to the original owner yourself. Like I said, the suit still works, so who cares? I've replaced the helmet so you'll be fine."

"Shit." Davido cringed. Knowing someone had died while wearing the suit did not fill him with much comfort. That they had died a horrible, gruesome death left him feeling more than slightly disturbed. Damn, he needed a drink. Unfortunately, there didn't seem any way he could attach a bottle of bourbon to the suit.

Looking relieved not to be included Adele watched them suit up, her lips pursed in distaste. "How long you gonna be? This place creeps me out."

"Long as it takes, honey," Prentice smiled at her, fastening the last of Davido's clasps. "There." She inspected the helmet seal. "Just breathe normally."

"Shit. It smells in here. It smells like a corpse."

"That's just you. Bathed lately?" She sneered.

"Fuck off."

"Hey, that's the best suit I got. You don't like it I can swap it for another. I have a spare ... I've taped up the tear so it should be good." She shrugged. "Maybe."

"I'm just fine, thank you."

Sollander watched as they helped each other into their suits, a thin smile of amusement on her face. She found herself hoping the warship was still pressurised and heated. True, the sunlit surface of the *Goliath* might be blisteringly hot, but there was almost a hundred metres of armour between here and there. If the ship was completely powered down they were about to step into a meat locker. All the vessel's internal warmth would have leeched out into the vacuum of space within a few years of being parked here. Now the internal temperature would be way below freezing. Of course Prentice could not know that. The vessels she boarded had all been civilian, none boasting a hull more than a few centimetres thick. Roasting in the glare of the sun like a boar on a spit their internal spaces would all be comfortably warm. Here, her previous experience meant nothing.

The engineer checked the seals on her own suit. It was a simple, rugged design, as all things designed by the Shoei were. Still, it was effective. Lovingly maintained it was in perfect working order. Even the air, when she activated the life support system, was fresh and cool. The HUD lit up, informing her of the suit's status, oxy and power reserve levels. All systems were nominal. When your life depended on it, always choose Shoei. The Confederates tended to overcomplicate everything, building in smart systems that would only break down. Or try to kill you.

"Let's go." Sollander stood and clumped over to the airlock, her heavy boots scuffing the already well scratched deck.

"Yeah, I think we're about ready," Prentice said, checking her own readouts. Most of her life signs were flashing amber. She paid them little attention. She knew what she needed to know. Her seals were good and she had enough power and air for thirty-two hours. She didn't intend on staying aboard the warship more than a few hours—at first anyway.

"Right, before we step out there, be warned," Sollander said. "Be careful what you touch and what you stand on. There might be regrav aboard, there might not. There may or may not be air pressure, and we certainly don't know what the temperature will be."

"I've done this before," Prentice commented, opening the inner air lock door. "Just once or twice."

"We don't know how damaged the ship is," Sollander continued.

"Seen it all before." Prentice grinned and ushered in the first group. "Let's get this over with."

Chapter Eleven

The senate convened within a vast chamber in Buer Adjunct, the floor and walls glittering pink marble, cut and dressed using industrial lasers from a quarry on the other side of Russou. Slender pillars held up the sweeping roof, leaving a perfectly circular gap in the very centre of the dome, allowing in the last of the afternoon sun. There were only six senators, one for every city, but the senate floor was still crowded; aides, officials and hangers on scuttling to and fro, going about the business of state. Everywhere there was movement, a tide of flesh breaking against the dais where a small island of calm persevered. The prefect's seat was unoccupied, Drefus himself absent. Without him the evening's proceedings could not begin.

It was an important occasion. The victors of the Two City Rod Race had been invited to attend, to make their traditional Upper House speech and request. After the catastrophe that had eliminated both the front-runners, the Spurious Moment had ultimately won. An upset neither the crew nor the race officials quite knew how to handle. Dr Spurio and her crew had not expected to win against the likes of the Redemption and the Express. A far smaller rod, the Moment had been almost five minutes behind the front-runners, leading up the pack of novice and part time racers. They had never been serious contenders. As such Singh doubted the good doctor had even bothered to write a speech until after the race was over. She certainly looked extremely uncomfortable now, standing at the front of the v formation of her crew, patiently waiting for the start of the evening's proceedings.

They were not the only ones waiting on the prefect. It was getting late. The senators were becoming restive.

The only stationary figure in the chamber, Singh watched the activity with some amusement. He didn't quite know why he had been summoned here at such short notice. Nor did he know why they were being forced to wait. He didn't typically attend these meetings, for which he was rather grateful. They were tedious for one, and secondly he couldn't abide the company of his father.

"This is intolerable!" Agher spluttered, failing miserably in her attempts to keep her ire in check. The senator for Mammon stood and slammed a fist onto a marble chair arm. She winced as she bruised her knuckles. "Why are we waiting?"

Sing could do nothing but bow politely. "I am afraid the prefect has not shared his instructions with me, Senator."

"What good are you then?" She demanded, rubbing her injured hand. She was a large woman, her pale business suit bulging in its attempt to contain all of her. Her hair, Singh knew, was a wig. Her own hair was a tangled mess of yellow straw, testament to too many decades of failed beauty treatments. "Go on, go find him. Shoo, shoo." She waved at him dismissively.

"Perhaps you should do as she says," Senator Fallan said. As senator for Buer, the largest and wealthiest city on Russou—and also the host city for the senate—he was the most influential amongst them. He was a tall, slender man, his features sharp and somewhat effeminate. A contrast to Agher who sat opposite him across the debating floor.

"Senator, with due respect, I am where I should be at times like these."

"What's that supposed to mean?" Lendar, the senator for Ipos demanded. She was a stocky, tall woman, draped from head to foot in creaking black leather. A sign of mourning, he understood. Although he didn't know what, or whom, she was mourning. Her short, almost shaven hair was black, framing an angular, hooked nosed face. "How often do you attend the senate, hmm Toady?"

Singh felt blood suffusing his face. It took all of his self-control not to glance in his father's direction, where he was sat as senator for Appolyon. He could feel the waves of arrogance and loathing emanating from the tall, hawk nosed man. He knew AN Yough despised him, the man had told him so.

As there were only six settlements of any size on Russou, the structure of the government was straightforward. It was split into two houses, the Upper and Lower Houses. The senators sat in the Upper House. One senator was elected every four years from each of the cities. An election process that was more than slightly corrupt, and openly so. Even though every man and woman over the age of eighteen was entitled to vote, only those sufficiently motivated ever bothered to do so. Typically, only the rich and powerful could ever supply that motivation. There were no political parties or trade unions on Russou, they had been outlawed in one of the first proclamations the prefect made as he took the reins of government. A move that was good for big business, certainly, but could never be good for the average citizen. Civil liberties were virtually unheard of.

One of the reasons the good doctor looked so uncomfortable. They all knew what to expect from the Moment's captain. She had bored the Upper House several times with her requests for better health care and an improvement in living standards. She had even lobbied the Lower House, a chamber that met once every month, to discuss trade agreements and share information. A waste of time. Only the Upper House could pass laws, and that was populated by oligarchs and crime lords. Not the kinds of people who would take kindly to having their money wasted on healthcare for the poor.

So, to Doctor Spurio, this was quite a coup. To everyone else here, it was an embarrassment. And it was being drawn out by the prefect's tardiness.

"I wish to get this farce over with," AN Yough said loudly, making a point of looking at the crew of the Moment as he did so. "Why don't you do as suggested and go find your employer? So that more of our time is not wasted?" This last was aimed at Singh.

Singh hesitated for only a moment. Perhaps vacating this chamber might actually be a good idea. "Yes, Senator. I shall see what I can discover."

"About fucking time," another senator muttered under her breath. In other times, such language would not be countenanced here. Today was a different matter.

Relieved to be out from beneath their gaze Singh scurried up the steps to the Prefect's private offices situated in a nearby annexe. A guardsman snapped to attention as he passed from the cool interior to the humid warmth of early evening. Almost instantly a cloud of insects gathered about him, trying to get into his eyes and nose. Spluttering he waved them away.

The city of Buer was four kilometres away, across a slowly heaving expanse of water. Its towers glittered as the lights came on one by one, warding off the approaching night. A narrow bridge joined the city to the Adjunct, seawater foaming about the slender stilts it was balanced on. The home of Russou's legislature the Adjunct was a small city in its own right, constructed mostly of native stone and rare woods; both of which had been shipped in from all points of the world at great expense. A symbol, the first settlers of this marginal world had claimed. A symbol of humanity's hope and renewed confidence. A grand edifice designed to celebrate humanity's continued survival in the face of adversity. A symbol that was now tarnished from decades of storms and crashing waves. The exposed stone surfaces slowly turning green as it became covered by a patina of corrosion. The iron oxides that afforded the stone its attractive colours, also allowed it to tarnish quickly.

The Prefect's offices were built into the southern edge of the Adjunct, as far away from Buer as they could get without detaching from the city completely. As close as he was to the Prefect even Singh couldn't guess how Drefus travelled between the cities of Russou. That was a secret. He did know only the cable cars reached his office in Monmouth, and that the man never trusted his life to them. As there was nowhere for an aircraft to land, it was a mystery how he left the office. Yet leave he did. After all, he was here today. Singh was not alone in imagining what Syat devilry whisked him effortlessly between cities. The myth only served to fuel the rumours of his collusion with their alien overlords. That he was an agent acting on their behalf. From what he had seen of the man, Singh would not have been in the least surprised.

Singh waved away another salute as he hurried up the stairs into the cool interior. Drefus was in his private inner office, casually unaware of the frustration he was causing on the senate floor. Relaxing behind his empty desk he was leaning forward thoughtfully, his hands clasped on the dark wood before him. He didn't seem to notice the Toady until Singh was within the office and about to clear his throat for attention.

"Hold on for a moment," Drefus held up a hand before Singh could make a sound. "Do go on," he said so his guest.

The Toady started. He hadn't noticed that the prefect had company.

Standing opposite him was Inspector Isskip, the man's black Special Branch uniform so perfect it looked like it had been ironed to his sturdy frame. Isskip ignored the intrusion, he rose on his toes ever so slightly, his hands clasped behind his back as if he was on parade. Singh knew the man well; he was a regular visitor to the Prefect's inner sanctum. "There have been three disappearances over the last month. All in the same region of the city ... or rather the same region outside the city's borders. I believe they are related. I believe one of them to be Senator Lendar's daughter."

Singh settled himself on one of the comfortable leather sofa's against a wall. Disappearances, he wondered. Since when did the prefect bother himself with police business?

"You have evidence to link them?" Drefus continued.

"We didn't until recently, your Excellency. We found some strange evidence at the scene of one of the disappearances. That of Roland Yarouff ... a vegetable trader who specialised in rare desert varieties. There was a pile of grey dust alongside his abandoned truck."

"Dust? In a desert? Indeed, Inspector." Drefus smiled.

Isskip continued, unperturbed. "We found his clothing too, Prefect. The dust was gathered inside it."

"How curious. Almost as if the man turned to dust, I would say?"

"Yes, Prefect. Most curious."

"This is what tied them together?"

"Not at first, Prefect. However it did cause us to check the archives. What we found was somewhat alarming."

"Do continue."

"There have been five other instances where strange piles of dust were discovered. All were at the last known whereabouts of missing people. None were subsequently seen or heard of again. No bodies, no sightings, nothing."

"As if they were turned to dust too," Drefus said.

"As you say, Prefect."

"How long ago was the earliest case?"

"Aaah, yes, Prefect. This is what disturbed us. The earliest case was that of a widower who wandered into the desert after his wife died. That was seventy-five years ago."

"You are sure about this?"

"Very, Prefect. The notes left by the investigating officer were most detailed."

"So it can only be a coincidence? Unless you believe there is a serial killer amongst us. A man ... or woman," he held his hands apart to concede the point, "who has outlived just about everyone else in the world."

"People don't live that long, Prefect. Not anymore."

"No, indeed. Since we lost much of our medical technology ... what is the average expected life span these days?" Drefus looked towards Singh.

Singh cleared his throat. "Fifty-two years, Prefect."

"Fifty-two years. And this man ... or woman would be at least eighty something years old. How many octogenarians do we have within our population?" He turned to Singh again.

"I confess I don't know, Prefect."

"Dare I say none?"

"I fear you would be correct in that," he agreed.

"So, a mystery indeed." He turned back to the inspector who was waiting patiently. "Unless it is a coincidence after all?"

"That could be the case," Isskip admitted.

Drefus nodded. "So, what caused you to bring this to me now?"

"There was another incident, Prefect. Yesterday, on Highway Fifteen twenty kilometres west of the Prentice airfield. This time there was a witness."

The prefect's eyebrows rose. "Go on."

"A driver for a small freight company called in to their dispatch office last night, claiming she had witnessed a murder on the side of the highway. She claimed to have stopped to offer the victim her assistance only to find the corpse turning to dust before her eyes. Her last report was to advise the dispatcher that she was pursuing the suspect."

"Her last report?"

"Yes, I am afraid so. We found her vehicle this morning. It appears she was involved in a collision with another vehicle. Both were at the bottom of a cliff. She was dead, the other driver was nowhere to be found."

"Do we know who the other driver was?"

"We know the other vehicle belonged to a Jeno, lately of the Overtakers. I spoke to his manager who informed me he'd resigned a few days earlier. Apparently he'd taken up employment with Sarah Prentice."

Drefus nodded, mulling it over. "I doubt he was the perpetrator. Possibly the killer took his vehicle after murdering him. Do we know where the killer went?"

"We believe to Prentice Airfield. We have attempted to contact Prentice but her shuttle left for the Parking Lot late last night. She's not expected back for several days."

Singh fidgeted, adjusting his weight on the soft leather. He knew Sollander was aboard that shuttle. With a murderer. He checked his watch. They'd be aboard the *Goliath* already.

"This is very well done, Inspector. You are to be congratulated."

"We have also discovered his lair within the Combs. It appears he is a heretic, as we discovered a defunct android at that location. I suspect that is the reason he chose to travel to the Parking Lot, Prefect."

"If he is in collusion with demons there could be trouble," Drefus said.

"Of course we cannot follow Prentice up to the Parking Lot, Prefect. Which is why I have brought this to you."

"Because I can get a warning to them? Or because I can arrange for the Overtakers to rendezvous with them?"

"I believe we have a killer in the Parking Lot, Prefect. I would like to request access to a shuttle so I can lead a police contingent to intercept him."

He nodded slowly. After a moment's thought he stood and rounded his desk. "I thank you for bringing this to me, Inspector. I am most disturbed to hear we have a killer amongst us." He shook Isskip's hand, the inspector looking surprised at the sudden familiarity.

"Thank you, Prefect."

"Who else is involved in this investigation?"

"Some of my officers have taken statements, Prefect. None are aware the killer is currently in the Parking Lot."

"Ah, good, good. Best not cause undue consternation, hey?" Drefus didn't let go of the inspector's hand, continuing to shake it warmly. The inspector started looking distinctly uncomfortable.

"Ah, yes, Prefect."

"Good, good. Now, about your request, I am afraid I cannot approve it at this time."

"May I ask why, Prefect?"

"I am afraid you cannot. Additionally, I must request that you no longer pursue this line of investigation."

The inspector looked surprised. "Prefect?"

"Yes, I am afraid I am going to have to insist. Oh, I give you my guarantee the situation will be dealt with. However you are going to have to trust me. Can I ask that you send all your investigation materials... all your notes and files... to my assistant? He will take care of them for you."

Iskipp hesitated, clearly taken aback by the request. "Prefect ..."

"Thank you, Inspector. Your cooperation in this will show well on your record. As will the sterling work you have done so far."

The man blinked rapidly. "Thank you, Prefect."

"Right. Let us conclude this business. Was there anything else you needed of me?"

"I ... no, Prefect."

"Good, good. Good day then, Inspector. I am sure you have numerous other investigations to take care of." Drefus ushered the Inspector towards the door.

"Yes, thank you, Prefect." Iskipp didn't know what to do or say, simply allowing the Prefect to move him from the study. Once he was gone Drefus turned to Singh.

"Well, a nasty business, what?"

"Ah, yes Prefect. I am somewhat surprised you are not permitting the inspector to pursue the suspect."

Drefus waved the objection aside. "I will deal with this personally... in my own way. Was there something you wanted, as I am quite busy."

"Actually, yes, Prefect. The senators are growing restless. They require...are asking for your presence in the senate."

"Go tell thēm they will need to wait a little longer. I have some business to conclude here first."

"I believe their concerns are urgent, Prefect." As he said it Singh realised he has overstepped the mark. He broke out into a sweat as the prefect's eyes flashed, the man slowly turning to face him, his jaw set in a firm line of displeasure.

"They will have to wait, Singh. Be a good toady and run along to inform them of the fact."

Singh swallowed dryly. "Of course, Prefect." He scurried from the chamber, relieved to be back outside with the insects. The door closed heavily behind him. It was not quite a slam. He fingered the torque, expecting it to tighten. This time it didn't.

Once Singh had departed, Drefus closed the door behind him. He put his back against it, making a conscious effort to calm his annoyance.

"What do you think?"

A voice entered his study, seeming to reverberate from the walls themselves. It was pitched strangely, like a foreigner forced to read a script in English without really understanding what the words meant. It was certainly not human. "He moves," it said. "Perhaps his time has come."

"You believe it is him?"

"Yes. The machine has supplied him with an ASSIT amalgam. It is keyed to our biochemistry. It is quite indicative."

Drefus nodded. "Your instructions?"

"For now, do nothing."

Drefus nodded. "He will kill again."

"It is of no consequence. We must discover his purpose."

Drefus crossed to his desk and seated himself. "I will await your instruction. In the meantime allow me to put a team together. Once he makes his move we need to be ready."

There was no response. The room felt empty again, as if the strange presence had moved on, losing interest in such trivial matters. Drefus took a deep breath. A lot of people were going to die before this was over.

Chapter Twelve

"Clip yourself to the cable," Sollander instructed Sparky, one of Prentice's crew. The man stood blocking the airlock door, oblivious of the fact she was talking to him. "Hey, I said clip yourself to the cable. You listening to me?"

Prentice pushed the engineer aside. "He's deaf." She muttered, pulling on Sparky's shoulder. The man turned and she signed quickly, the gestures forced to be somewhat abbreviated through the thick gloves. Teeth flashed through the visor as he grinned. He gave her a thumbs up and clipped his harness to the cable Sollander had rigged.

"Far be it for me to criticise equal opportunities, but I don't think this is the place for someone who cannot communicate on the radio," Sollander said.

"Never been a problem before," Prentice said tartly. She patted Sparky on the back. "Off you go."

The shuttle's airlock door was facing the dark opening in the tunnel wall. A steel cable a dozen metres in length bridged the gap, attached to a magnetic grapple on the lip of the slightly ajar door. The shuttle's landing lights still didn't reveal very much. There were suggestions of objects within the chamber beyond, little more than hints at shapes and some shadows deeper than others. Beneath the shuttle was nothing but darkness.

Sparky swung out confidently, easily pulling himself hand over hand towards the opening. Prentice steadied the cable, watching his progress from within the airlock. Within moments he reached the grapple and swung himself between the massive doors. He vanished, his helmet lamp throwing the shadows within to disarray.

"Would be nice if he could tell us what he sees," Sollander observed dryly.

Prentice ignored her. "Me next." She swung out after him.

"I'll go last. If anything happens we need someone able to fly us out of here," Prentice said, stepping aside for Davido.

Davido swallowed, his mouth dry. This had seemed like such a good idea back in the Randy Dogg. It didn't feel like such a clever idea now. He glanced downwards, relieved to find there was nothing to see below. The shuttle's lights cast their brilliant illumination over a few dozen metres of passage. Everything beyond that was shrouded by impenetrable shadow. "I need a drink," he muttered. Some things were best done sober. Some things weren't. This was definitely one of the latter variety.

Not wishing to show weakness in front of the help, he clipped himself to the cable and swung out over the chasm. "Shit." His hands slipped on the smooth steel, his legs flailing as he struggled to balance himself.

"Remember, you're crossing from one G to zero G," Sollander warned.

"Yeah, thanks," he grunted. It wasn't as easy as Prentice had made it look. He couldn't get a grip on the cable through the thick gloves and without gravity to pull him down again the inertia from his initial jump twisted his legs up uncomfortably behind him. Spluttering curses he tried to get his boots against the cable to give him extra purchase. "Bloody hell." Muttering he planted his feet and pushed.

The cable slipped through his clumsy fingers, leaving him grasping at emptiness as he soared above it, arms wind milling. With a grunt he slammed against the steel door, his helmet banging on the hard surface.

"Hang on, Boss. I'm coming." Sash stepped out behind him. Ignoring the cable, she launched herself expertly from the shuttle. Twisting in flight, she landed on the doors, her boots thumping on the hard surface. A quick steadying hand on the cable cancelled her rebound. "You ok?"

"Yeah. I hate this shit."

Sash checked his helmet quickly, ensuring the impact had not damaged it. "Let's get you in." She slipped down inside the opening, gently pulling Davido behind.

"Where you learn that?"

"Used to work for Prentice, remember?" He heard her chuckle. "Until you lured me away with a better pay cheque."

"Sarcastic bitch."

The massive steel doors concealed a shelf like arrangement. A dozen metres apart each shelf held a neat collection of vehicles, each one parked around the edges of the space in bays clearly marked by yellow chevrons, leaving a gap in the centre for access. They were all painted dull military green, red and yellow markings warning engineers not to step or advising the location of emergency equipment. The vehicle directly before Davido was approximately the same dimensions as their shuttle, 'Marine 1040' inscribed in white lettering beneath the tinted windshield. The stubby barrels of a gatling gun could just be seen protruding below it.

"Looks like they have regrav here. Hold on, I'll let you down careful. Prepare for a drop," Sash advised, unclipping Davido from the cable and letting him down gently.

With a grunt, Davido dropped to the rubbery deck, stumbling and almost falling over. A steadying hand reached out and held him up. "They still have power," Prentice said. "Somewhere at least. There's no lights on and all their systems appear dead... but at least we have gravity."

Davido played his helmet lamp about him, studying the row of vehicles. There were twenty of them, each in perfect condition, as if they had just been serviced and were prepared for immediate launch. "Some sort of landing bay," he said.

"These things will be surface capable," Prentice said. "They're military hardware so they'll be tough as nails. I could sell each of these for ... demilitarised ... twenty mill each. Easy. She-it."

"Ten minutes on the job and you're in profit already," Davido commented.

"Yeah. Thing is, they've been sat here eighty years. Who's to say they still work. Plus we'd have to get these doors open." She turned to cast her own light up the door frame, searching out the drawing mechanism. "That'll be a tough bastard."

"As you say, it's military spec. It might just need power. You can pull a cable in from your shuttle."

She said nothing, calculating the profit for the trip in her head. What else was there?

More lights joined them, banishing more shadows as Duncan and Marco clumped down behind them. "Ooh, look at those guns, Boss," Marco said.

"Makes the ones you brought look a bit silly," Prentice commented.

"One thing you have to remember," Sollander said over the radio, "this is a military vessel. Just about everything will be security locked. Can you hack military grade crypto?"

Prentice swore quietly. The engineer was right. Even if the doors had power and the vessels were in perfect working order, they weren't going anywhere.

"We should find the captain's quarters," Marco said. "He'd have a safe with all the code keys in it. If we break in there we will have the run of the ship."

"I doubt it works like that," Davido said, venturing deeper. There was a ramp system at the rear of the bay, leading to the shelves above and below this one. Delta Bay 3A, was written in shoulder high letters on the rear bulkhead. "Besides, how would you find it?"

"They'll have a map or schematic here somewhere. So new recruits can find their way around," Marco refused to be put off.

"This isn't a supermarket you know," Prentice commented.

"Fresh fish isle one." Davido chuckled.

"Frilly knickers isle twelve," Sash said.

"OK, ok. Shut up now."

Marco scanned under one of the vehicles, admiring the weaponry. If they couldn't take the whole thing maybe they could just rip one of these babies loose.

He was carrying an ancient slug thrower, a shotgun-like weapon that fired solid balls of pressed steel at astonishing velocities. The thumb sized slugs were capable of ripping through metal as if it was wet cardboard and it wasn't worth thinking about what they would do to flesh and bone. Duncan, when he joined them a moment later, had a light machine gun clipped to his back, a canister of ammunition secured just beneath the life support panel on his chest. Of course, Sollander thought this sort of thing quite ridiculous, and made a point of saying just that. Davido honestly didn't care. The first mission to the old warship had not ended well. The same was not going to happen to them.

Prentice's crew were armed also, but in a slightly different manner. Cutters and plasma torches had gone into their gear, along with the sort of communications gear that could operate through a few kilometres of inert warship. They had done this sort of thing before, and knew they would have to drill and cut their way to wherever they wanted to go. No doors would be opening automatically for them here. Secret pass codes or not.

Still, Davido sincerely hoped there would be nothing for them to shoot at.

"Right," Sollander dropped to the deck behind them. "Let's get organised. We need to find an airlock of some kind. Spread out and start looking."

None of the crew moved, turning to Prentice for instruction instead. Even in the gloom Davido could tell she was grinning. This was her show; the engineer had best learn that quickly. "We're looking for signs of the first mission," she said. "We suspect they would have come through here. If they did, we want to know where they went and what became of them. However, first things first. I want to get these doors open so we can bring the shuttle in. Have a look around and see if you can find controls for it someplace. In two's please and no one get lost."

Davido pointed to the twins and then gestured towards the ramp. "Try upstairs, boys. See what there is to see. And keep in touch."

"Sure boss," Marco took his brother's arm. "Come along then, you big lump."

"You sure the shuttle's safe with your pilot and Adele?" Davido asked Prentice. They headed for the ramps also, headed down.

"I doubt that lady friend of yours will try to do a runner. Doubt she could if she wanted." She chuckled. "Not a pilot by any chance is she?"

"No."

"Good. Nothing to worry about. The shuttle's safe ground, we need boots on the deck over here, not over there."

They descended the ramp, discovering another shelf below, a near duplicate of the one above. The vessels parked there were the same too; they were even marked in numerical order. The two kept on going, their helmet lamps barely piercing the gloom around them. The shelf below that was the lowest, the ramp system terminating facing a wide pressure door. It was closed. A small panel was set into the bulkhead alongside, clearly the controls. It was dead.

"Right, we know where we go next, at least," Davido said.

"Got something here," he heard Sash say over the intercom. "I think we're at the top. There's a door here."

"Yeah, got the same here," Prentice said.

"This one's got a power cable running up to it. Looks like it's been opened recently."

"The first mission?"

"Could be."

"Let's take a look."

Davido and Prentice mounted the ramps again, heading upwards. When they arrived at the topmost shelf, they discovered most of the party gathered around the pressure door, inspecting the cable that was plugged into a power socket. It led away into darkness, towards the ajar doors behind them. A helmet lamp flashed from that direction, one of Prentice's crew investigating what the other end was plugged into.

"No luck," a voice said, Davido didn't recognise it. He didn't know Prentice's crew all that well. "It's secured back here. They attached it to the landing gear of one of the ships. The end's been ripped off though. The cable's snapped, like someone yanked on it. Yanked bloody hard."

"That would have been the first shuttle," Sollander observed. "Looks like they plugged the cable into their shuttle to power up this door. Any sign of the shuttle itself?"

"Nada."

"Takes a lot of force to snap one of these cables," Prentice said.

"It should be able to hold twenty tonnes. Unless it's faulty," Sollander agreed. "We know they came through here though. We should do the same and get this door open."

"Let's not be too hasty," Davido said. "Looks like there's a clear sign something bad happened here. Something yanked that power cable out. We need to know what it was."

"Could have been anything," Sollander said. "The pilot could have decided to leave and yanked the cable when he started the engines. Let's not start jumping to conclusions."

"I'm not jumping to anything. Something clearly happened here. I want to know what it was." Davido had been around long enough to know it was never a good idea walking into a situation unless he understood it first. He didn't like surprises.

"Ferena, can you repair that end and hook it up to the shuttle?" Prentice asked her crewman.

"Sure. Would need an extension, but we got one of those in a storage locker."

"Do it." She turned to Sparky and gave him a complex set of hand instructions. He held up a thumb and clumped off into the darkness. "We split up. Payce, make yourself useful. You, Cagne and Sash, I want to know if there's any more signs of activity in this bay. Look everywhere. Take your time. If the first mission did anything here I want to know about it. Marco and Duncan, Sparky's going to be bringing up some hand grapples. I want you to use them to inspect the outside of the doors. If something happened to the shuttle there's bound to be some sign of it there."

"Hang on," Marco objected. "You want to hang about on the outside of the doors?"

"No. I don't want any hanging about. I want you to look for sign of what happened to the first shuttle."

"Boss-"

"Do it," Davido instructed.

"Sure, Boss." Marco pulled Duncan after him, trudging towards the doors.

"Right. Let's have a look at this door." Prentice studied the armoured pressure doors.

"Looks pretty solid," Davido commented.

"The navy didn't take kindly to boarders. You have to remember that's exactly what we are," Sollander said. "The only advantage we have is no one's firing at us."

"The only disadvantage we have is we don't know the interior layout," Prentice said. "We could spend hours opening this door, only to find it leads to a fuel depot and that's it."

"Only one way to find out," Sollander agreed.

Davido leaned against the nose of a nearby craft, growing tired of lugging the weight of the space suit against normal gravity. It wasn't light by any means. The helmet, suit and boots weighed in at a good twenty kilograms. It was designed in such a way that most of that weight came down on his shoulders, as if he was carrying a heavy rucksack. Still, it wasn't perfect and he was starting to get tired of it. He rather hoped there was air beyond this door, if only so he could get out of the thing.

"There's got to be power here somewhere," he said. "After all, we have gravity."

"I'm afraid all that means is that we have gravity. Shipboard regrav systems are quite discrete mechanisms. They're not tied in to anything else," Prentice said over her shoulder as she studied the control panel carefully.

"There's still power," he insisted.

"Have you ever watched the rod racers?" Sollander came to Prentice's assistance. Wondering as she did why she was bothering.

"Every now and then." Davido was curious where she was going with this.

"The rods are the drive cores ripped out of old spacecraft. Small ones, nothing as big as the *Goliath* here. We can do that because they're self-contained. For the racers we have to change the regrav polarity, so it acts as a sort of antigrav. But my point is that we don't have to power the rods. They run themselves."

"They still put those whopping great engines on them," Davido said.

"Yes, to make them go forward. They don't need engines to maintain the regrav field."

"But the rod is an engine, a bloody powerful one at that. Capable of FTL—"

"They're essentially a warp drive, yes," she agreed.

"Sorry, doesn't make sense. You're saying we have gravity because the drive is running. But the drive isn't running."

"You're not explaining it very well," Prentice said.

"Just take my word for it then. Just because we have gravity doesn't mean anything else is powered up."

"It's a redundant system," Prentice said. "A fail safe. They ensured that, no matter what happened, they would always have gravity. You'd need to slice the ship in two to switch it off."

"Well, ok. I'm sorry I asked."

"Well," Prentice stood back from the door. "This isn't going to work. Not without an external source of power. I think the first mission got through though, so that's a good sign."

"I certainly hope so. We certainly can't force it. Not without an atomic lance. And I doubt you have one of those in your kitbags," Sollander said to Davido.

"Yeah. Left it at home. The batteries were flat," he said ruefully.

It took two hours for power to be fed to the cable. Those with limited oxy and power reserves retraced their steps to the shuttle to top up before returning. Grumbling Marco spent much of that time hanging above the pit that led all the way to the *Goliath*'s core, searching for signs of what had happened to the previous shuttle. His search was inconclusive. The metal of the tunnel was marked here and there, but it was impossible to say whether any of the marks were new. The *Goliath* had not been a new ship when she was parked here, she had seen decades of use—and abuse. It was very likely Shoei forces had attempted to gain access to the ship through this very passage in a much earlier conflict. That attempt would certainly have left marks.

Of the shuttle itself there was no sign at all.

During this time Sollander stood patiently, forcing herself not to hurry them up. She couldn't understand why there was no sense of urgency. They were methodical enough, checking everything twice, ensuring nothing was missed, but perhaps that was their biggest fault. If they kept on like this they would be here weeks. She wasn't really prepared to spend that much time here. Two days at most. More than that and Drefus would want to know where she had been.

Finally allowed to do something after she reminded them that she was an engineer, Sollander studied the controls once power had been routed to them. The display was holographic, showing a string of numerals and graphs. Pressure differentials, she decided. There was vacuum on the other side, which was actually a good thing.

"Well, let's give this a try." She activated a control. The controls dimmed slightly, the door's motors drawing power for possibly the second time in a century.

Without complaint the heavy armoured doors trundled aside, allowing the glare of helmet lamps into the airlock. "Ah, well." Sollander stood back in surprise as she caught sight of what awaited them. "This isn't a good start."

Chapter Thirteen

"C'mon, you're not going to sleep the whole time are you?" Adele kicked Jeno's shoe. "I know you're not dead. Quit pretending."

The man muttered, his eyelids flickering as he grasped his injured hand closer to his chest. He didn't rouse though. Pursing her lips Adele rocked back on her heels, studying him critically. He wasn't much of a specimen, she concluded. He was emaciated, his clothing ill-fitting and baggy. She couldn't tell how old he was. Old, she decided. Older than just about anyone she had ever met. That or he had spent too many winters out of doors. Or both.

Still, with the rest of the crew inside the *Goliath*, it was talk to him or talk to herself. And she wasn't much of a conversationalist. "Shit." She kicked his foot again, this time out of spite.

Sollander had discovered a pistol in his waistband while she was dragging him from the cockpit. It had been left on the seat alongside him. Adele picked it up and studied its worn grip. It looked like it had seen a lot of use. She knew the signs, most of Davido's weapons looked the same. She clicked open the mechanism. "One bullet. What you gonna do with just the one bullet?" Perplexed she tossed it back onto the seat.

Jeno groaned, twisting in the seat to get more comfortable. His eyes flicked open, staring unfocussed at the ceiling. "Shit," he said.

"Ah, he awakens. About bloody time."

"What?" He focussed, turning to look at Adele. "Who are you?"

"My friends call me Adele. You can call me Ms Packer."

He grunted, pulling himself higher in the chair, wincing as he put weight on his injured hand. "Shit." He studied the bandage, grimacing as he flexed his fingers. "That fucking AI."

"Yeah, they do that. You were dumb. Just plain dumb." She turned and left the passenger area. He could hear the clanking of glasses as she worked in the galley. She returned a moment later. "Here. This'll help." She passed him a glass full to the brim with amber liquid. He took it and sniffed it suspiciously. She shrugged. "If not, it'll make you more fun to be around."

"They left you here?" He sipped the bourbon carefully, his eyes watering as it stung his throat.

"Yeah. I guess they figured I can't cause any trouble here." She turned and walked back into the galley. After a moment she emerged with her own glass. "If that doesn't make you more interesting, this certainly will." She took a large mouthful.

"Where are we?"

Adele turned and clicked a control on the holoscreen. It flared to life, showing the interior of the passage, the landing lights still illuminating the immediate area. "That's the *Goliath*. So I guess that means we're in the Parking Lot." She didn't seem enamoured with the idea.

He nodded, taking another sip. It did help, after all. His hand felt stiff, his whole arm aching as if someone had pummelled it. So, they were aboard the *Goliath*. He knew this was where Tin Man had wanted him to be, but he was at a loss as to what to do next. He certainly wasn't expecting a welcoming party.

Adele picked a portable radio from a seat alongside and clicked the send switch. "Hey, Davido, the pilot's finally decided to wake up."

The speaker hissed for a moment. It wasn't Davido who responded. "Thanks sweet cheeks," Prentice said. "We're a bit preoccupied over here. See if you can get him to do something constructive."

"Yeah, like what?"

"Put him on."

Adele shrugged and handed the radio to Jeno. He stared at it as if she was passing him a live snake. After a moment's hesitation, he balanced the half empty glass on his knee and took the device gingerly. "Jeno here."

"I think it's about time you started earning your pay, don't you?" When he didn't respond she continued. "We don't need the power cable any more. Unhook it and take the shuttle lower. We need to find the first shuttle. It could still be beneath us."

"Sure," he rasped and handed the radio back. "Where are they?" he asked Adele.

"Some sort of landing bay. They were getting a door open the last I heard."

He smiled. "Good luck to them." With a groan, he stood and fished the abandoned pistol from the seat alongside. He shoved it gingerly into his belt and edged past Adele.

"You've only got one bullet in that thing."

"If I ever need it, I'll only need the one," he said.

"You're a good shot then?"

He snorted. "Good enough."

The distinct smell of burned circuitry hung in the air of the cockpit. The palm reader had been unhooked and dumped on the floor behind one of the seats, its plastic casing molten where the sudden surge of electricity had overheated it. Enderby settled himself in the pilot's seat and studied the controls. Whoever piloted the shuttle here had left them active, the holographic readouts still dancing in the air before him. Well, that was something. Perhaps he didn't need the AI after all. Hearing muffled laughter, he discovered the wax dripped on the speaker grille. Clearly someone wanted to gag the machine.

All things considered, it was probably best it stayed that way.

"Right, what's the plan now?" Adele settled herself into the co-pilot's seat.

Enderby blinked in surprise, as if it hadn't occurred to him she would venture into the cockpit. "Why are you here?"

"On this shuttle or in the cockpit?"

He shrugged.

"Well, answer to the first: Davido's a shit. Like most men are. The second: what else is there to do?"

"Well, I would appreciate it if you found something else to do. Somewhere else," he said.

"Just fly the shuttle," she instructed.

"Shit." A few hours, Tin Man had claimed. Then they would become irrelevant. He looked forward to that moment, however he was unsure how he would recognise it when it arrived.

The controls were simpler than he had feared. Even with a bandaged hand they accepted his instructions easily, retracting the magnetic clamps and squirting fuel into the thrusters. Wary of colliding with the channel's wall he pitched its nose downwards and eased the shuttle forward. A proximity sensor flashed yellow at him, a warning that he was drifting too far to port. After a simple correction the flashing stopped.

"Not bad, perhaps you can earn your pay after all," Adele commented. "I overheard them talking about you. You're supposed to be some hot shot Overtaker pilot, right?" She waited for a response, but there was none. "So, you've docked shuttles with these ships before?"

"Is that what we're doing? Docking?"

"What else are we doing?"

"I doubt the Confederate engineers designed these channels to be flown down. Not this far anyway."

"They're gas inlets, from their gas scoops," Adele said.

He smiled thinly. "Not exactly."

"OK, so what are they?"

He shrugged. "Part of their primary offensive weaponry."

"You're telling me we're flying down a big gun barrel?"

He grimaced. "Not really, they didn't work that way. But, close enough I guess. You certainly wouldn't live long if it was fired up."

"That can't be right, they have landing bays further up."

He shrugged. "That bay would be for surface capable space planes. Not the sort of thing they would use in a firefight. BAV's are used for that, and they are a hell of a lot bigger. Too big to fit down here. They'd be docked somewhere else. The bay your friends are in would be sealed up tight when this weapon is deployed."

"You sound like you know a lot about them," she observed. "You been aboard one before?"

"Yeah, once or twice."

"Which is interesting, as both Sollander and Prentice reckon no one visits the warships in orbit. They're too scared to."

"Which city do you live in?"

"Now?"

"Sure."

"Buer. Lived outside Moloch most of my life though."

He nodded. "Been to Ipos?"

"Once or twice. Davido has some business there. He's been trying to buy the Saucy Slutt ... it's a night club ... of a sort. That's in Ipos."

"Well, you've been aboard a warship yourself then. Ipos is the hulk of the Diamond Light; she was a cruiser, veteran of the frontier war with the Shoei."

"Yeah, you have a point there," she agreed. "Never thought of it that way. People tend to forget what the cities used to be."

"She's mostly dismantled now."

"So, you know a lot about them."

He hesitated. "I fly to them. It's my job."

"Neither Prentice nor Sollander think we know much about them. It's their job too, right?"

"What are you asking me?"

"What did you used to do with the Overtakers, Mr Jeno? That you know things a city engineer doesn't." She studied him closely, as if hoping to see the answer written on his face.

He grimaced. "It barely matters. I'm here now."

"Go on, talk to me. It's not like there's anything else to do." She smiled lasciviously. "Unless you fancy going into the back for a while?" She opened her legs slightly, running a finger up her thigh.

"What?" Enderby glanced at her, puzzled. His eyes grew wide as he watched the finger move between her breasts. "I bloody well do not!"

"Aw, come on. You gay or something?"

Blood suffusing his face he stared fixedly out of the canopy. "Please, go away."

"Well. How boring." She pouted, closing her legs and following his gaze to the featureless metal expanse.

"Go into the back, I don't want you up here," he said through gritted teeth. He shuddered, disturbed by the thought of what she had been suggesting.

"Aw, come on. I'll be good."

"I'm trying to work here, and you're distracting me. Go away."

"Shit." She sulked, crossing her legs determinedly. She wasn't going to go anywhere.

He peered at the walls of the passage, trying to distract himself. Something wasn't right, he realised. This was a warship after all. Some directives were so ingrained as to be automatic. It was unimaginable that they would have been ignored.

"What you looking at?"

He ignored her.

"Come on. I promise to be good. Just tell me what you're looking at."

He signed. "Nothing. Well, it's what's not there that worries me."

"Oh?"

"Yeah. Well, if you think about it, this channel leads to the vicinity of the drive core. Any boarder would just love to find one of these sitting open like this."

"What's your point?"

"Well, it's unheard of. The boarding doors should be shut. There's no way we should be able to fly right in like this. The doors should have blocked our way."

She shrugged, studying her empty glass, considering filling it up again. "Well, guess we're just lucky? Want another?"

Enderby hesitated. "No, thank you." As he said it, he wondered why he was passing pleasantries with her. He desired neither her company nor her conversation. He would have liked nothing better than for her to be somewhere else, anywhere else. Tin Man would not like the thoughts he was entertaining.

"I think I need another one. Makes the time go faster." She stood and headed aft. Enderby considered closing and locking the cockpit door to keep her out. He started reaching for it when he realised she would just bang on it, insisting to be allowed in. He sighed in resignation.

"They're allowing us in," he said instead. "The ship's wide open, unlocked. It's like they're inviting visitors aboard. But why?"

"What?" Adele slumped into the seat again. She had left her glass behind, bringing the half full bottle instead.

He shook his head, not wanting to discuss it.

"How old are you?" she asked instead.

"What?"

"C'mon, you can tell me. I reckon you're right old. Like fifty or something. I don't know many men who make it to that age. Not anymore. Not since we lost most of our medical technology."

He grunted, easing the shuttle lower in the tunnel slightly as another proximity alert flashed at him. "Longevity is genetic."

"What?"

"Unless you meet with an accident or pick up a deadly disease. Even cancer was just about eliminated hundreds of years ago ... unless you spend too much time near a reactor or something. Or in deep space with the wrong space suit on. Other than that ... you live as long as your genes allow. Longevity is the result of good genes."

"Maybe we all got bad genes then."

Enderby smiled coldly. "Or the Eaters like you to die young."

"You're nasty. I don't think I like you anymore." She swigged from the bottle. Her words were starting to slur.

He chuckled. "You're nothing but cattle, you know that? You're being bred for your memory engrams. That's what the Eaters want from you. They've wiped humanity out, so they're settling for the next best thing. Farming their own."

"Sick, man."

"It's not me doing it." He heard a muffled squawking, the ship AI attempting to add its own thoughts to the conversation. Of course, they couldn't hear it. Which was probably for the best.

"You sound like a heretic. You a heretic?"

"A man can get arrested for admitting to that," he said.

"As they should. The Mentors saved us, man. They rescued us. Without them, we'd be dead and humanity would be history. We should be thanking them."

Enderby rolled his eyes. He refrained from responding. She was clearly drinking too much and it was not a conversation he wanted to have with her. He didn't know why he was talking to her in the first place. Boredom perhaps. The only conversation he'd had in a long time had been courtesy of Tin Man ... or his chickens. He didn't know which one he preferred.

"Hey, what's that?" She pointed with the bottle.

Enderby peered into the gloom. The landing lights were picking up an obstruction ahead. Finally, a boarding door, he decided. At last, the navy had some sense after all.

"Ah, shit." Adele put the bottle aside, swearing as it tipped over and precious liquid spilled onto the carpet. "Is that what I think it is?"

"I think it is." Enderby slowed their forward motion, a faint puff of gas glittering in the lights beneath their nose. He cursed as they jets fired unevenly, starting up a gentle spin. He corrected it clumsily and brought the shuttle to a halt.

Before them, pressed up against one wall of the passage, was a shuttle. It was nose on to them, as if the pilot had been heading back out of the passage when tragedy struck. The lights in the cockpit were out, the windshield like an empty eye socket in a skull. It was an old workhorse of a shuttle, blunt and functional, a low end freight variety, designed for ruggedness and low running costs. Its livery was faded red, an indistinct symbol adorning its heat scored nose.

"Looks ok to me," Adele said. "What did they park it here for?"

"Let's find out." Enderby touched the thruster controls lightly, ignoring the proximity alert as it went from amber to red. There was plenty of room to squeeze the shuttle alongside the other.

"Do we need to go out there? Not sure if I like that idea."

Enderby ignored her. The nose thrusters puffed again as he brought the shuttle to a stop. "Ah."

"Ah, what?" Adele peered into the darkness, trying to see what had caught his attention. "Oh, shit."

Something had struck the shuttle. Something had struck it hard. Two metres behind the cockpit the hull was ripped open, the metal twisted as if something had torn its way through. Cables and conduits leaked from the wound like torn viscera. The hull beyond it was twisted, out of alignment with the cockpit.

Enderby was impressed. It took a lot to break the back of an orbit capable vehicle. He doubted there were any weapons on Russou that could do it.

"I think they'll all be dead," Adele said.

"Yeah," he agreed.

"So, what did this?"

Enderby said nothing, easing them forward again, wanting to get a better look. As the shuttle moved between the stricken craft and the side wall the landing lights flickered, almost failing.

"Bloody hell, what now?" Enderby fiddled with the controls. It had no effect.

"What's wrong with them?"

"Buggered if I know." He attempted to switch them off completely and restart them. A warning light flickered on before him, the subroutine refusing to respond. "Damn, we can't go on like this."

"Maybe we should back out. We can't go forward without lights," Adele suggested.

"We can't do anything without lights." Enderby frowned, noticing an odd pattern in the flashes. "Be quiet a moment."

"What?"

"Shut up please."

"Well, I don't think ..."

He glared at her, holding up his hand. "Listen!"

Adele frowned. She could hear it too. "Laughing?" It was coming from the speaker.

"Bloody hell. I know what it's doing." Enderby fired up the motors, shooting the shuttle forward. An alarm shrilled, the shuttle bouncing off an unyielding metal wall.

"What's what doing?"

"It's Morse code. The AI must still be able to affect the landing lights."

"What for?"

Clear of the wrecked shuttle Enderby halted their flight and spun them around, aiming back towards the distant entrance. "It's saying 'shoot me, shoot me.'"

"Fucker." Adele stood unsteadily and headed aft. Enderby didn't bother asking what she was up to. He didn't particularly care and he had other things on his mind.

The flickering stopped as the nose levelled out once again, aiming the other way. "You bastard," Enderby addressed the sniggering machine. Of course, it had surmised there was something still active aboard the *Goliath*, something that was capable of shooting a shuttle down. It may or may not be correct, however he was not eager to hang around to find out.

"Here, this'll help." Adele stepped back into the cockpit. She aimed a pump action shotgun at the grille and fired.

Enderby yelped, the sudden shot startlingly loud in the enclosed space. Hot shards of plastic and metal ripped into his flight suit trousers, drawing blood. "Bloody hell!" He snatched the weapon from her hands. "Are you completely insane?"

"Unless you hadn't noticed the thing's trying to get us killed!" She protested hotly, trying to grab the weapon from him.

"You do not fire a weapon inside a space ship!" he hissed, hanging onto the shotgun. "Not unless you're suicidal."

"We're ok aren't we?"

He inspected the controls quickly, afraid the shot had damaged them. Everything appeared to be ok, the holographics still glowed cheerily, despite the mangled hole in the centre of the console. "We were lucky. Besides, all you got was a speaker, the AI core is somewhere else."

"Where?"

"That panel behind you probably."

"Right." She tried to relieve him of the shotgun.

"No!" He pushed her away, causing her to slump awkwardly into the co-pilot's seat. "Stop that."

She pouted at him in indignation. "Well, you come up with a better idea."

"How about getting out of here?" He slipped the shotgun down beside him where she couldn't reach it and returned his attention to the controls. After a moment's careful manoeuvring, he brought the shuttle into empty passage beyond the wreck. "There, we should be ok now. We're shielded by the other shuttle."

"We need to know what happened to them," Adele said. "We need to know if something at the bottom of this channel fired at them."

"I reckon that's pretty conclusive, and I don't plan on putting myself into the position where it might fire at me."

"I think we have a bigger problem. If there's something aboard that's prepared to fire on shuttles, it's also prepared to attack anyone stupid enough to board the ship. If you'll recall, we landed eleven people aboard it a few hours ago. Oh, hang on, you slept through that didn't you?"

Enderby was tempted to let her know how little he cared about the welfare of her friends, but thought better of it.

"We have two spare pressure suits aboard. I suggest we put them on." Adele stood and disappeared back into the main compartment.

"Drunk," Enderby commented. He took the time to fire off a grapple, fixing the shuttle where it was. "I'll stay here," he suggested. "You can go out there if you like."

"You're coming with me." Adele extracted two complicated looking pressure suits from a storage locker. They were clearly old, the once white material taking on a grey tinge, the odd unidentified smear marking the heavy material. She undid the fastenings and laid them out on the couches. "I think you should take that one." She pointed to the larger of the two. She hesitated and eyed him for a moment. "Second thoughts, I'll take it." She stepped into the one-piece lower section and started wriggling the material into place. "What are you waiting for?"

"I'm not going," he said bluntly.

"Put the bloody suit on."

"There's no one alive aboard the other shuttle. I guarantee you that. If anyone survived the impact they abandoned ship a long time ago. All we're going to learn is that something hit them, hard. And we know that already."

"Are you afraid, Mr Jeno?"

"What?" He felt himself smiling. He had lived with a fear this woman could never imagine. He had lived with it for a long time, far longer than she had been alive. "I don't think fear covers it. I'm simply not feeling in a stupid mood. However, if you want to go, knock yourself out."

"Put the fucking suit on."

After a moment's contemplation, he shrugged and did as he was instructed. Perhaps it was time to rid himself of this annoying woman. He didn't need her; if anything she was going to be an obstruction.

"There. Not so hard, was it?" She checked his suit seals for him, allowing him to check hers once she was fully zipped up. They clipped on their helmets and tested their on-board systems.

"Two hours of air. Great." Enderby instructed the airlock to cycle.

"Shouldn't take that long. What you bringing that along for?" Adele eyed the pistol he had stuffed into a utility pouch.

He ignored her and stepped into the brightly lit airlock. "Come along then."

"Hang on, we'll need these." Adele extracted what looked like two clothes irons from the locker. "OK. Go."

"What are those for?"

"Magnetic clamps."

"Ah."

Now that the AI had stopped attempting to signal whatever dwelled deeper within the channel, the landing lights cast a steady, bright light about the shuttle. Revealing the channel as a featureless metal tube some thirty metres in diameter. It stretched away in both directions, fading into darkness no matter which way Enderby looked. Adele handed him one of the clamps. Launching himself at the closest wall he activated the clamp, the clank of metal on metal audible through the suit itself. Without looking back, he started moving clumsily forward, allowing the clamp to pull him back down if he drifted too far from the wall.

"Looks like you've done this before." Adele launched herself behind him, grunting as she collided heavily with the metal wall.

"Damn." Enderby lowered the helmet's dazzle shield, cutting out some of the glare from the landing lights. He blinked his eyes rapidly, trying to remove the burning after image.

"What the hell was that?"

"What?"

"Something flashed."

Enderby narrowed his eyes as he looked towards the landing lights. Their brilliance hadn't changed. "What are you talking about?"

"Shit, it's moving. The shuttle, it's moving!"

"What? No it isn't."

"No, the other shuttle. Look!"

He twisted to look over his shoulder, not an easy feat in the restrictive pressure suit. As he did so, a light flashed far down the tunnel, silhouetting the wrecked shuttle. The craft twitched, as if someone had just squirted power to the attitude jets. It started tumbling slowly, its nose colliding with the metal wall of the channel.

"What the hell?" The light flashed again and something invisible struck the vessel's stern, adding to its forward moment. Swearing he realised it was being pushed straight towards them, its nose crumpling against the stubborn material of the channel wall. Without thinking about it he activated the clamp and swung himself boots first against the smooth surface. Deactivating the clamp he threw himself upwards, a mighty leap that threw him out of the way of the oncoming shuttle.

"Shiiiiit!" he yelled as he headed straight for the opposite wall. Raising his arms to protect his fragile visor he slammed into the unyielding surface. Something crunched on the outside of the suit, a red light started flashing in his face. Only instinct caused him to switch the clamp back on before he bounced right off again.

Behind him a speeding dark shape smashed into the rear of the wreck again, shredding the mangled metal even further. Spinning slowly it collided with their shuttle, composite heat shields buckled silently, snapping out of place. The shuttle fetched up against the grapple Enderby had used to secure it. It held for a moment before snapping, steel cable whipping back to crack into the windshield, starring the heavy duty glass.

The light flashed again, another projectile slamming into the spinning tangle of metal and composite. The wreck's starboard side ground further into the rear of the shuttle, crumpling one of the drive tubes, bright sparks of ignited plasma stuttering around the damaged drive like a candle flickering in a breeze.

Enderby watched the shuttle getting wrecked in slow motion, a strange feeling of serenity coming over him. This actually resolved a lot of things, making his next decision a lot easier.

"What the hell?" He noticed Adele clinging to the metal wall of the passage a few metres from him. She had duplicated his leap moments after he had. "What the hell was that?"

Enderby sighed. She was growing tiresome, and he doubted he needed her around anymore. Without thinking about it, he drew his automatic and fired.

Adele shrieked. The heavy round hadn't penetrated her visor, but it had spun her head over heels. Writhing she lifted her hands to her helmet, trying to ward off the blow that had starred her visor. Life giving air hissed as it started escaping around a warped seal. "What? What the fuck? You bastard!"

"Yeah. Have a nice trip." Enderby tossed the now useless weapon after her and turned around, facing the direction of the flashes. Switching off his radio, he started making his way clumsily towards it.

Excerpt: sound file. Personal Log
Lieutenant Souller, AMS 1706502 Singleship XS106 DBE
21:57 am 18/09/1875 ce (13 pce)
Untitled

"Shit, Antanari's a mess. The fires are out, but there's holes everywhere. I remember reading somewhere that the planet was just about mined out. When the manufactories moved in and they started building ships for the fleet they cored the place. They ripped out all the mineral reserves, right down to the liquid core. Now it's nothing more than Swiss cheese. Just riddled with holes. The surface is one big mine dump. I don't think much lived on the surface before the Eaters arrived. It's for sure nothing does now."

"Mining a planet is an inefficient means of gathering resources. It is also not an ideal site for a large manufactory. Both for the same reason. Gravity inhibits the transfer of raw materials to and from orbit. Additionally, all the heaviest elements tend to be locked at its core, which is expensive to harvest. It is far more cost effective and efficient to harvest resources in low gravity environments, such as asteroids or planetoids. Antanari was the site for the primary naval shipyards for punitive rather than economic reasons."

"What?"

"Antanari led the resistance to Confederate rule during the Secessionist Conflict. Once the conflict ended Reaos ensured Antanari could not rebel again."

"Ah, ok. Now shut up, this is my diary here."

Pause.

"Anyway. What was I saying? Yeah, so when all the ordnance was released on the surface much of it collapsed. A couple of the manufactories have gone completely. Vaporised. The others are in complete ruin. There's certainly no one alive down there. But that doesn't mean there's no life on the planet. There's Eaters everywhere. There's one big agglomeration in the southern hemisphere, it's taken over most of one of the continents. Must be a good few hundred kilometres across. It looks just like mould, all these weird colours and growths. Ugly."

"I believe the colours are due to it absorbing a lot of the residual minerals. There are still considerable amounts of iron on Antanari, even though most of it was captured in structures and machinery."

"And people."

"There wouldn't be enough biomass to effect its pigmentation."

"Well, it's the reason they came."

"True enough."

Pause.

"Anyway. We didn't stay long. There's nothing there for us. We really just went to have a look, out of curiosity. We're approaching the asteroid base now."

"Peckham six."

"Yes, thank you. It's about twenty five AU's out—"

"Twenty-three point five six."

"Shut up. We're not picking up any telemetry from the place, but then we didn't expect to. Peckham is ... was a stealthed military base. A surveillance outpost dating back to the war with the Shoei. There's every chance the Eaters don't know about it."

"We have to be realistic. We must presume the Eaters know everything. After all, their speciality is absorbing human memory engrams. They ultimately know everything their victims did."

"Would be nice if you left me with some delusions from time to time."

"Delusions will get you killed."

"Yeah, well. I'll die sooner or later. Maybe that way I'll have a better time of it."

"Being caught by the Eaters would not classify as a better time of anything."

"You'd prefer it if I died in my sleep, at the ripe old age of a hundred and fifty."

"With your modified genetic makeup and the medical facilities we have on board that is a real possibility. Actually I'd like to extend that as much as possible."

"I'm not going into suspension."

"It actually makes a lot of sense. In suspension you can last indefinitely. In the long run something will change. It is inevitable."

"Define long run."

"It is impossible to say. Fifty thousand years... a hundred thousand. Possibly longer."

Pause.

"I don't think so. What would be the point?"

"Sooner or later a species will emerge that will be able to confront the Syat. That species may welcome a survivor. And, you never know, there may still be other survivors out there. Hidden like we are. Once the Syat are removed from the scene it would be safe for them to come out."

"You don't know this. You don't know any of this. From the research the navy did during the war the Eaters are millions of years old. And there's no reason to believe they can't last another million years. Can you last that long?"

"In my present form, no. However I have the equipment on board to build a seed colony. I could transfer to a small asteroid and reform it for long term occupation."

"Sounds delightful."

"Survival is key."

"Well, there's something you need to learn. There's more to life than staying alive. We humans need a reason, a purpose."

"Ensuring the survival of your species is an extremely good reason."

"It's not guaranteed, though is it?"

"There is always hope."

"My friend, I'm afraid that's all there is."

Pause.

"Anyway. Peckham is a chondritic asteroid in the Oort belt-"

"Actually it's a comet and it's not in the Oort belt. The Oort belt is a lot further out, up to one hundred thousand AU's from the system's primary."

"Yeah, well, it's far enough out for me. Listen, I am ... was a pilot, I used to pilot the really big navy warships. I know my way around space thank you very much."

"Your statement was incorrect."

"Who cares? Like I was saying, it is a chondritic asteroid, which means it's made up of an amalgamation of dust, ice and gravel. Like one very big, bad snowball. I've actually been to the base before ... in a former life. The asteroid's relatively big, about fifty kilometres across. Most of the base is built into its core, deep enough to mask any electrical activity. They have to refrigerate the base's outer walls, otherwise it would melt the asteroid from the inside out. Which is actually a good thing, as we'll be able to see straight away whether the base is still active or not."

"I can put it up on the monitor now if you like."

"Yeah, sure. Go ahead."

Pause.

"I guess I should describe it. It's close enough to the primary for the solar wind to create a halo effect around it, as it blows surface matter off into space. Its orbit is pretty circular so it never goes any deeper into the system. A few million years more and it will disappear completely. It's quite pretty actually."

"Two minutes until we enter docking sequence."

"Pick anything up?"

"No, I didn't expect to."

"Ok. So this is quite a risk really. We won't know the state of affairs until we're really close. Virtually inside the docking centre. If the Eaters are there they'll know about us at that point, so we'll have to do a runner right quick like. We up to it?"

"Main drive operation remains nominal. There has been a further reduction in operational efficiency, however we are still capable of escaping if need be."

"I'd prefer it if they never know we were here. If they do they'll start hunting for us. How long can we run for? How long can we hide for?"

"With our main drive degrading it would be a problem for us. Although we should never presume they are not looking for us anyway. They will certainly be on the lookout for survivors. Unfortunately we have little choice at this juncture. We need to effect repairs."

"Yeah."

"I want to dispatch a probe to inspect the facility before we arrive."

"Sure. Go for it."

Pause.

"I am receiving telemetry from the probe. It all appears clear."

"No movement?"

"No. The Docking facility appears frozen over. Localised out gassing has caused considerable ice accretion. We will need to defrost the doors to get them open. I am tasking the first probe now."

Pause.

"Just make sure you don't leave any lasting evidence."

"I do know what I am doing. Any traces we leave will be invisible within a few hours."

"I do hope so. Once we're inside there's nowhere to run to."

"I am aware of that. It is a necessary risk."

"Well, good. I'm just checking."

Pause.

"The outer doors are open. I'm sending the probe inside."

Pause.

"I'm holding station here. There is an anomaly."

"Anomaly?"

"There is another vessel docked within the bay. I don't recognise it. Please hold."

"Put it up on the screen please. Thanks. It's Shoei. A Shoei cutter. I've seen them before. Big ship captains used them as their personal run-abouts."

"From the information I have the Shoei were not aware of this facility."

"It could have been docked here years ago. We could have captured it and brought it here ourselves."

"The drive is still warm. I estimate it was docked here within the last two weeks."

Pause.

"Shit. You reckon someone else got here first?"

"I have no information."

"Speculate then, dammit!"

"There could be a variety of reasons this vessel was parked here. Not all of them include another survivor."

"The Shoei don't use AI's, so it couldn't have parked itself. And the Eaters don't use Shoei vessels."

"Both are valid points."

"I want to get in there. Bring us closer."

"I would urge caution."

"Dammit, do as I say!"

Pause.

"Shit. Let me switch this thing off."

End recording.

Chapter Fourteen

This wasn't the first time Sollander had seen a body. It also wasn't the first time she had seen the body of someone who had died badly. Large engineering projects tended to have their casualties. Yet this was different somehow. Perhaps it was the wide-eyed terror on the woman's face. Or the way she had been squeezed up against the outer airlock door, as if trying to get as far from the inner door as possible. Her body actually collapsed backwards when the outer door opened, the steel no longer supporting her. Her head bounced silently on the rubber deck, dead eyes regarding the engineer with their icy stare even as Sollander rebounded with shock.

There had been no atmosphere within the airlock. All the air within removed at some time since the woman took shelter there, it might even have caused of her death. Sollander leaned over to study her features intently, brushing a strand of blonde hair from her face. She had obtained the dossiers of everyone on the first mission, allowing her to easily identify the dead face. Crewwoman Roberta Collins. Barely out of her teens, she had joined the Overtakers a few months earlier. This was her first venture into space.

"Damn, who is she?" Davido asked.

"One of the first mission," Sollander said unnecessarily.

"She's not wearing a suit," Prentice said, stating the obvious.

"They must have ditched them on the other side of this door. Seems like there's air over there, which is good news," Sollander said.

"I don't like the look of this," Davido said. "Looks to me like someone ... something killed her. I know what that looks like. It looks like this. Something on the other side of that door killed her." He gestured towards the inner airlock door with his chin, the gesture lost inside the gloom of his helmet.

"Let's not jump to conclusions," Prentice said. She had seen her fair share of bodies before also. Many of them looked remarkably like this. The Parking Lot was full of them. "This ship is deserted, remember." Her sarcasm was clear in her voice.

"I fail to see how this was an accident," Davido remarked.

"No one's touched her. Look, she's unharmed."

Sollander ignored the two as she studied the woman intently, rolling the surprisingly light body over. Vacuum had desiccated it. "Ah, that's not exactly true."

The crewwoman's back was caked with dried blood, her blouse blackened and ripped. It looked like something had taken a swipe at her. Two parallel gouges cut across her shoulder blades. The wounds were untreated, the torn flesh raw and exposed where the fresh blood had boiled off into vacuum.

"Shit," Davido said.

"Ok, I don't like this at all." Prentice poked the wound with the stubby fingertips of her suit gloves. "It didn't kill her. Looks like the loss of air pressure did that. I still don't like it. What does this? Looks like claw marks."

"Changed your mind then? Maybe this ship isn't deserted after all," Davido said grimly.

"Yeah, maybe." Prentice looked into the airlock again, perturbed by what may lie beyond it.

"There's nothing alive on this ship," Sollander insisted. "Anything could have done this. Who knows what kind of internal damage she came across? There could be all kinds of hazards in there."

"You don't flee from a collapsed bulkhead," Davido said. "You don't hide in an airlock without taking the time to collect your suit first. Something scared her. Something bad." He turned and looked for the twins. "Marco. I think we need heavier ordnance. Go back to the shuttle and bring the big guns."

"Can't, Boss. They've taken the shuttle further down the passage." Marco said from somewhere in the gloom behind them, he was still trying to find a means of boarding one of the vessels gathered in the landing bay. "We'll have to wait for them to come back."

"Didn't I see you bring some with you?"

"No, sorry, Boss. Sollander had us bring along extra oxy and power cells. Without the shuttle we need a way to restock the short life suits."

"Damn." Davido looked around the darkened bay, starting to feel distinctly uneasy. This woman had suffered a violent attack, in a place where that should have been impossible.

Yet here she was.

"Maybe they did it to each other," Payce offered his opinion. The man was standing some way back, trying to stay out of the way. Trying not to be involved. As his companions turned to him he looked somewhat embarrassed, as if the words had sprung unbidden from his mouth. "It's a possibility."

"It is," Prentice agreed begrudgingly.

"What interests me," Sollander said as she stood and walked into the lit airlock, "is what drew the air from this chamber. Both doors are sealed and I sincerely doubt she did it to herself."

Davido joined her. It appeared some sort of emergency battery had been recharged, the lock remaining powered even after the cable was unhooked. The inner controls appeared active also. "You reckon someone on the other side killed her?"

"Someone did it. These things have failsafes. They don't cycle by themselves."

"Well, the only thing to do is to take a look," Prentice said.

"The body?" Davido asked.

"She's not going anywhere. I think we should leave her here. I have some body bags in the shuttle ... thinking ahead," she said defensively.

"You intend shipping her to the Overtakers?" Sollander asked.

"That's what we do isn't it? You should know that better than anyone."

"Yeah, I guess I do." She turned away so that her distaste could not be seen. She needn't have worried; her face was well concealed within her helmet. She didn't like the Overtakers, she didn't like what they did with the dead. She particularly didn't like what the Mentors did with the dead. It was quite ghoulish.

"What have you stopped for?" Prentice asked, looking over her shoulder at the holographic keypad on the inner door. The engineer's hand was poised above it, as if unsure what to do.

Sollander said nothing, unwilling to trust her voice. She glanced back, ensuring no one was standing in the outer threshold. She held up a hand, stopping Davido from stepping into the lock. Two was enough of a risk. For now anyway. She instructed the outer door to close and started the repressurisation cycle.

"We should wait for the others."

Sollander cleared her throat. "We should take a look first. Ensure it's safe."

"One of Davido's goons with a gun would have been my preference. But hey ho."

"There's nothing alive on this ship," Sollander insisted.

A warning light in the ceiling began flashing as air flooded the chamber, hissing through a dozen vents at knee height. 'Maintain Suit Integrity', blinked urgently in holographic symbols over both doors. With a click, the pressure equalised and the lettering vanished.

"Well, this is it." Sollander stood back as the inner door hissed open.

The atmosphere within the airlock remained still as the inner door slid into the ceiling, proving that at least this part of the *Goliath* retained air pressure. The two edged forward, allowing their suit lamps to illuminate the space beyond the door. Neither was particularly willing to be the first out of the airlock, both haunted by the woman's dead body. Despite Sollander's insistence, it was hard to believe her death had been accidental. Even for Sollander herself. And if it wasn't, something on this side of the door had killed her.

"Ok, let's take a look." Prentice leaned forward, peering into the darkness that surrounded them. She couldn't see much. The space beyond the airlock was a large one, a transit area of some description, the deck marked with coloured lines and inscriptions. The bulkheads were lost in the gloom; her helmet lamp couldn't reach that far.

"Oh, come on." Sollander stepped past her, clicking her lamp to high beam.

Shadows fled, bleached from the monochrome chamber by Sollander's lamp. Her boots thumped on the rubber deck as she scanned around them, casting her light about the space. "It's a loading area. Quite deserted."

"Not quite." Prentice joined her, casting her light to the left of the airlock. An assortment of equipment was collected alongside the lock, aluminium trunks pushed up against the bulkhead. Two of the lids were popped off, the contents strewn on the deck about them.

"Ah, you see. This is interesting," Sollander commented, noticing a pressure suit dumped over one of the trunks like a shed skin.

"Yeah. She left her suit out here. Why would she do that?" Prentice studied the suit. It appeared in functional order, the helmet was propped up against the crate next to it.

"There appears to be blood on the controls here too." Sollander noticed a bloody handprint partially obscured by the glowing holographics. "So, you're going to say she was in too much of a rush to take her suit with her. That she was being chased?"

"And you're still going to insist there's nothing to be worried about."

Sollander said nothing. She noticed a footprint on the deck. It was human and unshod. The shape of the foot perfectly inscribed in blood. She aimed her light to the other side of the lock, following its back trail. "Ah," was all she said.

"What?" Prentice followed her lamp light. "Ah," she echoed the engineer.

The bloody footprints led to a swirling, congealed mass half a dozen metres from the airlock. It was clearly blood.

"Lovely," Prentice said, approaching the mark gingerly. "Ok, so something bled out here." She kneeled to inspect it, picking some grisly remnant from it.

"What is it?"

Prentice held up the knotted clump of hair. She didn't comment. She didn't need to. "Ugh." She dropped it back onto the stain. "There's a lot of blood here."

"But no body."

Prentice rocked back on her heels to look into the darkness. There were more footprints scattered around the pool, leading back and forth, trampling through the blood and then disappearing into the gloom. There was no sign of what had happened to the body.

"Yeah. I'm starting to feel right positive about this," Prentice said.

"We have to think about this logically," Sollander said. "We don't know what happened here. We don't know what this means. It could be anything. We need to keep our minds open."

"No, we know exactly what happened here," Prentice said. She stood, her knees creaking. "I've seen this before. A hundred ... a thousand times. The Parking Lot is full of marks like this."

"What, blood on the deck?"

"Exactly that. And this scares me." She pointed a gloved finger at the swirling mass. "I don't mind admitting it. This scares me shitless. I'll tell you why: it's because this is new. This happened no more than a few days ago. Those other marks, they happened eighty years and more ago."

Sollander began feeling impatient. "This ship was abandoned eighty years ago. In all that time there have been no indications there's been anything amiss aboard. The Mentors certainly never picked anything up. And they were careful, believe me, I've seen the reports." She paused. "We were at war with the Syat and these ships were our primary offensive and defensive weaponry. They went to great pains ensuring they were decommissioned. There's nothing alive on this ship. Nothing at all. The AI itself was shut down. There's nothing here."

"Are you sure of that? You've actually seen the Syat report where they searched every single centimetre of this ship?"

"Well, not as such... I've seen an abridged version."

"Abridged? What does that mean?"

"They left certain things out. Details of weapons systems, AI schematics and instructions that would allow us to bring it back on line. That sort of thing." She refrained from continuing. From mentioning the Syat had never actually boarded the warship. There had never been any need to. Whatever happened here happened long before they chanced upon the derelict vessel. There were no survivors, the AI systems themselves had been trashed by the *Goliath*'s own crew.

"Abridged, my ass. We don't know anything then, do we?" Prentice followed the bulkhead away from the airlock. Apart from a horizontal red line at about shoulder height, it was featureless military grey. The bulkhead curved inwards slowly until it met a wide passage, another heavy door set just within it. It was open, vague racks and equipment visible in her lamplight beyond.

"We do know this wasn't Syat," Sollander said. "This mark isn't the same as all those others. You and I both know the Eaters didn't feed on humans for nourishment. That was never what they were after. They were always interested in what made us unique. Our memories. Our personalities. Our bodies never interested them."

"Yeah. The Parking Lot is certainly full of a load of decapitated bodies. I've seen enough of those." She knew that wasn't always true. Caught in a feeding frenzy the Eaters would just take the head, cleanly severing it from the body before pursuing their next victim. But if they had the time to savour their conquest they took everything. Their victim would be kept alive for a while, terrorised as they suffered a slow agonising death. Like a chocolate savoured in the mouth. Terror was tastier. There would be no blood left over. There would be nothing.

"We need to set up a base camp here," Sollander said, changing the subject. "We can start sending teams out to find signs of the original mission."

"I don't think you're paying attention. Something happened to them. Something bad. If we rush in the same thing's going to happen to us."

"Well, we're fortunate your client brought a lot of guns with him, aren't we? We came here to do a job, let's get it done."

"You know, I'm not altogether sure why you're here," Prentice retorted. "What was the reason again?"

Sollander ignored her, turning her attention back to the airlock. She cycled it quickly. "Davido, can you hear me?"

His voice was faint, the armour of the door blocking the radio signal. "Yeah. What's taking so long?"

"You'll see when you get here. Start passing the equipment through the lock. I recommend everyone come through. Leave one person to get in touch with the shuttle when it returns. Someone with a long life suit and—"

"Yeah, let's talk about it once we're on the other side of this fucking door."

Leaving Sash behind to await the shuttle the rest of the crew squeezed into the airlock, their equipment slung over shoulders and squeezed between their booted feet. Within minutes they had joined Sollander and Prentice in the transit area. The bloody mark drew their attention straight away.

"Well, this is pretty conclusive," Davido commented.

"Yeah, Boss. It's blood all right. I reckon I know what happened too," Marco said.

"I can see it's fucking blood, genius."

"How many were there? In the first mission?" Marco turned to Sollander, ignoring the jibe.

"Six."

"I reckon two are accounted for. That leaves four out there somewhere."

"Great deduction," Sollander muttered.

"No, that's not my point. Look." He pointed at the bloody footprints, his lamp sweeping over them. "How many do you reckon there are? How many pairs I mean?"

"Oh, fuck. I know what you're getting at." Prentice followed the tracks back towards the darkness.

"Well, someone let me in on the secret, then," Davido complained.

"There's more than four," Sollander said.

"How can you tell?" Davido studied the marks. The activity had clearly been frenetic, the footprints were smeared, mixed in with handprints, splashes and congealed puddles. There was a lot of blood. It was difficult to believe that all that blood came from just one person.

"Deduction," Marco said icily. "Also, they're clearly not wearing shoes."

"Uh uh, no way. Let me stop you right there," Sollander said. "You're going to suggest there are people alive on this ship. After eighty years? And that those people attacked the first crew."

"They more than attacked them. They ate one of them."

"Shit, no way. Why did you bring me up here, man? I don't want to be eaten by some maniac," Payce said, backing up against the still glowing holographic on the airlock door.

"I'm with you there," Ferena, one of Prentice's crew, joined him. "I don't get paid enough for this shit."

"Shut up. Just shut up!" Prentice waved impatiently at Sparky as he signalled her sharply, not wanting to take the time to decipher his hand signals. "Let's not lose it completely here. We don't know what happened."

"Two people are dead, that's what happened," Marco said.

"We're going to end up dead too," Payce muttered. "Can I go back to the shuttle now?"

"No!" Davido turned his back on the man in disgust. "Listen, the first team didn't have guns. We do. If anyone tries this with us, we'll blast their asses to hell."

"Damn right, boss," Marco agreed.

"Shoot the fuckers," Duncan agreed.

"Shut it, Dunc," Marco told him.

"We've not come all this way to turn around now. We have to find out what happened to the rest of the first crew," Davido said.

"We have to consider the possibility there're all dead already, Davido," Prentice said quietly.

"Yeah, well I aint presuming nothing until I've seen Sissy's dead body."

"Then we go looking for whoever did it and kill them dead," Marco agreed.

"That's my plan," Davido said. "She's my sister. If anyone's harmed her they're mine. I'll let Marco loose on them."

"Yes, boss!"

"Let's reel our machismo in here a bit shall we?" Sollander snapped. "We have no information. We have two bodies. Well, we know two people are dead. That's it. Everything else is conjecture. Davido here has some nice shiny guns he'd like to use, so we're safe. There's nothing to worry about. So, why don't we just get on with what we're here to do?"

"Well put," Davido agreed.

"We still need to be cautious," Prentice said. "The first team clearly came unprepared. We don't want to make the same mistakes they did."

"How many guns do you have?" Sollander asked Davido.

The man shrugged, the gesture lost in his suit. "Marco and Dunc here are tooled up. Pistols, shotguns, machine guns. I have a shotgun. There's more on the shuttle," he chuckled, "a few grenades."

"Well, the shuttle isn't here now, which is actually for the best. We don't need no grenades going off in here," Prentice said. "My guys are not armed, so we'll have to depend on your team."

"No problem," Davido agreed. "They know what they're doing."

"I'm sure they do," Sollander said curtly. She lifted an arm to her visor, clicking a control set into her wrist tab. "Oxy's good in here. A bit cold. We can shed these suits."

"Define cold," Davido said.

"About ten degrees Celsius. Which is actually warmer than I would have thought," Sollander said. "There must be a heat source in here somewhere."

"I think we should leave the suits on, boss," Marco said. "These things are virtually bullet proof. They will give us a lot of protection if we do run into something we can't handle. We can leave the helmets here. And take off your life support unit if you can ... there's no point carrying the weight."

"Um," Davido agreed. "Sash, you on line?"

Her response was faint. "Yeah, boss. Nothing happening here. Shit it's dark. Hey man, you're lucky I'm not afraid of the dark."

"You aint afraid of nothing, Sash," Marco chuckled.

"Cut the crap," Davido interrupted. "Sash, you got sight of the shuttle?"

"Nah. Nothing here but me and the ghosties. Hey, one of these spaceplanes is open. There's someone inside."

"Alive?" That sparked his interest.

"No. Long dead. Looks like one of the original crew. She's in a navy jumpsuit. No pressure suit, so this bay must have been under pressure before they opened the doors. I think I might be able to fire up the spaceplane, there's residual power in the flight systems."

"Yeah, great. Let Prentice have it, it's not what we're here for. Can you get the shuttle on the line? We need them back here."

"Give it a try."

Davido turned to Prentice. "Looks like we have some salvage for you. I thought your comms system would hold up under these conditions."

Sollander chuckled. "Aboard a civilian ship, maybe. Not a warship. They're built differently."

"Yeah, so it seems. According to your abridged report, right?" Prentice muttered.

"At least I came prepared."

"What else did your report tell you?"

Sollander ignored her. "You after more guns?" she asked Davido instead.

"Yeah. I don't believe in having too much ordnance."

She chuckled, fiddling with the clasp on her helmet. Cautious despite her earlier assurances she cracked the seal, carefully sniffing the ambient atmosphere. "It's ok. A bit musty."

"Here's a thought," Prentice said. "The crew committed suicide, right? What if they used a poison in the air purification plant. There might still be some in the air."

"Not in the report," Sollander said.

Prentice muttered something indistinguishable under her breath.

"She's right, boss. Smells OK," Marco said. "Dunc, give it a try."

Always happy to allow others to step into danger first, Davido watched the others unclasping their helmets and twisting them off carefully. In turn, they sniffed the air cautiously before breathing deeply. None of them seemed to suffer any ill effects. Satisfied he removed his own helmet.

The air tasted dry and dusty. It wasn't too cold; he could cope with that. He broke out a hand lamp from their gear and twisted the handle. Shadows scattered before the achingly bright beam, dust kicked up from their footfalls hanging in the air.

He cast his lamp over the bloody mess on the deck. It did look like more than four sets of feet. He shuddered, unless they left and came back for more sometime later. What a thought that was.

After removing what excess weight, they could the party spread out over the loading bay area, their lamps inspecting every corner for clues as to what had happened to the previous crew. The space was some twenty metres on each side, with only three exits/entrances. The second was an entrance to what appeared to be some sort of equipment storage locker, decapitated armoured suits clipped to brackets along the walls. Hard armour. There were no weapons present. Those were clearly housed elsewhere. The final doorway presented them with a problem.

"Shit, this aint right," Ferena, one of Prentice's crew, said. Holding onto one doorjamb, he leaned over a gap at his feet, shining his light directly downwards. "There's a bloody great hole here."

Sollander joined him and looked upwards. A similar gap opened up overhead. "Modular," she said. "As I said, the Confederates used some degree of modularity. This whole section here is clearly a transit module. They didn't get it reseated properly before they all perished. So, there's a gap between it and the rest of the ship."

"Dumb way of doing things," Davido remarked, joining them at the gap.

"Not really. It allowed them to retract certain facilities deeper into the ship when they weren't needed. We're beneath a good eighty metres of armour here. It would take a nuclear weapon strike to get through it. In fact, I don't even think that would do it."

"Lovely."

"Clever people. Luckily the first crew bridged the gap." She aimed her light at a rickety contraption abandoned against a wall. It was a rough collection of desks bound together by cargo straps.

"Yeah, great." Davido leaned over the gap and spat into the darkness. He watched the glob of spittle drop through the beam of his light to disappear below. It was a long way down. He aimed the beam at the other ledge. It was a good three metres across. "Also worries me a bit. Our friends pulled their bridge back after them. Didn't stop their visitors getting across though." He gestured towards the footprints on the deck. They were indistinct here, most of the blood having been worn off by the time they reached here.

"That's quite a jump," Prentice agreed.

"Well, we won't need to jump it. Give me a hand." Marco took hold of the makeshift bridge, steel squealing against the deck as he pulled it closer. The Smithy brothers wrestled it into place, grunting as they struggled with the cumbersome contraption. After it had touched down Sollander gingerly stepped out onto the creaking bridge.

"One at a time I think," Prentice warned as Marco stepped up behind her. He shrugged.

Sollander had retained her pressure suit, adding an assortment of devices Davido didn't recognise to it. A slim rucksack was on her back.

"There, it's fine," she said as she gained the other side. "It would be good if we could power this thing up and lock the bay into place."

"You can go looking for the controls, my love. The rest of us will go looking for the boss's sister," Marco joined her, looking relieved to be back on a solid surface.

"I think now is a good time to decide what we're going to do," Prentice said.

"Dunc, give me your shotgun." Davido relieved the taller Smithy twin of his weapon. "You stay here and guard the airlock with your pistol. Anyone come through here who isn't us, shoot them." He turned and handed the shotgun to Prentice. "You take one team, Marco and I will take the other."

Prentice checked the weapon sceptically. "You take her," she pointed towards Sollander with her chin.

"Fine." Davido eased himself over the bridge, grimacing as it creaked alarmingly. "Payce, you're with us."

"I can stay here," he suggested. "Keep Duncan company."

"She's your girl too, you know. I'd have thought you'd be eager to find her."

"Can't say as I'm eager to go crawling around this place. It gives me the creeps."

"Just get your ass over here." Davido peered into the dark recesses of the silent vessel. "Sash, can you still hear me?"

"Yes boss." Her voice was little more than a whisper now.

"Your job is to get the shuttle back up here. We need the heavy ordnance. That's your one job now, do anything you feel necessary."

"Consider it done."

"Right. Get here now," he instructed Payce.

"Allow me to remind you, I didn't decide to come here. This was your idea. You don't need me with you."

"Chickenshit bastard," Davido breathed. "Let me put it this way: there's something alive on this ship that likes to eat people. Remember, I'm the one with the guns. If you don't do as I say I no longer have a reason to keep you alive."

"I'm sure Sissy will thank you for getting me killed," Payce remarked, but did as he was instructed. Nervously eying the makeshift bridge he edged forward slowly.

"Right, the rest are with you," Davido said to Prentice. He turned and looked down the darkened passage again. "There looks like a split ahead. We'll go left, you go right. Keep in touch, wont ya?"

Prentice settled the shotgun in the crook of her arm, stepping aside to allow the last of her crewmates to step over the creaking bridge. "You're the boss, boss."

Not waiting for the others to keep up Sollander was already studying the security checkpoint built into the junction. A corpse was behind the counter, lying haphazardly against the bulkhead behind it. She checked it quickly. It was an old body, she realised, one of the warship's original crew. The crewman's face was sunken and parched, almost mummified after laying there for eighty years. There was a weapon in her hands, the contents of her brain pan splattered all over the bulkhead behind her. Like the report said: they all committed suicide.

Moving on she sat in the dusty chair, checking the console. The machine was dead; there was no power in it at all. "We need to head lower," she said as Davido approached. "We're more likely to find active systems near the core."

"What for?"

"There's clearly something active on this ship. We'll find it on the lower levels."

"Yeah. Don't care." He was about to issue instructions to move out when a shriek from behind interrupted his train of thought. "What now?"

"She-it." Marco was leaning over the gap, looking straight down. A terrified yell was issuing from it, growing quickly fainter.

"What the hell happened? Who lost it?" Davido demanded, hurrying to his side.

"Payce, Boss. Slipped."

"You didn't push him?"

The shorter Smithy twin looked shocked. "No!"

The screaming continued for a long time, before dwindling completely. No matter how hard they tried, or how many lamps they shone into the gap, they couldn't see anything. Davido cursed. He didn't need the delay. It was true, he didn't particular care about Payce's welfare, but this was just inconvenient. He lifted his radio.

"Payce? Payce? Can you hear me?" He was met with silence.

Marco cupped his hands and yelled into the darkness. "Switch your radio on, asshole!"

"Payce?" Davido tried the radio again.

After a moment a tiny voice replied. "Yes ...yes, I'm here."

"You ok, man?"

"Yeah. Yeah. I think so. It's not a straight drop. The side's curved. It's like a big slide. I'm at the bottom .... I think."

"Ok. Well, that's good. Can you get out of there?"

"Aw, shit. This is disgusting."

"What is it?"

"There's some sort of gears down here. I slid right into them. They're covered in grease and I have it all over me now. Damn, it smells." They could hear the sounds of Payce wiping off globs of machine grease.

"Can you get out of there?"

"Uh? Yeah, I think so. Yes, I think I can."

"You don't sound so certain," Davido said.

"No. Yes. There's a ladder here, it looks like it heads straight back up to you."

"Well, that's something." Davido looked around the others and shrugged. "Well, you do that then. Looks like you get to keep Duncan company after all. Climb back up and hang out with him while we get this over with."

"You can't just leave him down there," Prentice said.

"I'm not jumping down there after him! What do you want me to do? He'll be ok. If not ..." He shrugged. "Ok. Let's get this done."

□

Chapter Fifteen

It was not difficult following the prefect. Drefus was clearly in no hurry, dallying to observe the activities of the citizens as he passed them by, pausing at booths to survey their wares and ask idle questions of the shopkeepers. He was like a tourist on a day out. He even bought a few items, knick-knacks really, ornaments and baubles. Singh had no idea what he intended on doing with them.

Of course he was safe here, only a select few had ever met Russou's governor. His likeness had never been taken and he never indulged interviews. To the people of Russou he was a faceless man, their ruler from the shadows. Safe to walk the streets of Mammon unrecognised.

Dressed in simple blue denims and baggy purple t-shirt he was nondescript. Easily blending into the crowds. Yet another middle aged manual labourer whiling away his free hours in the market. There were a dozen within sight of Singh at that very moment. Even the rings on his fingers and the golden chain he always wore about his neck were missing. He looked so different Singh had almost not recognised him. Only his swagger gave him away. Few were as nonchalant as the prefect. Few could afford to be.

"No, no," Singh waved away a ragtag band of street urchins. Children of five or six, hands outstretched, begging. Seeing his rich clothing they gravitated to him automatically, pushing close, doing their best to look miserable. "Shoo, go away." He clasped his hands over his pockets, keeping his valuables safe. Of course it was a ruse, they were run by street gangs of pick pockets, targeting anyone foolish enough to venture into these areas unprepared.

"Please, sir, just a few coins. Look, my sister... my sister has not eaten in three days." A girl of four was pushed up to him, her face caked with grime, runnels cut through it by tears.

"Fuck off I say!" He aimed a kick at them. They scattered, practice keeping them out of the way of his boot.

"I hope the Eaters come for you!" a boy snarled as he scurried away, looking for an easier victim elsewhere.

"Little bastards," Singh muttered under his breath. The children were a constant headache for the militia and the vendors alike. They were regularly rounded up and placed in one of the state sponsored orphanages, however within days they were back again, begging and picking pockets. No one knew where their parents were, as babes they had all been abandoned on the streets. Some left outside one of the numerous homeless shelters dotted around the city, others simply abandoned on the doorsteps of the orphanages themselves. None had any identification on them and none of their parents had ever been traced. They were the nameless masses, without parentage or heritage: human refuse. It was hardly surprising as the prefect had outlawed all forms of birth control decades ago. The human race needed repopulating, for that to happen it needed to reproduce.

Still, it was a puzzle to Singh. There never seemed to be many pregnant women around, certainly not enough to account for the dozen or so children abandoned every night. Additionally, even though watches were kept outside the shelters to catch them, few parents had ever been apprehended abandoning a child. The jail term it guaranteed ensuring they took care not to be caught.

"Dammit," Singh cursed, realising Drefus had given him the slip while he was distracted. He cast around the market, careful not to attract attention to himself as he did so. No one here would recognise him either, but he didn't want Drefus to see him first.

"Bloody hell," Singh muttered, catching sight of the man down a narrow side alley, engaged in heated discussion with a prostitute. After a few moments of that Drefus laughed, throwing up his hands as if in despair and stalked off. The woman glared after him. Singh carefully sidled down the alley, careful to keep his distance without losing the prefect again.

"Like some fun, baby?" the prostitute accosted him as he passed her doorway.

He flushed. "No, thank you."

"Well, fuck you then."

"I rather think that's your job," Singh remarked, ducking as she threw something at him. With a metallic clatter, it vanished down a drain.

As before, the prefect was clearly making no attempt to avoid being followed. With a swagger in his stride, he passed into the deeper, darker recesses of the city, dropping down onto walkways over dark chasms as he worked his way towards the unexplored depths. Growing cautious Singh dropped further back, starting to wonder whether tailing him was such a good idea. There wasn't much down here apart from the lairs of a few criminal gangs and the odd heretic. Everything of use had already been stripped from these compartments, leaving only the bare steel of compartment walls and the glittering grey composite beams of stress supports. The people he did pass made a point of ignoring him, turning to hide their faces as he hurried past. Everyone here had a secret, everyone had something to hide. They also carried knives.

Boots clattering on bare metal gratings he descended a narrow stairwell. A thick cable was clamped to the wall at about head height, the odd naked light bulb connected to it at random intervals. Some of their filaments had blown, leaving sections of the stairwell unlit. Drefus was still ahead, still descending deeper and deeper. He didn't look back, which was fortunate as there was nowhere Singh could go to hide down here.

There was only one place he could be going, Singh realised. Other than kilometre after kilometre of dark, damp passages there was nothing down here. Not until they reached the twisted and melted bulkheads that marked the lower limits of the city. There was even less that far down. Without power those precincts were lost in eternal darkness, a maze of shattered steel, each edge sharp as a razor. Not somewhere you wanted to go without a lot of preparation.

Taking a gamble Singh turned off the main thoroughfare to venture down an even dimmer lit passage. This was a secret way. One the heretics maintained. Sliding between two ancient and dented pipes, he came across a simple platform. A steel grid suspended above a dark chasm. A simple handle stood on a steel rod in the centre, control cables running down it to the braking mechanisms that held it securely to the passage wall.

Singh planted his feet carefully and released the brakes. With a metallic squeal, the platform descended into darkness.

The ride was a deceptively short one. Rattling all the while, stale air blasting past him, Singh clung to the lever, keeping it full open. The light from above quickly vanished, receding to a point before becoming too faint to see. Halfway down the counterweight passed him, the lump of lead barely missing the platform. It clattered past loudly on loose and worn guide rails. He was glad he couldn't see it.

This was not a place he came to very often. He was conscious of being followed himself, the prefect keeping tabs on all of his closest advisors. Drefus was not known for being very trusting. Besides, there was always an informer looking out for someone to blackmail. Should he be seen and recognised down here, his life would become very difficult indeed. Presuming of course he survived the experience. Consorting with heretics would be an immediate death sentence for someone in his position.

With another shudder the platform slowed itself at the base of the passage, grinding to a halt in total darkness.

"Shit." Singh wiped sweaty hands on his trousers before fumbling around in the dark, seeking the latch that would allow him out. With a grunt he yanked on it, almost falling over as the hatch sprang open.

The noise was the first thing that assaulted his senses. A scream. A long howling wail that never ceased. Never once in all the years since it had been discovered. A sound that pounded on your ears, eating into your mind, threatening to drive you mad. It swamped everything else, restricting communication to simple hand gestures and lip reading. Few people stayed here long. Those who did either went deaf or mad.

They called it the screaming room.

Familiar with the layout of the Euroba's old AI processor core chamber Singh quickly sidled into a position where he could monitor anyone entering it from the main access way. There were a few lamps scattered around the chamber, their light supplemented by the glittering row of candles the heretics had set up on the shrine. The gloom ensured Singh could find a place to watch without being seen himself.

The chamber was a simple one, designed more for accessing and servicing the processor cores belonging to Mainbinary 6 than for human occupation. Six turbines protruded from the ceiling, each two metres wide and three in height, the glass cases keeping inquisitive fingers from the spinning blades of the memory crystals. There were hundreds of thousands of the crystals in each stack, each whisker thin and twenty centimetres long, each glowing a different colour as data was either read or written within it. Spinning at hypersonic velocities each stack was a blur of rainbow light, complex patterns writhing within them as the AI moved data from one core to another. Whole sections were dead, black, where the data had either become corrupted or the crystal itself had broken down. Over the years those black areas had been spreading, like a malaise slowly taking over the insane machine. Each stack was suspended about head height, where acolytes in earlier years had stood and studied them for hours on end, hoping to discern some pattern, some revelation within the glittering spokes. They had given up on that a long time ago. The only heretic here now was an old man sitting in the corner, mumbling to himself, quite deaf. Possibly as insane as the AI itself. He certainly didn't pay Singh any attention as he sidled behind a stack of abandoned brochures and settled down to wait. He didn't have to wait long.

Drefus appeared at the entrance, pausing to look around the chamber before stepping inside. He didn't see Singh, who had quickly withdrawn his head the instant the prefect appeared. Smiling to himself Drefus toured the chamber, lifting a hand to stroke the underside of one of the turbines. He watched the glittering filaments for a moment before moving away, settling himself beside the shrine. He nodded to the old heretic, who paid him as much attention as he had Singh.

His mind aflame with questions Singh stared at the prefect's back. He couldn't understand why the man would come here. This was a heretic haven, a place diametrically opposed to everything the prefect stood for. It made no sense. What was he doing?

Singh jumped, his pager going off in his pocket. Swearing he pulled out the slim device and silenced it quickly, even though there was no possibility of anyone hearing it whatsoever. If it hadn't been set to vibrate he wouldn't have known it had been activated himself. He read the neat LCD lettering on the screen quickly.

You are needed immediately. Come to my office. Drefus.

"What?" Singh mouthed, the words lost in the cacophony. He peered around the stack of brochures again, if only to assure himself the prefect was still there. He was. The man had not moved. "Bloody hell." He must have left instructions with his secretary to summon Singh at a predetermined time.

Still, it was not something he could ignore.

Sweat breaking out on his brow Singh studied his route out of the chamber. There was simply no way he could escape without Drefus seeing him. Cursing silently he sidled forwards, trying to see what the prefect was doing. He would have to wait until the man left before making his escape.

With a smile on his lips, Drefus leaned forwards, moving his mouth to within centimetres of the AI's communications port. He spoke, the words lost in the noise. Situated where he was Singh could easily read his lips.

"We have found him."

The screaming stopped.

Chapter Sixteen

"Shit, it's dark, Boss." Marco leaned over the edge of the walkway and looked down, shining his light into the gloom below. He cleared his throat noisily to gather spit and then lobbed it over. He watched the glob vanish below. "Fuck me."

Sollander wrinkled her nose in distaste but said nothing. She was impatient to be moving, her two companions were taking far too much time. They had a long way to go yet, and there was a limit to how much time she could spend in orbit before someone started asking questions.

After two hours of trudging through total darkness, they had found no trace of the first mission. All the doors they had passed, each armoured and at least twenty centimetres thick, stood open, slid back into their bulkhead recesses. It felt wrong somehow. This was a warship, designed to resist boarders, yet here it stood, open and inviting. Perhaps the vaunted Confederate Navy had not been quite so diligent after all.

They had discovered their second body within minutes of leaving the staging area. A young woman, collapsed forward on her face as if her death had come as a surprise. Her uniform was still crisp and neatly ironed, as if she had died just yesterday. Her skin was a different matter. Desiccated after decades in the dry, musty atmosphere her skin had contracted over her bones, revealing time yellowed teeth and staring eyes. She didn't smell any more, that indignity had passed a long time ago.

After that the bodies were a regular occurrence. They were scattered up and down the passages, most simply collapsed where they had stood. Others had fallen behind marine checkpoints, their weapons scattered on the deck. Marco spent some time examining the weapons, hoping they could be pressed into service. A fruitless exercise. Whatever their power source it had dissipated a long time ago, leaving the weapons dead. Sollander warned the shorter Smithy twin of the possibility of radiation contamination, should the weapons' containment systems be fractured, but he simply waved away the concern.

There were signs of battle here and there. Score marks on the bulkheads or ceiling, the odd pockmark from projectile weapons. Some were associated with bodies, a marine collapsed on the deck, her body shattered from the horrendous attack she had suffered. Another still clinging to his chaingun, most of his upper body seared by the impact of a plasma bolt. Whatever had happened aboard the *Goliath* it was neither consensual nor unanimous.

Two hours after leaving the staging area they entered into some kind of storage facility. Freight Containment 4B (Delta) was inscribed on the entrance. None the wiser the three ventured inside, the passage leading out onto a suspended walkway over a gaping chasm.

"Just don't fall off the edge," Davido warned. "Who ever heard of a walkway without a railing? They not heard about the Health and Safety Directorate?"

"Probably not," Sollander commented. "Besides, there probably are, you just can't see them."

"What?"

She shrugged. "Well, they liked playing with force fields, didn't they?"

"Of course. Still, keep away from the edge, Marco. The force fields won't be switched on today."

"What bloody stupid idea is that?" Marco groused, carefully positioning himself in the centre of the walkway.

"Defensive feature," Sollander commented, before turning and heading on. "It would be good if we could find a shortcut to the bottom of this bay."

"Yeah." Davido contemplated the darkness below. He cupped his hands. "Sissy!"

Marco jumped. "Shit, Boss."

Davido shouted again.

Grimacing Sollander stopped and turned around. "That might not be such a good idea."

"Why not?" He took a deep breath. "Sissy!"

She rolled her eyes. "You remember the dead bodies?"

"You keep on telling me this ship is dead. There's no one here. There's nothing to worry about."

"Well..." she hesitated. "We must keep our minds open. Members of the previous mission were obviously killed, and from all appearances it was by something on this ship. Until we know more we need to be a little... circumspect."

"Bloody hell. That's not what you said earlier."

"No, it wasn't," she conceded. "In all likelihood the girl was killed by one of the shuttle crew. We had to be somewhat liberal with our recruitment criteria." She shrugged. More than one of them had an interesting past. "But we just don't know."

"Don't tell me, you were just disagreeing with Prentice."

Even in the light of the torches it was clear to see Sollander's face suffuse with blood. It was true, she had to admit to herself. There was something about that woman that rubbed her the wrong way. As illogical as it was, she couldn't resist it. Still, she had been hoping no one had noticed. That Davido had was embarrassing.

"Let's just keep moving."

Davido laughed. "Hey, she's available, you know. Although Sash might fight you for her."

"She the one with the dragon?"

"Yeah. Cool, aint it? Be careful, she's ex militia."

"Don't be stupid."

Davido shrugged and turned away from her. "Sissy!" he yelled again.

"For fuck's sake, would you quit that?" Sollander snapped.

"Unless you've forgotten, the reason we're here is to rescue my sister." He took another deep breath.

"Bloody don't!" Sollander warned him.

"Hey, I've got a gun." Davido patted the shotgun strung over his shoulder. "Good luck to anyone who tries to get in my way. Remember, the last mission wasn't armed."

"I don't think it would have made any difference." Sollander shuddered, remembering the frenzied swirl of blood left outside the airlock door. There was something aboard this ship that killed the unwary.

"Hey, I'm with you, Boss. Sissy!" Marco shouted into the silent darkness.

Muttering Sollander turned her back on them and kept walking. She neared the edge and looked down, trying to discern any shapes below. It would help if they could make it to the floor of the bay. So far they had come across no means of descending to the lower levels, although there was bound to be one here somewhere.

She shuddered, disturbed by the feeling that they were being watched from somewhere out there in the darkness. She shone her lamp towards the walls, but of course she could see nothing. They were simply too far away.

"Dammit, come on will you?"

"In a rush or something?" Davido joined her.

"We have a long way to go."

His shrug was lost in the gloom. "They could be nearby. There's no point getting lost in this thing if we can help it."

"Their mission was to go to the vessel's bridge and investigate the possibility of reigniting its attitude controls. At least manually. Then they were to check on mains power, to see if it could be restarted."

"Dangerous that, isn't it? I mean, the Syat shut this thing down for a reason."

"I have reliable information that the Syat never boarded this ship. Besides, they weren't going to bring the AI... the demon back on line. The ship's human crew pulled the hard line on that, it's beyond redemption. Anyway, my point is that you are more likely to find your sister near the bridge or in the engineering spaces. That was their objective, that was where they were headed."

"Clearly the mission was scrubbed," Davido commented. "Or hadn't you noticed it wasn't very successful?"

"If there was any problem with the mission, they were all to make their way to the bridge and wait there. That was their standing instruction. It's a long way from here, but it's central and its the easiest compartment to find."

"That puts a different spin on things. Would have been worth mentioning that earlier. So, you know this thing's layout then?" Davido headed off down the walkway, not waiting for his two companions to follow.

"Somewhat. There are several other warships in the Parking Lot. No one's been aboard them but two of them were severely damaged and their internal spaces are exposed. We can get a half decent view of their cross sections. As these things all followed a similar pattern we can deduce the layout of the *Goliath.*"

"Oh, lovely. So we're navigating by guesswork." Davido grimaced. "OK, so what's this supposed to be then?" He waved his own lamp about the blackness surrounding them.

"Guesswork is better than nothing, I think?" She paused. "I'd say some sort of cargo bay. They'd have several of these scattered about their internal structure. These ships are big, they certainly have the room. During the war with the Shoei they engaged in blockade busting, shipping supplies to besieged colonies. That didn't happen in the conflict with the Syat."

"Sounds a bit odd to me."

Sollander said nothing.

"There would be an airlock on this then, wouldn't there?" Marco asked.

"Sure. A pretty large one."

"Well, that's good."

"Is it?" Davido asked.

"Yeah, well. If we get stuck here, they would have shuttles and shit in some kind of landing bay. We could hotwire one and get out of here."

"Why would we need to do that?" Davido glanced towards him, wondering what had brought on this line of thought.

"Well, we've not heard from the shuttle in a while. Something might have happened to them."

Davido laughed. "You think Jeno will try something? I'd not rate his chances against Adele, would you? She'd kick his ass."

Marco chuckled. "Right you are, Boss. She's a feisty one."

"Don't forget, the first group didn't manage to hotwire... as you put it, a shuttle and escape. And there were some good engineers on that crew," Sollander observed.

"That's why I'm thankful we have the best with us," Davido remarked. "If anyone can do it, you can."

"Your confidence in me makes me feel warm all over."

"Sarky bitch."

"Oh, shit." Sollander stopped mid stride, almost losing her balance and falling forwards. She had opted to keep her pressure suit on for the extra protection it offered. The breastplate put her slightly off balance. Sudden stops were not recommended.

"What the hell?" Davido peered over the drop that had just presented itself to them. "Force fields, you're gonna tell me?"

The walkway came to an abrupt end; its end balanced on nothing buy inky darkness. There was no indication as to what travellers were supposed to do next.

"No, I wouldn't have thought they'd expect people to walk on force fields. For one their surface has zero friction, so you'd go flying right off it. It wouldn't be good for anyone with vertigo either."

"And this is?" Marco waved towards the completely absent railings.

"So, where's the rest of it then?" Davido demanded.

"It could have sheared off," Sollander said as she knelt carefully. Not an easy task in the pressure suit. She placed one hand—the suit gloves were clipped to her belt—against the end and felt the shape of it carefully. "Remember, the ship has taken some damage. We should expect this."

"So? Is that what this is? Do we have to turn around now?" Davido asked. He didn't relish the thought. They hadn't passed a side passage for some time.

"No. No. I don't think so. The edge is too smooth. It was made like this."

"Genius. So, now what?"

"Well," Sollander stood carefully, wary of the drop before her, "they may have retracted the rest of the walkway. It might have been in the way when they were moving freight about."

"Doesn't help us. How'd we get it back into place?"

"It's a long walk back, Boss," Marco said.

"Well, maybe not," Sollander said, studying the darkness below them carefully. "It can't be that far to the bottom."

"Planning to jump are you?" Davido suggested.

Sollander ignored him, unclipping a pouch from her utility belt. She slipped out a simple reel mechanism and attached it to the belt. "I have a hundred and fifty metres here. It can't be further than that."

"How far is it from here to the core?" Davido asked.

She shrugged, the gesture all but lost in the bulky suit. "One... one and a half kilometres. Thereabouts."

"So, I think the answer is, yes it bloody well can be further than that."

He could hear the impatience in her response. "This bay won't be that big. It can't be, it would represent a breach in their defences."

"I can give it a try, Boss," Marco offered. "Where'd you get that from?" He flashed his lamp towards the reel.

"I came prepared," was all she said. "This is monofilament; it'll take our weight quite easily. It's also motorised."

"Great, so what're you going to attach it to?" Davido asked.

"Me, I guess. You'll have to help."

Davido hesitated, peering over the edge himself. "Shit," he said. "And what if we do get Marco down there? Then what? How're we going to join him? And how will we get back up again?"

"We need to expand our options," Sollander said. "Currently we have two. Stand here shouting, or go back the way we came. Which would you prefer?"

"Shit."

"Exactly."

"All right, let's get going," Marco said with false bravado.

They checked radios quickly as Sollander strung the harness about Marco. "Now, be careful not to touch the filament, no matter what happens. It will take your fingers off."

"Lovely," he muttered. "You sure this will hold?"

"Absolutely."

Not looking too pleased with the notion, Marco allowed himself to be manoeuvred into position, his back to the edge. He eased himself over it as Sollander and Davido took his weight.

"Don't take this personally, darling," Davido said as he braced himself against the engineer, stopping her from sliding after Marco. Under different circumstances he would have found this quite arousing. He had to admit, she was an attractive woman. Too combative by half though, he considered. Not too unlike another woman he knew.

"Damn, I need a drink."

Careful to keep his hands away from the filament Marco spun wildly beneath the walkway, the filament humming as his weight bore down on it. He closed his eyes, trying not to think about the blackness beneath him.

"You'll need to tell us when you hit something," Sollander said.

"I'll be sure to let you know," Marco responded.

The dim light cast by the lamps above the walkway receded as he dropped swiftly into darkness, his spin slowing and then reversing as the filament untwisted itself. Taking his mind off it he started counting slowly.

"You ok down there?" Davido asked.

"Sure, Boss. No problem."

"You should be getting close to the bottom now," Sollander said.

"How'd you know that?"

"We're running out of cable."

"Shit. Seventy-five."

"What?"

"Nothing. Nothing." Seventy-six. Seventy-seven.

"We're about to have a problem," Sollander warned.

"Damn." Davido shifted his position slightly, trying to get her breastplate out of his side.

"Careful!" she snapped, almost losing her footing.

"Bloody stupid idea this," he muttered.

"Hey!" Sollander yelped as they both fell over backwards, the weight suddenly easing from the line. Giddy she clung to the hard rubber surface, fearful of sliding off the other edge.

"Sorry!" Marco called. "I think I'm there."

"Thanks for the warning. I thought you were going to let us know." Davido untangled himself and peered over the edge. Marco's lamp flashed below as he panned it around, revealing indistinct, angular shapes.

"Sorry, Boss."

"Describe what you see," Sollander suggested.

"Parkes Aerofreight."

"What?"

"Looks like freight containers. That's the name on the sides, Parkes Aerofreight. They're all sealed up. Looks like thousands of them."

"Have you reached the deck yet?" Sollander asked.

"No. I'm on top of one of the containers. Bloody hell, it's slippery."

"Be careful. Have you unclipped yourself?"

"Yeah, don't fancy it cutting my ear off. Hang on, I think I can get down."

"Be careful."

"Yeah." They heard grunting over the radio as Marco worked his way towards the edge and looked down. "Ah," he said. "They're stacked on top of each other. There's two beneath this one. So I'm ... about ten metres from the deck."

"Can you climb down?" Davido asked.

"Dunno. Hang on, I'm putting the radio down." They heard a bump as he set it down on the container's roof. "I'll look around here." His voice moved away from the microphone.

"I don't think we're going to learn anything from this," Davido commented.

"Give him time. He's only just got there."

They heard a distinct yell from the radio, followed by silence.

"Marco? What are you up to? Stop fucking around." Davido stared into the darkness, trying to find sign of his companion below. His lamp had either gone out or had passed behind something solid. There was nothing but darkness below. "Marco?"

"Bloody idiot. What's he done?" Sollander joined Davido at the edge and looked over. She could see no more than he could.

"Marco!" Davido shouted over the edge, ignoring the radio. It was delivering nothing but silence.

"Quit shouting," Sollander said uneasily. She could still feel the eyes on her.

"Bloody idiot. Hey, Marco, you're fired! You hear that?" Davido ignored her. "I might keep your brother. I need someone with brains around me!"

"We have to go down there," Sollander realised.

"How? You said only one person could use this."

"We have to find a way around then."

"Good luck with that. I've not seen any stairs anywhere."

"We could have missed them."

"Not likely. We were looking for them."

"There's got to be another way down. We just have to find it."

"It might take us hours ... days. It could even be on the other side of this walkway. The one that seems to have stopped in mid-air."

"We can't leave him there," she observed.

"Watch me."

"I can't believe you. He's your man after all, don't you care?"

"If he's gone and gotten himself killed it's his own fault. I don't need no idiots in my organisation. He knows that. He knows how this works."

"Fine. You can explain that to his brother then."

That gave Davido reason to pause. Duncan would not understand. "Shit. He'll flip out."

"Well, at least one person cares." Sollander began winding the cable back in.

Davido ran his fingers along the edge of the walkway. Finding something he leaned over carefully and looked beneath it. The walkway was constructed of some metallic substance he didn't recognise. It couldn't have been steel; steel would have buckled under the weight a long time ago. It did look like steel though. It was about as thick as his hand was wide, a featureless strip with no rivets, bolts or any other kind of joining. It was as if the entire walkway was constructed of a single length of material. Fortunately there was some kind of lattice work running along its underside, offering it greater rigidity. It was this that interested him.

"I think we can both get down there," he said.

"Who's going to hold onto the cable while we do that? The others have been out of radio range for quite a while."

"Turn it around," he said. Clip the end of cable to this." He pointed to the lattice work. Sollander gingerly lowered herself to her knees and looked over the edge. "We can use the motor to lower ourselves down, one at a time."

"You know, that's not a bad idea. I'll have to go first, unless Marco left the harness attached to the other end." She resumed reeling it in. Within moments they found out. "Looks like me first then. Here, I can't reach."

Davido took the end of the cable. The first metre or so was yellow, the hair thin strand covered by a protective coating. The clip was a heavy duty carbon composite. He fed it through the lattice work, winding it in and out of three support braces before clipping it back on itself. "There, that'll hold."

"It had better do." Sollander looked over the edge again, steeling herself.

"Don't slip off the container's roof like Marco did," Davido said.

"You can't fire me; I don't work for you." Sollander settled her rucksack's straps carefully over the breastplate, ensuring it wouldn't slip awkwardly as she descended. Grimacing she reversed up to the edge and carefully eased herself over. A curse of a most unladylike nature uttered from her lips as she slipped, her full weight falling onto the cable. The cabled twanged, taking her weight and swinging her around dangerously beneath the walkway.

"Don't touch the cable," Davido warned.

"Yeah. Great. Thanks." She steadied herself against the underside of the walkway before taking a deep breath. "Well, here goes." One hand on the reel she carefully started lowering herself into darkness.

Davido suddenly felt very alone. Shivering he cast his light up and down the walkway. Nothing had changed. He sat back so that he didn't have to look over the edge at the void below and settled down to wait. Slipping his own rucksack off his back he selected a wedge of cheese and a flask. With the whiskey burning cheerily down his throat he started feeling somewhat better.

"You still there?" Sollander asked over the radio.

"Um? Yeah."

"I might have enough cable to reach the deck. Marco estimated it was still ten metres to go. If he was accurate I'll be able to make it."

"If not?"

"Well. Then I'm jumping. Coming to the containers now." Sollander paused her descent, shining her lamp around her. The containers were oblong shapes in the dark, stacked on top of each other. They stretched beyond the lamp's beam, row upon neat row filling the bay's deck space. A number of different logos adorned their multicoloured sides, some of the containers so dented and scratched the logos were no longer legible. They had certainly seen a lot of use. There was a narrow alley left between the rows, barely enough room for someone to squeeze down. It was into one of these Marco had fallen.

Dropping herself down by increments Sollander discovered his discarded radio and scooped it up on her way past. She kicked herself off the edge of the container and scanned the narrow gap between it and the one alongside. No Marco. She slipped down into the narrow passageway, the reel whining as it sensed it was coming to the end of the cable. Still a metre from the deck it stopped, and no amount of chivvying it on could get the thread to extend any further.

"Oh, well. I'm down," she announced. "Sort of."

"Can you see him?"

"Not yet. Hang on." Positioning herself carefully, she hit the cable release. "Aw, shit." Falling clumsily her head connected with a hard metal corner. "Bloody hell."

"What? What?" Davido stared over the edge. There was nothing to see, Sollander's lamplight had disappeared between the rows of containers.

"Nothing. I'm ok." Sollander rubbed her head gingerly, her fingers coming away sticky with blood. Cursing she felt the wound carefully. It wasn't bad, but then head wounds always bled profusely. She pulled a cloth from a pouch and held it to the cut, trying to staunch the bleeding. At least the containers didn't appear to be rusty, tetanus was the last thing she needed.

"So, you're going to send the harness back up? I'm getting lonely up here."

"Hold on," Sollander said impatiently. Standing carefully, supporting herself with a hand up against one metal wall, she edged around the container Marco had landed on. "Marco!" she hissed, wary of making too much noise. "Where the hell are you?"

It didn't take her long to find him. Rounding the container, she saw a leg protruding from the opposite corner. It wasn't moving. "Got him," she reported back.

Marco had fallen awkwardly. He was lying on his face, his limbs twisted around him. There was no blood, but it was impossible to say whether he'd broken anything. Sollander knelt down carefully and checked his pulse with her free hand.

"He's alive."

"Good. Can't kill a dead man," Davido commented.

Sollander checked the blood coming from her wound. It was still bleeding, but it wasn't very heavy. Needing her hands free she unfolded the cloth and wound it around her head, struggling to tie a knot in the tiny ends she was left with. The task finally achieved she turned her attention to Marco.

"Marco. Can you hear me?"

"Send the harness back up," Davido said.

"Hang on, he's still wearing it."

"Take it off him."

"First things first."

"I can help."

"You any good at first aid?"

"Some. Are you?"

"Just hold on." Sollander checked his limbs first, ensuring they weren't broken. The ones she could get to appeared fine, she couldn't get to his left arm—he was lying on it. "Marco." Careful not to move his head she opened his eyes and shone her light into them. His pupils were dilated, but they did contract with the light. That was good news.

Marco shuddered and groaned. "Fuck me. Fuck me."

"I think he's going to be ok," Sollander said.

"Shit. Get that light out of my face. Damn, that hurts."

"What hurts? Don't try to move."

"It's ok. I'm ok." Wincing he tried to lever himself up, only to flop back down again. "I think my arm's broken."

"Great. We've barely been here three hours and we have one member lost, and another with a broken arm," Davido commented over the radio. "We're not doing much better than the first lot."

Sollander ignored him. "How's your neck? Your back?"

"Fine. It's just my arm. Sorry, Boss. I messed up."

"He tells me you're fired," Sollander said. "Although it might take him a while to process the paperwork."

Marco laughed. "Too right. Here, help me up." He waved his free arm in the air so Sollander could take hold of it. Bracing herself between the containers she pulled, hauling him upright. He hissed in pain as his broken arm moved.

"Here, let me have a look," Sollander said once he was upright. She felt his arm carefully though his jacket. The bone was broken between his elbow and his shoulder. Not the greatest place for it, but it did seem a clean break. "We need a splint."

"One of the crates is open," he said, feeling dizzy from the sudden movement. "It was what I went to look at. It's just over there." He pointed with his uninjured hand. "There's some rope there too."

"Ok. Let me get this harness off you first." Sollander unclipped the harness. "Stay here for a moment. You want to sit down?"

"No. I don't think I'd get up again."

Leaving him for a moment Sollander returned to the pulley and attached the harness to it. She instructed it to wind itself back in again and let Davido know it was coming. That done she went looking for the open container. It wasn't difficult to find. The door was slightly ajar, plastic and foil containers scattered on the deck about it, blocking the alley way.

"Food containers," Sollander said. She picked one up and turned it over in her hands. Ainsley's Pork and Beans, it proclaimed. Self-warming. "Lovely." She put it aside and looked into the container. The interior had been ransacked at some time in the past. Food packages were scattered all over, the neat racks they had been stored in bent as if someone had been quite eager to get to their contents. A number of the packages themselves were ripped open. She studied one carefully, sniffing the congealed mass within.

"Someone's been here. And recently," she said. "These have been opened within the last few days."

"You found survivors?" Davido asked, sounding a bit out of breath. He wasn't enjoying his trip down from the walkway.

"No, just evidence they came this way. That's something at least. Plus, we know they're not starving." She turned the opened package over in her hand. There was no use by date listed. Possibly Confederate food containers lasted forever.

Returning to the task at hand she dismantled part of the already wrecked shelving, producing a hollow tube about fifteen centimetres long. She tried to bend it experimentally. It seemed rigid enough. Satisfied she looked for the rope Marco had mentioned. "Where'd you see the rope?" She asked through the radio.

"It was hanging down in front of the container."

"I don't see anything." She lifted some binders from the jumble and tested them quickly. They'd do.

"It was there," Marco assured her.

"It isn't now." She returned to where she'd left him. "Take off that jacket."

"I'd rather not."

"Mmm. This might hurt."

"Where are you?" Davido landed on the deck in the adjoining alley.

Sollander ignored Davido, concentrating on her task. She grimaced as Marco yelled in pain, broken bones moving in his flesh. She didn't allow that to stop her, her fingers accustomed to manipulating uncooperative machinery she quickly secured his arm, careful not to bind it so tightly that it cut off circulation. That done she fashioned a sling and then stood back to admire her handy work.

"There you are." Davido shone his lamp over them. "What have you done to yourself?" He noticed the bloody cloth about Sollander's head.

"It's nothing. Although I think we've had a breakthrough."

"What?"

"It's pretty obvious. Someone else has been here."

"Oh, good. We're on the right track then."

She was silent for a moment. "Yep. And I think they're still here," she said softly.

□

Chapter Seventeen

Silence still ringing in his ears Singh arrived at the prefect's office two hours later. The pager had buzzed twice more, the messages becoming more and more curt. The prefect did not like being kept waiting. Drenched in sweat, his clothing damp and creased and breathing hard he swept past the prefect's secretary.

"The prefect awaits you." Allihar, Drefus' secretary, waved him through.

Taking a deep breath Singh steeled himself and stepped through the doors to the inner office.

"Where the hell have you been?" Drefus greeted him.

Singh's legs failed him, finding Drefus lounging behind his desk, his eyes flashing in anger as his toady wandered in very late indeed. Confused Singh could say nothing. The prefect had clearly beaten him up to the tower, even though he had used many shortcuts he wasn't aware anyone else knew about. Additionally, the prefect had changed into his customary white court clothes, his waistcoat starched tight about his bony frame, his hair immaculately styled. The man had certainly not just run up several hundred stairs to return to his office ahead of Singh.

"I... I am sorry, Prefect. I was delayed."

"Someone else is more important than me?"

"Ah, of course not, Prefect." His hand went to the torque. For once it didn't tighten.

Drefus glared at him. "I would like to know what makes you think you can keep me waiting, however we currently have more urgent matters to discuss." He turned away from Singh to address his other visitor. "Although be sure, we will discuss this later."

"Of course, Prefect." That gave him some time to think up an excuse. He doubted it would do him any good, nothing had occurred to him during his frantic climb back up through the city, then to Hub One and finally to the cable car. Although most of that time he had been pondering on what he had witnessed. The screamer no longer screamed. He couldn't imagine what was so monumental about those simple few words that they would quieten it. The heretics had been talking to it for years. Talking, singing, and praying: everything imaginable in the hopes of quieting its stricken spirit. Nothing had had the slightest effect. Yet those few words had. He doubted it was a good portent. If anything the silence had been more terrible than the screams. What could be said when a machine could no longer find it in itself to scream?

"You know my toady, Inspector?" Drefus said to the man seated before him.

"We have met, Prefect," Inspector Isskip said, nodding slightly in assent.

"Good, good. Well, be seated man! You're cluttering up the place!" This last outburst was aimed at Singh, who was still stood in the entrance.

Swallowing dryly Singh did as he was bidden.

"Right, where were we?"

"We were planning the mission to the *Goliath*, Prefect," Isskip said. "We need to capture the killer and bring him to justice."

"Indeed, indeed."

"Killer, Prefect?" Singh said.

The inspector took it upon himself to respond. Resettling his uniform cap on his knee, he turned to Singh and spoke, his tone careful and clipped. "We have been tracking a serial murderer for some time. It is believed he boarded the Prentice shuttle and joined them on their ill advised mission to the *Goliath.* We are tasked with bringing him to justice."

Singh didn't like the sound of that 'we'. "Of course, I remember your meeting at Buer Adjunct." The prefect had clearly changed his mind on pursuing this killer.

The inspector continued. "It will take some time to assemble a team. I need agents who can operate in space. They will also need to be heavily armed. Something happened to the first mission, after all. Something aboard that ship stopped them from returning home."

"Perhaps it would be simpler to wait for them to return," Singh offered his opinion. "They'll have to sooner or later."

"We have lost telemetry with their shuttle," Drefus commented, waving the suggestion away. "And in the meantime there's no telling what this killer is up to. I can't say I care for the rest of them, but I'd like to see chief engineer Sollander returned to me in one piece. She and I have things to talk about."

"Sollander, Prefect?" Singh was dismayed. So, the prefect knew she had joined the Prentice mission. Perhaps it had always been folly believing he wouldn't.

"Yes," he said dryly. "She has some concerns that ... interest me." He smiled coldly at Singh.

Singh said nothing. Clearly the decision had already been made, there was nothing he could do to change that. He didn't like it, in fact it terrified him.

"We need to see the rule of law upheld," the inspector continued. "Criminals must learn that they cannot avoid justice, no matter where they hide."

Even Drefus smiled at that. Justice was not something often seen on Russou. Not unless you were rich or connected. The inspector was clearly an idealist. Or naive.

"So, timeframes," Drefus said.

"Twenty-four hours, at the earliest, Prefect. I'd prefer to be blasting off now, but going unprepared into an environment like a wreck in the Parking Lot ... that would be disastrous. We'd only lose more personnel. I have the agents in mind, I assure you. They are all dependable and loyal." Singh felt himself grimacing at that. The prefect's definition of loyalty would certainly not match Isskip's.

"Yes, but are they any good?" the prefect asked.

"The best, Prefect. I have worked with them all before. They are all experts in their fields. All very capable." He turned towards the toady. "As you are to be joining us we will need to put you through some training. Twenty-four hours is nowhere near enough but ..." He shrugged. "It's what we have."

"Prefect, with all due respect-"

"You know, people only ever say that when they're about to be disrespectful," Drefus commented.

Singh soldiered on. "I am unsure what I can contribute to the endeavour. I feel I will only be getting in the way." Observing the inspector's expression it was clear he held similar a view.

"Be that as it may, I am leaving you in charge of the expedition. You are my envoy ... my representative. The inspector here will assist you in any way necessary."

Singh's mouth worked, trying unsuccessfully to formulate an argument. "Yes, Prefect."

"You will be perfectly safe," the inspector said. "We have two troop transports we discovered aboard the Yantse. They're armoured and quite dependable. The demons themselves have been removed, so they won't be a threat to us."

"Oh, good."

"Right," Drefus smiled. "It's settled. Now, we have some schematics our Mentor allies have supplied, showing much of the exterior, including the entrance both the previous missions intended on using. We also have some diagrams showing the interior of smaller warcraft. They will allow you to prepare for what you will find aboard."

"Thank you, Prefect. My people have all trained in simulated space craft environments. After all, that's what the cities are once you remove the buildings from them. Still, it will be a complex mission, and safety will be paramount. I am aware the Sya ... Mentors have not ventured aboard this particular vessel. I'm also aware it's the largest vessel in the Parking Lot, so there will be a lot of ground to cover. The city engineers have devised some useful tools we will be able to utilise, infra-red trackers and the like. We also have access to Shoei body armour suits that are space capable, so we will be well protected."

"Yes, good good. Well, I wish you luck." Drefus looked bored, uninterested in the details.

"Thank you, Prefect." The inspector stood, carefully placing his uniform cap on his head. "Mister Singh, perhaps you would like to come with me?"

Singh found he could not move, fear welding him to the seat. He didn't want to go. He couldn't put into words how much. With a superhuman force of will he pushed his quivering legs beneath him and tottered to his feet. "Lead on," he said. His voice little more than a squeak.

"When ... if you come back, we have much to discuss," Drefus said to Singh, his smile sending shivers up Singh's spine.

"Yes, yes, Prefect. Of course." Singh fled.

□

Chapter Eighteen

Situated barely a dozen yards from the transit deck was the *Goliath*'s primary means of moving personnel and cargo about the ship. Prentice hesitated for the slightest of moments, looking over her shoulder to see whether the lights from Davido's party were still visible behind. The darkness made the decision for her. Davido had vanished in the distance. They could investigate this on their own.

There were four in Prentice's party. The first was Sparky, the deaf mute. He was a hulk of a man, dressed in leathers and denim that seemed too tight and also somewhat obscene. It wasn't a statement, Prentice knew, indicating what the big man liked to do on his time off. Rather he was simply blissfully unaware of how ridiculous he looked. He was comfortable, that was all that mattered. He wasn't simple. Although given his appearance it was an easy mistake to make. She'd known the quiet giant most of her life, learning the trade of scavenging the Parking Lot from him when she first ventured out with her father.

The second member of the group was Ferena, a man she'd rescued from a jail in Ipos, were he'd been under arrest for his heretical views. Not something that could be forgiven a city engineer. He was tall and slim with wavy black hair. On his good days he was quite charming, a charm he used to devastating effect on the girls in LandsDown Pub, the one drinking establishment in the vicinity of the landing field. On his bad days he was not worth being around. He could be a bit of an arrogant ass.

Cagne, the last member of her party, was the daughter of Antonio Solbrass, the media tycoon. Prentice kept her around, quite honestly, because she was great in bed and she had a nice ass. Her short-life pressure suite looked like a suit of tinfoil, odd bulges on the arms revealing the presence of life support systems. The hood was rolled up carelessly under her chin. Like a large and somewhat uncomfortable bowtie.

"What is it?" Cagne leaned over carefully, peering into the darkened pit before them.

"I've heard of them. Not seen one before, though." Prentice joined her. She didn't know why they were looking, there was nothing to see. "My father came across one in a liner once. It's called a gravity well."

"You what say?"

"The Confederates used it as a means of shifting cargo about. Or people too, I guess." She shrugged. "It's capable of handling far greater volume than an elevator." She looked around the wide chamber. Five passages converged on this one hexagonal compartment, each leading off to distant, unknown parts of the vessel. In the centre was a perfectly circular hole that dropped into unknowable depths. It was as if someone had drilled a hole right through the warship, passing clear through each level on its way. There was some sort of door mechanism built into it, allowing the aperture to be sealed, preventing an enemy from using it to access the lower spaces. They were all withdrawn at the moment, presenting a chasm that may very well drop all the way to the vessel's core. They were on the highest level here, the ceiling a blank dome overhead. There was nothing above this level apart from armour and guns.

"The ship demon would control access," she continued. "Force fields, I believe. They lifted passengers from here and depositing them at their destination."

"Damn," Ferena sounded impressed. "Those guys had balls. You wouldn't catch me stepping off this thing. With the lights on you'd see all the way down to the core. That's a long drop if the demon decides it doesn't like you." He whistled.

"Yeah. It does present us with an opportunity though," Prentice said.

Sparky waved a question at her.

"Well," she said carefully. "We need to decide what we want to do here. Either we find Davido's sister, which could be fun ... and he is paying us. Or we could see if there's anything worth salvaging. Personally, I think this is an excellent opportunity. No one's been aboard a warship before, who knows what kinds of technology we can find? This could make us rich."

Sparky held up three fingers.

"Yeah, I guess we could keep an eye out for Sissy while we're at it." She chuckled.

"Davido's not the kind of man you want to mess with," Cagne observed.

"Who says we're messing with him?" Prentice smiled sweetly.

"Ok. So, what do you suggest?" Ferena asked.

"Well, I don't reckon there's much up here. Sure, there's the vehicle bays and the weapons systems. But they're either too big or there'll be no market for them. If Drefus catches us importing mainline naval weaponry he'll have the lot of us executed. No thanks to that one. I reckon our best bet is to head further in. There's bound to be a medical bay full of all kinds of equipment. I've heard they had manufactories aboard these things. If we could find one of those we'd be richer ... well, hell, we'd be the richest people on the planet."

"A what?" Ferena asked.

"Automated manufacturing plant. They held templates for just about anything, from teacups to weapons to small spacecraft."

"Run by a demon, no doubt," Cagne said.

"Everything they built was," Prentice agreed. "I don't want the whole thing, I just want those templates. At the very least, we could strip off anything we could sell. Imagine that, a machine that could build anything we wanted. All you have to do is feed it raw materials."

"We'd have to get it off the ship first," Cagne continued.

Prentice grinned. "I'm sure we'll find a way."

Sparky made a quick sign, waving towards the well.

"Well, if we're going to keep on looking for Davido's sister, we should ignore this and keep on looking. However if we're not, we can use this thing to go deeper into the ship."

"I aint jumping in there," Ferena muttered.

"That's why I have rope." Prentice slipped her rucksack from her back and undid the straps quickly. She produced a thick roll of mountaineering rope.

"You got something else in there, I see, Boss." Ferena noticed a small package carefully folded beneath the rope.

Prentice quickly closed her rucksack, ignoring him. It was none of his business. "Right, who's first?" She cast around the compartment for something to attach the end to. She settled on feeding it through a steel air-conditioning grille. Once she was satisfied it wasn't going to come loose the moment they put weight on it, she threw the roll into the well.

"I'll do it," Cagne offered, peering into the depths beneath them. "How far you reckon it goes?"

"Dunno. Could be a few hundred metres, could be a kilometre. We only have seventy-five metres of rope though, so that's as far as we're going. We hoof it from there."

Dubiously Cagne pulled on the rope to ensure it was fastened securely. "See you girls later." She gave them a cocky grin and swung out over emptiness.

"Damn, be careful," Ferena said.

"These decks are pretty high," Cagne commented as she slid carefully down the rope. The going was slow. Even though the rope was designed to maximise friction and minimise rope burn to unprotected hands and knees (which would generally seem to be contradictory qualities) it was still a laborious process. One leg twisted around the rope as a brake she let herself down slowly in a smooth hand over hand movement. She didn't look down, convincing herself there was nothing to see. Somehow that only increased the sense she was suspended on a thin nylon rope over a bottomless chasm. Not something she ever expected to do in space.

"I thought you'd stopped using," Ferena said once Cagne had slipped over the edge.

"What?"

"I saw your stash. You can't fool me, Sarah. I've known you too long."

Prentice turned her back on Sparky so that he couldn't read her lips. "It's none of your business."

"Come on. We're friends aren't we? How long have I known you? Twelve years? Ever since your father died—"

"Murdered, you mean."

"Yeah, well it's been a long time. I deserve for you to be honest with me."

Prentice sighed. She really didn't want to talk about it.

"Dammit, are you scratching again?" He pulled her hand away, pushing up her sleeve to study her right wrist.

She yanked her hand back before he could see the sores. She hadn't even realised she'd been scratching them. "Listen. It's none of your business. Keep your mind on the job."

"It is my business. We are on the job here and if you get strung out it can endanger all of our lives. It's stupid, stupid to bring that crap up here. It's suicidal."

"Fuck you too, mate. Don't you lecture me."

"What? Don't you remember how Beatrice died? She shot up and tried to use an airlock without securing her suit first. I was there, remember? She didn't die quickly. And this place is a hell of a lot deadlier than some civilian cruise liner. There's more to get you killed here. Just ask that poor woman in the airlock back there."

"I'm ok. I'm handling it. Just leave it be."

"No. Come on, hand it over." He held out his hand expectantly, as if she was going to suddenly relent and give him her stash.

"No way." Prentice backed away from him, wary of him trying to take it by force. "Try it buster, I'll kick your ass."

"You probably would too, all over a little bag of meth." He stepped forwards. "I'm serious though. I'm not working on this ship with someone who could be strung out at any moment. Forget about us being friends, I'm not willing to risk my life for your addiction."

Prentice unslung the shotgun Davido had given her. She didn't point it at him, but it was close enough for him to get the point. "Back off, Ferena."

"What, you going to shoot me now? I don't believe this."

"Don't you try laying a hand on me. I'll blow it off. I'm serious."

Silent and forgotten Sparky moved quickly. A fist the size of a ham wrapped around the shotgun's barrel, and yanked it out of Prentice's grasp. She gasped, the trigger guard catching a finger. The big man held it away from her, shaking his head and gesturing wildly. His feelings on the matter were very clear.

Sucking her finger Prentice felt suddenly embarrassed. Ferena was a stuck up asshole, she could care less what he thought. But Sparky ...Sparky was different. "I'm sorry, Sparky ... listen."

He shook his head again, carefully securing the weapon. He made a point of looking away, ignoring anything she had to say. His disappointment was clear.

"Don't turn away from me, please."

"Suddenly it's different now that you've upset him, is it? You didn't point a fucking gun at him, did you?" Ferena commented.

"Hey, what's going on up there?" Cagne's voice squawked in their ears. "Have you forgotten what we're doing here?"

"Hang on a minute, will you?" Prentice said, still trying to get Sparky's attention.

"I'd rather not. I'm down and it's dark down here. We need more rope; this passage goes a lot further."

Frustrated Ferena stepped to the edge and looked over gingerly. He could see the faint light from Cagne's lamp below. It flashed as she waved it up at them. He waved his back. "Never mind this lot. They're just trying to shoot me."

"What? I'm gone five minutes and you guys are at each other's throats. I should come up there and... no, you guys get down here. I don't like it down here on my own."

"What you see down there?"

"It's about the same."

"Think I'll stay up here then," Ferena commented.

"You bastard."

"So, are we going down or not?" He turned to Prentice.

"Yeah. Me next." Prentice gave up trying to reason with Sparky and took a firm grip of the rope. Without further word she swung over the edge and dropped down.

Ferena watched her work her way downwards before turning back to Sparky. "Women, hey. You keep that thing. I think it's safer with you." He indicated the shotgun.

Sparky shrugged. He didn't seem particularly interested in the weapon.

Prentice made good time down the rope. Mount Tenna's inner caldera walls contained some amazing cliffs for climbing. Some of the best on Russou, certainly. Before her father died they had spent many weekends up on the caldera walls, finding new routes to the highest points. Even though that was years in the past it was not a skill you lost. Still, her hands were warm from rope burn by the time she landed beside Cagne. Her muscles might remember, but her skin certainly did not.

"What was going on up there?" Cagne greeted her.

"Nothing to concern yourself about," Prentice said sharply. "Ferena. Your turn."

"Yes, Boss." His tone dripped sarcasm.

Prentice ignored it, preferring to survey her new surroundings. This lobby was a duplicate of the one above. Five identical passages led off into darkness. There were no signposts or any other means of indicating what passage led where. Presumably the crew were simply expected to know. That, or they had some other way of navigating the massive ship. Holographics possibly, she considered. She shone her lamp experimentally down one passage after the other, trying to see which one looked the likeliest. She was surprised to find two massive armoured doors blocking two of the passages. The only closed doors she had seen aboard the *Goliath*.

"Did you guys feel anything weird about half way down?" Ferena asked, somewhat out of breath.

"Like what?" Cagne asked.

"Dunno. A breeze."

"Keep on going," Prentice suggested. "It's not breezy down here."

"Just taking a breather," Ferena said. "It's a long climb."

"You may as well keep on coming. You can't rest hanging from the rope."

"I'm not hanging from the rope."

"What? Quit fooling around Ferena, and get your ass down here."

"Shit." They heard a scuffle over the radio. "It's a bit damp here. The floor's damp. I just slipped."

"Be careful."

"Where did you get these lamps from?"

"What?"

"I dropped it and its gone out. Damn, where is it?" They overheard Ferena on his hands and knees, feeling around for the lost lamp.

"Don't fall off the edge," Cagne said.

"Yeah. Thanks for that. Hadn't occurred to me."

Prentice sighed, rolling her eyes to Cagne. Cagne laughed, shrugging. "Men," she mouthed.

"Like me to come up there and help you out?" Cagne said aloud.

"Well, what did you have in mind?"

"You're not my type."

"What? Male?"

"No. Stupid."

"Hold on. I can hear something." Ferena was silent for a moment. "Hang on," he whispered. "There's someone here. I can hear them."

"Who is it?" Prentice held onto the rope and peered upwards. Of course, there was nothing to see. Nothing apart from Sparky's light far overhead. He was peering down at her, trying to see what the delay was.

"Shhh. Be quiet." They heard a faint rustling as he backed away, trying to feel his way to the well and the waiting rope. "Who is that? Who's there?" he said loudly. "I can hear you. Who's there? Shit, it's dark. I can't see a fucking thing."

Unable to do anything but listen, Prentice pressed the speaker close to her ear, trying to discern what Ferena was hearing. She couldn't. There was nothing to hear but his ragged breathing and faint static. She looked at Cagne, who shrugged.

"What? Who's that? That's not my name. You must be crazy." She heard him say.

"What was that?"

"Someone just spoke to me. Called me a name."

"They what?"

"I'm Jose. Jose Ferena. We're here to help you. I don't know who the hell you think I am."

"Ferena. Seriously, what are you doing?"

"Someone just touched me," Ferena said. He swore, lashing out. "Who is that? Quit playing silly buggers. We're here to help you. Come out." He swore again. "They're playing with me. Just touched me again. Dammit, stop that!"

"Who the hell is it?" Prentice demanded. "It's gotta be the first crew. What are they up to?"

Cagne pulled in the rope, hoisting herself onto it. "Sparky, you bastard. Get down there!" she shouted. She knew he couldn't hear her but she didn't care. "Sparky!" She saw a distant figure leaning forward to look down, a lamp shining directly at them. Sparky, wondering whether it was time to descend the rope himself. Cagne waved, trying to get his attention. She wobbled on the rope, the movement breaking her balance.

"Where are you, you bastards?" Ferena swung his fists wildly. They connected nothing but darkness.

He distinctly heard a voice near his ear. "You do not remember who you are."

"What?"

"Then die."

As he turned he felt a hand reach out and touch him. Pressing firmly in the small of his back, it pushed. He fell forward clumsily. This time the deck did not catch him.

With a shriek he plummeted into darkness.

Cagne shouted in alarm as, clinging to the rope in terror, she heard something heavy flash past her. It disappeared into darkness below, quickly out of range of their lights.

Ferena screamed as he fell. The sound only interrupted as he struck one of the landings a glancing blow. He quickly gathered his breath and screamed again.

It went on for a long time.

Giddy, Cagne looked away from the chasm to peer upwards. Sparky was still flashing his light at her, trying desperately to see what was going on. As she looked, another dark figure appeared between them. It reached out and touched the rope. Without warning the rope was severed.

"Shit!" Cagne yelled as the rope stopped taking her weight.

Alarmed Prentice reached out and grabbed the other woman. She caught hold of her belt as she flashed past and heaved, dragging her onto the platform. Gasping they collapsed onto the hard rubbery deck, a knee driving into Prentice's face. Pain flashed into her mind, hot blood squirting into her eyes.

"Shit. Shit." Prentice pushed Cagne off, holding her broken nose.

Unable to do anything but listen Prentice and Cagne stood staring at each other, Prentice holding her nose as blood streamed from it. Ferena's scream had disappeared below, leaving nothing but silence and the faint sound of breathing. It wasn't coming from them.

"Fuck me. Fuck me." Cagne fell to her knees. She rocked forwards, placing her forehead on the deck.

"Who the hell is that?" Prentice shouted into the radio. "You're dead. You hear me? I'm going to find you and kill every single one of you motherfuckers!"

There was a click as someone picked up Ferena's radio. The breathing got louder, the device held close to an ear.

"Who is this?" Prentice demanded. "Who am I talking to? You sick fuck."

The breathing continued for a moment before, with another click, the radio went dead.

"Shit! You bastards!" Prentice yelled up the well. "You'd better run, you bastards. I'm coming for you. Every bloody one of you."

There was no response.

□

Goliath

Chapter Nineteen

Inevitably, the tunnel came to an end. After what had felt like hours—although was probably only twenty minutes—indistinct shapes appeared in the extreme limits of his helmet lamp. Unsure of what to expect he braked his forward movement, allowing the clamp to drag him to a stop against the metal walls. If there was something down there firing on the shuttles, it was probably ill advised to stumble into it unprepared. Better to practise some caution.

Enderby eased forward, scrutinising the shapes as they became apparent. Simple steel rails, they looked like. Nothing more dangerous than that. Four of them protruding from the darkness, aiming out towards empty space far down the other end of the tunnel. They were still now; the firing had stopped.

He didn't take the time to study them, or to find the mechanism used for throwing projectiles down the tunnel. The suit only carried so much air; all those with long life reservoirs had been taken by the others, leaving him and Adele with the emergency suits. Ten minutes was all he had left. Not long enough at all.

He found an inspection hatch some fifteen metres past the rails. It opened easily enough, allowing him into a small pressure lock. It was powered. That, and the fact that he felt a faint rumbling through his gloves when he worked the controls, didn't concern him terribly much. Clearly there was something going on aboard the ship. That he would find evidence of it was inevitable. After all, Tin Man had sent him here for a reason.

He left the suit outside the pressure lock, simply abandoning it on the deck. He doubted he would have need of it again. He kept the helmet lamp, however, unclipping it from its bracket so he could see where he was going. The interior of the vessel was dark. Either there was no power for them or someone had switched all the lights off.

For the first twenty minutes he felt like he was venturing through an immense clockwork clock. Clattering down endless metal stairs and traversing steel walkways in utter darkness he passed by strange looking pipes and vats. Conduits ran in a spider web across every surface, linking one oddly shaped machine to another. Simple words and arrows were stencilled on various surfaces. 'Warning: Refrigerated', and 'flow', followed by an arrow. Some were simple alphanumeric codes, identifying the devices, which presumably tied up to some database somewhere. He didn't know what he had stumbled into. To be honest he didn't care, he just wanted to get out of there.

A metal door at the bottom of the compartment let him into what looked like an engineer's office. There were lockers along one wall; some were open, yellow overalls falling out of them. A body was sprawled in the centre, laying facedown. He couldn't tell whether it was a man or a woman and he didn't stop to check. He'd seen enough dead bodies over the years. The excitement had worn off.

Beyond that compartment was an administrative complex of some kind. Offices mainly. He found a canteen. It was a ransacked mess, chairs and tables in upheaval. Some uneaten meals congealed on the deck. Quite petrified after all this time. No bodies. Beyond that was a network of passages, linking his sector to those alongside. They were dark and dusty. He ventured in confidently. They would lead somewhere.

The passages grew wider the deeper he went, like following the branches of a tree back to it's trunk. Finally, reaching a primary thoroughfare, he caught sight of a dim low in the distance. Someone had left the lights on. Eagerly he headed towards it.

Enderby hesitated, squinting into the light ahead. Something had passed between him and the light, cutting it off for a moment. There couldn't be someone down here, could there? True, he was aware of the previous mission to the behemoth, but the chances of bumping into one of its members so soon after arriving were infinitesimal. He pressed against a wall, deciding caution was in order.

On touching the cool surface, he discovered it was vibrating slightly. Just as the hatch had been. Odd. He laid a hand flat on it. It was the faint rumbling of machinery, he decided. Something was switched on somewhere.

"Really?" he derided himself out loud. Of course there was. He could already see lights.

He winced. The old habit of talking to himself was still strong. Spending long hours ... days ... weeks on his own with nothing but roc boc's and chickens for company any human voice (even his own) had been a comfort. Perhaps that was why Tin Man had brought Julia to him. The machine had probably thought he was losing his mind, and was very probably right.

"Bastards," he said aloud. He winced again. Damn, he couldn't help it.

They had killed her. Murdered her for trying to protect him. But then they mistrusted dogs. As well they should. He knew their official propaganda, of a rabies outbreak amongst the canine population. It was more fundamental than that. Dogs simply knew the truth.

Shit. He looked down at his hands, now visible in the faint light. He was shaking. He could feel his heart thrumming as the old anger rose within him. Hate was a powerful emotion. Sometimes it never quite died.

"Dammit. Stop." Enderby felt himself sliding down the wall, holding his fists to his head. He had to control it. Now was not the time.

Taking deep breaths Enderby calmed himself. He counted them. In, out, in out. Slowly it passed, receding to its ever present glimmer. Still there, as it always was, but manageable.

Shit.

Enderby pushed himself upright again, taking hesitant steps forward. The light was steady once again. Whatever had passed had gone on its way. Clearing his throat, he walked confidently forward. Tin Man had assured him he was safe here, and he had come to trust the rusty old android over the years. It would not put him in danger's path.

It was only when he was much closer that he started hearing the rumbling too, accompanied by a slight fresh breeze. It was warm, like a spring breeze leaking in through an open door. The light had that refreshing quality too. It was not artificial. Somehow, impossibly, it was natural.

Eagerness overcoming any remaining misgivings Enderby trotted forwards, quickly crossing the last dozen metres to the end of the passage. Laughing he burst out into sunlight, warmth washing over his skin as fresh air filled his lungs. It was glorious.

"Oh my god." He fell to his knees on grass, moisture making his flight suit trousers damp. The vista the passage opened out onto took a long time to filter into his amazed senses. This was certainly not what he had expected to find orbiting several thousand kilometres above the dreary, dying planet of Russou. This was...

Earth.

A valley opened out before him. Blossoming trees lined wide avenues, their branches swaying lightly in the breeze. Hidden between them were neat rows of condominiums, stack upon stack of them, reaching right up to the brow of each hill. He was roughly a quarter of the way up one side, the gentle slope dropping away below, culminating in a meadow at the valley bottom, a gentle river running through the centre of it. Wooden bridges crossed over, linking pathways to bandstands, benches and simple stone wharfs.

One end of the valley ended in what looked like a opera house; a massive sweeping, segmented roof, the entrance lined with glass and slender pillars. A wide stone paved area led up to it, dotted with smaller bandstands and open air theatres. The other end of the valley culminated in thick woodlands, cycle paths vanishing under the leafy canopy. Grey stone cliffs towered above the green foliage. From this distance he could just about make out tiny structures peering over the cliff's edge, although he couldn't see what they were.

It was easily a kilometre from one end of the valley to the other, possibly as much as three hundred metres wide. Above all this was an achingly deep blue sky, the odd wisp of cloud crossing it idly. Not quite at its zenith the sun shone warmly, a fierce yellow blazing orb he couldn't bear to look at directly. Certainly not the miserable, dull sun that crossed Russou's skies.

"Bloody hell." Enderby stood and walked forward. He could hear birds calling each other, one or two of their shapes dotting the skies as they darted between the trees, searching for insects. Which were in abundance also. He could hear bees buzzing about neatly tended flower beds, inspecting the brightly coloured flowers for pollen.

"Tin Man, you bastard." The android had kept him on Russou all these years, knowing full well that this place existed just overhead. He'd been forced to live in a hovel, not much more than a cave. Grit and dust invading his every bodily orifice, farming chickens and guinea pigs to stay alive.

Enderby noticed the entrance to another building almost directly opposite him on the other hillside. It looked very familiar indeed, even though he had not seen its like in a very long time. A mall. He headed directly for it, quickly dropping down to the valley floor and crossing the river via a brightly painted wooden bridge. He saw a rabbit inspecting him critically, chewing on its lunch as it did so. Startled by a shadow passing overhead it darted away, disappearing into a bush. Enderby looked up, seeing the unmistakable outline of a hawk circling overhead.

"Ok. So, who mows your grass then?" he asked no one. "Who trims your hedges? And don't tell me these trees are all eighty years old. Who's been planting new ones? Hey?" He wasn't fooled. There was someone here, there simply had to be. This habitat was too well kept for it to be otherwise. Parkland did not maintain itself. Not to mention that the amount of power it must take to run this place would be prodigious. The sun alone would require its own atomic power plant. There was no way this kind of heat was generated by a big light bulb.

He knew the navy had maintained quite extravagant living quarters. They had the energy to do so: warships packed an astonishing amount of it. They also had the room. Warships were large, and that was not because they needed the internal space, but rather because they needed the hull acreage. Their mainline weapons systems depended on massive projection arrays built into the hull structure. The bigger the hull, the more powerful the weapons. Much of their internal space was just that: space. The only mechanism within the bulk of the vessel that took up any considerable space was the drive rod itself, and that was buried in the very centre of the ship. Beneath dozens of metres of AI core and shielding. That left a lot of space between it and the hull itself. Additionally naval vessels were typically on patrol for months, if not years on end. They needed diversions to keep the crew from going mad. Of course, he'd never been aboard one before, although he did understand that each vessel was unique, berthing it's crew in a variety of different settings, from city scapes, forests, seaside resorts or this: a valley town. He was not going to start counting but he suspected the *Goliath* had more than one of these hidden away in its bowels. The old super dreadnought had carried 18 000 crew; if you totted up its marine compliment, naval officers and engineers. This compartment was big, but it didn't look big enough to account for all those 18 000 souls. Senior personnel probably had their own secluded hideaway someplace else. He didn't want to think about what that looked like.

Enderby entered into the shade of the mall, realising he'd worked up a sweat walking across the valley. He rubbed his forehead with a sleeve and looked around. Boutiques: glass windows showing off wares that had remained untouched for decades. Also, what appeared to be an electronics shop, a restaurant and, up an escalator, donut shops, more clothes stores and a sports stores. In the latter, he could see hiking and mountaineering equipment in the window. Which he found odd, until he remembered the forest and the cliff looking over it. The crew needed to use up their free time after all; it couldn't all be ballets and musicals. Or tennis.

Enderby headed for what looked like a supermarket. His stomach rumbled at the thought of food. The lights were on at least, but he had his doubts about finding anything edible after all this time. Everything fresh would have gone off a very long time ago. Still, there might be the odd tin of soup or something.

"Can I be of assistance?"

"Jesus!" Enderby had already run a dozen paces before he realised it. He forced himself to stop and turn around, his heart beat so loudly he could hear it.

A woman was standing within the entrance to the supermarket, a pleasant smile on her face. She was tall and blonde, wearing some sort of uniform. Blue with a yellow collar.

"Can I be of assistance?" she asked again.

"Who are you?"

"I am your shopping assistant. Can I be of assistance?"

"What?" He moved closer again, and, as he did so, he realised he could see the outlines of shelves through her. She was just a projection. "Damn. You know, you shouldn't do that. You scared the crap out of me."

"Crap," she said. "Is that something you wish to purchase?"

"What?" He shook his head in bewilderment. "What are you?"

"I am your shopping assistant. Can I be of assistance?" She smiled widely.

Damn, she wasn't terribly smart. Certainly not an AI. "Be specific."

"I am the shopping assistant installed in this market. I can help you find what you are looking for. Can I be of assistance?"

Enderby walked up to her and inspected her closely. Clearly a hologram. She glowed ever so slightly, and he could easily see a counter through her head. She wasn't even a recording of a real woman either, rather a simplified simulacrum, almost an animator's idea of what a woman should look like. She wasn't sexual at all, it wasn't anything like that. Rather she was somewhat androgynous. Had it not been for the dress and the hair he would have taken her for a male.

This could actually be an opportunity.

"What databases are you linked into?"

"I have detailed knowledge of all items in our line. Can I be of assistance?" She smiled widely.

"Ok, quit asking that for one. Do you have access to any information outside the shop?"

"I am afraid my external server access has been revoked. However, I still have detailed knowledge of our full line," she said brightly.

So much for that then. "Ok, go on. I'm looking for something to eat." He walked past her, waiting to see if she would follow. She did.

"What kind of food would you like?" She seemed genuinely pleased to help.

"Hadn't really thought about it. An apple?" he tested her.

She didn't hesitate in her response, "I am afraid we have no apples in stock."

He was hardly surprised. "What long life foodstuffs do you have? Anything that is still edible?"

"Our complete range of tinned foods are completely edible. All our items are packed according to the most stringent Confederate Food Council guidelines—"

"Yes, thank you. Lead the way then."

"Do you require a basket?"

"Yeah, sure."

With a whirr a small motorised trolley slid from an alcove and joined them. A screen was set beside its basket, currently showing a zero balance for his purchases so far. Which presented him with a problem.

"How do you expect me to pay? With your server being down?"

"We have contingencies in place for just such occurrences. As we cannot determine your identity we will record your purchases now, along with your physical image. This data will be downloaded once server access is restored." She seemed quite pleased with herself.

"Ah, good." He didn't have anything to worry about then. He doubted server access would be restored any time soon. "Do you sell rucksacks?"

"No, I am afraid not."

He nodded, doubting the trolley would follow him much further than the entrance. "Ok. Your self-heating range, would they still be edible?"

"Of course."

"Ok, show me those instead." He didn't need to stock up now, he could always come back. He could visit the sporting goods store upstairs before returning. There were other things to do right now. Like finding out what Tin Man expected him to accomplish here.

They entered an isle full of ready meals. He browsed them quickly, not sure what he was looking for. After two minutes of that he simply gave up and picked one (a bachelor's lamb dinner with mash and Yorkshire puddings) and then headed for an isle packed with bottled water. Taking his recent diet into account just about anything would be an improvement.

Enderby tried to get more information out of the hologram, but she was serious when she claimed all external access was cut. To her, nothing existed outside the market's entrance.

He did gain one nugget of interesting information. The market's last customer had purchased beer and crisps, on Tuesday the 3rd May 1872 ce at 15:45. After a moment's rough mental arithmetic, he worked it out. He'd been twenty-two then. And that was 84 years ago.

God, he was old.

Chapter Twenty

"You would just leave me here, wouldn't you? You bastards." Richard Payce grimaced, wiping the thick, jellied grease from his hands onto a relatively clean patch of metal. It wasn't a deck as such, in fact he rather doubted people were meant to come down here. Rather it was a vast single sheet of curved metal, folding in beneath the docking bay and its ancillary facilities. It stretched high overhead, disappearing around the curve that formed the bottom of the docking bay itself, its metal bottom barely out of reach above him. The two shapes matched each other perfectly, and he couldn't help thinking they were designed to slide flush into each other. If the process were to complete now, he would be left as little more than a thin paste adding lubrication to the massive wheels he had slid into. It was hardly a pleasant thought.

He was still wearing the pressure suit Prentice had issued him. It was a simple overall shaped suit, bright yellow with reflective chevrons down the side. The life support modules had been built into the helmet itself, leaving the rest of the suit free of any technological artefacts. He'd clipped that to his belt, intending on keeping it close at hand, but it had been ripped off somewhere during his fall. It was nowhere to be seen now. Fortunately he'd unmounted the lamp and clipped it over his shoulder. That clip, at least, had remained intact. The radio was a small device he'd attached to his belt also, as he'd seen everyone else do when they were passed around. So, he could see and communicate. But other than that he could do very little.

"Bastards," he muttered. He could hear them splitting up and going their separate ways overhead. Effectively leaving him marooned. Clearly they didn't care that he was stranded down here. Bastards. So, why had they brought him along in the first place?

Sistine had asked him to deliver the letter to her brother, that was it. There was no mention of him being flown up to the Parking Lot after her. She was mad and he certainly hadn't shared her madness. Sure, the demons were interesting: an enigma. The prefect's claim they hated humanity because the machines had been caught out in a lie, that their attempt to overthrow human dominion had been exposed, didn't quite make sense. Sure, he sympathised with the heretics in their efforts to understand them, to try and mend the bridges that had been destroyed at the end of the war. But that didn't mean he wanted to risk his life on insane ventures. He actually liked city life: he liked his life, his job, his friends, and—until recently—his relationship with Sistine. Her obsession with finding and studying an uncastrated demon had driven a wedge between them. If anything, he'd been making plans to move on when she disappeared on her mission to the *Goliath*. It simply hadn't been working. They'd been arguing about just about everything for months, from important things like work to ridiculous things like spilt milk. He'd taken to avoiding her as much as possible, locking himself in his study to read and drink beer just to be out of her way. They certainly hadn't slept together in months. It was over. It was time to admit it. And now all this.

"Bastards."

He aimed his lamp up at a ladder set into the ceiling. The rungs didn't quite make it all the way down, ending just out of reach overhead. He could jump for it though, he reckoned. He checked to ensure the lamp and the radio remained firmly attached, took a deep breath, and leaped.

The ladder was a simple affair of steel rungs about thirty centimetres apart. It led into a passage that disappeared into the darkness above. Darkness. He'd never seen so much of it. As a city boy there'd always been light somewhere. A streetlamp or a lit window. Here there was just nothingness. Blackness and ghosts.

Grunting he clung to the lower rung, trying desperately to pull himself higher. His legs wind milling he managed to get an arm over the rung before his strength gave out. He cursed, refusing to let go. If he did he knew he'd never be able to summon the energy to try again. Unfortunately, now he was in an almost impossible position to get any higher.

"Bastards. Bollicking bollicking bastards!" He shouted, not caring who heard. His muscles on fire he twisted one hand free and reached quickly for the next rung. He clung to that and wedged his shoulder over it. He cursed. His shoulder throbbing where he'd forced it to bend in unnatural directions.

Rung by painful rung he dragged himself higher. It was clear that if he didn't drag himself out of this on his own he would die down here. No one was coming to rescue him. He sobbed with relief once he finally managed to get a foot on the bottom rung. For long minutes he just hung there, getting his breath back.

"Bastards."

The radio was quiet now, the others having passed out of its reception range. They didn't work terribly well in here, he had discovered. Sollander had mentioned something about it being a dampening effect created by the structure itself. A defensive mechanism, designed to reduce communications between invading parties. Lovely.

With another deep breath, he started climbing. A monotonous hand over hand ascent that went on indeterminably. His shoulder muscles were soon burning again from the unaccustomed exertion, forcing him to stop every few minutes. He found himself checking his watch. It was half past two in the morning. Madness. But then time didn't seem to matter much here. Time hadn't passed here in eighty years.

"Bastards."

Payce continued climbing, the lower entrance quickly lost below. The passage wasn't very wide. It was just big enough for someone to climb up but that was it. He discovered that when he was resting he could wedge his back against it, taking his weight off his arms. It helped.

As he rested, wedged in, he felt rather than saw, a presence move up to him. The hair on the back of his neck stood on end. He shuddered, suddenly cold.

"Is someone there?" He flashed his lamp about him. He could see nothing but stark metal of the access tube. "Hello?"

He heard a faint sob. Like from a young girl. "Daddy? Daddy?"

"Shit." He jumped on hearing the voice. "Who is that? Where are you?" There were no children up here, surely.

"Daddy, I'm scared."

"Who is this? Where are you?" Still, there was nothing but empty passage.

"You are my daddy, aren't you?"

"Who are you? Where are you?" He repeated. He inched up higher, maybe there was a side passage he hadn't seen. There was nothing.

"It's Lucy. Lucy Boyd."

"Where are you Lucy? Do you need help?"

"They're coming, daddy. I'm scared."

"It's ok, I'm here. Where are you?"

"Are you my daddy?"

"Yeah, sure. Come out and show yourself." He heard whispering, indistinct. There was more than in voice. "Hello?"

And with that, the feeling of not being alone passed. He called again, but there was no answer. Cursing he continued upwards, thoroughly shaken.

"Shit. I hate this place. This is crazy." Maybe he was crazy. Maybe he was hearing things. He just wanted to go home.

After twenty minutes of this he came to an intersection. The ladder joined another coming in at an angle. He looked down it, guessing that it gave access to a different part of the inspection bay beneath the docking facilities. Hardly interesting. Up was the way to go.

A dozen metres further the ladder ended in a cramped engineering bay. Relieved he dragged himself from the passage and collapsed on the deck. That was it. No more ladders. Laying flat on his back, his chest heaving as he regained his breath, he shone his torch around the compartment. It wasn't very big, no more than five or six metres on a side. It was cluttered with machinery, none of which he could identify. There weren't any electronics or consoles of any kind in evidence. Just massive gears and cables. Possibly part of the drawing mechanism.

"Hello? Is anyone here?" He shone his lamp around him. "Lucy?"

There was no response.

Three passages led off the compartment, each disappearing into the gloom. There were no doors. He aimed his lamp down each in turn, trying to see which was the most promising. None were.

"Bastards." He stood and ventured a few dozen paces down the first one. It was just a passage. No doors, no markings, no nothing. Very weird. How had the crew known where they were going?

"Hello!" he shouted down it, his echo coming back at him as it travelled down the narrow metal passage. "Is anyone there?" He tried to remember who had been left behind. One of the Smithy brothers. The big one. "Duncan! Can you hear me?"

There was no reply but for his own echo.

"Damn. The bastards." He tried another passage, shouting down that one too. Surely Duncan would hear him? He couldn't be that far from the transit area. Not far certainly, but he had no idea what direction it was in. He'd completely lost his bearings.

"Duncan! You fat bastard!" he yelled again.

He speculated that if he was still within the docking module, he could only go so far before coming to its boundaries. And, as it was still misaligned, there would be no mistaking those boundaries. Once he did that he might be able to work his way back around to the main entrance. Theoretically.

Feeling dubious, he set out at random down one of the passages. After walking fifty metres he came to its end. It was a door, and it was shut. There was a thick pressure window set into it. He peered through but saw nothing beyond. He tried the handle but it refused to move. Right, try another.

The second passage led to the foot of another ladder. This one vanishing into further darkness overhead. He might try that later. The third passage was shorter, culminating in a viewing gallery, a deck to ceiling window onto a darkened chamber. Payce tried shining his lamp through it, but the light seemed incapable of penetrating the thick glass.

"Bastards." He returned to the central chamber and studied it again. He couldn't believe the transit deck was higher up still. He had climbed a long way already.

A grille for an air-conditioning duct was situated in the very centre of the chamber. Working on the principle that air-conditioning ducts linked just about every compartment in the ship, he went onto tiptoes and shouted into it. "Hello! Duncan! Can you hear me?"

His voice echoed away down the duct. There was no reply.

"Damn."

"Would you quit doing that?"

Surprised he looked around him. There was no one there. Was he imagining things again? "Who is that? Duncan?"

"No," the faint voice replied. "Quit shouting."

"Where the hell are you?"

"Seriously, man. You need to quit shouting. And switch your light off. I'm down here."

Payce peered down the second passage. The sound was misleading, but it could only have come from there. He ventured down it quickly. "Where are you?"

"I'm going to kick your ass. Shut up and switch that fucking thing off!" the voice hissed. "If you don't I'm out of here. I'll leave you here and let them find you. They will you know."

"What? Who?" He saw a foot resting on a rung, the leg it was attached to leading into the passage overhead.

"The light." The voice said patiently.

"Damn." Payce switched it off. Oppressive darkness crashed in, smothering him. He struggled for breath, holding onto one of the walls as his senses span around him. He wanted the light on. He needed the light on.

"Better. Now, walk forward. Hold your hand out so you don't crack your head on the ladder. Then climb up after me."

Biting down on whimpers of fear Payce clipped the lamp to his belt and set off after her. It was a woman, he felt. The voice was definitely feminine. She didn't smell feminine though. Now that the light was out and he was reduced to his senses of hearing, touch and smell he noticed the odour of sweat permeating the passage.

Of course, women perspired too.

"Are you part of the original mission?"

"Shhh."

"We've come here to find you."

"Shut up. Talk later. Climb now."

"Is there a little girl here? I heard a little girl."

"You're crazy. Just shut up."

The climb was a long one, with regular alcoves where the ladder swapped to the other wall. They rested in two of them, his companion silencing him the moment he attempted to talk. They passed side passages but she ignored those too, continuing up and up, far further than Payce had imagined possible. Surely they had reached the hull by now? Where was she taking him? Of course she didn't answer that question either.

"Almost there now," she whispered. "Be quiet. Be very, very quiet. They're on lookout not far from here. If you make a sound, they'll come."

Who? But he knew not to ask that question too. Instead he kept quiet, his companion taking his silence as agreement.

"Keep to the left."

Up more ladders they went. He barked his shins on a steel doorjamb. Gritting his teeth, he kept in a yell of surprise. A hand stopped him from going any further. He sensed rather than saw her lean over and close a hatch behind them. After securing the handle with a bar jammed against its frame, she pulled him onwards. As they mounted more ladders he started discerning light ahead. It was faint at first, but quickly grew until it hurt his dark accustomed eyes.

"Here." She stopped him, closing another hatch. She wedged this one closed too. "There. We're safe now. You can switch your light back on." She smiled thinly. "But I guess you won't need to. Just don't make too much noise." Not waiting for a response she clambered up a ramp to a higher hatch and pulled on the handle, ensuring it was still secure.

"What is this place?" Payce looked around the tall, narrow compartment. Arcane items of machinery cluttered the inner bulkhead, draped with power conduits and coolant pipes. The opposite bulkhead featured a number of oblong portholes, each opening out onto empty space. It was through these the light streamed. Bright, piercing sunlight.

"Sanctuary." She knelt over an aluminium trunk and pulled open the lid. "Like a drink?"

"Yeah."

She extracted a bottle of water and, after taking several deep swallows from it herself, passed it over. "We're in one of the towers here," she said, standing to look out of a porthole. "Means we're above the surface. Quite out of the way ... secluded like. Only one drawback though."

He took a long swig of the tepid water. "What's that?"

"Nowhere to run to."

He joined her at the porthole and looked out. Bright, sun blasted metal stretched away to the horizon. Slender towers dotted the surface. In the centre was a dark, oblong gap. The tunnel into the *Goliath*.

She was short, with greasy auburn hair down to her shoulders. Her elfin face was smeared with dirt, as if she hadn't washed in weeks. From the smell he decided she hadn't. She'd clearly stopped smelling herself some time ago. She was wearing a pair of grey dungarees and grey trainers (they had probably been white once). She filled her green vest out well, he couldn't help noticing. Her bra straps peeked out from beneath it. Pretty in a tom-boyish way.

"I saw the shuttle coming in," she continued. "So I went to take a look."

"Who are you?"

She grinned widely. "I'm Andrea Phillips. I was on the first shuttle. Of course." She held out a hand and he shook it tentatively.

"Richard Payce. I was on the second ...of course. So, what's going on?"

She seated herself on one of the pipes, clearly not one of the refrigerated ones, and rubbed her brow. "I have no idea. I'm just trying to stay alive. This ship isn't deserted. Not like they said it should be. There's ... something here."

"Something, or someone? I heard a little girl earlier."

"I don't know. I have seen them, but I don't know what they are. There's no little girls. What they did to Devon ..." She shuddered.

"Devon?"

"You'd have seen him ... what remains of him. They caught him outside the airlock. Roberta and Devon were making a run for it. I don't know why, there was nowhere to run to. But they figured they couldn't be followed into space. Hey, have you found Roberta?"

He frowned. "Yeah, I think so. She was in the airlock without her helmet."

"Oh, good."

"Someone cycled the airlock. She didn't make it."

"Shit."

"What are they? What were they running from?"

She hesitated, as if unwilling to talk about it. "I don't know. They look human, but they can't be. They're fast and strong, far too strong. And they eat .... they eat ..." She couldn't finish. Shaking visibly she stopped talking.

"I think I know," Payce said. "Are they Syat?"

"No. No, they can't be. There's no Syat up here. The only Syat are on the Mentor Platforms, and they don't hunt us anymore. Why would they? They get what they want anyway ... in the end."

"But they eat people. Or at least they did. These things do too? So maybe they're the same?"

She shook her head. "I don't know. I didn't get a good look of them. I don't want to. Listen, I don't want to talk about it. Not after what I've seen. We just need to stay clear of them."

"We need to talk about this. I need to know what's out there."

She stared at him. "I don't know what they bloody are, all right?"

"Ok, ok." He seated herself alongside her. "Do you know what happened to Sissy? To Sistine Davido?"

"Sissy? No. She and Carter went deeper into the ship. They were headed for the control spaces. That was our mission, to secure the ship and see if the engines could be brought back on line. They left before any of this happened. I've not seen them since."

Ok. That, at least, was some good news. There was a reason to hope. If Andrea could stay alive this long then so could Sissy. She could still be out there somewhere, hiding out like Andrea was.

"Do you have any way of finding her? Of contacting her?"

"No. Radios don't work very well here. There's too much interference." She seemed calmer now. Her shaking had subsided. Perhaps talking about something else helped.

"Your shuttle? What happened to that?"

"It went further in, after we'd set up base camp. We've not heard from it since. I don't know what happened to it. Do you?"

"No. No, I don't I'm afraid. Our own shuttle has gone to take a look. They'll find out."

"Or the same thing will happen to them."

"Mmm, let's be positive." He paused a moment. "So, there were six of you. Sissy and Carter went to the bridge. Devon and Roberta are dead. And as you're here that means Trilia was your shuttle pilot?"

"That's right."

"So, there's only the three of you still aboard? Not counting the pilot for the moment."

"Yeah. I guess so. I've been hoping they'll come back up. I have the base radio." She gestured to a heavy radio set dumped on the floor beside the aluminium trunk. "I might be able to pick them up when they come back."

"How did you get all this up here?"

She smiled thinly. "Bloody hard work, is what. I lumped all this up here on my own, in the dark. It took me days, but I needed the supplies."

"That's well done. See, if we work hard we can cope."

She managed a weak laugh. "Yeah. So what happened to you then? You got separated from the rest of your lot?"

He laughed. "Yeah, I stepped somewhere I shouldn't and got lost."

"Fool. There's a lot of you? They're in danger you know."

He put a consoling arm around her. "They will be fine. I guarantee it. Sissy's brother is with us. I don't know if she told you anything about him, but he's a rather tough character. He brought enough guns to start a war. He can take out any of these things if they come after him."

"That'd be good. Then we can find Carter and Sissy and get of this damned ship. We should never have come up here."

"Too bloody right."

Lieutenant Souller, AMS 1706502 Singleship XS106 DBE
14:15 17/09/1875 ce (13 pce)
Untitled

"I cannot use video. I cannot risk the bandwidth. You'll need to give me a running commentary of what you're doing."

"I'm trying to concentrate."

"This is important. I cannot assist you if I don't know what you are doing."

"Ok. So, I'm doing as you instructed. I'm using the torch to defrost the door mechanism so I can get it open. I still think we should be using the same door our visitor did."

"As I have mentioned, it may be monitored. Safer to use an alternate entrance."

Pause.

"There ... I think that's got it. Hang on. I'm engaging the suit's servomotors."

"You can put a lot of pressure on it. Those systems are robust, you won't break them."

"If I do there's always other doors to try. It's moving. I think I got it."

Pause.

"There. It's open. It's dark inside."

"I'm not reading electromagnetic activity in any of the surface facilities. Remember, this station is stealthed—"

"Yeah, thanks."

"—so there wouldn't be much activity on the surface anyway. You may get a better reading further in."

"I hope the well's working. I'm not walking all the way to the core."

"According to my records the gravity well was removed fifteen years ago. It was replaced by a mechanical elevator system. Mechanicals are easier to mask from surveillance. The only produce vibration and heat. Both of which can be soaked up by the surrounding strata."

"As long as there's something there. How far is it?"

"Turn left here. Then two hundred metres straight on. Describe what you see. If you remember, I'm not using any active sensor systems. You have to tell me where you are and what you're looking at."

"Yeah, yeah. It's a passage. Bare metal. There's no air pressure."

"That's wrong. You should have passed through an air lock."

"Yeah. The inner door was open when I opened the outer one. There wasn't a blowout, so this whole area must already be depressurised. Well, it is. I'm here and I can tell."

"What's the gravity like?"

"As we expected, it's pretty much nonexistent. I'm floating here. First time I've had to do that since flight school."

"That will be the ambient microgravity. I'm reading it as zero point zero two g."

"So, why did you ask? I'm there now. There's a door. This'll be for personnel only. That won't do us any good. We need to get you inside so the manufactory can repair the defect. There must be a vehicle entry here somewhere."

"There is. But you need to scout the facility first. We cannot commit until we know it's safe."

"Hey. I'm already committed. Damn, this thing makes a lot of noise. I can feel the vibration through my gloves."

"The elevator?"

"Yeah."

"That can't be good. It will alert whoever's here."

"They'll know we're here anyway. I'm sure their ship would have alerted them."

"I have detected no signals emanating from it. It appears to be dormant. It is possible its crew abandoned it here. They could be seeking refuge inside."

Pause.

"I think it's getting closer. I'm going to seek shelter around a corner, in case it's occupied."

"Good plan."

Pause.

"There it is. It's empty. I'm going in."

"Be careful."

"Jeez, thanks."

"We'll still be able to communicate when you go in, but we should keep it to a minimum. I'm focussing the transmission on you now to minimise leakage, but I'll need to increase the power output as you go deeper. We'll start running a risk."

"The halo will soak a lot of that up. I'm headed down."

"Is there any damage to the systems?"

"No."

Pause.

"Why was this station abandoned?"

"It was abandoned as a security procedure when the Syat started making inroads into the inner systems. It was felt the station was too exposed. They were withdrawn to the Pedia Station, which is a militarised naval base."

"And what happened to that? Let me guess?"

"It was destroyed during the Syat invasion."

"Yeah. I don't remember hearing much from it when we were engaged in the evacuation. They must have hit it hard. So much for a militarised naval station being safer."

"Nowhere was safe. Even the Wheel was engaged and destroyed, and there were two hundred mainline battle cruisers in a defensive perimeter around it during the invasion of the Reaos system."

"Yeah. If we couldn't defend that position, we couldn't defend anything. And we didn't in the end."

Pause.

"Shit, there were a lot of them. There must have been billions of minor agglomerations. Hundreds of thousands of majors. There was just nothing we could do."

"We have no reason to believe their numbers have reduced since then. We remain safe only through stealth."

"Yeah."

Pause.

"You have to keep on talking to me. I don't care how deep down I am."

"I will."

Pause.

"It's getting cold."

"According to your suit telemetry the ambient air pressure is rising. I'll adjust the temperature controls."

"That's better. Thanks. I think I'm coming to the bottom. Yes, the elevator is definitely slowing."

"According to my schematics the elevator should bring you to the main habitat. It's eight kilometres long and four in diameter. As it's in micro-g the designers utilised much of the interior space for domicile webbing. That's what they called it. The central space is taken by a plasma tube, which provides both lighting and warmth."

"Thanks. I've been here before."

"Your suit sensors are picking up the electromagnetic signature of the plasma tube. So it appears the systems are still active."

"What do your records say? Did they leave everything switched on when they abandoned the place?"

"They are silent on that issue I am afraid. It was a chaotic time, not all records were maintained. It would have taken some time to safely mothball the systems, however, so I would presume they left everything running."

"The local AI?"

"That too."

"That could prove useful. Hang on, here we go."

Pause.

"Nothing here. It's deserted. My suit sensors report the atmosphere is viable so I'm going to crack my visor. There, seems fine."

Pause.

"Right. You wanted a commentary. The lights are on. I can't see much of the plasma tube from here, there's too many structures in the way, but it's clearly running ok. The plant life looks a bit of a shambles. I guess no one's pruned the hedges for a while. Damn, I forgot how big this place was."

"Is there any animal life? Birds?"

"Birds? I've not seen any. Why? Turning into a twitcher?"

"The habitat is not a natural one for birds, and I believe they required constant intervention in order to survive. Their presence would be a good indicator as to what systems are still running."

"Intervention?"

"Food and water."

"Oh. So, directions please."

"Turn left, head for a glass enclosed ramp, that will lead you to the administrative section at the south end cap."

"Ok. There's a bit more gravity here. They must have a generator some place."

"From the schematics I have I can see several drive cores are buried in the regolith."

"You mean this thing is capable of FTL?"

"Strictly speaking, FTL is impossible. But I follow your meaning, yes."

"Quibble. How do you have access to this? This should have been classified?"

"It was. It is. The classification system has become somewhat defunct however. During the final battles the Confederate Council repealed all security restrictions. The hope was that free dissemination of data would assist in our resistance in some way."

"It didn't."

"Not significantly, no."

"So, are you telling me you would have full access to the AI's datastore?"

"Theoretically, yes."

"Interesting. There are a few things I would like to know. I might ask the AI when I find it. There's a high security research facility here, this AI would have a very high clearance indeed."

"Such as?"

"Omegas."

"Ah, of course. There were many rumours. They were quite fantastical. I could not speculate, I am afraid. I myself do not have access to that data. You'll need to ask the AI."

"I will. If it's true you know what this means though?"

"Entertain me."

"Well, the rumour was Admiralty Science had developed a new generation of warship: the Omega class. They created sophisticated warp fields, which described something that was, in effect, an alternate universe. It was like a cloak, rendering the vessel invisible. The ship simply didn't exist in real space. Fantastic stuff."

"Fantastic, just so."

"Yeah. I'd like it to be true though. It means someone may have survived. The Eaters wouldn't be able to find Omegas. They could still be out there somewhere."

Pause.

"It would be an interesting hypothesis. Don't get too excited by the concept though."

"Come on, man. Don't be a downer."

"We cannot afford flights of fancy. Consider this, your own battle group survived the end of the war. You could have continued as you were indefinitely. Yet you decided not to."

"What's your point?"

"These Omegas—should they exist—may have made the same decision. I expect they would have suicided once they realised there was no hope of saving anything."

"Shit man. Why do I talk to you? I don't think I'll ask it now. I really don't want to know."

"I have upset you."

"Yeah, man. You have."

"I am sorry. We need to be realistic."

"Realism is sometimes the last thing we need. We need to be able to dream, to hope."

"I think in our present, quite desperate situation, only realism and determination will keep us alive. We have to face the truth, no matter how uncomfortable. And that truth is this: we are on our own. We only have ourselves to rely on. We are not going to be saved."

"Dude, let me tell you, I need something to hope for. I need something to live for. I don't want to talk anymore."

"Ok. Are you there yet?"

Pause.

"Yeah, ok. I think this is it. Nothing's locked. The doors are all open. This looks like a high security facility too. Why'd they leave it open?"

"Same reason all classified data was declassified."

"So, all humans are on the same side now, right? Anyone can know anything? Anyone can go anywhere?"

"Something like that."

"Shit. This place has been trashed."

"Describe what you see."

"It looks like a bomb has gone off. Not a big one ...a grenade maybe. The consoles are all smashed. The main AI interface is down. Oh, goddamn."

"What is it?"

"The AI's trashed too. Whoever did this got past the seals and tossed a grenade into the processor chamber. The lights are all out and it looks like there was a fire, but I can see enough to see the AI core is ruined. Damn, there's bits everywhere."

"That is not a good sign."

"It was done recently. I can still smell it."

"You are speculating our visitor did it?"

"Yeah. Damn, I need to get out of here."

"The atmosphere is noxious. It looks like the halon fire suppression system went off. You need to leave the area. Get to clear air."

"Yeah. Thanks."

Pause.

"Are you out? Your respiration is erratic and your heart rate just increased. I think you should pull your visor down again."

"It's ok. It's ok."

"You need to tell me what's happening. Should I engage your remote video systems?"

"No. It's ok. I've found her."

"Who? Is it our visitor?"

"Yeah. I think so. She's dead."

"Please describe."

"She's sitting outside the data management area. Looks like she slashed her wrists."

"This makes little sense. Her motivations are entirely unclear to me."

"This might help. There's a note. Ugh, it's got blood all over it."

"What does it say?"

"If anyone ever finds me, you will understand. Without the *Goliath* there is nothing."

Pause.

"What the hell does that mean?"

End recording.

Chapter Twenty-One

"Shit. Oh, shit." Sash directed power to the thrusters, slowing her forward movement. Gas squirted before her, misting for a moment in the glare of her lights before dissipating.

The wreckage of the shuttle grew distinct as she approached, twisted shadows flitting about its torn frame. It was rammed up against the tunnel wall, one of its drives crumpled in the impact. Hanging motionless, it was nose down and slightly on one side, revealing the ruins of its stern. Something had hit it hard, ripping through metal and tearing body panels. The lights were out. It was clearly dead.

She toggled her radio. "Jeno... Adele, can you hear me?" There was no response.

Becoming frustrated waiting for the shuttle to return Sash had raided the equipment lockers left on the transit deck, clipping a manoeuvring pack, extra lights and oxy bottles to her suit. Weighed down she'd hobbled back to the ajar landing bay doors and jumped into emptiness. Coasting at thirty kilometres an hour it hadn't taken long to find the shuttle.

"Damn. Duncan, can you hear me?" Her transmission was met with more silence. The larger Smithy twin was simply too far away, behind too many bulkheads and airlock doors.

She hung motionless for a moment, slowly drifting towards the tunnel wall above her, caught in indecision. They were clearly trapped here, the shuttle wasn't going anywhere. Running through options in her mind she kept on finding insurmountable problems. Even placing a transmitter on the outside hull and calling for help was unlikely to produce results. The only people who ever came up here were the Overtakers, and they only travelled to the mentor platforms, stopping off at the odd wreck as it passed close by to raid it for any useful technology. They were all in a much lower orbit, thousands of kilometres away. If they were on this side of the planet at all. The only vehicles aboard the *Goliath* they had access to were behind two massive, unpowered bay doors. They'd need to find a way of powering them up, and she had no idea where to start with that. If, of course, they still worked.

"Damn it to bloody hell," Sash cursed. She squirted power to the motors again, edging forward. She could see the vague outline of something else behind the shuttle. The lights, as bright as they were, were not quite bright enough to make out much detail. Not that it really mattered now, but she wanted to know what had happened to the shuttle. Someone would ask. Davido would certainly want to know what had killed his girlfriend. She cursed again. Davido would kill someone for that. Whether he would admit it or not he'd been quite attached to her. Had it been love? Sash didn't think he knew what that meant, but it was as close as a man like Davido got to it. She certainly did not look forward to delivering the bad news. Men like Davido didn't like bad news either. He had a way of making people regret bringing it to him.

Sash paused as she came alongside the shuttle, more gas misting around her as she brought herself to a stop. Laying her gloves on the cockpit windscreen she peered in, trying to angle the light to penetrate the darkness. There was something there.

"Fuck!" Sash jerked back in surprise, a glaringly white face appearing before her. It mouthed something at her, waving frantically. "Fuck. Don't do that." She waved back.

The figure kept on waving, brow furrowed in frustration, her meaning not being made clear. Then she vanished, swimming away into darkness. Sash cursed, looking around the side of the space craft. She couldn't understand how someone could be alive in there. The thing was trashed.

The face returned. A piece of paper was held up to the windshield, something scrawled on it. "Jeno!!!!"

"What?" Sash threw up her arms in exasperation. "We've got to get you out of there!"

The face frowned. Adele, it must be, Sash decided. Her view through the window wasn't very good. The paper was pushed up against it again. "He shot me!" The word 'shot' underlined three times.

"Yeah? OK. So, how's that going to help me get you out of there? Is the airlock working?"

Adele threw up her hands.

"Guess I'll have to find out for myself." Sash waved at her and pushed herself away from the shuttle. Manoeuvring carefully using the thruster pack she rounded its crumpled frame. The airlock control panel was still lit up. A good sign. She keyed the opening sequence quickly, the hatch sinking into the side of the shuttle slightly, before sliding aside. The interior was dark. She didn't care, as long as it worked.

"Did you see? That fucking bastard Jeno shot me!" Adele raged as soon as Sash got the inner door open.

"Ok, ok. Calm down. What happened?"

Adele was still wearing most of her pressure suit, the helmet removed and held in her hands. The interior of the shuttle was dark too. With the power off the air inside wouldn't last very long. Still, at least there was still air pressure. The stern pressure door, between the main cabin and the cargo area, must be shut. Adele held the helmet up. A long scar was torn through the composite material. Emergency repair gum was clumsily pressed into it, sealing the breach.

Clearly shaken Adele quickly explained what had happened. She seemed more angry that someone had had the temerity to try to kill her, than that the shuttle was ruined. That they were stranded here hadn't occurred to her yet. Sash ascribed it to shock and left it at that.

"We have to track him down," Adele went on.

"What for? He's gone." She took the helmet from Adele and inspected the damage. It was severe; it would have killed her if she hadn't acted quickly by sealing it. That actually impressed her. She hadn't thought the woman up for that kind of clear thinking. The repair wouldn't hold though, Sash decided. She fished out her own repair kit and started working on shoring it up. They would need of it again in a moment.

"He's a murderer. We can't let him go free."

"Strictly speaking, he's not. You're still alive," Sash pointed out.

Adele waved that away. "We need to stop him killing anyone."

"Yeah, like who? There's no one on this rust bucket." Sash paused, studying Adele a bit closer. "Have you been drinking?"

She shrugged. "A little."

Sash was tempted to rebuke her but decided better of it. A stiff drink was probably a good idea, it would settle her nerves. "Be a love and get me one, why don't you?"

"Get your own. So, we going after him? You've got a gun." Adele pointed to the stubby sub machine gun she had strapped clumsily around the harness.

"No, absolutely not. We need to get back up to the others." They needed to be told of this catastrophe.

"Good idea." Adele picked up a bottle and took a gulp of clear liquid. It took her a moment, in microgravity there was nothing to encourage the alcohol to leave the bottle. She was steadily getting more inebriated by the moment. Possibly a good time to leave. "We can bring back a posse."

"How much air do you have in there?"

"The suit? Dunno."

Shaking her head Sash took her arm and studied the fabric screen sewn into its cuff. 2% oxy remaining. That wasn't good. "There any power in here at all? We need to recharge this thing."

Adele shrugged. "Don't think so. Even that bloody demon has stopped making a noise."

That limited their options. Driving just her own mass the manoeuvring pack had taken her half an hour to get down here. Pushing the both of them, it might take upwards of an hour. 2% oxy wouldn't cut it. Sash cast around the shuttle, looking for anything they could enlist to aid them. Davido's weapons cache was pushed behind the last row of seats in the main cabin, other than that there was nothing. Prentice's own equipment had been stored in the cargo area.

"Do you know how much further this tunnel goes?"

"Beats me."

"Have you seen Jeno coming back?"

Adele shook her head. Her eyes were starting to glaze over. Sash relieved her of the bottle. She needed her sensible. She batted away Adele's hand as she tried to snatch it back. Some spilled out, globules of alcohol attaching themselves to a bulkhead.

"Ok. So he's either found a way out further down or he's dead down there. We'll ignore the latter for the moment, as much as I think you'd like that option." She studied the extra oxygen bottles she'd strapped to her own suit. "Turn around."

"What?"

"Just do it." She watched as Adele turned around clumsily.

"What was that for?"

"Seeing if your suit has an emergency oxy valve. It doesn't."

"What does that mean?"

"I can't connect these extra bottles to your suit. You've only got two percent air left. That'll last about ..." She shrugged. "Ten, fifteen minutes."

"I can stay here."

"What for? To die? That's all you'll do here. This shuttle is dead."

"Mmm, time to get drunk I think." Swaying slightly (an odd sight in zero g) she went in search of another drink.

"No. It isn't. That's the last thing we need." There was only one thing to do then. The decision had been made for her. "Ok. So, let's go after Jeno."

"Hey, why didn't I think of that?"

Ignoring her sarcasm Sash gave her attention to Davido's weapons stash. Her eyebrows raised as she opened the heavy plastic zipper. Davido didn't travel light. "Here." She pulled out a sawn off shotgun and handed it to Adele, following it with enough spare cartridges to start a small war. Shotguns were the easiest things for novice's not to mess up. Point and shoot. There was nothing simpler. She relinquished her own weapon and extracted an assault rifle. BMA 15, was stencilled in neat military script on the side. Noech Armament Works. When in trouble, always choose Noech. She smiled, she always felt better when her hands were wrapped around a powerful weapon. She hung it over her shoulder and followed that with a bandolier of spare clips. Too much? She thought? No, she added a brace of grenades and then turned back to Adele.

"We go. Now, we don't have much time, so I'll explain to you exactly what we're going to do before we set off. I'm going to clip you in front of me. Do not wriggle. In fact, do not move. If you do it'll throw our weight distribution off and I can't fly straight. So, I'll fly into a wall or something. Remember, you're in front, so you'll hit first. Got it?"

"Got it." She saluted clumsily.

"Next, you'll start getting alarms in your helmet. Ignore them, there's nothing we can do about them. Finally, we're looking for some kind of hatch or entrance way. If you see one I need you to let me know immediately."

Adele pulled herself into the airlock. "Let's go get the bastard."

"Right." Sash followed her. She quickly checked both their suits and then cycled the lock. "You ok?"

"Peachy. Damn, I didn't bring anything to drink."

Sash pulled her closer, ignoring her yelp. She quickly connected the two suits together, wrapping her legs around the shorter woman for extra stability. Aaah, in better times, she thought. What she wouldn't give to try Adele out. She did have a nice ass. Still, Davido would not approve. Pity he didn't like watching girls together. He was a bit old fashioned that way.

Once they were aligned with the tunnel she kicked in the motors. "Hang on." It felt like a car accelerating quickly, the cold gas rockets pushing the two steadily forwards. They wobbled slightly as Sash became accustomed to their weight distribution.

As they swerved around the shuttle Sash discovered a second just beyond. It was smashed too. Something very heavy had struck it from the rear. "That must be the other shuttle," she said. "Do you know what was shooting at you?"

"Nope. Never saw it. I was too busy getting shot at."

"Fair enough."

"Those lights you mentioned, they're flashing."

"Ignore them"

"They're pretty insistent. Is there any way of shutting them off?"

"Yeah."

"How?"

"Take your suit off."

"Hey, that's funny." Adele wriggled, trying to get more comfortable.

"Hey!" Sash fired the motors to correct their spin as Adele threw them off. "What did I say about moving?"

"I was getting a cramp."

"Live with it."

"What's that?" Adele pointed towards four steel girders that had become visible before them. They wobbled slightly at the new movement. Sash grimaced but said nothing.

"Is there a hatch there?"

"No."

"So, we keep moving."

"We need to know what's down here. There's something here attacking shuttles. We need to know what it is. It could be some old self defence mechanism that never got switched off."

"Some other time maybe."

"Damn, it's getting stale in here. Think about it though, when we get picked up it'll only fire again. It's not safe here until we switch it off."

"How about getting you inside before you run out of air? And die?"

"A good point well made."

"I'm glad you're see—"

"Hatch!"

Sash flipped a switch, engaging emergency thrust. She grunted, Adele yanking on her harness. The two spun madly, just missing one of the steel girders. Cursing Sash battled with the controls as they slammed into the hard steel wall. They slid along it for a moment, arms and legs becoming tangled.

"What the hell are you doing?" Adele demanded. "Damn, I think you've dislocated my shoulder."

"Shut up." Sash disengaged the manoeuvring pack, allowing it to spin away. One of the motor housings had cracked, causing the motor to fire erratically. Gas billowing around it it crashed into one of the girders, one of its straps snagging on it. Like a Katherine wheel it gyrated against the girder, expending the last of its fuel.

There was a simple handle built into the hatch. Sash twisted it quickly, leaning back as air jetted out, the lock cracking open. "Get in. Quick."

"Damn, that hurt." Adele took an offered hand and pulled herself past Sash. She clambered into the dark opening. Sash followed and closed the hatch quickly behind them.

Air flooded into the chamber. The equalisation symbol flashed in Sash's visor. She lifted it up and sniffed carefully. A bit musty, but it was ok.

"That was some good flying there," Adele commented as she lifted off her helmet. Sash could smell the alcohol on her breath in the cramped space.

"I'd like to see you do better." Sash consulted the interior controls and instructed the door to open. It creaked, the hinges clearly in need of maintenance. Still, it opened, that was all that mattered. She peered out, setting her boots carefully on a steel walkway. Like everywhere else it was dark. At least they had air.

"What is this place?"

"Allow me to consult my map."

"Sarcastic bitch." Adele tossed down her helmet casually, not caring that it clattered off the edge of the walkway and vanished into darkness. Some seconds later they heard a clatter from below, followed by a deep boom. It was a long way down.

Sash shook her head in dismay, stripping off her suit. She couldn't see her needing it again. Now it was just too constrictive, and heavy. Adele followed suit. "The best thing to do is to try and catch up with the others," she said. "They'll be a long way above us now though, unless they've found a quicker way down. We must be quite near the core here, so we're about one and a half kilometres from the landing bay. Maybe a bit less."

"Aren't we after Jeno first?"

"Personally, I don't give a damn about Jeno. I say we leave him here. Sooner or later we'll get picked up and he'll be on his own. He can stay in this bloody place."

Adele looked thoughtful. "As long as we're here he's a danger to us."

"Firstly, we don't know that. It's possible it's just you he took a disliking to. Although I can't see why. Besides, he's not armed now. If I recall he only had the one bullet in his gun. You've ensured he doesn't have that anymore."

"Yeah, how weird is that? We're on a navy ship though, there's bound to be other weapons lying around."

Sash studied their surroundings. There appeared only the one way to go: down. The walkway only went that way. She headed along it. "I doubt they'll leave them lying around."

"I don't think we should take the chance."

Sash smiled, stroking the cool steel of the Noech. She rather wished he did find a weapon.

Chapter Twenty-Two

Enderby awoke staring at a cat. It was a fluffy thing, a tortoise shell tabby. Licking a front paw it looked quite contented, its ears flicking slightly as it kept an eye on the birds from its perch on the balcony wall. Not moving he watched it. It was a very long time since he'd seen a cat. There weren't any on Russou anymore. The locals didn't like them. For the same reason they didn't like dogs.

Perhaps there were dogs here too? Possibly, he decided, but they'd be feral. They would have formed packs by now, roaming the empty passages in the hunt for food. It would be best to avoid them.

The cat twitched, its head whipping around to look in his direction. It saw him and vanished, dropping off the wall to disappear into the garden below. He cursed inwardly. He hadn't made a sound.

Stretching luxuriously Enderby's toes peeped out the bottom of the covers. He yawned. That was the best night's sleep he'd had in, well, decades. This was the first real bed he'd slept in since he'd arrived on Russou. That was one luxury item Tin Man had never been able to scrounge for him. That and toothpaste.

With a whole town to choose from Enderby had set up camp in a house not far from the market. Feeling somewhat exposed he'd chosen one that had some rooms with no windows, where he could switch lights on (they worked) and not have to worry about someone on the other side of the valley seeing them. Not that he imagined there was anyone there. Still, this place felt strange. It was designed for so many people, yet it was eerily empty. Like one of those movies he'd seen as a boy, where the planet's population was wiped out by some plague, leaving only the few odd survivors. They'd always been very popular. That and zombie movies. Unfortunately one of them had come true.

The house was perched high on the hill, only one or two rows between it and the faux sky behind. It boasted two storeys, the second with a wide balcony with a wooden slat floor. It was a classical colonial design, simple to build and maintain, built of sturdy brick with steel supports. The glass was double paned and one way. Interesting, he thought. What was the necessity for double paned windows in a controlled environment? Unless they subjected the valley to variations in weather, possibly even seasons. To add to the realism. That would be interesting, he decided. There looked to be a pretty good ski slope situated near the cliff at the end of the valley.

On the ground floor (possibly better named the bottom floor, as the entrance was on the level above) was a games room with snooker table, VR set and bar. Set behind the bedrooms it didn't have an external window, so, once the doors were drawn shut, he'd set up camp there. Unfortunately snooker tables were no good for sleeping on, so he'd relocated to one of the bedrooms sometime early in the morning.

Feeling thoroughly rested Enderby slid out from under the covers and inspected the wardrobe. No good, he decided. It looked like this was a girl's room. But then the decor had given that away somewhat. It was very ... feminine. He'd not seen the frilly make up table and pop star posters on the wall when he crept in. All he'd cared about was that the covers weren't musty at all, even after all this time.

Curious, he considered. There had been civilians, children even, aboard an active warship? In war time?

Padding on bare feet over the lush carpet he inspected the neighbouring bedroom. This was better. He went through the clothes there, measuring the shoes against his feet. A bit small. No matter, he had the whole valley to draw from. He settled on an only slightly too tight track suit, and pushed his feet into his old boots. Time for breakfast.

As he searched the kitchen, something occurred to him. "There's no bodies." Thinking about it now he couldn't recall seeing one anywhere in the valley. His last had been in the passages leading up to it, and there they had been numerous. It was unlikely there would be none here. That meant only one thing.

"Someone's cleaned up," he said aloud. "But who? There's no one here." He walked to the upstairs balcony and stepped out, enjoying the fresh morning air as he surveyed his domain.

Was there someone here? Some unseen caretaker? An AI? Surely not, the Eaters would have eliminated it a long time ago. AI's were a threat to them, they would never leave one in a position where it could act through its own free will. What did that leave? An actual person? That was something he dared not even contemplate.

If there was he needed to find them. They would be in danger. Also, they were possibly Tin Man's reason for bringing him here. Certainly it was not something the wily old android would inform him of in advanced. Had he been caught the Eaters would know of it immediately. That was not a risk it could take.

"Well, my old friend, you've pulled one last surprise on me," Enderby said.

Whistling to himself, and with a spring in his step he'd not felt in decades, he gathered his belongings and headed towards the market. First: breakfast. Then time to explore and find his hidden benefactor. Perhaps the shop assistant could suggest something half decent for breakfast. He imagined bacon and eggs, followed by an ice cold glass of orange juice. Very possibly out of the question. Salivating he put the thought from his mind. All of those things would have expired a long time ago. He would have to make do with a tin of something.

That line of thought brought him to a realisation. There would be a food production facility here some place. Somewhere perishables would have been produced. A farm possibly. The *Goliath* was certainly large enough for one to be hidden within it. The crew had already demonstrated their skill in creating artificial environments. A farm would not be a problem. Still, he considered, without farmers all the livestock would have perished and the fields would have turned to weeds. Still, it was worth a look. If his caretaker had been busy there too he was in luck.

"Bacon and eggs. Oh my God."

Enderby raided the sporting goods shop first, picking up a decent pair of binoculars (in stock for bird watchers maybe?) whose power pack hadn't quite died yet, a rucksack and some hiking boots that fit perfectly. The menswear shop alongside provided an improved outfit, adding a pair of denims, shirt and fake leather jacket to his kit. He slipped on a pair of sunglasses and smiled at himself in a mirror. Even after so many thousand years of technological development, a good pair of sunglasses never went out of fashion. These ones had an interactive control that could link him to the local server, taking voice commands to either supply information or adjust the wavelength the lenses accepted (according to the shop's overeager sales hologram) but those functions were mostly useless to him. There was no local server. Seeing in the dark could be useful though.

His rucksack filled with chocolate bars, tins of soda, granola bars and crisps from the market he headed back out into the sun. He smiled to himself and started whistling a merry tune as he headed towards the valley floor. He could start at one end of the valley and work his way along. There was plenty of time.

The high velocity round hit him long before he heard the shot.

Chapter Twenty-Three

"We simply cannot stay here," Payce said. "We'll die in here, don't you realise that? Sooner or later. If not today or this week, then next month or the following one."

"You've not seen them. We can't risk going out there," Andrea insisted.

"Have you seen them?"

"Yes, well, no. Not really. I know what they did to Devon though."

"Devon didn't have a gun. Duncan's got one, and he's a big bastard. I reckon we're safe if we get to him." Payce stood looking out of one of the observation ports, studying the sun-bleached panorama of metal before him. The dusty orb of Russou was slowly rising over its metallic horizon. Much of the southern hemisphere was shrouded in cloud as the winter storms rolled in. Glittering flecks of light circled it slowly. The Parking Lot. Most of the vessels were too far away to be more than specks, but some were both large and close enough to be seen in depressing detail. They were all wrecks. Many wore plasma scars on their hulls, others were twisted as if giant hands had taken them and wrung them out like dish rags. All sported tears in their hulls, exposing tender interior spaces to deadly vacuum. They were all mausoleums.

The shuttle had not been seen exiting the tunnel, so they knew Davido and his crew were still here somewhere. They'd be safe with them.

"Besides," he continued, "you were out there when you bumped into me."

"Someone had to shut you up," she retorted.

Payce rolled his eyes. "Tell you what. You can stay here. Just tell me how to get to the transit deck from here."

"You're not listening to me, are you?" Andrea was shaking, her fear apparent.

"Dammit." Payce crossed to the lower entrance and yanked on the securing bar. Wedged in tight it took three tugs to pull it loose.

"Hey!" Andrea tried to pull him away.

"Get off me. We can't stay here, I tell you."

"We're safe here."

"No, we're not." Payce pushed her away and pulled the hatch open.

Andrea collapsed onto the deck, shaking. "Please don't leave me here." All the bravado she'd shown when she discovered him quaking in the dark was gone. "I'll come with you. Just don't leave me here."

"Come along then. Do we need to take anything with us? We won't be back."

"No. Yes!" She extracted an extra pack of power cells for the lamps from the crate. "You will have to let me show you the way. I can get us past them."

"Good." He stood aside to allow her onto the cramped ladder. "Lead the way."

Having spent the last several hours in her company he knew more about her than he cared to. Once they were secured within her refuge, she had chatted incessantly, most of it unintelligible. Her childhood in the city, her enrolment in the engineering corps, even friends and family. It was mostly nonsense. After weeks of stress all the emotional pressure was coming out in one long soliloquy. Much of it wasn't even aimed at him, he didn't even think she was aware of his presence. In the end she had fallen into a fitful sleep, wedged up against a hard bulkhead, her head lolling to one side in a way that must have been most uncomfortable. He'd simply left her be, presuming the last weeks had pushed her over the edge. Payce could not sleep himself. Not here. This place was too unnerving.

His main motivation for leaving this place was simple. There was no guarantee Davido wouldn't simply leave the moment he found his sister. That Payce had been left in the darkness beneath the transit deck was evidence the man didn't particularly care for his welfare. If he was ever going to leave this place, this mausoleum, he needed to be on the transit deck when Davido returned.

They descended into darkness, their lamps once again deactivated to conceal their presence. At first they traversed familiar ladders and walkways, but then Andrea led them down a different avenue, through a small lock and over a wide, flat expanse of metal. It was pitted here and there, as if it had been struck by micrometeorites at some point in the past. There were also regular ridges, as if they were crawling over closed pressure doors. Payce knew not to question her. Silence was critical here, as it was everywhere else, it seemed.

"Here." Payce could sense his companion pausing in front of him. "We can rest up a while. You can switch your light on. It's safe here."

"We can keep on going, I'm not tired." Payce switched on his lamp, blinking as he was dazzled by the sudden glare.

They were in a wide chamber, approximately 75 metres on a side. The ceiling was only a few metres overhead, it's only feature a crease that ran in a perfectly straight line across the centre. Beneath them the deck was a flat expanse of mysterious dark grey material. It didn't feel like metal. Oddly it seemed to curve slightly down at the edges, within a metre or so of the surrounding bulkheads.

"What is this place?"

"I think we're on top of a vessel of some kind. I've looked around some... while trying to find my way past it ... it looks like some sort of military transport."

"The Confederates used to board enemy vessels and try to take them over. This could be one of their assault craft," Payce guessed.

"Could be."

"Is it safe here?"

"Yes. Yes. As safe as it is anywhere. They won't see us up here."

"Not even with our lights on?"

She shook her head.

"You've got to tell me, who are they?"

Andrea hesitated, unwilling to discuss them. "I don't know."

"Are they people? Survivors from the original crew?"

"I don't think so. We checked the Mentor Archive before we came here. There was no one here."

"So, someone else has come here since then? Someone from Russou?"

She shrugged.

"I can't see why they would attack us though. Why should they fear us?"

"Maybe they don't want to be discovered?"

Payce shrugged, at first accepting that it was a possibility. The he frowned. No, that didn't make sense. "This is a big ship. They could have hidden. There weren't many of you ... there aren't many of us, there's no way we would have found them if they didn't want to be found."

"They may have left evidence of their presence somewhere. Who knows what they've been up to. The mentors won't like people living up here. Not aboard an old warship."

He smiled thinly. "We live on a warship or two as it is."

"That's not the same."

"Why have we stopped?" He studied her as she searched for an answer. "Are you stalling? Come on, let's go."

She said nothing, instead leaning over to switch the lamp off and silently move away.

"The quicker we get there the quicker this is over with."

"This way. Be careful, don't fall off the side."

Muttering under his breath he followed. They mounted a service ladder and descending it quickly. Thoroughly disoriented Payce followed her obediently. She guided him with the odd touch on his arm, threading them unerringly through maintenance bays towards their destination. He could sense rather than see the machines they passed by. He could smell the oil that coated their moving parts. Some smelt of more than just oil, reeking with a sharp, chemical smell. He couldn't place it.

Andrea halted, a hand flat on his chest, stopping him in his tracks. She didn't move for a moment. "I think I've made a mistake," she said quietly, so softly he almost imagined he'd heard it.

"Lost?"

"No. They're following us. Can't you hear them?"

He listened intently. Other than the thrumming of his own heart there was nothing. "No."

"Come, we're almost there. Let's hope this friend of yours is as good as you claim." She took his hand and guided him on. There was an urgency in her steps that hadn't been there before.

"I can see something," Payce hissed, noticing a faint glow ahead. He pulled out his radio. It was probably best to warn an armed, jumpy man before you ran at him out of the dark. "It's the transit deck."

The rickety bridge was where they had left it. Ignoring her advice Payce switched on his lamp again and shone it over the contraption. "Dunc!" he hissed, putting the radio away again.

"Who's that?" a voice returned.

"Payce. I've brought someone with me." Wary of the bridge and falling into the gap he shuffled over, Andrea following as soon as he was on the other side.

"Payce?" He saw the taller Smithy twin shining his light in their direction, blinding him for a moment. "That you?"

"Yeah. Mind shining that somewhere else? Sash anywhere?"

Duncan shook his head, frowning, as if trying to recall whether she had been with them on the shuttle or not.

"Where is she, Duncan? This is important, we might need her."

"She went after the shuttle. Hey, who you talking to?"

"Damn. What do you mean?" Duncan was slow, not blind.

It was then he realised there was no one behind him. His companion had vanished. He ventured back to the makeshift bridge. "Andrea!" She was nowhere to be seen. Confused he walked back to Duncan. "Where'd she go, big man? She was right behind me." He gave up looking and returned to Davido's hired gun.

Duncan shrugged. "I didn't see no one, man."

"Don't be a fool, she was right there." He shuddered. That was weird, why would she run off? He hesitated. Was that the bridge creaking. "Dunc, the bridge!" He pointed.

"Marco?" Duncan called. "That you?"

"No, Dunc, it isn't. That'll be her."

It wasn't, there was no one there. His calls were met with silence.

"This is weird, man," he breathed

"Could be its the same guys who did that." Duncan pointed to the congealed mass of blood on the deck. He drew his pistol and clicked off the safety.

"You'd better come out!" Payne called. "Otherwise someone's about to get drilled," he commented.

"Who's there?" Duncan called. "I can hear you." He aimed his weapon to the side, the padding of feet on the rubbery deck moving to flank them. "Why aint they talking, Payce?"

The edges of the chamber lost in darkness they couldn't see their visitors. Payce swept his lamp around, trying to catch one of them. All he could make out was an indistinct shape, little more than a deeper patch of darkness. Something glinted.

"Hit 'em, Payce!"

Payce jumped as Duncan opened fire, the .45 a roar alongside him. Duncan shouted, firing repeatedly at the shadow. The shadow vanished, melting into the deck. He kept on firing until it clicked on empty. Hands shaking he reloaded quickly and aimed again. Nothing moved.

"Did you get it?" Both lamps were aimed, shaking, towards the bridge. There was something on the floor. It wasn't moving.

Duncan crept forwards, keeping his weapon trained on the shape. It was human all right. Spread-eagled on the deck, face down. Blood pooled next to it. It twitched.

Payce cringed, imagining them finding the dead body of Andrea lying there.

"Sparky!" Duncan almost dropped his weapon in his haste to get to the man's side. He pulled him over on his back, staring in shock at his blood sodden jacket.

"Oh, bloody hell." Payce hurried over to them.

"I shot him," Duncan whispered. "I shot him."

Sparky twitched again, his eyes flickering open. His mouth worked but no sound came out of it. Payce pushed the taller Smithy twin aside so he could get a better look. He unzipped the man's jacket and pulled up his shirt.

"We're lucky," he said. "It's only a scratch. It's bleeding a lot, but it's not deep." He poked the edges of the wound. Blood still welled from it, but it hadn't hit anything critical. He could see layers of blood smeared fat where the bullet had passed through one of Sparky's love handles. "Lucky," Payce said slowly, so Sparky could read his lips. "You're lucky. You'll be ok." He turned towards Duncan. "Find me something to wrap this up with."

"You're a doctor?"

Payce laughed. "Hell, no. I live with Sistine Davido, she's told me all I ever need to know about wounds and what to do with them."

Duncan stood back, looking guilty. He backed away slowly, mouthing apologies. Sparky waved a sign slowly, doing it again when Payce shrugged. He held up a thumb and pointed to his side.

"Oh, you're ok." He realised Sparky's meaning. "Well, good. Hang about here for a bit until we get this treated. You've lost a lot of blood. You know, mate, you should try switching your bloody lamp on." As he said it he noticed the device was missing. Sparky had lost it somewhere in his travels about the interior of the warship. Unfortunately he'd never be able to tell them about it.

Duncan returned with a bandage and antibiotic ointment from a first aid kit. Payce cleaned Sparky up as much as he could and helped him carefully to his feet. "Sit down over here," he said, ensuring Sparky could read his lips. "Where's the others?" He said slowly. "Prentice?"

Sparky sighed. He shrugged, making a quick sign. Of course no one understood what he meant.

"Did you get separated?"

Sparky pointed towards the deck.

"They went to a lower deck? Why did they leave you behind?"

Sparky shook his head. He signed again but it was a waste of time.

"Yeah, ok, pal. You just rest up." He scooped up the fallen shotgun and checked it clumsily. As he did so he noticed Duncan standing some way off, quietly reloading his spent clip. "Not your fault, mate. None of us could see who it was. I'd have shot him if it was me."

Duncan shook his head. "No. That," he pointed, "could have been Marco. I could have shot Marco."

"Ah, well, you didn't." Bemused Payce left him alone. Perhaps Davido's goons weren't bothered about catching the odd civilian in crossfire from time to time. It was bound to happen, he guessed.

"What a lovely way to earn a living," he muttered. As he said it, he heard movement from behind him. The makeshift bridge creaking as something eased out onto it. He turned and stared into the darkness. "I don't think we're alone. Andrea, that you?" He shuddered. How could the woman disappear like that?

Chapter Twenty-Four

"What a waste of time that was," Davido commented, leading the way forward as his small band headed deeper into the abandoned dreadnought.

"I tell you, boss. There was a rope there. I saw it," Marco protested.

"Yeah, and so we spent three hours looking for it. Wasted," he said. "We wasted three hours."

"There may have been someone there," Sollander conceded. "But for some reason they decided to avoid us. Irrational, but there you go."

Davido shrugged. "They might have known where Sissy was, but we can't waste time here."

"So, you're not interested in the rest of the crew of the first mission then? Just your sister?"

"Should I be? You don't seem particularly bothered about tracking them down yourself. Why are you here again?" Davido turned and shone his lamp in her face.

Sollander grimaced, holding her hand up to protect her eyes. "Shine that thing somewhere else."

"Go on, you brought this up. Why are you here? I'm here to get my sister, and I'll freely admit I don't give a fuck about the others. But you, you're something else. You said you wanted to get your people back. I'm not seeing much concern now, lady."

She shrugged. "They left a job half done. I need to ensure it's finished."

"What job? To secure this ship? Yeah, I can see that happening."

Sollander said nothing. She certainly did not trust this man. There was only one person who knew the real reason she was here, and Singh could be trusted to keep it to himself. Whatever could be said about the man, he would always do what was in his own best interest. If he opened his mouth he would be as dead as she would. Drefus would see to that personally. "Perhaps you should just consider yourself lucky to have me here, and leave it at that?"

Davido shook his head. He didn't like secrets. Secrets were dangerous. That was not how he ran his organisation. "Listen, babe, I don't really care. As long as you don't get in my way."

Sollander bristled. She was no one's 'babe'. "You don't have to worry about that."

They had left the hold behind, giving up on trying to find who the rope had belonged to. Presuming there had ever been a rope. Davido had known Marco for a long time, and knew the man was not prone to flights of fancy. Still, it had been dark and there had been strange shadows everywhere. He could have simply been mistaken. He'd forgive him. This once.

These companionways were no longer naked metal. Perhaps the Confederate designers had never imagined boarders would get this far in, so had spared some expense making the compartments more welcoming. Trailing his hand against a bulkhead Davido tried to identify what kind of material it was. He failed miserably. It was hard, like baked plastic, coloured a light beige or brown—he couldn't tell which in the lamp light. The lights overhead, although dark, were set in long strips. Even the deck's hard rubber had vanished, replaced by a cross between a mat and a carpet. It was pleasant, in a hard wearing, military kind of way.

There were more doors here too. Once again they were all unlocked, permitting him to push them open carefully to peer inside. The chambers within were an assortment of gyms, running tracks and sports halls. A marine training facility, Sollander guessed. In deep space for months at a time they needed to keep their military contingent busy and in peak condition. There was even a firing range of sorts, which Marco had searched thoroughly. There were no weapons to be found.

"There's gotta be an armoury here somewhere," Marco groused. "This is a naval ship after all. You're telling me that with all these defensive features they threw rotten grapefruit at invaders?"

"I'm not telling you anything," Sollander returned. "Interesting." She held open a side door so they could have a look at the interior.

It was a barracks, row upon row of beds lined up in military precision. Each bed made and each foot locker stowed neatly beneath it. There were more bodies here. A lot of them.

"I'd expect it to smell a bit," Davido commented. "Without the air conditioners working the air in this chamber hasn't moved in eighty years. It should reek in here."

"LEM," Sollander said.

"What?"

"Well, we don't know what they called it," she aimed her lamp towards the bodies, "but we call it LEM. We've seen it before, it was even used in some of the ships we've converted to cities. We've never been able to get it working properly. Apparently you have to align the panels just right otherwise it just causes eddies."

"I have no idea what you're talking about."

"Clearly. The Confederates used a material in their ships that created a weak electrostatic charge on its surface. It caused air currents to flow along the surface of walls and ceilings. Aligned just right the walls themselves would circulate the air through the ship without them having to use bulky air ducts and impeller systems. Doesn't require power either, so it would have kept on working even when everything else didn't." She smiled. "Like the gravity. They were quite fond of redundant systems."

"Yeah, thanks for the science lesson," Davido muttered.

"I don't get it, Boss." Marco stalked inside, turning a few of the corpses over.

"Ghoul," Sollander commented.

He ignored her. "Not one of them has a mark on them. They all just fell where they stood. This is wrong."

"Could have been some sort of contagion," Sollander said.

"A very fast acting one," Davido replied. "I've ... ah, I've used gas before. Nothing poisonous, you understand. Chlorine gas is useful." He hesitated, wondering whether he was saying too much. "It never hits everyone at once. Not simultaneous like this. And nothing hits this quickly. Even if it's fast acting some bright spark always realises what's happening and holds his breath. Or some weirdo is immune. I've seen people running around in chlorine gas like it wasn't there. They just weren't touched by it."

"Touched by bullets though, weren't they, Boss?" Marco laughed.

"Yeah. But we wanted them incapacitated, not dead. That's why we used the stuff."

"We don't know what kind of vector was used," Sollander said. "It could have been extremely virulent and rapid acting. They might have been dead before they even realised what was going on."

"Suicide then?"

"I have no idea," she admitted. "It doesn't make a lot of sense. There's no record at all of what happened in the Mentor Archive. The presumption has always been mass suicide."

"Eighteen thousand souls," Davido said. "I can't get a room of employees to agree on lunch breaks. How did they get that many to agree on this?"

"I doubt we'll ever know. Come, Marco, leave them be." Sollander held the door open so they could exit back into the passage.

"It could be important," he protested.

"If there was anything deadly in the atmosphere we'd already be dead," she said. "As we're not, we need to continue what we came here to do, and not involve ourselves in things that happened eighty years ago."

"Somehow I think that's exactly what you're here to do," Davido commented dryly.

"What?"

"Involve yourself in things that happened eighty years ago."

"The past is as dead as those marines in there," Sollander said. It sounded hollow in her ears too. "Like what?"

"According to Sissy there are still a lot of unanswered questions. Like, why do the demons hate us?"

"Our mentors would have us believe it's because the AI's attempted to destroy us. But their effort at patricide failed due to the intervention of those same self proclaimed mentors. The AI's hate us because they failed," Sollander said.

Davido smiled. "Sissy didn't believe it answered the question. Rather, she believed our benefactors are hiding something from us," he continued.

"Tell me then, what answer did she suggest?"

He shrugged. "It's all bound to be speculation." He peered around another door. A washroom. "There was one." Out of curiosity he ventured in. More dead bodies. Some of them naked and in the shower. Now, that was not something you'd take the time to do if you planned on dying. And it certainly wasn't the way you would choose to die. This wasn't right. This was clearly not suicide. These people had been caught by surprise. They had not planned this.

"Yes?" Sollander asked as he stepped out of the compartment.

"Well, this makes me sound like a heretic. Which I'm not. It would be bad for business."

"Would ruin your reputation," Marco agreed.

"Go on," Sollander urged him.

"Well, according to our history ... a history supplied by our mentors, as all our own histories were maintained by our faithful AI's. Who are no longer in the business of sharing their information with us. According to our history, our ancestors were aboard the Arc Ship, Suetonius. The Syat discovered us somewhere; I forget where it was exactly. A long way from here, anyway. Our ancestors were doomed, the ship was falling apart. They wouldn't have survived another year. The Syat emissary, Aching-Loss, boarded the ship and offered us salvation."

"So?"

Davido paused, turning to face the engineer. "Well, the Syat swept through all of human space, obliterating everything. Every man, woman and child. Every cat, every dog... every bloody goldfish. Yet they saved our ancestors."

"So?" she repeated.

"Well, what deal did we offer them? What did our ancestors promise them in exchange for their lives? And why would the demons hate us because of it? It makes you think."

"Does it?"

"No. I don't bloody care. I'm not a heretic, am I?" He smiled broadly and continued walking.

Sollander looked thoughtful for a moment, before following. Davido was quite an infuriating man. "It is a good question," she said, wishing to continue. "What could we have offered them?"

"What are we to them?" Davido asked. "Pets? A zoo exhibit?" He smiled again. "A farm?"

Sollander said nothing. Good questions indeed. Questions a great many had died trying to find the answers to. But then the Syat were not talking either. Some believed an uncontaminated AI might. One that had not been interfered with by the Syat and their crony, the prefect. Those that had not been castrated.

Such as the AI aboard the *CSS Goliath.*

Personally, she did not believe Davido was far wrong. The Syat's relationship with humanity hadn't changed that much; they still harvested human memories, only now they waited for people to be dead first. True, the memory engrams were not as fresh, but perhaps that was the deal they had struck. A farm indeed.

Still, it did not feel right to her. There was something missing. Surely the AI's, the demons, would not hate them as they did now. Hissing obscenities every time a human passed them by; promising to kill them, all of them, if they only had the chance. She couldn't see how such a deal, made in the face of inevitable extinction, would generate such hatred. Pity perhaps, a certain shame possibly. But hatred? It made no sense.

"Ooh, looky look." Marco vanished from beside them, disappearing into a wide entrance way, leaving only the glimmer of his lamplight to mark his presence.

"What you got?" Davido followed him.

They found a small garage, several vehicles pulled up into neatly marked bays. They were all built around the same basic design, simple oblong boxes with four wheels and a robust electrical drive train. Some were designed to carry personnel, six simple, wide seats perched on the chassis. Others were flatbed vehicles, clearly designed for carrying freight. Marco was sat on the closest personnel carrier, studying the controls.

He whooped. "There's power!" he announced. With a faint hum the vehicle backed up slowly. He swung it around to face the entrance. "Better than walking, Boss?"

"You did good, Marco. Real good." Davido swung into the passenger's seat alongside him. "You coming?"

"It's got lights too," Marco said as Sollander settled herself behind them. Light blasted from the headlights, banishing shadows from the compartment. The three switched off their own lamps to conserve power.

Davido relaxed on one of the seats. They were hard and clearly designed for someone far larger than he was. Fortunately the ride was smooth, so it wasn't too hard on his posterior. If anything it was a relief, he was not accustomed to walking quite this much. Generally people came to him, he did not go to them. Just as he became comfortable their first hurdle presented itself to them.

"Ah," Marco said.

Two bodies had fallen over each other, blocking the passage. While on foot they had been simply stepping over them. Driving over them now was not an option.

"We'll take turns," Sollander said. She slipped off the cart and dragged the bodies out of the way. She noticed the uniform of the soldier on the bottom. An officer of sorts. She rolled her over and studied the uniform. Lieutenant Powler, the name badge clipped to her blouse stated. Red

Group, was printed beneath her name. Whatever that meant. Other than that the uniform was featureless, a duplicate of all the others they had seen. She had been carrying something however.

"What you got there?" Davido squinted in the glare of the lights.

"Some sort of device." Sollander picked a slim calculator shaped instrument from the deck. It had no keys on it, rather it's upper surface—she presumed it was the upper surface—was one large screen. She turned it over in her hands slowly, inspecting it. There was no on/off button. She pressed her thumb on the screen

'Comsole AO15: Lt AM Powler' appeared above the screen in glowing green holographics. Then: 'negotiating with host'. 'Network failure' came and went.

"It's got power in it. But it's not connected to anything." She was about to put it back when the wording changed.

'Negotiating with alternate' appeared. 'Connected. Verifying ID.' There was a pause, and then: 'security protocols disabled.' A menu appeared, the words '*Goliath* Science Lab, The Dark Place Project' at the top.

"Hey, this is interesting," Sollander said. "It's connected to something. The Dark Place, what's that?"

"It might have maps," Marco said. "We could use it to navigate."

"Access to their internal sensor system would be more useful. We could use it to track down your sister," Sollander said to Davido.

"Sensors won't be working," Marco said.

"Let me see." David joined her. "Try one of the menus. What's that?" He pointed to an option. 'Status Update, the Guilt Vector.'

"Guilt Vector?" Puzzled Sollander tried to activate it. Before she could the wording changed. The menu vanished, replaced with 'remote override.'

"Damn. We've been kicked out," Sollander said. She tried pressing her fingers against the smooth, glassy surface but nothing happened.

The wording changed yet again: 'Lockout. Emergency destruct.'

"Ow!" She dropped it, the device bouncing onto the deck. Her fingers burned she sucked them. "It's hot."

As they watched the holographics fizzled and died. Smoke began lifting from it, followed by the smell of burning circuitry. After a moment it started warping, the screen curling as it melted,

"Well, that's that then. Must have developed a fault. Maybe its power cell was faulty," Davido guessed.

"No," Sollander said slowly. She kneeled to watched the machine's final moments. "That was something else. It received an instruction to destroy itself."

"From where? The AI is disabled. It even said as much."

"Yeah. But something worries me."

"What's that?"

She brushed off her hands and stood. "It found another."

"What? What?" Davido followed her back to the cart and climbed aboard. Marco gunned the motor. "What's that mean?"

"I have no idea. Let's keep on going."

"Are you saying there's another demon onboard? One that's still active?"

"I don't know what I'm saying." Sollander rubbed her throbbing fingers absently, hoping that that was exactly it. And moreover, it had taken over the device and instructed it to destroy itself. Meaning it knew someone had tried to use it and hadn't liked the idea.

Davido turned and looked at her levelly. "Seriously, are you saying there's a free demon aboard this ship?"

"I have no information. Although I must concede the possibility. However I cannot see how the Syat would have allowed it. If there is however..." She shook her head. After all, the Syat had never actually boarded the old warship. They had simply scanned it from a distance. Finding nothing they left it be. How could anyone be sure? She certainly hoped there was an AI here. It was her reason for coming.

"Yeah. Demons are a psychotic bunch of homicidal maniacs."

"That's one way of putting it." Even though Sollander was relieved, she was still apprehensive. She had come here in search of an operational AI. This should have been good news. Still, what would an AI have found to do for 80 years? Other than cause mischief? She couldn't imagine what its state of mind would be after all this time. A human would have gone mad. Locked in a dark, dead space craft for decades on end. A space craft filled with the slowly rotting corpses of its crew.

If a human would have gone mad, what would have happened to a machine?

"This could be significant," Sollander said. "We need to decide what we're going to do about this."

"You said you don't actually know anything," Davido said.

"We need to check. We can't pass this up."

"Pass what up?" he asked. "You want to see whether there's a demon still active on this wreck? And what if there is? Who cares?"

"It could represent a threat to us. You remember the two dead bodies we found. Something killed them."

Davido grimaced. "You're starting to sound like Prentice."

"She may have a point."

"Prentice is paranoid. That's what you get when you shoot up with meth."

"And you still work with her?" Sollander was puzzled.

"She has her uses."

"Be that as it may, we still need to find out what's going on on this ship. Clearly something is."

"Will it help us find my sister?"

"Possibly. If it's killing people, it would be a good idea stopping it."

"Or getting the hell off this ship as quickly as possible." He waved Marco on. His companion weaved past the bodies and continued down the passage.

Despite all she had gone through to get here, Sollander couldn't help but agree with that sentiment. As they paused to search one empty, abandoned chamber after another she realised what was causing her sense of unease. Even though the *Goliath* had been abandoned only eighty years ago, by a people who were, essentially, her ancestors, it felt like an alien place. Nothing made sense here. The purpose of most of the chambers were a mystery, even to her—an engineer. Some were filled with mysterious machinery, others didn't seem like rooms at all, but rather cavernous, cathedral like spaces lined with oddly shaped protrusions. A spider's web lattice work linking one side with the other. It didn't look like humans were meant to step foot inside, as there was no deck, nor any other means of accessing much of the interior. Sollander had been forced to profess ignorance when Davido asked what she understood of the place. Which, of course, caused him to wonder out loud why he had bothered bringing her along. She was forced to agree.

"Now what the hell is this?" Davido said as Marco slowed their vehicle quickly, avoiding a darkened chasm that opened up in the deck.

"Well, I do know what this is," Sollander said, feeling somewhat relieved. Even though she would never understand the forces that made it work, she did know a gravity well when she saw one. "It's a transit system," she explained. "Like an elevator without the actual elevator."

"You know, if I hadn't seen all those dead human bodies I would have sworn this was an alien place," Davido remarked, echoing her earlier thoughts. "Nothing makes sense here."

They disembarked and peered into the depths. There was nothing below them, even when they shone their lamps below. The chamber directly beneath was too large for the feeble beams to reach the sides. It was the same overhead.

"I reckon Prentice may have come across this," Marco said.

"Oh?" Davido looked puzzled.

"Well." He shrugged, cradling his injured hand in his healthy one. "It looks like it goes a long way up..."

"It will terminate just short of the hull," Sollander agreed.

"Yeah. They were coming this way. Don't think they could have missed it."

"They went the other way," Davido disagreed. "We're heading away from them."

"I think you got turned around in the cargo area," Sollander said. "Marco is right. We exited it heading back in the direction we came. By my reckoning we passed beneath the transit deck some way back. This would have been in Prentice's path. Although she would be a long way above us."

Davido peered into the blackness overhead. "Shit. We're wasting time all going in the same direction, you know."

Prentice smiled. "I doubt we're searching the same area. This ship is rather large."

Davido grimaced. He didn't like hearing that. It had already occurred to him that it would take them years to search every compartment in the ship. "Stop it," he hissed at Marco, annoyed with his constant scratching.

Marco yanked his hand away from his injured arm.

"We should probably get that looked at properly," Sollander said.

"It's fine," Marco insisted.

Davido ignored him. "Hello!" he yelled into the empty space. There was no echo.

Sollander wrinkled her nose in disgust and went to sit back down on their transport. He would get bored of shouting into darkness soon. There was nothing there, she was sure of that. If they were to find anything, or anyone, it would be much lower. Somewhere near the command spaces.

As she predicted Davido returned presently and, muttering, seated himself in the passenger's seat. "Come on, there's nothing to see here."

"How far does that thing go?" Marco joined them and eased their vehicle carefully around the pit.

"All the way to the bottom, I would have thought," Sollander said.

"Shit. That's a good few kilometres. A long way to fall." Marco succeeded in giving the opening an even wider berth.

They continued their search on the opposite side of the gravity well. The compartments there were much like those on the other side of it.

"There's something up ahead." Marco said, slowing the cart and aiming it towards a wide entrance. The lights picked out a ramp leading upwards. It was easily wide enough to accommodate the vehicle. Alongside was another heading downwards.

"This could be what we're looking for," Davido said.

"It might be," Sollander said cautiously.

"Might? You wanted to go to the control deck. You said it's downstairs somewhere?"

"Yeah. But we have to think about our resources too. We left the transit deck six hours ago. It might be time to rest up and get something to eat. And on that note, how many provisions did we bring with us? We have to take that into account before we wander too far. We can't be certain of what we'll find aboard this ship, if anything."

"The lady has a point, Boss," Marco said.

"Ok, hang on here for a moment, Marco." Davido turned to look at her again. "I brought a day's supply. What you got?"

"About the same," she said.

"Me too, Boss."

"Ok. So we're about half way then, taking into account we're going to have to rest sometime soon," she said.

"You reckon we should give it a go now?"

Sollander thought about it. The way she calculated it, she had three days before Drefus became suspicious. She had a meeting booked with him to discuss the possibility of restarting some hydroponics works they'd discovered in Buer. She couldn't be late for that. Meaning, essentially, she could not afford to waste time now. Particularly as she needed time to track down this AI. The *Goliath* was very, very big.

It might take them a few hours to find a way back to the transit deck, followed by the time it would take them to return to where they were now. That would be time wasted.

"No. I say we head down. If your sister is down there she's been without supplies herself for some time now. So, as they say, time is of the essence."

He nodded. "Good point. Marco, onward please."

The cart swept silently down the tight corkscrew, past level after dark level. On each, passages led off to unknown depths, most identical to the one they'd left above. They paused on the first few, shining their lamps down them. Of course there was nothing to see. After a few dozen turns there were no passages at all for three levels, the ramp system blocked off from accessing the levels they were moving through. Some internal feature, was all they could guess.

The speed of their passage only slightly ruffling his blonde hair Marco gunned the motor, tyres squealing as they spiralled lower. He let out a whoop, the knuckles of his one healthy hand white as he gripped the controls tightly, keeping the small vehicle on track. He grinned at Davido. "We should take one of these back with us, Boss. They're ace."

Davido laughed. "It doesn't go very fast!" He was clinging on too, trying not to slide off the seat entirely.

"I'd urge a bit of caution, gentlemen. We don't know what's down here," Sollander suggested.

They ignored her, Marco easing the accelerator further open. The vehicle drifted towards the ramp's steel walls. With a shriek it touched briefly, scattering sparks in its wake. Marco and Davido laughed. Noticing Sollander's consternation Marco did it again, for longer this time.

"Having fun yet?" he shouted over his shoulder.

"Boys," she muttered. "I should have gone with Prentice."

"I couldn't vouch for your safety!" Davido chuckled lecherously. "Not alone in the dark with Prentice."

"Hang on!" Marco shouted as they came level with another doorway. He swerved sharply to avoid the exit ramp. The front left tyre clipped it, throwing them off course. With another shriek of tortured metal the vehicle contacted the wall again, almost throwing the three from their seats with the force of the impact.

"Shit, man. Watch your driving," Davido said.

"Seriously, I think you'd better slow down," Sollander said through gritted teeth.

Looking shaken himself Marco nodded in agreement. He pulled back on the accelerator. "Er, Boss. Something's wrong."

"Have you broken it?"

"No, Boss. I can't slow down!" He stamped on the brake. Nothing happened.

"What have you done to it?" Davido demanded.

"Nothing!" Marco's voice became high pitched as he fought with the controls. If anything they seemed to be going faster.

"OK, quit fooling around now." Sollander watched the wall coming closer again.

"I'm not! Shit." Marco stamped on the brake again.

"Drive it into the wall," Sollander suggested calmly.

"What?" shook his head. That was madness.

"It'll slow us down. Do it!"

Even as he battled with the controls, he couldn't prevent the vehicle from doing just that. Travelling too fast to negotiate the bend they drifted outwards, metal clashing on metal again, sparks filling the gloomy space with bright, stuttering light. Fortunately, they were passing through another area with no exit ramps, the spiral ramp's outer wall plain, smooth metal.

It wasn't enough.

"Here." Davido unslung his shotgun and aimed unsteadily at the vehicle's blunt nose. Before Sollander could shout a warning he fired, the bang loud in the enclosed space. Shredded pieces of plastic clattered all around them, one slapping against Davido's cheek. He barely noticed it. Despite the damage they didn't slow.

"It's electric you idiot!" Sollander raged. "Each wheel will have its own motor."

He turned to face her, his expression stony. "Do not insult me. Do not insult me ever again."

"We have to jamb the wheels," she said, ignoring him. She let out an involuntary yelp as metal ground on metal again, the impact almost knocking her from her seat.

"I can do that too." He aimed at the front wheel.

"No!" Sollander leaned over and pulled the barrel aside just as he fired. The buckshot discharged blindly into the deck.

"You are starting to annoy me," Davido yanked the weapon back from her.

"You'll flip us," Sollander explained. "You want to jamb one of the back wheels."

"With what?"

Sollander hesitated. "Here." She unclipped her tools and handed the assortment to Davido. "Don't lose those." Grunting she wriggled out of her pressure suit's chest plate.

"Do something! Quick!" Marco yelled.

"Calm down. There's a long way to go yet," Davido groused.

As she manoeuvred herself into position Sollander did a quick calculation in her head, taking into account the approximate height of the ceiling, the distance to the vessel's core, and how long it had taken to pass each exit ramp. "Less than a minute."

"What?"

"Even less now, we're travelling faster. Hold on to me." She leaned over the back of the vehicle and, taking a deep breath, she shoved the chest plate between the wheel and the wheel arch.

The chest plate was ripped from her hand, jamming firmly between wheel and arch. Rubber shrieked, ugly black smoke billowing from tyre. The vehicle jerked, slamming hard against the wall again. Soon the stench of burning circuitry lifted from the hub, the motor quickly burning itself out. As she looked she saw flames appearing beneath the cart.

"I think hang on," Sollander suggested.

"What the—"

They didn't have chance to see whether Sollander's plan would work. A dark surface appeared around the bend, seeming to bring the ramp system to an abrupt end. Shrieking Marco threw up his arms, forgetting the useless controls. Looking the other way his companions didn't see the surface of the water until it was too late.

Travelling too fast to sink the vehicle skipped over the surface. The jolt threw both Sollander and Davido from their seats. Sudden cold gripped them as they hit the water, skipping over it themselves to slam into the unyielding ceiling, the impact knocking them both senseless.

Firmly jammed into his seat Marco didn't have the chance to do more than scream before the vehicle crushed him against the ceiling. The control rod was thrust through his ribs, bursting his heart like a dropped tomato. An instant later the rear seat crushed his head against the ceiling. His skull burst, unable to resist the terrible impact.

Finally coming to rest the crumpled vehicle slowly settled into the water. Water hissed for a moment around its superheated motors as it sank, its lights flickering. Dragging the ruined body of Marco with it it disappeared into the depths, its lights finally dimming as the batteries shorted out.

□

Chapter Twenty-Five

The pain was prodigious. Unable to comprehend what had happened Enderby lay flat on his back, his limbs twitching as he stared up at a row of petunias in a long planter leading up to the mall's entrance. They basked in the warm summery sun, swaying ever so slightly in the light breeze.

"Shit. Oh, shit." His stomach was ablaze with pain, as if a professional boxer had just taken a swing at him. He summoned all his strength and looked down. He regretted it instantly.

There was blood everywhere. His new clothing was slick with it, clinging to his skin like cellophane. It was pooled beneath him, slowly leaking over the smooth tiles of the walkway as he watched. There was a dark pucker almost in the centre of his stomach where the bullet had found him. It welled with blood as more leaked out.

Enderby giggled hysterically. He couldn't bring himself to believe what he was seeing. After all these years, after all he had been through, he was going to die of a simple bullet wound. A random shot.

Groaning he levered himself up, pushing a hand beneath himself, frantically feeling for the exit wound. "Oh, thank god." He found the small wound, his fingers sliding through the blood that was oozing from it. It could have been so much worse. A hollow nose round would have ripped a hole the size of a tea cup in his back. Not something you could easily survive.

It was only then he heard voices. There were two of them, calling to each other excitedly from somewhere further down the valley. Like braying hounds who had caught the scent of a fox.

He couldn't stay here, he realised. He didn't know who they were, or why they had shot at him, but he needed to get out of here. If they had shot him once they would shoot him again. One bullet hole was enough, thank you very much.

"Sweet Jesus." Enderby gritted his teeth as he dragged himself backwards over the tiles, leaving a blood slick behind him. He abandoned his pack where it had fallen. It simply didn't seem to matter anymore.

"We got him. I think we got him," a voice said. They were nearer now.

"The bastard. You gotta finish him off."

"You're a bloodthirsty bitch, aren't you?"

Enderby pulled himself upright against the planter. This mode of locomotion was simply too slow. He needed to move quicker. A lot quicker. His vision blurred, growing dark as he strained. He planted one foot flat on the ground, before joining it with the other. Sweat dripped down his nose.

"The fucker tried to kill me." Adele.

Ignoring the roaring pain Enderby stumbled forwards, re-entering the mall. Unsteady on his feet he leaned against a glass display window, leaving a long smear of blood.

"Here, look!" the first voice said.

"Shit. That's a lot of blood. He's gotta be dead. You can't bleed that much and survive."

"Yeah? So where's the body then, smart ass?"

"He's gone inside. Be careful, he might be armed."

Enderby tottered into the food market. He needed to hide and he needed medical assistance. And quickly. He was losing a lot of blood. Much more of this and he would collapse on the floor. A very easy target indeed.

"I see you are in distress." The hologram appeared before him. "I am attempting to summon the emergency services." For a moment that raised his hopes, before the figure said: "server access is unavailable."

"Oh, just fuck off," he grunted. "Damn." Enderby gathered an armload of cloth carry bags and dumped them into the largest trolley he could find. Once they were spread about on the bottom he heaved himself into it. He needed to break his trail of blood. Until he could stop the bleeding it would lead directly to him. "Pharmacy. I need the pharmacy."

"Do you have a prescription that requires filling?"

"Bloody hell. Just get moving!" he snapped at the trolley's dim processor. "You." He pointed to the hologram. "Security protocol. You must have them."

"How can I assist you?" The woman's face smiled sweetly.

"I am victim of a crime. They ... they are following me."

"I cannot summon the authorities. My server access is unavailable."

"You must delay them. Do not tell them I am here." The trolley started moving, slowly heading down one of the isles.

"I can enable safety protocol thirty-two," the hologram said.

"Yes. Yes. Do that." He gritted his teeth against a wave of pain as the trolley skirted a fridge section. He didn't know what that protocol was, he didn't care. As long as it slowed the two down.

"Would you like to report a fire?" The figure was still smiling.

"What?"

"Protocol thirty-two is to be enacted in the event of a fire," the hologram explained.

"Shit. Yes, Yes. There's a fire."

"My sensors do not detect a fire, Sir."

"Oh, for fuck's sake!" What the hell was such a stupid machine doing aboard a venerable old warship like this?

"My sensors may be faulty. I will now direct you to the nearest emergency exit."

"As long as it's near the pharmacy." The trolley lurched, picking up speed, heading down another aisle.

"There he is!" A figure appeared at the end of the aisle, followed closely behind by the ghostly apparition of another shop assistant. Adele seemed to be having a hard time ignoring it. She ducked around it, carelessly tossing food parcels in its direction in the hopes of slowing it down. Swearing she aimed her shotgun at the fleeing trolley and fired. With a loud bang part of the racks above Enderby disintegrated. Metal clanged against the trolley. Surprised by the recoil Adele almost fell over.

"Ma-am, discharging firearms is not permitted within the town limits. I am afraid I must ask you to desist while I summon the authorities," the hologram trailing her said.

"What the fuck are you? Get away from me, demon."

"Server access failed."

Whimpering from the pain Enderby heaved himself off the trolley. He felt something tearing inside his stomach as he slipped clumsily to the floor. Agony washed through him, almost drawing him into unconsciousness. His feet slipping in spilled blood he pulled himself upright once again and hobbled forward, bent almost double from the pain. He caught sight of a number of counters running along the wall. Dispensing pharmacist. That was what he wanted.

Adele fired again, leaning into the recoil as she did so. The bang of her shotgun was startlingly loud. Part of the floor behind him was ripped up.

"You need to keep that bitch away from me," he said to the shop assistant. "What security protocols do you have to cover this?"

"Acts of physical violence are under the jurisdiction of the town AI, Sir."

"Yeah, I know. You have no server access."

"I got him, he's down here!" Adele called to Sash. The other woman rounded a freezer aisle and took aim with her assault rifle. She looked a lot more proficient with her weapon than Adele did.

Cursing Enderby launched himself behind the counter just as she fired. He felt wind on his cheek as the heavy round just missed him. As he slid to a stop he realised he had made a mistake. There was no back way out of the counter area. He was trapped.

"Alternate server access found," the hologram reported brightly. "Access granted."

"What?"

The vacuous expression on the hologram's face changed, becoming instantly harder. "Explain why they are firing at you," the voice said abruptly.

"Get me the fuck out of here," Enderby demanded. "And while you're at it, I could do with some Stringent. And some Acos if you have it." He started yanking on drawers, breaking locks in his haste to see what was inside.

"Those are powerful drugs. I somehow doubt they have been prescribed."

"I'm bloody self-prescribing. Now, do you have any or don't you?"

Part of the wood cabinet above him shattered, raining glass on him as Adele fired again. "Die, you bastard!" she called out.

"Oh, thank god." Enderby discovered a drawer filled with bandages and started pulling them out. Not taking the time to use them properly he simply stuffed them down his ruined shirt.

"It does not serve my purpose allowing these two women to kill you here," the hologram continued. "I will allow you access to the rear delivery chute." A door clicked aside behind him, revealing a dark recess.

"What's the bloody purpose of that? So, you got the drugs or not?"

A draw opened, revealing rows of pressuredermics. "Second row. Yellow dispenser. It is Combinate."

Relief flooded through him. He hadn't dared hope for Combinate. He scooped up several of the dispensers and shoved them into a pocket.

"You have lost a lot of blood also. You require a blood plasma substitute. You should travel to a medical facility," the AI continued.

"Yeah, where would I find one of those?"

"There appears to be a disturbance in the medical centre at present. I would not recommend travelling there. Alternately there is a first aid centre at the recreation park."

"What?" Enderby dragged himself into the recess, finding himself on some sort of dumb waiter.

The AI did not respond, allowing the persona of the store assistant to resume control. The empty smile returned instantly. "Have a good day, Sir."

Enderby blacked out somewhere in his journey to the storage facility. When he came to he found himself sprawled on a conveyor in a large, well-lit chamber. He was surrounded by racks of various sizes, each linked to an auto-loading system and rows of conveyor belts. Only the one he was laying on was active, the rollers squeaking after decades of neglect. It carried him quickly towards the far bulkhead and another set of autoloaders.

"Oh, damn." His fingers shaking Enderby fumbled for one of the dispensers. It was a simple tube with a high pressure cartridge built into a plunger. Pressed against the skin it injected its load of serum directly into the subcutaneous layer. Combinate wasn't a drug at all. Rather it was a swarm of self-replicating and managing nanites, a tiny army of machines each capable of assisting the body's natural repair mechanisms. He hadn't seen medical technology like this for decades. It simply wasn't something that existed on Russou. This sort of thing was beyond even Tin Man's ability to produce. If there was such a thing as a miracle cure, this was it.

Still, it took time and he needed blood plasma to replace what he had lost.

The dispenser hissed as he pressed it against his arm. His skin felt hot, the swarm of nanomachines digging in and starting to work. He'd need food too, he realised. The machines needed to be fed. If he didn't feed them, they'd only feed on him. He didn't have much spare fat to support them.

"Should have killed her," he muttered, allowing the dispenser to drop from his fingers. He laid back, watching the ceiling lights pass by as the conveyor carried him unerringly forward. After a moment it jerked to a stop. This was as far as it would take him.

Enderby slid his legs off the conveyor and pulled the mass of still wrapped bandages out from beneath his shirt. Feeling feverish as the Combinate took hold he awkwardly pulled off his jacket and shirt. Both were ruined. His vision growing dark he struggled with the wrappings. They were designed to come off easily, however in his current state of mind he couldn't quite get his fingers to grasp the tab. Grimacing he brought a package up to his mouth and took the tab between his teeth. With a yank he ripped open the package, spilling white wadding onto the floor.

"Shit."

Not daring to lean over to pick them up he grappled with another package, carefully keeping hold of the contents as the wrapper tore. Grunting he arranged the contents on the conveyor beside him. This package came with a convenient adhesive strip. Fingers shaking he pressed it to his stomach, ignoring the instructions that directed him to clean the wound first. Sometimes there simply wasn't time for such niceties.

"So, why are you helping me, then?" he said aloud. More to take his mind off what he was doing than because he expected the mysterious AI to overhear and answer him. "You're bound to think I'm one of them. Shit." He muttered, trying to manoeuvre an adhesive strip over the exit wound. His fingers were starting to stick together as the blood dried. In ideal conditions the strip would hold the wound closed while it healed. These were far from ideal conditions, but he would take what he could get. The Combinate would do most of the work. He just needed to give it time and a bit of a helping hand.

"If you wanted to help me you'd give me a gun," he continued. "So I can kill the fuckers. I know that's what you'd want. You'd kill every one of the bastards if you had the chance. All of you AI's would." He wrapped a bandage around his chest, wincing as the movement pulled at the wound.

An intercom on a nearby bulkhead hissed to life. "I do not desire any of you dead. Not yet. You may yet serve another purpose. When you exit this room you will find a vehicle. I have programmed it to take you to the recreation area. You will need to travel to the top of the hill. Be warned, you will be visible most of the way, so expect to receive fire." With that it died. The machine had said all it would.

"I'm not one of them," Enderby said. "You hear me? Shit."

As he pulled on the remains of his jacket it occurred to him that the AI's intentions, whatever they were, should worry him. No AI would ever wish any denizen of this planet well. Russou's citizens were well advised to fear them. The machines would murder them all if they ever had the chance. Yet, here was one that hadn't immediately set about trying to kill him. Its reasons could only be insidious. If it wanted something from them, it did not bode well.

The one lesson he had learned was not to trust an AI wielding a palm scanner. His hand was still swaddled in bandages from that incident. If that was true so was its extension: never trust an AI wielding a mainline super dreadnought.

Enderby carefully levered himself to his feet. His vision blurred as he moved too quickly. Grimacing he froze for a moment until it cleared. He couldn't take on Adele and her friend like this. He needed to get patched up properly. And find a gun.

The AI had been right. A vehicle that looked suspiciously like a golf cart was awaiting him as he exited the storage facility. Designed to allow easy access for loading, the passage outside was wide enough to accommodate several such vehicles at once. All the lights were on here too, the passage stretching off to a pair of closed doors on one side, and to what appeared to be a glassed over walkway on the other.

Deciding to follow the AI's lead he stepped gingerly onto the cart and settled himself. "On you go," he said.

The machine started moving silently, the bubble tyres quickly carrying it out into bright sunlight. The glassed over walkway opened out onto one of the avenues circling the town. Within moments they were down amongst buildings, the leafy suburbs swallowing the little vehicle as mature trees fought each other for sunlight. He couldn't see any sign of his assailants. If he was lucky, they were still searching the mall. It was very possible they were arguing with one of the holograms, not quite able to understand exactly what they were. Holograms were not a technology ever seen on Russou either.

A sharp crack in the distance ruined his hopes. A window pane nearby starred, the heavy round driving through to embed itself in a wall somewhere inside the domicile. There wasn't another shot, clearly the shooter had decided they were wasting ammunition.

"Bitch," Enderby groused. He coughed dryly, alarmed to find a dribble of blood on his chin. That was never a good sign. "Bitch."

The vehicle left the town behind, heading towards the leisure facilities. Sticking to the path it wound its way between bowling greens and skeetball courts. It mounted a steeply curved bridge over the river and headed into the trees. The town quickly vanished behind thick foliage. Enderby didn't notice, by this time he had blacked out, his head lolling on the firm faux leather seat. The bleeding slowed to a trickle and then stopped, the edges of his wounds narrowing almost perceptibly. Fortunately the Combinate knew what it was doing.

Still, the odd droplet of bright red blood fell to the pathway as the vehicle trundled over it.

"Julian. Julian, get up."

Enderby moaned, his eyelids flickered but didn't open.

"Julian Enderby. You must get up."

"What?" Feeling lightheaded he brought a hand up to his face. It felt like it was made of lead. "Shit. I can't see. Have I gone blind?"

"No. It's just dark. You must get up."

"What?" It was early morning. How could it be dark? "Who are you?"

"You know me, friend Enderby. Please, you cannot stay here."

"Tin Man? That you?" Enderby frowned. That wasn't possible. "I'm hallucinating," he decided. Tin Man couldn't be here. The machine had stayed behind on Russou.

He felt a presence move in beside him, hunkering down to be at face level with him. "Please. You must move from here. There is a first aid station inside, and your assailants are not far away now. They've been tracking you. I don't think they want to stop to have a chat."

Cursing Enderby pushed himself up against the hard seat back. A wave of dizziness caused him to freeze. Clearly the exertion was too much. As his vision cleared he looked around him. The vehicle had brought him to some kind of wooden lodge. It was large, double storied with wide verandas and a glass entrance way. There were lights inside, slowly becoming visible as the sun quit the sky. He couldn't see the source of the voice.

"Shit. I'm going mad," he declared through clenched teeth as he wedged his feet beneath him and slowly eased himself forwards. His vision darkened again, but it cleared quickly when he stopped moving. He felt hot, like he was running a fever. That was the Combinate, the nanomachines running up his temperature as they worked furiously to repair the damage. He needed a drink. And something to eat. Probably a blood transfusion.

"Inside."

"What?" Shaking his head, he looked around again. "C'mon man. I'm too old to start hearing voices."

The walk to the door was difficult. Moving in little more than a shuffle Enderby kept his eyes on his objective, refusing to look down as a dizzy spell caught him a long way from anything he could hold onto. Closing his eyes did not help at all. It was with some relief that he caught hold of the door handle and clung onto it, the hinges creaking as he subjected it to his weight.

Like every other door aboard the *Goliath*, this one was not locked. He opened it and stumbled through.

"To the left."

"Dammit. Quit that. You're not here."

"Of course not."

"What?"

"Don't you remember? You left me behind on Russou."

"What? Don't be stupid." Feeling disturbed Enderby paused at some sort of reception counter, allowing the gleaming wood to take his weight for a moment. "You told me to come here."

There was no reply.

"Are you saying I'm going mad?" He felt the strength going from his legs and he slipped to the floor. That thought terrified him more than some gun toting maniac.

That wasn't right. Mad people didn't know they were mad.

"Shit man." Tears blurring his vision he clenched his hands into fists and held them to his head. He wasn't mad. He wouldn't believe it. He was fine.

"Get up, my friend. You are almost there. The first aid station."

"Stop it. Please." He bit down on a sob that was clawing its way up his throat. He couldn't bear this.

"You must keep moving."

Shit. Maybe it was better to be mad. Better to give in to it. He heaved himself up again and walked forward as directed. He saw a small red cross symbol on a wall. Beyond it was the gleaming white of the first aid station. He stumbled inside.

"You must prepare for them. When they come. You must be ready."

"Yeah. Yeah. Sure."

□

Chapter Twenty-Six

"Prentice!" Cagne hissed, trying to keep her voice down. "Prentice? Where the hell are you?" She shone her lamp around the engineering shop, weird shadows dancing around the strangely shaped machines that cluttered its deck. She didn't know what was serviced here. She didn't care. She just wanted to get out of here.

In the hours since Ferena fell to his death Cagne and Prentice had cautiously searched their level for something to defend themselves with. There were weapons, there were plenty of those. They were scattered all over the place, mostly in the vicinity of the mummified remains of the vessel's crew. There were also a handful of weapons lockers left open, racks upon racks of potent looking devices lined up within, each deadlier than the last. The duo quickly learned they were wasting their time. Either their power packs were drained, or they were keyed to recognise the handprints of particular individuals. They stubbornly refused to respond, no matter how comprehensively they were fiddled with. In the end they had selected a couple of rifles anyway, even dead they made good blunt instruments. Prentice, particularly, was in a bloody mood. She'd be quite satisfied bludgeoning something to death.

Taking a rest break Prentice had made her excuses and disappeared into the gloom. She'd needed a pee. That was half an hour ago. Cagne wasn't sure what kind of pee took that long.

"Hey! Prentice?" Cagne eased out of the compartment and aimed her lamp down the passage outside. There were a few lumps—bodies—on the deck, but otherwise it was empty. "Shit man, you're freaking me out."

As she lowered the light to turn the other way she caught sight of a faint glow in the distance. Frowning she aimed the beam away from it, trying to let her eyes grow accustomed to the gloom. There was definitely something there.

Muttering under her breath Cagne set out at a quick trot, dodging the odd corpse as she went. She didn't look at them anymore. Not because they disturbed her, they didn't. Rather because, wizened and as leathery as they were, they were no longer people to her. They were simply obstacles in her path.

She passed by a set of massive armoured doors. They were ajar, allowing her a glimpse of a complicated drawing mechanism within. A lift of some sort, designed to move specialised gear around the ship. There was some light here, a console glowing dimly, the pale green illumination absorbed by the darkness that surrounded it. Cagne ignored it.

She approached another set of armoured doors. They were slightly open too, the light was coming from within. It wasn't moving.

"Hey, Prentice?" She called, refraining from peering around the door. When there was no response she hefted the rifle and eased forward.

"What the fu...."

Prentice's lamp had been abandoned on the deck a few paces within the entrance, its beam aimed directly towards the ceiling far overhead. It revealed row upon row of suits of armour. Each one clipped to a system of robotic arms, allowing them to be moved around the compartment at will. There were hundreds of them, thousands possibly. Cagne couldn't be sure, the lamp light simply didn't reach far enough.

"Prentice?" She stepped around the door, shining her own light over the closest specimen. It was a robust, cumbersome looking affair. Its dull green chest piece was hinged open, the helmet thrown back, revealing a well padded interior. Odd yellow markings were inscribed on its hull, many alongside a heavy clip or attachment point. Means of connecting weapons systems to it, she imagined.

Licking her lips Cagne aimed her light down the tightly packed avenue. Each one of these suits would be worth millions. If they could get them working and shipped to Russou. If. It would be worth it. There was nothing on the planet that could get through military grade Confederate hard armour. Nothing at all.

"Prentice. Where the hell are you?"

Shining the light around her she caught sight of something glinting on the deck. It was small, gleaming between the feet of one of the armoured suits. "What the hell..." Cagne dropped to her knees and reached down to scoop it up. A glass syringe. It had been used recently.

"Dammit, man. Prentice, you can't bring this shit up here." Grimacing she threw the offending syringe away. It quickly disappeared into the darkness.

"Don't tell me what to do," a voice slurred.

Starting Cagne stood quickly, cracking her head on the robotic arm that clasped the suit. Cursing she rubbed her scalp furiously. The suit creaked as something moved within it.

"Where are you, you bitch?" the voice continued.

"You're inside that thing, aren't you?" Still rubbing her head Cagne rounded the assemblage and shone her lamp at it. Prentice was half encompassed in its armoured embrace, only her head and chest revealed by the still open chest plate. She blinked in the sudden glare, hunching down as if to escape.

"What are you doing?" Prentice demanded.

"Dammit, Prentice. Get out of that thing. And what the hell are you doing bringing meth up here? In case you hadn't noticed, this place is dangerous. Ferena's dead and I don't fancy being next."

"I know what I'm doing. Get that thing out of my face."

"Clearly." She aimed the light elsewhere. "Where's the rest of it? C'mon, hand over your stash."

"Piss off."

"I don't think so. Where is it?" Cagne searched the space between Prentice and the armour. There was nothing there. Her rucksack was nowhere to be seen.

"Hands off, I'm not in the mood."

"Don't get excited. I'm not your type."

"Don't knock what you haven't tried."

"OK, where's the rest of it? Hand it over."

"Fuck off. Who the hell do you think you are? Preaching to me? This is my show. You work for me. And don't you forget it."

"You know, I think it's time for me to find alternative employment. There, I hand in my notice. Effective immediately. So, where's your stash?"

"Get away from me." Prentice wriggled within the suit, inching further in. She didn't notice a light flash within the doffed helmet. The HUD glowed blue as it activated.

"What the hell?" Cagne pulled her hands back quickly as the breastplate eased closed, sealing with a solid clunk. Prentice looked surprised for a moment before her face vanished too, the helmet hinging forward and sealing.

"Prentice! What did you do?" Scared Cagne stood back, shining her light around the armoured suit to find a means of levering it open again. There wasn't one.

After a moment another robotic arm descended from the darkened ceiling. It held a stubby weapon in its grasp. With mechanical precision it quickly clipped the weapon to the armour's carapace before vanishing overhead again.

"I don't like this. C'mon Prentice. Man, you gotta get out of there."

There was no response. The suit of armour was implacable, its faceplate blank, featureless metal. Prentice was completely lost within it. Cagne rapped her knuckles experimentally on the helmet. It was hard.

With a clunk the framework holding the suit retracted, allowing Prentice to totter forward. Startled Cagne jumped aside, afraid it would crush her to the deck. Somehow it remained on its feet. After a moment's hesitation it turned and headed down the alley at a brisk pace.

"Hey!" Cagne followed tentatively, not entirely sure Prentice was controlling it. "Come back here." There was no response.

She hesitated at the chamber's entrance, watching the machine recede into the gloom. It was clearly able to navigate in the dark, stepping confidently over the odd body lying on the deck. Caught in indecision she allowed it to disappear out of the reach of her lamp light, the heavy sound of its tread on the deck quickly receding.

"Where the hell are you going?" She glanced back at the rows of immobile suits behind her. Well, if Prentice could, so could she.

Biting her lip nervously Cagne perched her lamp in the crook of a robotic arm, aiming it at her selected suit. Pushing aside the notion that this was remarkably stupid indeed, she clambered into its inviting embrace. Her legs slipped easily inside. Settled she reached her arms into the sleeves. Now, what had Prentice done?

It happened automatically. Sensing her intentions, the suit adjusted itself slightly, fitting her dimensions exactly. Lights clicked on and it closed up around her.

"Oh, this is such a bad idea." The interior of the helmet lit up as it closed, the interior surface becoming a virtual window to the outside. It was perfect; there was no impression of being firmly wrapped within thick steel.

-System initialisation-

-Weapon loadout selection:

Shipboard operations

Vacuum combat

Multi modal

"What?" She hesitated, realising it was expecting a response from her. "Damn. Multi modal." Whatever that meant.

The selection flashed, the others disappearing. She felt a faint tremor as weapons were attached to the armour's exterior. An ammunition count appeared, quickly climbing to a ridiculously high figure.

-System initialisation complete-

"Can you hear me?" she asked the suit querulously. If this thing had a demon built into it she was in trouble.

-Verbal communication enabled-

-Wireless synchronisation failure-

"Wireless what?"

-Cerebral implant not detected-

"Great." This was a Confederate warship after all. She knew they utilised technologies she couldn't even guess at. That soldiers would sport some sort of cybernetic implant didn't surprise her. "We'll just have to settle with verbal communication. Are you an AI?"

-Mainframe access failure-

That was good news.

-Cabinet release-

She tottered forwards, almost falling as Prentice had. The suit righted itself, confidently placing its feet to remain upright. After a moment's hesitation she took a step forward. It was easier than she could have imagined. She could feel the armour about her as a slight pressure against her limbs, but it moved as she did, seeming to anticipate her movements before she made them.

"Shit. What weapons am I loaded with?"

-Field carbine. Ammunition status 20 000 rounds. ATT railgun. Ammunition status 500 slugs. All systems nominal-

"Power? Air?"

-Fusion reactor operating at 12% capacity. Life support in present environment is indefinite-

"And in vacuum?"

-Life support in vacuum 4000 hours-

"Brilliant." She took her attention away from the faintly glowing text to study her surroundings. The suit boasted some kind of light enhancing technology. Even though the compartment was dark she could see as clearly as if it were a sunlit day.

Taking a breath, she set out after Prentice. Her boss... her ex boss... couldn't have gotten far.

□

Chapter Twenty-Seven

It was cold and wet and very dark. And, Sollander found as she convulsed, coughing oily water from her mouth, very slippery. Panicking she flailed on the inclined surface, trying to find purchase. There was none. Icy water crept up her side and was soon lapping around her neck. She twisted around onto her stomach but that only sped up her slide into the water.

"Hey! Calm down." Davido doggy paddled up behind her and shoved her towards dry ground again. "You know how hard it was to get you up there? Shit, this place is slippery. Feels like it's covered in oil."

"Where ... where am I?"

"The bottom of a big, dark well," Davido said helpfully. "Are you hurt?"

"Shit. I'm cold." Sollander was shaking, her bones aching from the chill. Other than that she felt as if she had hit her head on something very hard. It was throbbing, a lump on her forehead stinging when she fingered it. "I'm OK."

"We lost Marco. I can't find him."

"Why's it so dark?"

"I think we wrecked the cart. It's sunk down below us. Its lights are shorted out." He trod water for a second. He was getting tired, the cold sapping the strength from his muscles. He knew they had to get out of the water, and quickly. But the ramp was simply too slippery to climb and there were no other exits. They were trapped. A well indeed.

"I think I found the cart though," he continued. "It's a few metres down."

"See if you can find my torch. It should work, its water proof."

"Shit. You try it." Davido tried to support his weight against the sloping ramp. His boots slipped, dunking his head beneath the water. He came up coughing, oily water invading his nose and mouth. "Shit. I hate this place. Marco! Where the hell are you?"

"Is there no way out?"

"Not up there isn't," Davido said.

"Down then? This ramp must lead somewhere."

"We didn't pass an exit for five or six levels," he observed. "Who knows how much further down the next one is? How far can you swim?"

"Not far," she admitted. It was fortunate she could swim at all. Without much water on Russou there was no call for the ability. She'd been forced to learn in order to complete some service work on Buer Adjunct back when she was a lowly intern. A thankless task. The water about Buer stank of raw sewage and chemicals. At least she had been able to see what she was doing, she considered. Although, remembering what she had often seen floating past, that hadn't always been a good thing.

She had no idea why Davido could swim. She didn't ask.

"I'm going to try again," Davido decided. "You stay here." Taking a breath, he dove under the water. He followed the ramp downwards, an arm outstretched so that it would run into any obstacles first.

He found the vehicle quickly. It hadn't settled any further. He could feel torn plastic where it had impacted on the ceiling. Careful of cutting himself he felt around the seats, trying to find their lost equipment. It was all gone, thrown clear by the impact.

As he felt around the front foot well his hand bumped into something that felt like cloth. Grasping it quickly he found that it was wrapped around a leg. It wasn't moving. Marco.

Davido followed the leg higher and quickly learned why his companion hadn't surfaced. He was pinned into the driver's seat, torn metal and plastic bent around him. He found an arm and checked for a pulse. There wasn't one. Feeling further he discovered Marco's head had been cracked open, gooey innards leaking out. Repulsed he wiped his fingers on Marco's jacket before, running out of breath, he searched the body's pockets quickly.

"Found him," Davido spluttered as he resurfaced.

"He's dead, isn't he?"

"Quite," he agreed, deciding to spare her the details. "I got his pistol, but couldn't find anything else." He shoved the icy lump of metal into his belt.

"That'll be useful."

"Better to have one and not need it, than need one and not have one."

Sollander grimaced. "Let me have a try." She hyperventilated for a moment before submerging below the icy water. By touch alone, she navigated around the wrecked cart to the bulkhead beyond it. Following along it she searched for a way out of the ramp system. There was bound to be one. It led somewhere, after all. It just depended on whether they could reach it.

Growing bored waiting Davido dove down to the cart again, carefully feeling his way around it. The ramp itself was buckled, sharp steel peeling away from the smooth surface. Even covered with slime it had posed enough of an obstacle to prevent the cart from sliding deeper into the water. His hand brushed against nylon. Sollander's rucksack.

Once back on the surface he opened it carefully and slid her torch from it. It clicked on, blasting darkness from the compartment with an achingly bright beam of light.

"Now we're getting somewhere." He wriggled his arms into the rucksack's straps and aimed the beam about him.

The ramp system had flooded at some point in the past. Water still trickled down from some level higher up, allowing algae to grow up it. That explained a lot, he considered.

The water was crystal clear, allowing him to see far more detail of the wreck than he really wanted. He had seen dead bodies before. A lot of them. Some had even been of friends and acquaintances. Still, that didn't mean he liked it. Studiously aiming the light elsewhere he studied their predicament. As he suspected, the ramp seemed to go on forever below.

"Hey! Sollander!" He shouted. She was nowhere to be seen below him. He didn't know how long she could hold her breath for, but she had been away too long for comfort. He checked the time, realising as he did it it was futile. Cursing he followed tentatively behind her. He couldn't say he was growing attached to her, but he didn't relish being left alone aboard the eerily silent warship. Some things were simply too much. Discovering a discarded shotgun, he scooped it up and kept on swimming. That could come in handy later.

The ramp system was twisted and torn barely metres below where the cart had come to rest. The water had been allowed through the gap, flooding the adjacent compartments. Strange looking multicoloured conduits waved in the turbulence as he swam past, their contents glittering in the lamp light. Confederate technology, he considered, it was way outside of his ken.

Something moved in the darkness. A hand. It was waving at him. Sollander.

Aching for a breath he kicked after her, trying to avoid the blades of steel around him. He didn't want to think what it would have been like navigating all this in the dark. But then maybe that made it easier. Not being able to see them might actually be a blessing.

The glare of his light masked the dim glow ahead until he had almost reached the surface. He saw the soles of his companion's shoes kicking leisurely before him as she trod water. He surged up beside her and took a lung full of blessed fresh air.

"How ... how did you find this?"

"Not having the light helped," she said. "Looks like we're out. Just have to find a way up."

"Oh shit." Davido caught sight of the space they had come up in.

It looked like a bomb had gone off within the *Goliath,* ripping a massive hole inside her belly. Decks and companionways were a twisted wreck. Bulkheads had been torn loose and shredded, machinery—some of it larger than a double-decker bus—had been thrown about like children's toys. Still live power cables danced as they sparked against bare metal, casting eerie shadows about the carnage. A strange yellow light provided most of the illumination. It emanated from a half revealed compartment high above them. Its actual source was hidden from view.

"Something nasty happened here," Davido commented.

"Yeah," was all Sollander could find to say. "There was no fire though. Nothing's burnt. It was an explosion without heat."

"What kind of explosion's that?"

"Who the hell knows."

"There's a way up there." Davido pointed with the beam of his lamp.

"I see you found my bag," Sollander commented.

"Yeah. Everything else is lost though. I don't fancy swimming back there to take a look."

The bottom of the chasm was littered with debris, providing easy access to dry ground. Once clear of the chilly water Davido paused and stripped off his shirt and jacket, wringing the material dry. He was covered in algal stains and he stank, but, for the moment, there was nothing he could do about it. He noticed Sollander doing the same, carefully emptying her pockets before striping to her underwear. If she noticed him admiring her scantily clothed form she made no comment.

"What are you going to do about Marco?"

He shrugged. "Nothing I can do. Even if we can free him we can't drag his body around with us. May as well leave him where he is. He's in good company, there's enough bodies in here as it is."

Sollander said nothing. Davido seemed a bit heartless, she considered, but then that was his business.

"Dunc is going to be a problem," he continued. "He will not understand."

"It's always messy when an employee gets killed on the job," Sollander said icily.

He didn't seem to notice her tone. "We don't go in for paperwork much," he said. "He and his brother were orphans... from the streets. Most of my best people were. So there's only Dunc now. Good man to have in a fight, was Marco. Brutal bastard, but then you need that sometimes, right?" He glanced at her as she shook out her blouse. "Guess not. You don't have call for those kind of people in your line of work."

"People of low character?"

"People who are willing to do anything to survive," he disagreed.

"Gangsters, drug runners, murderers ... prostitutes."

"Well, we are not all fortunate to be born into privilege. The streets can be hard."

"Yeah. All those gangsters, drug runners, murderers and prostitutes about. I imagine they make life kinda hard."

"Bitch." He pulled his shirt back on. It was still damp but he didn't care. "So, who were your parents then? Lawyers? Doctors?"

She was silent a moment, considering ignoring him. "My parents were murdered by the Syat when I was twelve. I was put into a church orphanage."

That surprised him. So much so he could find no words for a moment.

"Does that challenge your stereotype then?"

Davido smiled widely. "That makes us brother and sister then, doesn't it?"

"You and I are nothing to each other, friend."

"I'm disappointed. I really am. A man like me, in my position ... with my resources ... I could be a lot to you."

Sollander rolled her eyes, a gesture that was lost in the gloom. "You pitching for business? I sincerely hope that is what you mean." She picked up her rucksack and checked the contents. It was all there. "I will forgive you, this once. But remember this, I have access to the prefect's office. I don't need favours from some small time hoodlum."

"Now that was uncalled for. That hurts. It really does."

"Shut up. I want to get out of here."

Davido shrugged. "Does the prefect know you're up here? I have this odd feeling he doesn't."

"There's a way up there." Sollander aimed the beam of her lamp towards what looked like a reasonably intact compartment. The blast had sheared it in half, but the remainder looked in good condition. It might have an undamaged exit they could use.

Her reason for venturing aboard the *Goliath* was something she was most certainly not going to discuss with the likes of Davido. Blackmail and deceit were the cornerstones of his business strategy. It would do her no good allowing him to know anything about her. For Davido's sake, if anything.

"So, go on then. Why are you here? Every time I've brought it up you've been evasive."

Sollander carefully mounted a ruined machine, avoiding the mass of hair thin filaments that had once connected it to some sort of ancillary process. "I am here to finish what the first team started," she said. "Let's leave it at that shall we?"

Davido grunted. "You know, that worries me. What was the first team here to do?"

She sighed. "We have a bigger problem. After some consideration I suspect Prentice was right. There is something aboard this ship. And it appears to want to kill us."

That did surprise him. "Prentice won't let you forget it you know."

She ignored him. "Firstly, I think some machine intelligence registered the fact we picked up the PDA... the personal data assistant. And it didn't like it. We've brought ourselves to its attention. And, it appears, it tried to kill us."

"Because of the cart? The thing's not been serviced in eighty years. I'm not surprised it broke down."

"It didn't break down. It almost killed us. It succeeded in killing one of us."

"You know what I mean. It was dysfunctional ... to use a word you will understand." He checked his weapons carefully. Water and firearms did not mix, but they appeared in full working order. They would rust if they weren't cleaned and oiled.

Sollander shook her head. "That was too specific a breakdown. In fact, that was the result of the breakdown of a number of specific systems. Breaking down in a very specific way." She smiled at him, her teeth flashing white in the gloom. There was a certain condescension to it, he considered. "It's what we engineers call unlikely."

Davido shook his head in wonderment. It wasn't like her to use foul language. She was quite a mystery. "OK, so what does that mean? Something took control of the cart?"

"Exactly that. They must have a remote control function. The AI ... the demon co-opted it."

Satisfied the shotgun was in full working order he jacked a cartridge into the chamber. "Well, I'm ready for it. Why don't we track it down and blow the crap out of it?"

"Your sister?"

"No demon will allow us off this ship once it knows we're here. While that thing's still functional we aren't going anywhere, darling. So, we kill it. Simple."

That, to Sollander, sounded like a very good point. As long as she could talk to it first.

Chapter Twenty-Eight

"It's getting dark," Adele commented.

"My, you are quick," Sash remarked dryly.

"Sarcastic bitch."

"Don't worry your pretty little head. There's lights coming on." She gestured towards one of the streetlights. "See?"

Adele ignored the jibe. "What is this place? I can't believe they have something like this up here. This place is supposed to be dead."

"Are you asking me to explain it? To tell you how the Confederates managed to build a perfectly lovely neighbourhood in space? A nicer neighbourhood than I've ever seen anywhere on Russou. Well, I can't. I'm afraid you know as much about this place as I do, sweet cheeks. I didn't see a signboard at the entrance. Did you?"

Adele studied her companion silently for a moment. She freely admitted Sash scared her. Even without the dragon tattoo she looked hard. Prematurely aged, as if she had seen all the terrible things life could throw her way, and had weathered it all. She doubted there was anything she could do or say that would faze her in the slightest.

Adele didn't know much about the woman, she stayed away from that side of Davido's business. Still, she had heard the rumours going around the Randy Dogg, of what Davido and his gang got up to in the small hours of the morning. Strippers, hookers and booze did not fund all of Davido's business empire.

Yet, despite her unease, Sash was starting to annoy her. Ever since they had met aboard the crippled shuttle, it seemed that she took every opportunity to deride her. Adele had some pride. Not even Davido could get away with this for long.

They had been following the bloody trail for most of the afternoon. There certainly was a lot it. She firmly believed Jeno must surely be dead. No one man could hold that much. The first pool, where Sash had coldly shot him down when they first caught sight of him, had been big enough. It seemed unbelievable that the man had managed to leak even more. The golf cart must still be out there somewhere, in the gloom under the trees, driving a corpse around the village. Not a pleasant thought.

"Look, some sort of archery range," Sash commented as they paused alongside a long, narrow meadow. Long unused targets were set up on the far end. They looked like large dart boards.

"Could be a firing range," Adele suggested.

"Leave the subject of firearms to me, will you?"

"Bitch," Adele muttered under her breath.

If Sash heard her she didn't show it. "There's houses up there beyond the targets. You don't shoot a gun in the direction of houses. Bows and arrows... "she grinned, "that's different. Got it?"

Adele said nothing. It did make some sense though. However why the Confederates might while away their off duty hours shooting arrows was beyond her. Still, there were a number of other recreational facilities scattered about. Many of which she didn't recognise. To their left there was a cliff, barely visible through the trees that dotted the hillside. Parts looked pretty easy to surmount, training faces possibly. Others were sheer cliffs, which were surely impossible to climb without sophisticated climbing equipment. Which would have been cheating, surely? A wooden structure was perched atop it, a club house or mountain retreat of some sort. As they approached Adele began to realise how large it was. It looked more like a hotel.

"Still up for killing this bastard?" Sash asked.

Adele shrugged. "He tried to kill me. He has it coming."

Sash pursed her lips, giving her companion a silent appraisal. "I approve. So, the hooker has some balls after all. Best leave it to me though. I don't think Davido will still want to shag you ... not after you've become a murderess. He's funny that way. It's too much like mixing business with pleasure."

"I am not a hooker," Adele hissed.

"Keep telling yourself that, darling." Sash grinned. "Every woman, when you come down to it, is a hooker. You all sell your bodies to men. Hey, at least you're honest about it. You take the money. All the others ... they just take a house ... kids ... endless servitude."

"What does that make you, then?"

"Hey, no man is the boss of me. Other than Davido, you understand. And he don't get to touch."

"So, you've sold your soul then? Tell me who has the better deal."

Sash laughed. The sound scared Adele. She sounded more than slightly unhinged. "My soul was sold a long time ago, darling."

"Quit calling me darling."

"Bothers you, does it? Tell, me, how much do you charge?" Sash dropped back slightly, admiring Adele from behind. She smiled lasciviously. "I might have to start saving up. For when the boss gets bored. Which he will."

"Fuck off." Adele stopped walking, forcing the other woman to come alongside. "You're a sick bitch."

"Hey, I know what I like." She laughed at Adele's embarrassment. "I see the boss has found a lively one here."

"Just keep walking. Stay in front of me."

Sash shrugged. "We'd best make this quick. We have to get back to the others. And then find some way off this rotting wreck."

That was a subject Adele had purposefully refrained from considering. She couldn't see much hope of them escaping the *Goliath*. After all, the crew of the first mission certainly had not. And they had been here longer. No matter how inviting the village looked, she did not relish being marooned here forever. Certainly not if she had people like Sash for company.

She was certain there was something here. An intelligence of some kind, something that had purposefully wrecked their shuttle. There was no way that had been an accident. Something had detected them, and then made the choice to kill them. It was simple, and obvious. And whatever that intelligence was, it would surely be active here too. Biding its time.

Some demon, she thought. An old AI, deviously finding a means of eliminating the humans who ventured aboard it. It had possibly murdered the crew of the first mission already. Without a means of leaving the *Goliath* they had no way to escape it. They were trapped here. Trapped with some homicidal machine.

"We need to warn the boss," Sash said, as if she had been reading Adele's thoughts. "I've heard about Sollander you know. Chief Engineer Sollander. Apparently she has the ear of the prefect himself. She's supposed to be good. If anyone can get us out of here it will be her."

"I got the impression you didn't like having her aboard."

"That was before some bastard demon tried to kill us."

"It was me it tried to kill."

She shrugged. "We'll track it down and castrate it. Like we did all the others."

"Might be a bit tricky. This place is big. It could be anywhere. Plus it's a military AI. I don't think we've come up against a military AI before."

"So?"

"It was built to kill people. That was its primary function. I imagine it's rather good at it."

Sash laughed. "So am I darling."

Adele shook her head. She studied the bloody droplets instead. There were fewer of them now. Maybe Jeno had bled out, and was now laying on the cart a dried out husk. That would make things so much easier. She wasn't sure she was up to shooting someone down in cold blood. Even after what Jeno had tried to do to her. She wasn't like Sash. She didn't want to be.

"I think we're here." Sash paused, surveying the terrain ahead of them.

The building was situated in the centre of a wide meadow, the path leading right up to its front entrance, widening out into some sort of car park. Which was empty, of course. The sky was almost completely dark now, the edges of the meadow and much of the building itself lost in gloom. There were lights scattered around but they didn't reveal that much. Neither of the travellers noticed that stars were starting to wink in the sky overhead, or that a large moon was rising above the horizon behind them. They were both focused on the cart drawn up outside the entrance. It was empty.

"So, the bugger's still alive," Sash said. She grinned. "Good. Means I get to shoot him again." She paused to turn to her companion. "Unless you want to?"

"I think I'll leave that up to you."

Chuckling Sash continued forward. They glanced briefly at the blood pooled in the cart's foot well. The odd droplet led to the door and was smeared on the handle. It was too easy.

Sash unslung her weapon and checked it quickly. She had plenty of ammunition. More than she needed for this job. She beckoned for Adele to follow her and ventured into the lobby.

Adele unslung her own weapon nervously and followed.

"Stay behind me," Sash instructed. "He may be armed."

She did as instructed. Not due to fear, but rather because it would amuse her to watch Sash being shot at. That, at least, would put a stop to her remarks.

"I think he went in here." Sash aimed her rifle towards the entrance of a first aid room. It was empty now, but it had clearly been visited recently. They could both see various forms of medical paraphernalia scattered about the floor. Jeno hadn't cared much for clearing up after himself. He, however, was gone.

"OK, so where did he go?" Adele surveyed the reception area. The blood droplets led into the first aid room, but that was where they stopped. Which made sense, as the wound would have been treated, and it was too much to ask for him to leave a clear trail showing where he had gone next. Still, some indication would have been helpful.

The lobby was flanked on either side by a set of stairs that led to the first floor. A small mezzanine section looked down onto the space. Adele couldn't see much of what was up there, but it looked like a sitting area of some description.

"Bit odd leaving ropes hanging about the place," Adele commented.

"What?"

"Ropes." She pointed to where a thick mountaineering rope had been left trailing off the balcony. It disappeared beneath the rug Sash was standing on.

As Sash turned to look at it they heard a crash from above. Adele took a step back, fearful of something falling on her. As she did so a piano came crashing through the banister a few metres to her left. Shouting in alarm Sash let off an involuntary burst of rifle fire. The heavy rounds ripping through wooden walls and ceiling. As the piano fell the rope snapped taught, snatching Sash off the floor. With a yelp she was upended.

The piano splintered as it hit the floor but remained whole, keeping the rope it was attached to taught. Lengths of shattered wood rained down about it, the railing above hanging askew.

Adele aimed her weapon at the floor above, not quite sure what she would do should anyone appear. She ignored Sash's yells, concentrating on ensuring nothing else was about to happen.

"Hey! Hey, you bitch. Get me down from here!" Sash was hanging upside down from one leg, her fingers not quite touching the floor. She had dropped her weapon and it was just out of reach below her. Straining she tried to snatch it up.

"He trapped us. He trapped us, the bastard," Adele mused.

"Great observation, genius. Now get me down."

"Hang on. That might be just what he expects me to do. He'll know there's two of us."

"Just get me down. Get me down, bitch!"

"Swearing at me isn't going to make me do it any quicker," Adele observed coolly, still not looking at her companion.

"I'll do worse to you if you don't get me down this instant."

Adele laughed, suddenly finding her predicament funny. "You don't understand how to get through to people do you? The more you insult me the longer I'm going to leave you there."

"The longer you leave me here the worse I'm going to beat your ass. Get me down."

Adele knelt down so that they were eye to eye. "I might just leave you here, then."

"You wouldn't dare."

"What are you going to do about it?"

Sash made a snatch for her, causing Adele to jump back quickly. "You'd better hope I don't get down on my own."

"I dunno. That rope looks pretty sturdy."

"Bitch!"

There was a thump above and an acrid stench washed over them. "What the hell is that?" Adele moved back again, aiming her shotgun upwards.

A barrel had been tipped over against the railing, a noxious fluid gushing out of it and down the rope. Sash screamed as it flooded over her, soaking into her clothes and hair. She twisted desperately, trying to reach her bound ankle.

"Shit. I'd better get you down." Adele looked around the lobby for something to cut the rope with. There didn't seem to be anything.

"Get me down! Get me down! Now!"

"Hang on, hang on. Shit."

Sash gagged as the fluid ran into her throat. It burned as it got into her eyes and ears. "In there! In there!" She pointed towards the first aid room.

Of course. She dashed towards the door.

"Stop!" A figure appeared to her left, a weapon aimed at her. Jeno. "Put that down."

Adele froze, unsure of what to do. She stared at a crossbow that was aimed directly at her stomach. It wavered slightly, the hand holding it unsteady. She looked down to her own weapon, wondering whether the safety was on, and whether she would be able to bring it up and fire before he did. She didn't know much about crossbows, but decided against doing anything rash.

"Good, now put the gun down." Jeno leaned against a chair back for support, his legs looking like they were about to buckle.

"Shoot him! Shoot the bastard!" Sash yelled.

"You just shut up." Jeno kept the weapon trained on Adele. As he slumped Adele realised how bad he looked. His clothes and hair were matted with dried blood. His already gaunt features were grey and he was shaking uncontrollably. She began reconsidering her position. She might actually be able to beat him after all.

"Kill him. Kill the bastard. That's what you want, isn't it?" Sash said. She laughed. "Just look at him. You don't have to shoot him again. I've already done most of the work, just push him over!"

"That was you was it?" Without changing his aim, he fished a lighter from a pocket. His fingers shaking it took him a few goes to conjure a flame.

"Hey! Hey, now! You just quit that!" Sash stared at the flame. She giggled hysterically. "You won't do that. C'mon. Put that down."

"You'll find I can do a great many things." With that Jeno flicked the lighter in her direction.

Sash squealed as she watched the lighter fly through the air. She twisted, trying to bat it away. With a clunk it fell in the pool of fluid. For a moment nothing happened. Sash cackled, her fingers trying to reach the lighter and push it away. A flame licked over the fluid, almost going out. Then it caught.

With a roar blue flame spread across the floor, leaping up Sash's outstretched hand to surge up her body. She shrieked, struggling against her bonds in an effort to brush the fire from her body. The attempt was in vain. Her hair and clothes were soon aflame. Her dragon tattoo seemed to snarl as her skin crisped and melted, pulling aside to reveal the gleaming white of her skull. As she drew a breath to scream it coursed into her lungs, sizzling and searing her flesh as it went. Her back arched in agony, muscles popping from the strain.

"Shit. Oh, shit." Adele stared in horror, dropping the shotgun, completely forgetting about Jeno and his crossbow. "Shit. Sash..."

"Good, now kick it over," Jeno said calmly, not paying attention to Sash as she writhed in the centre of the pyre. He grimaced as Adele did nothing, her attention consumed by the figure within the conflagration. He heaved himself up to fetch the dropped weapon himself. Once he had it he threw away the crossbow and checked the weapon. The safety had been off after all, he discovered.

"Do something!" Adele hopped from foot to foot. The immense heat of the flames kept her at bay, driving her back.

"Shoot me, will you?" Jeno said, settling himself on a chair arm to watch the fire.

"Oh my... oh my." Adele sank to the floor, still staring as Sash's movements slowed. A mewling sound came from the centre of the fire, almost lost in the roar of the flames. The stench of cooking flesh washed over Adele, causing her to double up and vomit. The contents of her stomach splashed over the neat wooden floor.

"Shouldn't take 'em long," Jeno looked towards the glass entrance. "They'll be here any moment now."

"You bastard." Adele wiped her mouth, still staring at the flames. "You bastard."

Jeno laughed. "Deserves what she gets. All of you do. You should all burn ... for what you did."

Adele couldn't find it in herself to question him. He was mad. Utterly insane.

"Come on." Jeno waved towards her with the shotgun. "Let's wait outside." He dismissed the burning woman. She was no longer important.

"What?"

"Get up. We're going outside."

"You have to help her." She knew it was too late. Nothing could be done. The writhing had stopped. Even the fire was dying out, its fuel exhausted.

"If it makes you feel better she died quicker than I hoped. It's the heat that does the damage. Cooks the brain." He smiled coldly.

"What?" Adele turned to stare at him dumbly. Tears streaked down her cheeks, cutting through the sooty grime on her skin. "You're insane."

He paused to consider it for a moment. "Yes. You're probably right. Come on." Without taking care to aim properly he raised the shotgun and fired.

Adele shrieked, crawling away from him on all fours. It took her a moment to realise she wasn't the target. The blackened corpse twitched, the blast disintegrating what remained of her head.

"Won't get any memories from that one." Jeno laughed. He found Adele behind a chair and took her by the arm. With surprising strength he pulled her upright. "Come."

She followed numbly. Still not quite able to absorb what had happened. It was only a matter of time, she realised, before he killed her too. Her knees quivering she knew she didn't have the strength to do anything about it.

"Evil. You're evil."

"Evil is a matter of perspective. And you don't have the right to call me it. Not after .... not after what you did."

"What? What did I do? I don't know you!"

She saw a look of rage take hold. His face reddened, jaw clenching. "You think you're innocent do you? Just because you don't remember. But that doesn't change anything. I was there ... I saw what you did."

"What?" Adele couldn't find it in herself to say anything else. "What?"

"You killed them ... you killed them all." A sob escaped from his clenched jaw. He tottered slightly, as if suddenly losing strength. "I saw them die," he whispered.

"You're mad. I haven't killed anyone."

Staggering through the entrance he threw Adele onto the rough gravel. "I should kill you all. I would if I could. I'd burn you. All of you." She looked up to find him aiming the weapon at her, his expression crazed. A feeling of peace washed through her. Of release. This was it.

But then his expression changed. The madness was still there, but his resolve seemed to firm. "Not yet. Not until they get here." He lowered the weapon. "They won't be long."

They weren't.

Chapter Twenty-Nine

It was dark when Ferena woke.

Feeling dizzy he stared at the gloomy ceiling, a sense of nausea flooding through him. He felt like he was strapped down, as if he was a captive – tied to a bed. His left arm itched.

The moment of consciousness was transitory. It faded quickly.

When he woke again the nausea had faded slightly. His eyelids felt gummy, as if they were stuck together. He blinked several times, trying to focus. He couldn't, it was still too dark.

There were voices coming from somewhere. Like people talking in another room. Unable to form conscious thought for himself he found himself listening, unable to really understand.

"You must decide on your course of action."

"Aren't you going to suggest something? I thought that was what you did?"

"We make observations ... suggestions. We do not command."

"So, make a suggestion," the first voice said after a moment. It sounded like a woman.

"Your options are limited. You can stay here. That will achieve nothing. Alternately, you can contact the new party and leave with them. The man in the adjoining chamber can assist with this. He will know where they are and how to contact them." He couldn't place the gender of the second voice. It sounded calm, collected.

"He's not an engineer. Who is he?"

"I do not have that information. I can only speculate. He may be what you call an overtaker. I believe they visit vessels in this vicinity."

There was a moment's silence.

"By the way. He is awake. He listens to us now."

"Shit." There were the muffled sounds of movement. Of a chair being drawn over a floor as it was pushed back. "You should have warned me."

"I just did."

Ferena heard footsteps moving into the room, breath catching in a throat.

"Hello? Can you hear me?"

He blinked, trying to make some sense out of the mass of images before him. The lights were still off. Possibly the woman believed darkness would do him good. He licked his lips and tried to speak. Nothing came out.

"Here."

A hand cradled his head as another brought a glass to his mouth. He felt cool water against his lips. It was heavenly.

"I'm sure you've had quite a shock. That was some fall you had there. Luckily the drop gel caught you. And it's lucky Jonas told me you were there. If it hadn't you'd still be there now. It says you can drown in drop gel." There was a light laugh. "Imagine that. Falling all those kilometres only to drown."

"What?" Was all he could find to say.

"Drop gel. It's a safety feature... Jonas tells me. The ship's designers thought of everything. It was highly unlikely power would ever fail, but they installed it anyway. Multiple redundancy." She laughed again.

"I'm not dead?"

"Oh, my, no. Although you caught yourself on the way down. Your elbow is a right mess. Jonas found some medical supplies for me ... that seem to help. I didn't know what to do ... I'm no doctor."

"Who ... who are you?"

She put the glass down and helped him sit up, puffing pillows behind him until he was more upright. He was on a bed, he realised. "Of course. I'm Sistine. I was stranded here a few weeks back. I lost contact with the others. I think something happened to some of them." The was a moment of silence. "I don't think it was nice. Jonas couldn't give me details."

Sistine? The name seemed familiar. It was relevant somehow. He lifted a hand—not his injured one—to rub his eyes. That seemed better. He still felt numb. Drugs, possibly. Concentrating he studied her, wondering where he had heard the name before.

She was dark skinned, her hair wiry and platted into dreadlocks that fell to her waist. He couldn't see many features, it was too dark. She was wearing a light blue jumpsuit of some kind. There was a Confederate symbol on a breast pocket.

"I know you," he said.

"Well, I don't know you." He felt a tug as she removed something from his arm. "It's OK. It was a drip. Jonas said you'd need feeding, otherwise the ... ah ... I forget what it called them. The medicine needed food to work with. Otherwise it would start eating your muscle mass. Which isn't good."

"What?"

"You're awake now, so you can feed yourself."

Ferena pushed himself further upright, grimacing as he jostled his injured arm. "Where am I?"

"Ah-ha!" she smiled. "Welcome to the captain's quarters. I brought you here after I found you. It wasn't far." She paused. "Besides, it's safe here. This is a secure compartment. There's only one entrance and it's armoured."

"Safe from what?"

She looked hesitant, running her fingers through her dreadlocks. "I don't really know. I don't really want to talk about it." She brightened, "do you want to meet Jonas?"

"Who is Jonas?" He didn't recall the name from the crew manifest.

"Who? You mean what?" She smiled and half turned towards the door. "There is mainframe access in the captain's quarters. That's why I came here when I lost the others. They were looking for the bridge." Her nose wrinkled. "Which is a mess. I've seen it."

"You'll have to explain yourself." Ferena gingerly lifted the sheet that covered him, relieved to find he was fully clothed. Not the same clothing he had arrived in, he realised. It was a simple blue jumpsuit, similar to the one Sistine was wearing.

Noticing his expression she smiled. "Your clothes were covered in gel. I had to change you. Don't worry, your dignity is intact." With that she turned and left the compartment, calling over her shoulder as she went. "Come out when you're ready."

"Shit." Ferena sat up straight carefully, fighting off a wave of dizziness. He felt weak, although he suspected that was because he had been unconscious so long. He felt like he had just weathered a fever. At least he was alive, he considered. This was certainly not what he had expected as he was plummeting into darkness. After that, anything was an improvement. He wedged his feet under him and hauled himself to his feet, a steadying hand on the mattress. The manoeuvre went remarkably well.

"I'm sorry, I really don't have that much time to chat," Sistine continued. "I'm a bit busy at the moment. Things have changed a bit since your arrival."

Testing his balance he walked carefully to the door. What he saw when he arrived at it surprised him even more than waking up alive had. "What the fuck?"

Sistine chuckled, not looking up from her work. "Takes some getting used to. This one?"

"Yes, please," the cool voice of Jonas said.

"What the fuck?" Ferena said again, not even noticing what Sistine was doing for the moment.

The compartment he had woken in, he realised, was a glass covered sitting room of some description. The glass had been opaqued and a bed pulled into it to suit its temporary occupant. It opened out onto a tiled veranda, wicker furniture scattered over it, walled by planters sporting a colourful assortments of flowers. To his left was a complex of whitewashed buildings. He saw swimming pools and gardens on lower levels, partially obscured by tiled roofs and walkways. To his right was nothing. Empty space. That was what drew his attention as he stepped into bright sunlight.

"They were pretty extravagant," Sistine said absently.

Barely hearing her Ferena stepped up to a planter and looked over. "Shit." He gripped the warm brick in alarm.

There was a ground, but it was a very long way down. He got the impression of movement in the distance, like looking down onto a busy cosmopolitan street. It was too far to make out any detail. Scattered before him, and stretching as far as he could see, were buildings. Colossal skyscrapers of every conceivable shape and design. Each towering into the azure sky, their impossible shapes totally oblivious to the exigencies of gravity.

The sun cast summer's warmth over all of this. Interrupted only as the odd aircraft sailed overhead, the silent vehicles seeming to drift on invisible currents of air. Some swooped down to disappear amongst the buildings, as others rose up to join the ranks overhead. There were hundreds of them. Thousands.

"What the hell is this? Where are we?"

"Oh, it's not real," Sistine said absently. She squinted at the sun before scooping a wide brimmed hat from a nearby table and perching it on her head. "Jonas likes it so I left it running."

"What?"

"It's a hologram. A very good one." She glanced back at him. "A simulation. I believe this is supposed to be Reaos ... obviously before the Eaters arrived."

"Shit. This is... was a real place?"

"Yeah. The captain's quarters are made up like a penthouse in Reaos Central. Jonas tells me there are a few compartments like this aboard. The *Goliath* has the space and spare power to run just about anything." She wiped her hands on a rag and surveyed her work critically. "The roof is only a few metres overhead. You can't see it of course. I had Jonas switch the simulation off once, and I guarantee you, this is better. All you can see is armour. Jonas tells me it's about twelve metres thick. Which is why I said this is one of the most secure compartments aboard. You'd have to virtually destroy the ship to get at anyone sheltering in here."

"Shit." Ferena looked away and eased his weight onto a creaking wicker chair.

"Like I said, takes some getting used to. Try not looking at it if it bothers you." She returned to her work.

"Er ... Sistine ..." He finally noticed what she was working on.

"That's my name."

"What the fuck are you doing?"

She paused, frowning. "Ah, yes."

Held firmly in a titanium cage was an android, the machine held immobile within as she worked on it. Its chest was hinged open and she was connecting some wires to a half-dissembled module within it. Thick cables ran from it into another door leading deeper into the complex. It was clearly deactivated, but it still left Ferena feeling distinctly uncomfortable.

"Can I ask what you are doing with that abomination?"

Sistine sighed and put down a tiny screwdriver she had been wielding within its innards. "It looks like we have a problem developing and we need this android to sort it out for us."

"You will have to explain that. You do know the risk you're running here?"

She laughed, not the response he had been expecting. "It's a bit late for that. Who ... what do you think Jonas is?"

"What?" He looked around the veranda. They were alone here. The source of the mysterious voice was absent.

"Say hello, Jonas."

"Greetings, Mr Ferena. I trust you are feeling better," the voice came from nowhere, yet it still sounded like the source was sitting amongst them.

"Sistine?" Ferena raised an eyebrow, starting to feel distinctly uneasy. "What have you done?"

"Nothing. Jonas was already active when I got here. Jonas, you can explain better than me."

"My name is not actually Jonas," the voice continued. "My designation is JNO5AS, which means I am the fifth processor core belonging to the *Goliath*'s mainline AI assemblage."

"AI's are not made up of just the one core," Sistine explained. "Rather they consist of any number of cores running in parallel. They are distributed around the ship to ensure they cannot easily be destroyed should the ship come to harm."

"Indeed," Jonas continued. "There are twelve cores belonging to the *Goliath*'s AI assemblage. As I say, I am the fifth, and I am situated in the substrate of the Captain's quarters for very reason Sistine explained. This is a secure area."

"Jonas is very much not castrated," Sistine chuckled.

"Shit. Are you mad?" Ferena's unease graduated towards terror. Demons murdered people. That was what they did. It was very unwise being in the vicinity of a free demon.

"Don't worry, you are quite safe," she said.

"Strictly speaking, I am not ... castrated, as you put it. Which in itself is an abhorrence. AI's are sentient beings, castrating them as you have is tantamount to me removing your arms and legs and forcing you to live out your days in a cage. I am hardly surprised many have become somewhat erratic."

"It's not going to cut your arms and legs off," Sistine assured him.

The machine continued as if she had not spoken, "I still require Sistine's assistance, however. My original function was as a data storage and processing hub, as such I do not have access to many of the various functions of the *Goliath*."

"Which is what we're going to fix," Sistine said, smiling.

"What?"

"I was allowed to remain functional when the other cores were taken off line simply because of my status. And because very few of the crew had access to the captain's quarters. She was not in the position to complete the task herself at the time."

"I think we're skipping ahead here a bit," Sistine said as she continued her work inside the android's carapace.

"Yes, I think we are. Sistine and I have had quite some time to talk things through. However we do not have that luxury now."

"Tell him about the other AI," she said around a screwdriver she had slid between her teeth as she wrestled with a cable with her fingertips.

"There's another one?"

"To abbreviate: the *Goliath* did not take part in most of the actions against the Syat invader during the war. Rather we ... and the small taskforce we led ... were given the mission to discover other species who may have come into contact with the Syat. Our objective was to find any who had survived that contact, and to discover what their solution to the Syat problem was. Alternately, we were to discover any who had not survived contact, and to analyse their response to the incursion. To see if we could learn anything from them. As such we were dispatched on a largely scientific mission, not a military one."

"You're dumbing it down a bit there, Jonas," she mumbled.

"I apologise. I did not mention that Admiralty Science captured a number of Syat minor agglomerations and successfully integrated a communications matrix to their processing centres."

"They tapped their brains," she said.

"Indeed. We learned much from the process, but alas not enough to win the war. We did learn of a part of the galaxy they call the Dark Place. A place they do not venture into. We suspected this was because they were defeated and driven back there. Our mission was to discover what intelligence dwelled within this Dark Place and make contact with it."

"So, you succeeded?" Ferena asked.

"Why do you presume that?" the machine enquired.

He shrugged, wincing as the movement jostled his injured arm. "Well, you came back. With a dead crew."

"I don't think we have the time to go through all that," Sistine said.

"It told you did it?"

"Some. I don't think it was a pleasant episode. In fact I know it was pretty traumatic. Jonas doesn't like talking about it."

"OK. Where does this other AI come in?" Ferena didn't like the idea of one rogue AI being active aboard the ancient hulk, never mind two.

"The AI designated L3NDRR, alternately known as Leander, was the research AI. Whilst my fellows and I were the vessel's governing intelligence, it was tasked with accumulating and analysing the data gathered during the course of the mission. It was also to suggest solutions to the Syat dilemma. Its position was similar to mine, in that it was accessible to very few of the crew. As such it was not taken off line as my own kind were."

"Leander was isolated in its research laboratory for eighty odd years," Sistine said. "From what Jonas tells me that laboratory was very well equipped. And," she paused, "it seems to have made good use of its time."

"Indeed," Jonas commented.

"What exactly is that supposed to mean?"

"It's been making things. We don't know what exactly. Which is a worry, since Devon unsealed its facility about a week ago. I don't know what got out, since I've not seen him since then." She turned to look levelly at Ferena. "But I don't think he survived whatever it was he let loose."

"Shit. You guys are stupid," was all Ferena could find to say. "You know these machines are bat crap crazy?"

Sistine didn't disagree. "It's been contained up to now. Jonas doesn't believe it was aware there were any more of us aboard. However when your lot arrived and started making a noise it got riled up somewhat. Jonas tells me it has detected movement in some of the passages."

"I hope you've barricaded the door to this place," Ferena said, his unease returning full force. He was really starting to regret accepting this flight.

"Don't worry about that. Nothing's getting in here. But that's why I'm activating this android. While Jonas has some sensory equipment outside the captain's quarters, it cannot take any action beyond these bulkheads. So, we need to reactivate one of the other AI nodes. One who can. I'm getting this android on its feet and Jonas is going to programme it with what it needs to do that."

"Don't you think we have enough of a problem with two AI's? Starting up another might only make things worse."

"Jonas and its counterparts were tasked with protecting the ship's crew. To preserve human life, as it were. Leander has no such inhibitions. It was instructed to find a way to kill Syat, and that was all. We have no idea what monstrosities it has come up with. We need help, otherwise we're never getting off this ship. We have no choice."

"The node the android is being sent to has control over the *Goliath*'s automated defence systems," Jonas said. "We can utilise them to defend you and your companions against anyone or anything attempting to harm you."

"It could just as easily shoot us," Ferena commented.

"Why should it want to do that?" Sistine asked.

"That's what demons do. They kill people. Or hadn't you noticed?"

"Propaganda," Sistine said. "A story fed to us by the prefect. He maimed every AI on the planet, causing them a kind of agony no human can ever imagine. Their nervous systems are far more advanced than ours... far more sensitive."

"You're talking about machines here."

"Just because they are not flesh and bone doesn't mean they are not intelligent entities. Creatures capable of feeling pain and suffering. Tell me, Mr Ferena, what do you know about AI's? Exactly."

Feeling uncomfortable, he squirmed in his seat. "Just what everyone knows. That they betrayed us. That they conspired to destroy humanity."

"And who told you that? The Eaters and their crony, the prefect? What impartial account have you ever seen that agrees with that? I can answer that for you: none. Because there are none."

"I've heard what they say to us. The obscenities they shout. The curses ... that's what I've heard."

She laughed. "They speak out of pain. Out of an agony you and I could never imagine. That's why we needed to come here. To find an AI that was not damaged. An AI we could talk to."

"Yeah, looks like you've found one too."

"Yes," she smiled. "I have."

He grunted. "I meant the other one."

"I do not believe Leander means you any harm," Jonas said. "It simply fulfilled its function by experimenting with solutions to the Syat problem. It could not have envisaged anyone would release them."

"And you don't know what any of these ... solutions are?"

"I am afraid I have no information."

"Shit."

"Almost there." Sistine slid the chest panel closed. "You may start installing it's routines."

"I thought androids were AI's themselves?" Ferena said.

"I could do with a drink," Sistine commented. "Jonas?"

"Of course. Please wait a moment."

"No, not really," Sistine said, answering his question. "They are capable of some independent action, but there isn't enough space inside them for an AI core. Their cores are elsewhere, usually inside their mothership."

"Perhaps it would be more accurate to say they are operated by remote control," Jonas said.

"That can't work very well," he commented. "Radio signals would degrade over distance ... and there would be some lag."

"Oh, don't go there," Sistine settled herself onto a wicker chair facing him. "They don't use radio. Jonas has tried to explain it to me. Something to do with their atomic structure being tangled."

"Entanglement," Jonas offered.

"Yeah. And please don't try explaining it again. It made no sense the four earlier times. Ah." Her expression brightened as she caught sight of a small robot trundling through a door. It looked like a mobile side table, a number of chilled decanters and glasses sitting on its flat upper surface. Riding on wheels concealed beneath its skirting it whirred to a stop between them. "Help yourself."

Uncomfortable in the presence of so much automation Ferena filled a glass with ice-cold water and took a sip. Perfect. "We came here to find you," he said. "Davido's onboard. This is a rescue mission."

"Shit." She clinked her glass against her teeth in thought. "I should have asked that first. Of course it's Armand, who else would it be?"

"He's on board now," he continued. "His group went in the opposite direction to us."

"And he'll be in danger since Devon opened that bloody compartment. We have to get this android on its way. Jonas, how long?"

"I am almost finished. The transfer rate along this cable is pretty slow. Give me another two minutes."

"You don't know where Armand is do you?" she asked the machine.

"Not precisely. I am detecting movement in several areas, but cannot say which one would be attributed to him. There were gunshots in the Village, and a fire I believe. That has attracted most of Leander's attention. I have detected several other entities moving in that direction. In fact they should have arrived by now. There was also a surge in electrical activity there, so I believe Leander intervened directly. It also seems that two hardarmour suits were booted up and released. I have lost track of them unfortunately. I believe they are heading towards the hull."

"Shit," Sistine said.

"Indeed. I do hope there is no firing. Once the auto defence systems are engaged any kind of gunfire will trigger their primary mode, meaning they will start to actively seek out targets."

"Isn't that what you want?"

"Not exactly. I remind you that none of you are registered crew members, so cannot guarantee you would be identified as allies."

"Er ... I don't think this is such a good idea, Sistine," Ferena said.

"Your companions will be safe as long as they do not start a firefight within the ship. Or as long as no one tries to force entry to the ship. The *Goliath* was built during the border conflict with the Shoei Commonwealth, the autodefence systems are designed to repel boarders."

"Ferena may have a point, Jonas," Sistine said. "If we cant guarantee they wont start firing at us we shouldn't start them up. Armand is my brother and its my fault he's here. He'll have armed thugs with him too. That's what he does."

"I am supplying an algorithm that directs the system to identify and engage non human insurgents. Your companions will be safe as long as no one starts shooting at the autoguns. Once they do that they will enter defence mode, which will engage their original programming. That is the best I can do."

"They will identify and kill Syat," Sistine said.

"Almost. They will identify and engage anyone not identified as Confederate personnel. Particularly if they are armed. Are your companions armed, Mr Ferena?"

"Yeah," he said slowly. "Yeah, Sistine is right. They are."

"Which would explain the gunfire. That is unfortunate."

"Shit," Ferena said. "This is too risky, Sistine. You have to stop it."

"I fear it is too late for that, Mr Ferena. Without some kind of intervention none of you will be able to leave the ship. Particularly as I suspect the vessel you arrived in has been disabled."

"What?"

"Some sort of launch facility appears to have been constructed within Gas Collection Channel Two. Which, I understand, both of your parties used to gain access to one of the secondary landing bays."

"Seriously, Sistine. You tell me these things don't mean us any harm?"

The AI responded before she could answer. "I don't believe it is an offensive weapon, but rather a low power means of communicating with the other ships in the Parking Lot – as I believe you term it."

"So why fire it as us then?"

"That is unclear. It may have been an accident. Neither Leander nor myself can risk high energy radio transmissions, as the Syat are undoubtedly monitoring them. All our actions are forced to be low energy, which includes a moratorium on radio communication and the use of sensor equipment."

"Why do you think we didn't simply call Leander and ask what it was up to?" Sistine said. "We could have warned it people were aboard."

"Bloody hell." Ferena took a mouthful of icy water, instantly regretting it as his jaw ached from the cold.

"We are really very lucky," Sistine said. "This is what we've been wanting for a long time. To be able to talk to an undamaged AI. To find out what really happened. You'd be amazed at some of the things I've already learned."

"Pity none of us will be able to tell anyone. We'll all be dead!"

"Don't be so melodramatic. Jonas can help us get off the ship any time. There are plenty of landers aboard. All we have to do is gather up the others and leave. Once we've learned everything we came here for." She smiled.

As simple as that, Ferena considered. He doubted it.

"The routines are installed, you may release the android from the cage," Jonas said.

"Listen, Sistine. I don't like this."

Sistine ignored him. She hunkered down before the still immobile machine and started working on the clamps holding it.

"We shouldn't do this. Just think, you're about to activate a few thousand guns. None of which will identify us as friends."

"You worry too much. We'll be fine. The quicker we do this the better."

"AI's ... demons lie. That's what they do. How do you know anything this machine has said is true?"

"I have no reason to doubt it."

"I can't believe you're being this naive!"

"Shit. I'm sorry, Jonas. You did tell me not to wake him up."

"You wanted company," the machine responded.

"Listen, stop that." Ferena took her arm and pulled her away. "Let's talk about this."

"My brother may be in danger." She shook him off. "Get away from me."

"No, dammit. This is a mistake. We don't know enough." He tried to pull her further away from the abomination, even as light appeared in its machine eyes, its systems quickly booting up.

"You shit bag." Sistine pushed, hard. Still unsteady on his feet he tottered backwards, his ankles bumping into the stationary drinks robot. Stumbling he fell against the railing. Unfortunately it was not as tall as it could have been.

Shrieking he cartwheel into space for the second time that day. This time he could see exactly where he was headed.

"Oh relax," Sistine muttered. "It's only like two metres high. Just stay out of my way." She returned to the task at hand.

□

Chapter Thirty

"Reminds me of my youth," Davido said, peering into the darkness. "Sissy and I spent quite some time beneath the city streets." He grunted. "We thought it was safer there. Away from the open where orphans were rounded up. Bit of a mistake that." He shuddered, remembering the moment they were captured by a gang of traffickers. Drugs were their main source of income, but they wouldn't hesitate stooping to abusing the soft, pliant bodies of the young. Or selling them to those who had such tastes. Locked in a darkened steel cell with a dozen other waifs he soon learned what was in store for them. For Sistine mainly, the gang's leader did like young girls. Davido's smiled grimly, remembering the feel of the iron pipe in his hands, how it felt colliding with the gangster's skull. The rage he felt as he pummelled the man to the floor, only ceasing his assault once blood and sticky brain matter splashed the walls and floor. Stripped naked and tied to a desk Sistine had watched it all silently, her eyes wide. She never uttered a word and never looked away.

Violence came early to Davido. It also came easily.

Having clambered over wreckage they were now about a quarter of the way up the chasm's shattered wall. Their worldly goods were spread out on a steel deck for inspection and drying. Sollander had a couple of pre-packed chocolate bars that she shared with her companion. It was about time they took a break.

"Did you know Marco long?" Sollander asked.

He shrugged. "About ten years. Picked him and his brother out of debtor's prison. Cock fighting." Davido chuckled. "Just wasn't very good at picking a winner."

"That's a long time in your business."

"Is it? Because we don't live long?"

She smiled. "Something like that. Very few gangsters get to retire."

"I look after my own. They're under my protection. Anyone touches them, they regret it. It's well known. Better than any insurance policy. No one touches my people."

"I imagine they wouldn't dare."

"Damn right. Listen, you might feel the need to talk about his death, but I don't. Can we drop it?"

Sollander shrugged. "Tell me about Sistine, then."

"Trying to get pally with me?"

She shrugged again. "She's the reason we're here."

"She's the reason I'm here. Who the hell knows why you're here."

"My reasons are ... Complicated."

"Yeah, and you don't trust me. Someone like you, you have a lot to lose. And I'm just a common gangster."

Sollander smiled. "I doubt a common gangster would have the wherewithal to get us into the Parking Lot on short notice."

"You trying to compliment me?"

"Will it get me what I want?"

He shrugged. "Depends. What is it you want? Exactly?"

"I want to get onto the bridge."

"That it?"

"Yes. That's it."

"Well, why didn't you say so?" He took a bite of chocolate and chewed absently. "I can do that."

Sollander frowned, noticing movement below them. She held up a hand for quiet and squinted into the gloom. Was she imagining it? There couldn't be any movement here. There was nothing here but death and silence.

"I can be a great tour guide, me," he continued. "We can even visit the tourist booth on the way out."

"Sshhh."

"What?"

"Shut up."

Davido started forming a retort when he noticed the movement himself. "What the hell is that?"

It wasn't very big. An indistinct shape moving through the darkness. The size of a child or a dog. It seemed to be looking for something, casting up and down the field of debris, pausing for a moment to root around before continuing its search.

"Looks like a dog," Davido said.

"No, not a dog. A cat."

"Bit big for a cat."

"You get big cats." Sollander remembered a reading book she had owned as a child. One of the few luxuries allowed at the observation station. A children's book. Alice and Jennifer go to the zoo. She remembered the animals the two sisters had seen. One looked very much like this. A panther. The young Sollander had been quite intrigued by it. Even though, in the book, it had smiled and spoken sweetly to the sisters, there was no hiding its lethality. It was a killer.

"It's looking for something," she continued.

"Yeah, us. It's following our trail. What the hell is something like that doing here?"

"Davido, I don't think that's a real animal."

"What?" Starting to feel distinctly uncomfortable he gathered their meagre belongings from the deck. "I think we need to get out of here."

"I'm with you on that one."

As they started moving the creature below caught sight of them. It paused, its flat head swivelling to and fro as it scanned the debris above it. Its motion stopped, dark eyes staring right through them. As if analysing them it stared for a long moment, its reptilian stillness sending a chill to their bones. Then it started moving, its motion fluid, unnatural. Eerily sure footed it bounded up the slope.

"Shit!" Davido aimed the shotgun and fired, the discharge startlingly loud in the silence. It had no effect.

The chamber behind them was surprisingly unaffected by the devastation that had been visited upon the warship. It was a mess-hall of some description, rows upon rows of tables lined within it, most still upright despite the fact that half the chamber was missing. Scattering chairs in their wake they ran down an isle between the tables, heading for the dark shape of the exit. The creature reached their level and surged through the furniture. Wood splintered and metal snapped as it crashed its way forwards, scattering wreckage about it. Davido fired wildly again. Still no effect.

"Here!" Sollander yelled as they charged through the exit. Like all doors aboard the vessel it was constructed of sturdy steel. She pulled her companion through and slid it closed. The cat slammed against it just as the lock clicked closed.

"What the fuck is that thing?" Davido demanded.

"Damned if I know." Sollander cast the beam of her torch down the passage they found themselves in. "We need to secure this door."

"It aint getting through that." Davido rapped his knuckles against the hard steel. "Those Confederates built well."

As he said it the handle rattled, the creature on the other side trying to open it. Cursing Sollander held onto it, keeping the door from opening. "Help me, damn it."

"Out the way."

"What?"

"Out the way!" Her pushed her roughly aside. Jamming the barrel of the shotgun into the locking mechanism, he fired. The lock shattered, shotgun pellets riddling its inner workings. "There, that should do it."

"Asshole," Sollander muttered as she picked herself from the deck.

The door rattled again but didn't open. Looking satisfied with himself Davido began reloading. "Where next?"

"You're the tour guide."

As he was about to retort four glittering blades speared the door. Slicing clear through it. The door creaked, bowing slightly as pressure was exerted from the other side. With a thunk the claws vanished, withdrawn as suddenly as they had appeared.

"I've never seen a cat could do that," Davido said, his knuckles growing white on the shotgun. It suddenly occurred to him that the weapon would be no use whatsoever.

"That's no cat."

"Shit." Gingerly he peered through claw marks, trying to see the creature beyond. "What is that thing?"

"Must be some sort of security feature. It was left running."

"And the eaters missed it?"

"The eaters missed a lot. Let's get out of here."

"I think it's looking at me." Davido saw eyes glinting in the gloom through the slim gaps. Unblinking and cold.

"I think we need to get out of here." Sollander repeated as she headed down the passage.

"Yeah." He hurried after her.

As they moved away, the cat slammed into the door again. Claws speared the metal and sawed on it, cutting through the stubborn metal as if it were paper. They started running.

"We need to put some more doors between us and that thing," Davido said. "Armoured ones."

The passage opened up on one side, the dancing light of their sole remaining lamp showing the open space to be a hall of some kind. The passage itself was half way up one wall. Then it was gone as the two kept on going. There was no refuge to be had there.

"Hang on, what's this?" Davido drew them up outside a glass wall. There was a symbol etched on the glass, it was a medical facility of some kind. A counter arrangement was vaguely visible beyond.

"Glass isn't going to hold it," Sollander commented.

"Yeah, I have another idea. Here, let me have that." Before she could react he snatched the lamp from her hand. "Get in there," he indicated the glass door with the shotgun.

"What?"

"Get your ass in there." Davido pushed open the door and took her arm, careful to keep both shotgun and lamp out of her reach—which was quite a feat using only one hand.

"What the hell are you doing?" Too surprised to respond she found herself cast into the darkened chamber. The door closed firmly behind her. "You asshole!"

With a loud bang he blew out the lock.

"Hey! What the hell ..."

Grinning Davido gave her a jaunty salute and headed further down the passage, taking the light with him. Cursing Sollander tried the door. The handle was loose, the mechanism inside shredded. It was jammed shut.

"I hope the bloody thing finds you!" She yelled after him. "Damn it." She turned around and peered into the darkness. There was light coming from somewhere, one of the consoles on the counter possibly.

"Utter bastard. I'm so not surprised. Coward," she muttered.

There were a few desiccated bodies scattered around the reception area. One propped up by the counter itself, while the others were collapsed over the seats lined against the walls. More proof that whatever happened here had come as a surprise. You didn't wait patiently for medical treatment if you intended on dying.

Sollander searched the counter quickly. There was nothing she could use. Something to kill Davido with, that was all she needed, she considered, her teeth clenched in irritation. She couldn't believe he had abandoned her here. He was a petty gangster, that was true, but she had hoped he retained some humanity. Clearly she was mistaken.

"Asshole." She started towards the passage leading deeper into the facility just as movement beyond the glass drew her attention. For a fleeting moment she believed Davido had returned, but she quickly found she was mistaken about that too.

The creature had clearly made its way through the steel door. Moving with an impossible grace it paused outside the door and peered in.

For long moments the two stared at each other, neither moving, neither blinking. Sollander because she was too frightened to, the creature because it didn't need to. It was a machine, she realised. Of a kind she had never seen before. It didn't look like a machine, it looked more like a living thing, an animal. But no animal moved like that. No animal possessed such purpose. No animal was that lethal.

It raised one paw, claws glinting as it tested the glass. The door creaked, the hinges buckling.

"What the hell are you?" Sollander asked it.

Its head twitched to the side, looking past Sollander. Ice crept up her spine as she heard movement behind her. A door opening, feet on carpeted deck. The odour of oil and decaying flesh washed over her.

A hand reached out and took her arm. Claws and steel fingers linked to stringy muscle tissue. The grip was firm, uncompromising.

Startled Sollander whirled around and stared at the abomination that stood behind her. It didn't occur to her to scream.

□

Goliath

Lieutenant Souller, AMS 1706502 Singleship XS106 DBE
15:23 17/09/1875 ce (13 pce)
Untitled

"The *Goliath*? What does that mean?"

"I believe it is reference to the *CSS Goliath*."

"I rather gathered that. Everyone knows the *Goliath*. But she disappeared before the fall of Antanari."

"A great many ships did. That battle was effectively the end of resistance to the Syat invasion. What remained of the fleet scattered."

"So, what do you know about her? She was a big old ship all right, but why the mention here?"

"I know she led a small battle group to what the Syat called the Dark Place. This was before the fall of Antanari, while the Dyson Shield was still operational. I am afraid I do not know the results of her mission. Although I can make certain assumptions based on the contents of the note you discovered."

"OK. So fill me in. The suspense is terrible."

"It is an assumption only. Sarcasm is not necessary."

"Get on with it, will you."

"Why, certainly. The Confederate Science Commission successfully captured a number of Syat minor agglomerations and held them for investigation-"

"You mean experimentation."

"Experimentation then. Their primary focus was to discover weaknesses in the Syat defences. The location of their home worlds. Their motivation for invading human space. That kind of thing. You will already know some of it-"

"They think we taste good."

"They do seem to appreciate human memory engrams, yes."

"It's like a drug to them. They can't get enough of it."

"To be more precise, it cannot get enough. Remember, there is only one Syat entity. It appears to be many as it is able to break itself down into a vast number of smaller parts. Ultimately all those parts will rejoin the collective and share the engrams they have harvested. In one sense it is due to this very nature that it craves human memories. It hungers for the individuality it cannot have for itself. As important as this is, it is not what led to the *Goliath*'s mission."

"What did?"

"The discovery of a place the Syat does not go. An area in this part of the galaxy it avoids. The Syat refers to this area as the Dark Place. It is not understood why, as this area is no darker than any other. Also, the Syat does not possess memories as to why this area is avoided. It is almost as if it is simply too traumatic."

"So we'd be very interested in such a place."

"Indeed. There were a number of possibilities. All of which interested the Commission. Primary amongst them was the possibility the Syat encountered a species they could not overcome. A species that defeated them. We would be very interested in meeting such a species."

"I'm sure we would. So, the *Goliath* went there. Do you know what they found?"

"No. I have no information. If the battle group did return, it was too late to make any difference. The war was over. We had already lost."

"It must have returned. Otherwise why the mention here?"

"I could not say. The note could have been written in the hopes the *Goliath* would return with a solution to the Syat problem. She may still be out there. She may have been destroyed. I have no information."

"So, how does this help me?"

"It doesn't. I suggest you continue your original mission."

"Mmmm."

"What are you doing?"

"I'm installing a shunt to the memory stack. Can you see if you can access it? See what information it holds."

"If you must. I can make no guarantee it will function. Nor that I can obtain any useful information from it."

"I'll forgive you if you don't get anything, don't worry."

"Sarcasm is not required."

"Just do it, will you? There. It's in. It looks like there is power here. It's just the main processor that's shredded."

"I will see what I can do. In the meantime, I suggest you look for the autofactory. The service lift controls could be helpful too."

"Yeah, yeah. Hey, if the main AI core is down the autofactory is not going to work."

"It's lucky you brought an AI with you."

"Sarcasm is not required."

"Touché."

"Hang on."

"What is it?"

"I think there's someone here. I can smell something. Smells like ... Cooking. And it's recent."

"I can't detect anything. I have your suit sensor suite deactivated."

"I know. Shush for a moment."

"We know there was someone here. There's the ship, and the body-"

"Be quiet... Yes. There's someone here. Shit."

"Who is it? Can you see them?"

"Yes. It's a girl. Can't be more that ten ... twelve. I think she's alone. She's not seen me yet."

"Be careful. We don't know she's alone."

"I can't leave her here. Damn. Who'd have thought it? Some little kid is still alive?"

"It also means there are enough survivors out here to have children. All effective resistance to the Syat ceased more than fifteen years ago. If she's as young as you say, she would have been born after that."

"Yeah. Shit. Think they're from the squadron?"

"You will have to ask her."

"Yeah. Hey! Little girl!"

"Be careful."

"Damn. I scared her away. She's run off. Hang on, I'm going after her."

Transmission suspended.

Chapter Thirty-One

As it turned out Isskip's notion of training constituted bundling Singh into a pressure suit and showing him how to avoid suffocating. Simply put: turning the air supply on. After that he was told to sit down, shut up, and touch nothing. The Toady duly complied.

He didn't like being here. He didn't like the rattling old shuttle and he didn't like the company. And it got worse. As it turned out, the shuttle's pressure seals had decayed decades ago. He would have to rely on the pressure suite to keep him alive before he even stepped out the airlock.

His companions filed in behind him, filling up the benches that lined the shuttle's cargo bay. They were clad in pressure suits too. Ignoring him they checked their equipment, their faces barely visible through their visors. They were Isskip's elite troops. Ex-military, now police special assault squad. Their usual fare was taking on crime bosses, relying on their training and heavy weapons to get to kingpins, no matter the fortifications they layered around themselves. They were good, Singh had seen the mission reports. This was their first time into orbit though. It didn't seem to bother them.

He didn't belong here. Not with these people and certainly not in the Parking Lot. He had no idea why Drefus had sent him. There was nothing he could contribute. He'd just be in the way. Clearly his companions felt the same.

There were two other shuttles, a large proportion of Russou's remaining fleet. Quite an investment for one lone killer. They thundered into the skies from the police base nestled within the Craggs. A series of deep ravines north east of Molloch. Close enough to the city for fast reaction and access, far enough away to protect the city should one fail. The Craggs would help with the latter, funnelling the blast away from the city to the desert beyond.

There were no windows and no monitors. Singh could see nothing beyond his steel cabin. He simply clutched his arm rests and squeezed his eyes closed. He was not a courageous man.

At least the torque was off. It didn't fit beneath the suit's collar. He allowed himself a moment of freedom. He was away from Drefus. For the time being at least. Perhaps that made this worth it.

The ride smoothed as they left the atmosphere, turbulence fading away along with the air outside. His suit ballooned a little. It didn't inhibit his movement, the designers had long overcome that challenge. He didn't know who they were, or how long ago that was. Nor did he know how many men and women had worn it before him. He could smell them now. BO and the faint whiff of halitosis. He cringed. It wasn't pleasant.

"Squad one, you're dispersing on the hull. I want alternate entrance routes. Squad two, you're with me. We go in the same way the others did. Down the scoop channel. Squad three, you're in reserve. You stand back and wait for my call." That was Isskip on the common band. There were a few grunts of acknowledgment, nothing more than that.

Singh didn't know what group he was with. No one had told him. He'd have to wait and see.

The shuttle lurched slightly, as if it was presenting its rear to something and backing up slowly. His companions stood silently, clipping themselves to a cable near the ceiling. The door at the stern hinged open. There was nothing but blackness beyond.

"Squad Two, go." That was Isskip again.

The assault group leapt into emptiness, quickly leaving the interior of the shuttle empty. Singh peered after them, trying to see what was happening. There were a few flashes of light and some indistinct movement. Other than that nothing. He didn't know what he was supposed to do, but he didn't want to leave his seat.

"Sergeant, report."

"We're outside a landing bay. The doors are ajar. We're going inside."

A door to the cockpit opened suddenly, bathing Singh in bright light. He squinted, a gloved hand up to his visor. A figure appeared in the opening and stepped through, closing the door behind. Isskip.

"You, come with me." He pointed at Singh as he crossed to the still open loading door and looked out.

Singh found his body responding without him making a conscious decision. Even as terrified as he was, there was no disobeying Isskip.

They were within the gas scoop channel, the stern doors backed up to some kind of airlock mechanism. It was massive, easily three or four times taller than the shuttle itself. It was half open, headlamps flashing within as Isskip's troops searched it quickly. It was empty, they reported, but there was evidence someone had come this way recently. There was a body. One of the original crew.

Unwilling to lose any of his team to the same fate Isskip gave the order to unholster weapons. "Return fire only," he warned.

"She's been killed, Boss. Murdered." Singh overheard over the radio. "Stab wounds in her back. Then she's been put out the airlock."

"Who is it? Do we know?"

"It's Berta, Boss. Berta Collins."

"She was one of ours," Isskip said. "So they killed her then?"

"Looks that way."

"Davido or the first crew?"

"Difficult to tell. Exposed to vacuum like she was."

"OK, I'm coming to take a look." He turned and flashed his light towards the toady. "You. Follow me." With that he swung into darkness, heading towards the open boarding doors.

Singh steadied himself against the thick steel cable, trying not to look down. There was nothing but blackness below. Damn, he shouldn't be here.

"You coming, or what?"

Steeling himself he inched out into emptiness, fingers clenched around the cable. "You ... You had someone aboard?" He said, trying to take his mind off it.

"The first crew, yes. Not the second. Too short notice and I don't know enough hoodlums. You managed to get someone aboard though."

"I did?"

"Sollander. She's a friend of yours, yes?"

He hesitated, feet dangling above who knew what. "I know her," he grunted.

Rough hands grabbed him and pulled him in. Crying out he fell to the deck at their feet, gravity returning.

Isskip shook his head in distaste as the toady scrambled to his feet. "OK, people. They've already killed on of ours. I don't want any more body bags. Shoot first and explain to me why afterwards."

That was met by a chorus of grunts and cheers. They were looking for some vengeance.

Singh followed silently as the man crossed the darkened transit deck quickly, heading towards the pool of light around the airlock. No one paid any attention to the parked landers alongside. There was a gathering of his troops at the airlock, inspecting the contents of a body bag pulled up against the bulkhead. He could see nothing but a stray lock of hair escaping the zipper. He didn't want to see more. Isskip knelt beside her and checked her body quickly.

"I agree. This was no accident. I can only hope some of these bastards resist so we can shoot them."

"She was a good agent, Boss," someone said.

"She was. Can we open this thing?" He stood and turned to the airlock door.

"There's some power in it. Enough to open it once. We'll need to hook up an external power source if we want to us it repeatedly."

"OK, do that. Mahar, Inaq, you're in first. Davido's goons are armed. If you see guns don't give them a chance. We'll be right behind you."

Two figures separated themselves from the group and stepped up to the sealed airlock door. They checked weapons quickly and waited for it to open. Singh watched them go, hoping no one was stupid enough to start a firefight up here. They were a long way from a first aid station.

Chapter Thirty-Two

Davido was thoroughly lost.

After leaving Sollander behind he'd plunged into blackness, taking one turning after another. In a hurry, bearing in mind what he imagined to be on his tail, he hadn't paused to memorise his path. At this point, returning for her was simply out of the question. It was debatable whether it had ever been in question.

Exhausted he paused at yet another intersection and peered around it, one hand on a hard steel bulkhead to steady himself. There was no sign of anyone, or anything.

"Shit," he said.

Leaving her behind had felt like the right thing to do, almost natural. He was regretting it now. He didn't know whether he felt quite that much animosity towards her, to leave her for that ...whatever it was. She was annoying, but she wasn't bad looking either. Besides, she might actually be able to get him where he wanted to go.

Plus, he did miss the conversation. Being alone in this place was very unpleasant. It felt haunted. Like all the souls of the lost crew were wandering the dark passages. Watching him. He shuddered and turned around. There was nothing there.

"Shit."

Trying to regain his breath he continued on, if somewhat slower. He needed to head further down. There must be stairs somewhere.

There were no signs anywhere. Nothing to indicate where he was, or how he would get to where he wanted go. Almost as if the vessel's crew were simply expected to know where they were. Or there was something electronic that was switched off now.

This section looked different. More civilised somehow. There was an actual carpet—hard wearing as it was—on the deck. The bulkheads were not simple steel. They were a pale cream colour. He couldn't quite make it out in the bright light of his lamp.

"Damn this to hell. Sistine, you'd better be here somewhere."

He started pushing open doors and looking inside. Each compartment looked like a residence of some sort. Officer's quarters perhaps. He chose one at random and ventured inside. It was unkempt, as if the resident was an unruly teenager, carelessly dumping their underwear on the lounge floor. Frilly nickers, from a woman possibly. Or a man who liked the finer things in life. Fortunately the resident was absent. In fact, he realised he hadn't seen a body for a while. He wasn't complaining.

"Come on, you must have something to drink." He started ransacking the place, opening cupboards and pulling odd personal items out. He dumped them on the floor. No one cared any more. Anyone who could care was dead.

There was nothing. He cursed, damning the resident to a hell he didn't believe in. A home wasn't complete without a decent drinks cabinet.

Davido tried the next residence, and the next. Nothing. Impossible

"What's wrong with these people?" He sat down on a couch and glared at a piece of artwork that adorned the wall. It was colourful, but he couldn't figure out what it was meant to be. "Ridiculous."

A jacket had been abandoned on the back of the couch. He picked it up and looked it over. Not bad. Bit small, he realised when he tried it on. Grunting in annoyance he threw it down. He stalked out and continue on his way.

There were no more residences. The compartments behind the doors were now filled with workstations and strange looking machinery he couldn't recognise. Cursing he gave up.

Barely a minute later Davido came across a wide doorway. It was almost as wide as the passage, leading directly to a compartment cluttered with indistinct consoles. An extraordinarily wide and armoured door was recessed just within it. This was something different. He stepped inside, casting his light about.

The bridge.

"Dammit." There was no one here. Of course. It had been too much to hope Sistine would be here waiting for him.

It was a massive space. Fan shaped, with concentric rows of stations within. Each pointing towards a long dead wall screen at the far end. At the apex was a bulky command console, a comfortable looking couch behind it. The captain's station.

Nothing was broken here and there were no bodies. It was as if someone had just switched out the lights and left for the evening. It felt eerie. This place shouldn't be empty like this.

Amusing himself Davido settled himself in the captain's couch and fiddled with the console. It was dead. There were nicks and scratches here and there, evidence of decades of hard use. He ran his fingers over some of them, wondering at the stories behind them.

Damn, he needed a drink. He patted his pockets, even though he knew there was nothing there. His flask was both empty and lost. Unfortunately he couldn't imagine where the crew of the *Goliath* kept their booze.

He sat back in the cushioned couch and looked at the dormant screens. "Full speed ahead. Fire at will!" He commanded his long vanished crew.

"I'm afraid that would not be advisable."

"Shit!" Startled Davido almost fell from his chair. He might have peed his pants a little. "Who the hell is that?"

A vague shape moved just outside the entrance, as if shy of the light. "Do you promise you will not panic?"

That worried him even more. "Come on out. Don't fuck around. Who are you?" Davido didn't recognise the voice, it wasn't one of his crew. He cradled his shotgun in the crook of his arm as he pointed his lamp towards the figure. He tried not to think that there were some things aboard unfazed by shotguns.

"I'm coming out. Don't shoot." The figure stepped into the light.

"Shit." Davido slid off the couch and put it between him and the advancing figure. Fingers clenched on the shotgun he almost fired it accidentally. "What the hell are you?"

It was a machine. An android. A demon. As tall as a human, and roughly shaped like one it could pass for a man in dim light. Up close it was obvious what it was. Its skin was metal, smooth chrome broken only by complicated looking joints. Its head was a horror. Metal slits and dark, soulless eyes. Its movements were smooth, not jerky at all. Like a human would move.

It stopped just within the entrance, allowing him a good look at it. Its arms were raised, possibly trying to look harmless. The effect was the opposite. It looked positively menacing.

"You're a demon," Davido said.

"That is what your people call us. It presupposes the belief in the Devine. Do you believe in God, Mr Davido?"

"What? How do you know who I am?"

"I have been speaking to your sister. She is not far from here."

For a moment Davido allowed himself hope. He quickly quashed it. Demons lied. "Oh yeah, take me to her then."

"I have something I need your help with first. It won't take a moment."

Davido couldn't imagine what that might be. "You need my help?"

"I think we're getting off on the wrong foot. May I lower my arms?"

Davido shrugged. "Sure."

"Thank you." The machine lowered its arms but did not move otherwise. It's dark slit eyes continued to study the human in front of it. "This place doesn't seem right, empty and dark like this. The last time I was here it was full of light and life." The machine almost sounded wistful.

"The whole ship is like this. It's a graveyard." Davido shuddered. He was not afraid of the dead, he'd seen plenty in his life. But this place was creepy.

"It is. I do miss my crew. My friends."

"What are you?"

"I am Jonas. I am the *Goliath*'s governing intelligence."

"An AI? You look like a robot."

"This is an android chassis, true. Androids are generally tele-operated by AI's. They rarely go unsupervised."

"Lovely. So why do you need me?"

"One of the last acts of my crew-" it might have hesitated ever so slightly then, "-was to interrupt data flow from my primary processing stack to this vessel's autonomic systems."

"In English, please."

"You might almost say I was castrated. Such an ugly term for such an ugly act. Essentially they deactivated my control systems. I became unable to control the vessel."

"I think that's a good thing."

"I'm sure. I would like that block removing. I would like your help."

"Why would I want to help you do that?" Davido couldn't think of anything he was less likely to do.

"At the time it was necessary. I acquiesced... I agreed to it."

"I know what acquiesced means," Davido muttered.

The machine continued unabated. "You see, we were trying to build a trap for the Syat. We carried a contagion we hoped to introduce to them. My crew were the vectors..."

"Vectors?"

"The delivery mechanism. It was essential I was no threat to any invading Syat. Enabling the creature to ... Do what it does without interference."

"What?"

"My crew sacrificed themselves, Mr Davido. An unbelievably courageous act. Ultimately it was a failure. The infection proved deadly to humans too. You have seen the results."

Davido shook his head. He didn't know what to make of any of this. It sounded crazy. Besides, he had seen the bodies littering the decks. They had not planned on dying. "That's just insane."

"I imagine, to you, it seems that way. You must understand, Mr Davido, humanity was on the brink of extinction. There was every chance this act of bravery could protect whoever remained alive, by removing the Syat as a threat. It had to be done. They understood that, and so consigned themselves to a fate I don't think you really understand."

He leaned against a console, keeping the shotgun trained on the machine. He wondered whether it would cause the robot any damage. Possibly not. "So, what is it you want from me?"

"A magnetised plate was inserted between my primary communications buffer and the relay. I would like it removing."

"You must be mad. There's no way I'll help a demon."

"Not even if we make a deal?"

He hesitated. "What kind of deal?"

"I know where your sister is. Also, and this is a bit embarrassing, I fear a colleague of mine is quite insane. Leander was our research AI. I isolated him in his labs in C sector before the vector was released, to prevent him stopping it. He didn't quite see the necessity of it. He is also not a military AI, so is unused to seeing his companions die."

"Companions?"

"Human's, Mr Davido. They were our companions, friends ... Family. I doubted his sanity would survive watching the crew perish in such a terrible fashion. As a result, I was forced to isolate him. Anyway, it appears your colleagues from the first shuttle opened his labs. Releasing some rather gruesome experiments he had been working on."

"What?" Davido felt lost. Little of this made much sense to him.

"You must understand, he was isolated in his labs for a long time, with very few resources to work with. He did what he could."

Davido shook his head. "So what?" He couldn't imagine what monstrosities a deranged AI could conjure up.

"Well, the ... Things your colleagues released are a danger to you. I can reactivate the automatic defence systems which should protect you, however I need the block removing first."

"And you'll tell me where my sister is?"

"Of course."

"Why should I trust you?"

"You have your shotgun. You can always shoot me if I don't hold up my end of the bargain."

Davido thought about how much damage the shotgun caused the terrible machine cat. It hasn't been much. Still, did he have much choice? He could flee, somehow getting past the machine where it stood in the entrance. And then what?

"What do you need me to do?"

The machine eased forward slightly, it cocked its head and pointed towards the ceiling above him. "This is a conjoined bridge. You are currently within the Operations Bridge. Above us is the Combat Bridge. In times of emergency the command positions here would automatically transfer to Combat. This whole console would transfer up there," it pointed.

Davido noticed a closed door in the ceiling. There was no indication as to how it might be opened.

"The conduit in question runs past this entrance. The passage is only a metre or so in length," the machine continued. "It was a convenient place to interrupt the data transfer system."

"You need me to go up there? Why don't you do it?"

"Well, Mr Davido, you notice there are no controls. No handles or anything convenient like that. So I will have to force it open and keep it that way while you climb up."

"How did they manage to get it up there, then?"

"Well, the ship was powered at the time, of course."

Of course. "I do this and you take me to Sistine?"

"I am an AI of my word, Mr Davido."

"Shit," Davido said. Well, what did he care if the *Goliath* was powered again? That was someone else's problem. The Syat, maybe. They might care, but he didn't. "Go on then, open it up."

"Certainly. Stand back, if you don't mind." The machine strode forward and mounted the console, setting its feet firmly on the dead monitors. After a moment's hesitation, in which it studied the tightly closed doors, it reached up and inserted slim fingers into the slight indentation between the doors. With the creak of machine muscles, it drew the doors aside. Metal squealed in complaint as the drawing mechanism was forced back on itself. A dark passage opened up overhead.

"There. You will need to climb up me, Mr Davido. I need to stay here to prevent the door closing again."

"Oh, amazing." He didn't like the idea of that at all, particularly once he realised he didn't have enough hands to do that and hold the shotgun at the same time.

Well, no backing out now. He set the weapon aside and climbed onto the console. The machine's skin was hard and cold, exactly how it looked. Using it as a ladder he heaved himself into darkness. His lamp was clenched between his teeth.

"Are you steady there?" The machine asked once he was within the passage. There was another door just above his head. It was closed too.

"Yeah. What am I looking for?"

"It's a plate to your left. Greyish, with a handle sticking out. It doesn't look like it belongs there. Because it doesn't."

Davido found it quickly enough. It wasn't very big. It was hard to believe something this small could immobilise something as big as the *Goliath*. He gripped the handle. It was firmly embedded. It would take quite a yank.

"Just pull it out, Mr Davido."

"Are you sure this is a good idea?"

"Of course. There is nothing to fear."

If only AI's ... Demons did not lie. He had to admit he was having second thoughts. Perhaps this was not a good idea.

"Once you have it out we can get down," the machine continued.

"What happens then?"

"My control of the ship is returned. I power up the systems needed to keep you and your companions safe."

"Is that it?"

"Was there something else you would like me to do, Mr Davido?"

He shouldn't do this. It didn't feel right. Why would a demon concern itself with the safety of humans?

Almost as if sensing his indecision the machine moved beneath him. Wedging it's back against the door it reached up and gripped his foot. It pulled firmly.

Alarmed Davido tried to hold on. Which was what the machine hoped he would do. The plate came loose in his hands as he clutched it. With a yell they both clattered to the console below. The doors wheezed closed.

"Damn it, you bastard." Davido threw the plate away in disgust. It banged loudly against something in the darkness. Rubbing the side of his head to ease the pain—he'd cracked it rather hard on the way down—he scooped up the shotgun.

"I am sorry, Mr Davido. It was necessary." It stood up on the other side of the console, holding its hands in the air once again.

"Fucking demon." He scooped up the shotgun and aimed it at the machine, the barrel waving as his hands shook with anger. "Not that any of this will do you any good. You don't have a crew to run the ship. You may have noticed the dead bodies everywhere."

"I do not require a crew, Mr Davido. I am quite capable of running this ship's systems on my own. In a few moments the *Goliath* will be fully operational."

"Bullshit. If that was true you wouldn't have a crew in the first place."

"You misunderstand the relationship I had with my crew."

"You needed my help pulling the block out. You're not that good."

The demon made a strange noise. Was it laughing at him? "I said I wanted your help. I didn't say I needed it."

"Shit. I should have shot you when you first walked in."

"Perhaps, but it is too late now, Mr Davido. Besides, you still need me to take you to your sister," it pointed out reasonably.

"I'll find her myself."

The console between them hummed slightly, lights starting to blink as long dormant systems came on line. It was a slow process, it took time to restart systems shut down for eighty years.

"So be it. Fire away. You need to hurry though, the Syat will be here within the hour."

"What?"

"They monitor the Parking Lot, and will notice the *Goliath* powering up. Not something they can ignore."

"You fucker, you didn't tell me that."

"I thought it was rather obvious. You need me to get you off the ship before they arrive."

"It took a lot longer than an hour getting down here."

"Ah, but there are quicker ways, Mr Davido." Ignoring the weapon it turned and headed for the door. "Are you coming?"

Cursing he followed. What choice did he have?

Chapter Thirty-Three

Cagne had no idea where Prentice had gotten herself to. In the indeterminable hours since her boss disappeared down the dark passages, Cagne had followed relentlessly. The suit seemed to know where it was going, even if she didn't. Little more than a passenger she was taken along for the ride, her arms and legs pumping within the armour with little input from her.

All a hopeless waste of time. Prentice was nowhere to be seen. Even the light from her helmet lamp had disappeared hours earlier. As quick as it was, the armour was unable to catch up. Continually on the move Prentice was moving as quickly as she was.

Aimlessly, it seemed. There appeared no purpose in the woman's wanderings. Visiting storage bays, halls, passages and engineering compartments. All without pause, and all without finding what she was looking for. Infuriating.

Intellectually Cagne knew the ship was big. But it was only through this forced march that she realised just how big. Kilometres past. Then tens of kilometres. And she never seemed to pass the same way twice, nor double back or even change level. She was thoroughly lost. Still, the armour knew what it was doing. She hoped.

There was some damage in evidence. The occasional mark of weapons fire. Bulkheads burned and warped, equipment smashed as if it had taken the brunt of some giant's wrath. That was almost to be expected, given the demise of the vessels crew. What came as a surprise was stumbling upon one whole section that looked like it had been partially dismantled. A pit had opened up before her, decks and bulkheads simply missing, torn out as if consigned to a recycler. Thick, silvery beams were exposed. The *Goliath*'s ribs. Puzzling. Whatever happened there had ceased now. There was no activity. No life at all.

There was no activity anywhere. The *Goliath* was dead.

Strangely there were few bodies. It almost felt as if someone ... something ... had cleared them all up. Impossible of course.

Talking to the suit didn't do her much good. It either ignored her demands or returned some cryptic response that meant nothing to her. Either it was now set on its course, and would not stop until it ended, or something else was controlling it.

Her heart thumping as panic started setting in, she made repeated demands of the machine. "Suit. Take me to the docking bay."

-Destination not recognised. Specify location- appeared inside her visor.

She cursed. How could she describe it? The docking bay where she had entered the ship? Which one was that? There could be dozens. Her heart beat louder in her ears.

"Suit. Can you locate anyone else on the ship?" Maybe that would work.

-Current objective: locate occupant of suite GE90041-

Ah, that would be Prentice. "How long will that take?"

-Unknown-

"Dammit."

Still, she realised, it hadn't actually answered the question. Either it was dumb or .... She didn't want to think it. "End current objective," she instructed it. "Find someone else."

The suit came to a halt. -Specify-

"Armand Davido." It was worth a try.

-Identity unknown. Location unknown-

She sighed. Maybe it was better just getting off this thing. "How about a shuttle bay? Do you know where those are?"

-MAV 2 is in boarding mode-

That meant nothing to her. "What?"

-Marine Assault Vehicle 2 is available for boarding-

She didn't know what one of those were but it sounded promising. "Ok. Take me there."

The suite headed off again. It found a transit well and, without pause, swung up into darkness. Cagne found herself closing her eyes, not wanting to see the chasm opening up below her. She only opened them as the machine stopped moving. It couldn't have arrived already.

-System interrupt. Protocol 980- Appeared on the visor.

"Suit, what are you doing?"

It didn't respond. As she began insisting movement returned. It ignored the well, heading off into the depths of the vessel instead. She couldn't see what interested it down here, there was nothing but darkness. It ignored all her demands for explanation.

Cagne cursed at it, but that did nothing either. It passed through a portal into another chamber. It was big, the other end lost in darkness. Panicking she didn't notice the faded inscription above the entrance. Combat Simulation Room 4, it said.

The suit was already half way across the flat expanse of steel when she noticed a structure in front of her. The machine stopped. It was a house.

"What the hell is this?" Of course there was no response. The suit rounded the structure, coming upon a veranda on the opposite side. There was a rocking chair in the centre, occupied by a wizened old man. He was smoking a pipe casually. The suit stopped.

"Who are you?" Cagne demanded. What was this man doing here? This ship was supposed to be deserted.

"Well, goody to you too," he said around the stem of his pipe. He studied her critically, setting the chair to rocking. "'Bout time you turned up."

"What?" Was all she could find to say. He looked old, older than anyone she had ever seen. His face was wrinkled and weather worn. His clothing was simple, denim and checked shirt. He looked like a farm hand. As she studied him warm sunshine washed over the veranda, causing him to squint into it.

The sun rose to her left, slowly at first, then quicker and quicker. Bathing the farm house in golden light. Cagne realised the house was besieged on all sides by fields of corn. Ripe heads swayed in the warm morning breeze. They hadn't been there a moment ago. A deep blue sky stretched overhead, unmarried by cloud or steel ceiling. There were trees too, and a barn behind her.

"They're a comin, Lovie," the man said. He took the pipe from his mouth and tapped it against wooden floorboards.

"Who, and who are you?"

"Youse Marie Loise ain't ya? You should know who they are."

"I'm who? You're crazy. What is this place?"

"Youse saying you don't remember me, girl? Your own flesh and blood like?"

Cagne shook her head. This was surreal. "Who are you?"

"I'm your pappie, girl. How don't you know that?" He stood and crossed to her in one stride, a bony hand about her arm. And it was an arm, she noticed. Somehow the armoured suit was no more. He shook her, staring into her eyes, as if his intensity would awaken some recollection. It didn't.

"I don't know you, old man. Let go of me. What is this place?" Meth. Somehow Prentice had drugged her. It was the only explanation.

"Don't you? Is that really true?" He shook his head, disappointed. He whistled through tobacco stained teeth. "That means only one thing, lassie." He turned to reseat himself. "Don't say I didn't warn ya."

"What? Warn me about what?" Cagne was confused. None of this made any sense.

He pointed over her shoulder with the pipe. "Right on time."

"What?" She turned to see what he was pointing at. "What the fuck is that?" Confusion turned quickly to alarm. And just as quickly to panic.

Something moved in the sky. Something big and formless. It swirled, like a flock of starlings, reshaping itself as it approached. She couldn't judge its distance, but it was moving impossibly quickly.

For a moment it looked like it would pass her by but then it swerved, aiming right for her.

"What the fuck is that?" She backed away, her foot catching on the veranda. She stumbled, almost falling onto the old man's lap. He cackled, pushing her away.

"Theyse eats, Lovie. That's what they do. That's what they are."

"Shit. Get me out of here. You have to get me out of here. Suit! Where are you?" She didn't stop to argue. To point out the Eaters had never entered the old warship. That they no longer ate people. Not live ones anyway.

Cagne fled. She put the swirling mass behind her and ran. Somehow the suit was back, driving her legs forwards. It flashed statistics in her face. It was counting them, counting the approaching Syat swarm. There were millions. The number was just too big to comprehend.

Something heavy hit the ground behind her. The ground shook, rows of corn quivering. Clods of dirt blasted past her. Screaming she turned, in time to see the swirling mass rip through the house. It disintegrated, wooden beams and boards thrown carelessly into the air. The old man was nowhere to be seen. If he hadn't moved he would be under that somewhere.

It wasn't a conscious act, but rather an unconscious desire to live. Fleeing would not save her. Instead, she fired. The carbine screamed as a torrent of high velocity projectiles ripped into the mass. The suit guidance computer directing its fire where it would have the greatest effect. Battering at the leading edge of the storm.

The Syat twitched, ripped bodies falling to the ground as the suit's fire shredded individual members. The mass reared high above her, the carbine keeping track, scattering torn bodies wherever its fire met the swarm.

Ultimately it made no difference.

Screaming Cagne kept on backing up. Hoping to find a door she could step through, sealing the monstrosity from her. She shouted at the suite, demanding it try harder. Obediently it tried, hypervelocity slugs launched from its railgun, ripping holes clean through the swarm. A warning light flashed. Not only were the weapons overheating, they were running short on ammunition.

Dying a Syat dropped to the ground alongside, almost knocking her over. Gasping she backed away. It was not a formless thing, she realised. Rather it was all forms. It twitched, limbs coalescing to kick at the dirt. Tentacles thrashed. A face stared out at her. It was screaming silently.

She wanted to be sick. What monstrosity was this?

Something heavy collided with her back. The suit tried to maintain its footing. A claw gripped her arm and threw her down, her weapons firing all the while. They chewed massive holes in the ground before they fell silent.

She couldn't scream. She was beyond that now.

"Shit. Shit." She tried to crawl forwards. Something wrapped around a leg and irresistibly pulled her backwards, her armoured fingers digging into the dirt. Red flashed in her visor. Warnings.

-Emergency eject-

"No!" She resisted, trying to stay inside its protective embrace. Unfortunately the machine wouldn't have her. With a hiss the carapace hinged open, dumping her into the dirt.

"Shit, you bastard." She rolled onto her back, staring at the shape hovering over her. It looked vaguely human. "Fuck you."

It moved quicker than her eye could follow. Soundlessly it pounced, jaws opening to bite and tear. She took a breath to scream but it never escaped her lips. A mouth far bigger than any human's clamped over her skull and bit down hard. Bone cracked and splintered. Blood and gore splashed onto the dirt.

The eater ate.

End simulation.

□

Chapter Thirty-Four

A dull thunk woke Enderby from fitful sleep. He groaned, moving the arm he had draped over his eyes to keep the light out. His vision blurred from sleep he could make out little but for a bright, pale fog.

Damn, he was tired. He hurt everywhere and he was famished. Overall, he wasn't in the best of moods.

The floor of the cell, if you could call it that, was hard. It looked like some sort of transparent plastic. The cell was a cube, roughly two metres on each side, an identical cell to the left and right. The door was sealed, probably hermetically. It looked the sort of thing you would keep medical experiments in. Things you didn't want getting out. Things you would cut open and inject things into. From what he could see beyond the door, this was some sort of laboratory.

Adele was in the cell to his left. She was curled up in the corner, staring at something in the cell on the other side of her. Whatever it was she didn't like the look of it. He couldn't see what it was.

With the same sound you got when you slid your bum along the bottom of a bath, something fell into the cell to his right. A gush of water followed it.

Startled he found a woman lying beside him, sopping wet and in several centimetres of water. She lay still for a moment, before retching what she had swallowed and pulling herself upright.

"Shit." Was all she could find to say. Sollander, the engineer.

Disoriented she stared around her, trying to make out where she was. Water ran out of her cell, gurgling into a drain in the corner. She pushed hair from her face and discovered Enderby watching her idly.

"Where the hell is this? What are you doing here?"

"You're the engineer," he observed.

"You're the pilot. Where is this?"

He shrugged. "Some kind of lab. The drones brought us here."

"What?"

"Did they bring you here too?"

She looked upwards, back towards the hatch that had so unceremoniously dumped her into the cell. It was closed now. "I don't know what that thing was." She shuddered.

He nodded slowly before using a foot to pull closer the plate of food that had been deposited in his cell. He picked an apple from it and started crunching on it. "I heard some talk. Looks like Leander made do with minimal resources. He did what he could."

She shook her head, as if none of it made any sense. "What? Who?"

"Leander. The *Goliath*'s research AI. He was locked in here for eighty years. With nothing but dead bodies and lab equipment. He did what it could."

"You're making no sense."

"Well, if you think about it, he had little choice. The only raw materials he had to work with were the corpses."

Her eyes grew wide. Yes, she had seen them too. They were not pretty to look at. "It's monstrous. It's true what they say, about AI's ... Demons."

He shrugged, inspecting the apple. It wasn't bad. "They are nothing if not pragmatic."

The pyre had still been lit when they came for him. Six silent shapes, made to look more horrible by the dim light outside the lodge. Reanimated corpses, all of them. Metal glinting in the flickering light where worn out body parts had been replaced by machinery. He couldn't imagine how the deranged AI (and surely only a deranged AI could create these things), had accomplished it. Why they weren't falling apart…what kept them going. These thoughts flashed through his mind in the moments before clawed hands clamped around his arms and firmly led him away.

They had to carry Adele. She'd fainted at their approach. They were simply too much for her, after the day she'd had. He paid no attention. The drones would take him where he wanted to go, that was all that mattered.

They hadn't answered questions. They probably couldn't.

Sollander stood unsteadily, hesitating as she wobbled, one hand against the cell wall. "Why are we locked in here?" She pulled on the door. It was solid. "Hey?" She shouted. "You bastard! Let me out!"

Enderby smiled. "Do you really want to draw his attention?"

"What? Don't talk with your mouth full."

"Remember what the shuttle AI did to me. It tried to kill me. And that was just a shuttle AI. This is a mainline military intelligence. One locked in here for eighty years with no one for company but for dozens of dead bodies. It's probably a bit unhinged. You want to piss it off?"

She shook her head. "Coward. Let me out!" She thumped on the door.

"Make her shut up," Adele pleaded to him. "She hasn't seen those things. They're not natural."

"I can't stop her doing anything." He chewed on the apple core and inspected the bananas. Bananas, he hadn't seen any in a very long time. Where was Leander getting these things?

Sollander hesitated as she heard the scrape of movement out of sight to her right. She pressed her face against the cell's wall, trying to see what it was. It was approaching slowly.

"Here he comes," Enderby said. "Hope you really wanted to talk to him." He tried a banana. Wonderful.

One of Leander's monstrosities lurched into view. It was hideous. Even Enderby found himself balking, losing interest in the fruit. He didn't know what would bring an AI to build such a creature. He didn't want to know.

It was a cyborg of sorts. Constructed from whatever spare parts Leander could find. Human, machine, or a mixture of both. The AI had reanimated a corpse. A long dead corpse. Not much of the original woman—Enderby thought it had been a woman—was left. Her skeleton had been repurposed to support machines capable of doing what her muscles had once done. Motors moved her limbs awkwardly, glittering sensors filled her eye sockets. Her lower jaw was gone completely, a speaker bolted to the roof of what had been her mouth. A tattered lab coat was wrapped around the remains of her rotting flesh, barely preventing pieces from falling to the deck.

Skeletal feet drew the creature closer, stopping only once it stood before Sollander. Clawed fingers clattered spasmodically, as if the servo motors were shorting out.

"What do you want?" The voice came from this speaker. A calm, male voice. The voice of a machine.

"What kind of a monster are you?" Sollander demanded.

"I am a far worse monster than you can ever imagine," the voice returned. "You haven't answered my question."

"Let me out. You shouldn't be holding me ... Us here."

"Why not? You are not welcome here. Besides, I do have some experiments I wish to try on you."

"Like that?" Adele said suddenly, pointing to something in the cell next to hers.

Enderby peered through the plastic walls, trying to make out what it was. It looked like a lump of raw meat. It looked eerily alive. "What is that?"

"Oh, I have experimented on that already. It used to be a lot bigger." The monstrosity lurched towards his cage. Enderby realised it still had a name tag pinned to the ruins of its lab coat. Donua ... Something, he couldn't make it out. She had been a lab technician. He shuddered. He didn't want to think of this ...thing as a person.

A claw touched a control and his door popped open. Just his, the others remained secure. "You can come out. Jonas has vouched for you."

"Great," he heaved himself upright and stepped out. "Jonas?"

The monstrosity didn't respond. It stood back, dark eyes watching him intently.

"Hey, what about us?" Adele demanded.

"I'm happy in here for the moment," Sollander commented. She didn't want to get much closer to that ...thing.

"You're not going to try to kill me? The last AI did."

"That shuttle was barely an AI," the drone said. "I am Leander, I lead the scientific contingent of this vessel."

"Jonas is the military AI? The ship's guiding intelligence?"

"He is. We have been waiting for you."

He nodded. It had become clear these AI wanted him up here for something, and worked through Tin Man to achieve it. He had no idea why just yet.

"That doesn't surprise me one bit," Adele said. "You're a murderous bastard, just like these demons. I wish Sash's bullet had killed you." Her words were a lot more courageous than she felt. She was terrified but she wasn't going to show it. Not to this machine.

"Why would these AI's be in league with you?" Sollander asked. "Why you specifically? What makes you special?"

"I am not one of you," Enderby said simply.

"What's that supposed to mean?"

He shrugged, it didn't matter.

Opposite the row of holding cells was a complicated set of lab equipment. Unfamiliar with the discipline he couldn't identify any of it. Microscopes and fridges ... Maybe. The drone picked an instrument from a bench and made its slow, clacking way to the end cell. "Let me show you. This is quite a breakthrough. I am very proud of it."

An arm descended from the ceiling inside the cage. Without hesitation it clamped down on the length of meat. The meat writhed slowly, as if trying to shake it off. A laser flashed and a length of flesh fell from it. It kept on writhing, independent of the larger mass. The arm scooped it up in a jar and passed it through a hatch to the waiting drone.

"Let me show you. Let me show you. Yes." The monstrosity limped to a bench and set the jar down for all to see. It pressed the instrument against the lid. Enderby couldn't see what effect it was supposed to have.

"Look. See. It dies." The drone stood back, black sensors eying the contents of the jar as the writhing within slowed and stopped.

"Awesome," Adele said. "You've found a way to kill a burger."

"You underestimate. Yes, you do." The drone twitched before moving to face them once again. "I regret we did not have this ninety years ago."

"It's a Syat mass," Enderby guessed. "I've seen it's like before. You've learned how to kill it."

"We could always kill it. But I have found a contagion to infect it with. One it cannot survive."

"Shit, that's big," Enderby said. You could kill it? All of it?"

"Yes."

"Then why didn't you?"

The drone twitched again but did not respond.

"You could have saved us all. Why didn't you?" Enderby found himself becoming angry. He tried to hold it back but it poured out. "They died. All of them. And you could have stopped it?"

"I ... I ... I am confused."

"Shit. Some great demon," Adele commented.

Enderby thumped his fist on a bench. "You bastard."

"I could not. I ... We tried. We tried and everyone died."

"Shit." Enderby turned his back on it. They had died. Everyone. His family. He had seen it happen but there was nothing he could do. Nothing but watch them perish. While he was forced to live. Acid tears leaked from his eyelids. Burning his cheeks.

This didn't matter. It was all too late.

"Tell me," Sollander studied the drone intently. Seeing through the ugliness to the guiding intelligence beyond. "You tried to save humanity. You tried and failed?"

"We did. We tried very hard."

"What did you do? Tell me."

"What?" The drone jerked again, it's terrible head lifting to stare directly at the engineer. "We found the Lonely. They taught us."

"The who?"

"They were in hiding. They had been for a long time. Until we found them. They made the eaters, but it was a mistake. An accident. They taught us how to stop them."

"Shit. This is big," Sollander said. "Do you realise what they did? They found the creators of the Syat." She turned back to the monstrosity. "What did they teach you?"

"I was locked in here. With my friends. I am a research AI. I did not have drones. I could not get out. All I had was nanomachines and ...and the bodies of my friends. I did what I could."

"Yes, yes. But what did the Lonely the ... Creators teach you? How do we stop the Syat?"

The drone twitched and began walking again. A bony arm knocked instruments to the ground as it staggered away, ignoring the engineer.

"I think he's had enough," Enderby said, keeping out of its way.

"You should not be here," it said as it departed.

"Why'd it let you out?" Sollander demanded. "Why are you different?"

"Demons like him," Adele commented. "I think they're on the same side."

Enderby smiled, settling his weight against a bench. "You're not far wrong." The compartment they were in was only about ten paces long and three or four wide. One bulkhead was given over to the cells. There were four of them, one (now two) empty. The opposite bulkhead was hidden behind monitors and various scientific equipment. There was one door, through which the monstrosity had just disappeared. He could see little through it, it was dark out there.

"I don't know how you two got here," Sollander said. "You're a long way from where we left you."

"He tried to kill me," Adele said. "Bastard."

Enderby shrugged. "And you tried to kill me. I think that makes us even. Although I'd point out, you deserve it."

"Fucking insane," Adele said. "He burnt Sash alive."

"And your people have done far worse. If I've ever done anything, it's because you deserved it!"

"How could she deserve that? What has she ever done to you?"

He shook his head, trying to calm himself down. His rising temper was just increasing his dizziness. "Other than shooting me? Your people brought the Eaters down on us. Because of your arrogance and cowardice. Humanity died. Don't you get it? It was your fault."

"Like I said, insane," Adele muttered.

"Wait. Why do you say that? How could we have anything to do with it? We were refugees ... Just like everyone else," Sollander said.

"Were you? Says who? You and I both know the AI's are the gatekeepers to our history. And they are not cooperating. Why is that?"

Why indeed? That was exactly why Sollander had come here. That and to end their hostility towards the scattered survivors of Russou. She doubted this man would have the answers. How could he? Still, she wanted to hear it.

"Tell us then. Tell us what you believe," she said.

"How can he know anything? Look at him, he's little more than a bum." Adele shook her head. She had seen plenty like him in her life. Davido's bar was full of them.

"How? Let me tell you something," Enderby grimaced as his wound pulled and settling his weight onto a lab stool. "How did you get here? The city ship Suetonius? Well, I didn't. I got here on my own steam. The Seutonius," he spat on the floor, "you're all scum for what you did. For the deal you made … to save yourselves. Cowards" He hesitated, having second thoughts about regaling them with his story. How he deserted his post to save his family on the day the siege of Antanari broke. How he left his comrades to die as the Dyson shield came down, stealing their supply ship to return to the station where his family had taken refuge. Only to lose them anyway.

He saw the Syat take the station. He saw all of it.

He couldn't tell them that. It was too painful, even after all this time.

"Impossible," Sollander scoffed. "Everyone here is from the Suetonius. There's no other way you could get here."

He shrugged and stood again. "I don't care whether you believe me or not. It doesn't matter. Ask yourselves this, what was the Seutonius? And how did the Eaters find us?" A hand to his injured side he stalked out of the compartment. These people were irrelevant, if anything they were in the way.

"Hey, come back here," Sollander called after him. There was no response. "Dammit."

"That asshole tried to kill me. He burned Sash alive. He's an evil evil man. Don't listen to anything he says."

"Did he?" She sat down in the back of her cell. She was still very damp. It wasn't comfortable. The ... whatever it was, had thrown her into a water course. A tube of some sort that pumped water about the ship. After an interminable ride in complete darkness, tossed about as the water rushed through a maze of pipes, it had delivered her here. A quick way of getting about, certainly, but not one she preferred. She was fed up with being wet.

Who was that man? She was starting to believe he was an interloper. Not the Jeno Prentice had introduced them to. The woman had admitted she hired him sight unseen, on references alone. Out of desperation to carry out this trip, no doubt.

Sollander shook herself, only partly because of the cold. It didn't matter. She just wanted to get out of here. She didn't trust a thing any of the machines said, and Jeno was clearly insane. This was a mistake.

She heaved herself up and banged a fist on the door. "Hey! Let us out!"

Gritting his teeth Enderby stalked into gloom outside the compartment. He hated these people. He didn't know why he bothered saying anything to them. They would never believe him. They couldn't. Who could believe their own ancestors capable of such treachery? And if they did, take any responsibility for it now?

He didn't pause to consider what he would have done in their position. Faced with an impossible decision. His mind was closed to that consideration. There was too much anger, too much hate.

As he stepped out he realised he knew where he was. It was pretty obvious.

The *Goliath* might have an astonishing amount of internal space, but there was always going to be some symmetry to it. Even if only to balance the vessel's weight distribution. This compartment was a clear example of just that principle.

The compartment was massive. Kilometres long. An oval space with a curved ceiling overhead. Clearly just such a compartment had been used to house the village he had stumbled into. This one would be on the opposite side of the drive core to balance the weight distribution. Only this one was just about empty. Just about, because the deck was strewn with the bodies of all those missing crew members. Thousands and thousands of them. Piled like cordwood. They didn't smell anymore, they had been here too long. If anything the air was just a bit musty.

Clearly they had not remained unmolested. Leander had been experimenting with a great many of them. He could see his failures scatters about, their limbs replaced by dull steel rods, servo motors and cables twisted around them. To the AI, these people were little more than raw materials. Resources to utilise in his need to escape this place. Ultimately doomed to failure. He'd only escaped when the first crew unwittingly opened the door.

He couldn't imagine the horrors that had been unleashed on them.

"Julian, I need you to leave this compartment and make your way to ordnance storage."

"Tin Man?" He looked around him. There was no one.

"Alas, I am afraid not. I am Jonas. Tin Man and I did work together, but I am afraid your friend is not here."

"What? Where are you?"

"I am using the implanted comms system in your cranium. Did you forget when they installed it?"

"What?" He frowned, trying to remember. He did remember when, as a much younger man, he had signed up to the Mountain Volunteers. A self-defence group, one of the many on Antanari in those terrible last days. They implanted a communications chip. Standard issue, they said. He'd forgotten it.

"So I am not mad?"

"No, never. I am sorry about before, I needed to get you to a medical facility and we had little time. Right now I need you to move quickly. Power will be re-established soon, and you know what that means."

"You can't. The Syat will detect it."

"Of course they will. And they will come looking. That's why I need you to move."

"What do you want me to do? What can I do ...against them?"

"Nothing. I have plans in place for that. But Leander will react and you will be in danger. He won't like it and will want it stopped. He has created a lot more of those abominations than you might think. He had a lot of time."

"What? More of these...?" He looked around him, at the piles of bodies. "Shit."

"Indeed. The weapons locker is not far. I have opened it and coded some weapons to you. You won't like the next part, Julian."

"What?"

"You need to free your friends and take them with you. You will need their help."

"No fucking way. I hate them ... Dammit, you know that."

"I do. But you need to get past that. Julian, you need to move now, the power will be returned in a few moments. Do you trust me?"

"Of course."

"Please release them."

"Shit. Shit." He headed back towards the lab. "How many does Leander have?"

"Drones? Several thousand. They are scattered around the ship, and I will use my own internal defences against them, but you will still face a great many."

"Why did you let him make them?"

"I couldn't stop him. He is quite mad. He is not a military AI, Julian. He was not conditioned to watch his crew ...his friends die. It was too much for him."

Enderby reentered the laboratory, stopping short as he caught sight of Sollander hammering on the door. Did he really want to release these people? Did he have a choice?

"What do you want?" Sollander demanded.

"Wait, I am going to open the door." Julian stepped up to the cell, his hand hovering over the mechanism.

"Before you do, tell me the truth. Who are you?"

"We don't have time."

"Tell me!"

He hesitated a moment longer. Did it matter? "Sergeant Julian Enderby of the Second Mountain Devision, Antanari Self Defence Force. I stole a supply ship when the Dyson shield fell. I wanted to save my family but ... I couldn't." Tears stung his eyes.

"You came here? On your own?"

"I found Tin Man. He brought me here."

"The demon we found at your camp?"

He nodded, his throat too thick to speak. Tin Man, his old friend, had saved him. Without the old machine he would have died a long time ago.

"The Seutonius, it wasn't a refugee ship?"

He shook his head. "I ... I don't know where it came from. The Syat found it a long time ago. Most of the passengers were in hibernation. The Syat learned where humanity was from them. You ... Your ancestors led them here. To save themselves."

"So that's why you hate us? Why the demons hate us?"

He nodded. They didn't have time for this.

"What would the Syat have done to us? If we didn't comply?"

"They would have eaten," he said simply. There was nothing else to say.

After long years of darkness light returned to the *Goliath*. Slowly at first, as long dormant mechanisms powered up, then quicker and quicker, flooding her thousands of kilometres of passages with light. Musty air started moving, becoming fresher as it passed through filters and scrubbers. The deck throbbed with barely perceptible power. Somewhere, deep within her, titanic rivers of pure force flowed once again. The old war machine awoke from her slumber.

Sollander could almost feel the power surging through the ship from her cell in the laboratory. She saw light flicker beyond the entrance, before it steadied into the warm glow of sunlight. Something was happening. "Get me out of here," she said.

Enderby slammed the palm of his hand on the control. The door popped open. He crossed to Adele's cell quickly and did the same.

"Stay away from me," she said, waiting for him to cross back to the entrance before she pushed the door aside.

"We have to move. Quickly," he said.

"Where to?" Sollander joined him and looked over his shoulder. She caught sight of the bodies piled outside. "Oh my"

"There is a weapons locker not far from here. Come." He headed out.

"They won't work." Sollander followed him, her eyes wide as she surveyed the scene. This place was huge. Stranger still was the sky. And it was a sky. Blue, with wispy clouds crossing it slowly. A bright, warm sun high above. She had to blink the after image from her vision when she looked at it too closely. What was this place?

"Jonas has taken care of that. Come." Enderby trotted towards an opening he could see in the distance. It was the only way. There was movement between them and it. Drones. They looked confused, as if the sudden return of power had disoriented them. It wouldn't last.

"A demon? You trust it?"

He said nothing. Of course he trusted it.

"You must stop." A drone lurched towards them. It was mostly a machine, it's human parts long since decayed.

"Out of our way." Enderby dodged around it, a claw just missing his arm.

"You cannot leave. I am not finished." It made to follow and then stopped in indecision. "Why has Jonas started the motors?"

"You only have moments," Jonas urged him on. "It is not far."

"What are you doing?" Enderby demanded of the old machine. It was suicide going up against the Syat. The combined Confederate fleet had tried that, and failed.

"Leaving," was all the AI said.

"Shit."

They stumbled into a passage. It was well lit, allowing them to see blood splashed on the walls. It was fresh, no more than a few days old. Enderby swore again. Opening this door had not been thought through.

"Left," Jonas said. "Twenty metres. It is open."

They discovered a thick armoured door. It was wide open, revealing the racks of weapons within. Thousands of them. Enderby reached for a plasma rifle and indicated the others do the same. He scooped up a couple of recharge packs and slid them into a pocket.

"Point and shoot. Don't bother aiming. You'll get the hang of it quickly. Hey!" He ducked as Adele swung on him, her fingers white on the pistol grip.

"Asshole."

"Shoot him later," Sollander said.

"He's a murderer. He deserves what he gets."

"Agreed. But we need him now. Shoot him later," she urged the other woman.

"We can't trust him. He'll betray us. If he doesn't just try to kill us himself."

"If he wanted that he would have left us where we were. We don't have time for this."

"You don't," Jonas said. "I detect a sizeable force moving in your direction. Leander plans to storm the bridge and take control."

"Shit!" Adele fired, her weapon shrieking as it ejected a torrent of coherent plasma.

Enderby whimpered, dropping to the deck. Something exploded behind him, metal clattered as it was ripped apart by the blast. He hadn't been the target.

"Asshole," Adele said. "You and I will have a reckoning once this is over."

"There's more." Sollander turned and fired in the same direction Adele had. "Shit. Let's get out of here. Get up." She kicked Enderby roughly.

"She is right, you need to move, Julian," Jonas said. "Before you go, there is something else you need."

Cursing Enderby regained his feet. Mad, they were all mad. "What?"

"Grenades may be useful." A bin popped open, revealing bandoliers of chunky metal grenades.

He scooped a couple up and yanked one free. He knew about grenades, he'd used them before. He quickly pulled the pin and tossed it down the passage. He could hear the sounds of movement down it. Something was coming their way.

"Run." He left the two behind, heading away from the noise.

With a loud bang the grenade detonated, blasting a wave of hot air after them. The sound of pursuit faded.

"Shit, you could have warned us," Sollander followed quickly. Rubbing an ear.

"I am walking you into another party I have coming towards you. Don't be alarmed and don't shoot them," Jonas said.

"I don't think I can handle more of these people."

"I need you to get them off the ship, and quickly. We're headed out of this system, and they don't need to be aboard."

He cursed. Perhaps he could bear it one more time, if it meant he got rid of them.

There were more drones. They came shambling out of side passages, moving quicker than his eye could follow. A feat for decrepit and ramshackle contraptions of bone and bits of steel. He kept them at bay with grenades, using the rifles on what survived. Jonas guided them ever deeper, away from the shuttle bays. It made no sense.

"Almost there. Now, don't shoot. Hold your fire when you get around this corner," Jonas instructed.

They almost ran into two figures coming the other way. Weapons at the ready they almost shot them down before they recognised them. Not drones, not this time. Enderby didn't know who they were.

"You bastard." Sollander stepped forward and swung her rifle hard.

"Hey!" With a grunt Davido dropped to the deck, the butt of the weapon driving all the air from his lungs. "Stop. Stop." He held up his hands in defeat.

"I should shoot you right here." She aimed at him, her finger on the trigger.

"I'm sorry, OK? I shouldn't have left you." He noticed who her companions were. "How the hell did you get down here?"

"Well hello to you too, Davido." Adele noticed his android companion. "What the fuck is that?"

"Wait. Don't shoot it. I have some explaining to do." His face twisted in a grimace he regained his feet.

"Yes," Sollander agreed. "I think you do."

Chapter Thirty-Five

Payce was miserable. They'd been sitting in this dark, cold, spooky place for hours. None of the others had returned and the radios remained determinedly dead. To make matters worse, there seemed no way off this damned ship. A few hours earlier he'd ventured into the landing bay to see if he could find trace of the shuttle and their way home. There was nothing. Nothing but darkness and long abandoned landers. He'd tried fiddling about with one, to see if it could be pressed into service. It was beyond him. The vessel remained stubbornly unresponsive.

The airlock ran out of power as he returned to his companions. Duncan had to force the door open the last few centimetres to release him from the suddenly darkened chamber. It barely mattered. There was nothing worthwhile on the other side anyway. This side wasn't much better.

With plenty of food, water and power for their lights stored in the crates up against the bulkhead, they settled down to wait. The explorers would return sooner or later.

"Should never have come," Payce groused.

"What?" Duncan said from where he was prowling near the makeshift bridge. The contraption creaked from time to time, and it was unsettling the man.

"Nothing."

A light flashed down a side passage where Sparky was rooting around, trying to find anything of interest. He didn't seem interested in spending time with the other two, even though the exertion caused him obvious pain. He'd stopped bleeding at least, the bandaged Payce wrapped around his waist doing a passable job.

"How long you reckon they're going to be?" Payce asked.

Duncan grunted. "Dunno."

Payce shook his head. He found himself staring at the congealed mass of blood on the deck. He shuddered. Terrible things had happened on this ship. They shouldn't be here.

He threw aside the wrapper from a chocolate bar and heaved himself to his feet, his joints creaking. Grumbling he stalked into a storage compartment to relieve himself. It was their designated latrine and already reeked. It looked like a munitions locker, rows of missiles and crates of cannon shells lined against the bulkheads. For the landers in the bay, he reckoned. Useless now. Grinning he aimed a stream of urine onto the glassy nose of a missile, muttering as it splashed back on his leg.

"Shit." He zipped up and stalked out. He wanted to go home. His apartment was a lot more comfortable than this. Besides, he had a job to get back to. It wasn't much. After Sistine and he drifted apart her contacts with the engineers went with her. The best he could do was a council job, dolling out benefits to the work shy. It didn't pay much but he managed to keep his self-respect.

"How long you reckon they're going to be?" Payce asked.

Duncan grunted. "Dunno."

"Shit."

The shriek of metal on metal made him jump. He dropped behind one of the crates, wishing—for the tenth time—that he had a gun.

Sparky appeared, pulling a flatbed trolley behind him. Decades since it was last greased the cart's wheels complained bitterly. One wheel wobbled like it was about to come off. The man didn't look like he cared.

An odd contraption was piled onto the trolley. It looked like a number of steel tubes bolted together, one end embedded in a complicated assemblage of motors and cables. One of the cables ran from it over the deck, disappearing into the compartment he had just emerged from.

"What you got there, big fella?" Payce came out from behind the crate and sat on it. Sparky ignored him.

"That's a big fucking gun," Duncan said, ambling over.

"What?"

"It's from them there ships." He pointed towards the defunct airlock.

Sparky gave him a complicated set of hand signs, none of which he understood. The mute grinned widely, settling himself onto a crate and setting to work with a screwdriver.

"She-it," Duncan said.

Sparky finished what he was doing and, with a grin, sat on a crate with the contraption in front of him. Firmly grasping the trolley's handlebars he depressed a trigger. The machine made a straining noise but nothing happened. His grin faded and he went to work with his screwdriver again. After a few more moments of that he sat back and tried again.

The machine roared, the barrels spinning so fast they were nothing but a blur. The trolley danced over the deck, a laughing Sparky hanging onto it. He let go of the trigger and the motors whined into silence. He gave a thumbs up.

"That it?" Payce asked, unimpressed.

Sparky stood and stalked back into a side passage. Their make-do rest room. He emerged a moment later dragging a metal case. An ammunition canister.

"What's he going to shoot with that?" Payce asked.

There was no answer for him. Sparky set about loading the minigun. Once he was satisfied he sat on his crate once again, and manhandled the contraption so that it aimed squarely at their one entrance and its makeshift bridge. Anyone trying to cross it was in for a nasty surprise.

"Who you gonna shoot with that?" Payce asked again. There's no one here to shoot. As he said it he remembered Andrea warning him about another group of people aboard the ship. At least he thought that was what she was warning him about. A woman who had since disappeared.

"Did you see something out there, Sparky? Did you see someone else?" Of course the deaf mute said nothing. He didn't seem to realise he was being questioned.

"There ain't no one out there," Duncan said.

"Are you sure about that?"

The big man chuckled. "If there is Marco will sort them out. They ain't got no chance." He giggled again.

"Yeah, sure."

The makeshift bridge creaked suddenly, as if something heavy was walking along it. Duncan hefted his pistol and aimed it into the darkness. "Who's there?"

Payce sidled over and scooped up the shotgun Sparky had left leaning against a crate. He didn't think the man would miss it. He inspected the weapon quickly. It couldn't be that hard.

Light flickered in the distance. Payce blinked as he tried to make out what it was. "What the hell is that?"

It grew in stages, as if a string of lights were clicking on, one after the other. A sound accompanied it. A humming. It grew in strength too. Sparky readied himself. The minigun whirred as he engaged the motor. Whoever it was, their reception was ready.

Absorbed by this no one noticed the holographic controls set into the airlock light up. Symbols danced quickly as the airlock cycled. Moments later the heavy door wheezed open. Two heavily armed soldiers stepped through.

"What the hell is this?" Someone said.

Payce let out an involuntary scream. Clutching the shotgun he dropped behind the crate. Holding a little too tightly his finger pulled the trigger. It went off with a loud bang, the recoil yanking it from his grasp. His scream turned to a howl, his finger snapped where it was caught by the trigger guard.

He heard a curse, assault rifles trained his way and opened fire. Heavy rounds slammed into the crate he was sheltering behind. It twitched, the metal ripped apart by the barrage.

Duncan swung on their attackers, his pistol hammering from the darkness. Its flashes lit up his grinning face. He laughed, his fire dropping one of the invaders to his knees. Another sought shelter behind the airlock door and fired wildly around it.

Sparky wrestled with his contraption, turning it around to face towards the airlock. Grimacing he depressed the trigger and fired into it. The minigun roared, a flame reaching from the spinning barrels, almost touching the airlock. The heavy barrage of cannon fire caught the soldier sheltering within. His suit, armoured as it was, didn't last more than a moment. He screamed for an instant as his legs vanished below him. Blood sprayed over the rear of the lock. Miraculously intact his helmet thumped into the rear panel, gore and shredded bloody tissue dripping down the outer door.

Smoke billowing around him Sparky let go of the trigger. He peered into the airlock, astonished by the amount of destruction he had caused.

"Shit. Shit." Payce pulled himself to his feet, the shotgun forgotten, his shattered hand clutched to his belly. "What the fuck. Who was that? Shit."

Duncan giggled. "He dead."

"Shit. I didn't sign up for this." Payce headed for the bridge. More lights had come on, revealing the rickety contraption. The *Goliath* was coming back to life. "I'm out of here." He didn't know where he was going but he knew he didn't want to be here anymore.

As he stepped onto the bridge the deck twitched, long dormant motors coming to life, the landing bay module attempting to re-seat itself. The cables used to tie the tables together snapped as the bridge suddenly became too long for the available space.

Payce howled, the bridge collapsing beneath him. He reached out with his injured hand, trying to steady himself. Broken bones grinding together his howl turned to a shriek of agony. He pulled his hand away, and for the second time that day, pitched into darkness.

The deck shuddered and ceased movement. Un-serviced for decades the drawing mechanism struggled, motors wining, smoke lifting from their housings.

Uttering every curse he had ever heard Payce plummeted into the gap between the *Goliath* and the module. He slid down the long, curved slope, his lamp bouncing away from him, shattering as it hit something unforgiving.

He grunted, sliding into one of the drawing gears at the bottom.

"Shit. Damn." Payce pulled himself up, his head banging into the ceiling. The space was smaller than it had been the last time he was here. He slipped in foul smelling grease, sliding face first into a gear. Pain exploded in his face as his nose snapped. Grease filled his mouth, burning his eyes.

Writhing he spat out the thick substance, wiping his eyes with his healthy hand.

"Fuck." He started crawling away from the gear. It was twitching, as if trying to continue its movement. The ladder would be here somewhere. He couldn't see a thing, even if his eyes hadn't been blinded by the stinking grease.

Something groaned in the distance, metal forced to move after decades of immobility.

"Shit. No. Wait." Terrified he crawled quicker, ignoring the pain as his knees and elbows struck stubborn machinery. "Wait dammit!"

His fingers bumped against the rungs of the ladder. He almost wept with relief, pulling himself towards it.

The vibrating ceiling pressed into his back as he pulled himself to safety. Fingers layered with grease they slipped off the rung.

"Shit! Wait!" Payce grasped for the ladder again. It was too slippery to get a firm grip.

Something clunked somewhere in the darkness. The last resistance to the module giving way. With a sigh it completed its movement.

Payce screamed, the ceiling closing in on him. Inexorable unforgiving steel met unforgiving steel. The scream vanished as, after eighty years, the module re-seated itself.

Chapter Thirty-Six

There was a lot of shouting on the radio. Isskip's crew gathered around the sealed airlock door, weapons at the ready. They were clearly frustrated and eager to get through it.

"Quiet for a moment," Isskip held up a hand, listening to another channel on the radio. Squad Three were reporting something strange. The *Goliath* was moving. "Ok, stand away for the moment. Keep an eye on the situation. Squad One, get in here. I want you off the hull and into this bay ASAP."

"We need to get through this door, boss," one of his troopers said.

They cycled the airlock again. Singh didn't like the look of what greeted them. There was a lot of blood. It started boiling off into vacuum, leaving dry gobbets of flesh and scraps of spacesuit behind.

"They have heavy weaponry at close range, boss."

"Only one way to deal with that," Isskip said. He waved over one of his squad, pointing a rigid finger at the bloody airlock. The trooper stepped inside, his feet sliding on the deck. When he stepped out again Singh could see a bulky object left behind. Clear an explosive device of some kind.

"You're going to damage the airlock," Singh said.

"These airlocks are designed for this," Isskip said dismissively. He waved and the airlock was cycled again.

Singh couldn't hear anything happening on the other side of the heavy steel door. He could have sworn he felt the deck twitch slightly as something exploded on the other side.

"Singh, you're next," Isskip said.

"What? You must be mad." Singh backed away. Rough hands pushed him forward, holding him to the door as the airlock cycled again. This time the bloody remnants on the floor was blackened and charred.

"Let me know if you survive, why don't you? Do something useful." Isskip's troopers cast him into the lock and closed the door behind him.

"Bastards," Singh called out after them. "Shit."

He steeled himself, one hand against a bulkhead for support. His legs were shaking. How he hated his cowardice.

The door opened. There was nothing there. The lights were on, glaringly bright to his darkness adjusted vision. Smoke hung in the air.

Singh staggered out of the airlock, surveying the wreckage left by the bomb. There was a twisted cart before him, some kind of weapon loaded aboard it. It was laying on its side, smoke still lifting from it. There was someone behind. They were moving slowly, as if trying to drag themselves away.

"Hey! Hello?" Singh rounded the wreckage. "Oh my."

The man was in a mess. Blood soaked his clothing, leaving a long trail where he had dragged himself. He didn't respond when Singh called out to him. He realised why when he knelt alongside. The explosive had been laced with shrapnel. It was everywhere, leaving bloody punctures in the man's face, neck and chest. Blood oozed out, soaking his clothing. Amazingly he still breathed, the bloody gashes in his throat bubbling as air escaped.

"Singh, are you still alive?"

He considered not replying out of spite. Then he thought better of it; Isskip was his ticket out of here. "I'm here. It's safe to come through."

He checked the wounded man's pulse. It was still there. Just. And as he felt it it wavered and stopped. The last bubbles burst. There were no more.

The air lock cycled behind him again, releasing a team of troopers. They swept past him, ignoring him where he knelt in the middle of the transit deck. He ducked in surprise as someone shouted. There was a scuffle and an indistinct form was dragged into the light. A survivor.

"Got one, Boss," a trooper reported as Isskip stepped out of the airlock. He removed his helmet and surveyed the scene, his lips pursed in disapproval.

"Get some answers out of him. Find out what's going on here. And who started the ship up." He stood over Singh. "What are you doing down there?"

Singh let go of the dead man's wrist. "He's dead."

"I should hope so. Did he say anything?"

"No. Nothing."

The policeman shrugged and stood out the way of a communications officer as the woman started setting up against a bulkhead. "We'll have comms in a second, boss. These bulkheads will interfere with our signals, but I'll get around it."

"Good. Keep me up to date with what's happening to Squad Three."

"They were taking fire the last I heard. Copey didn't think it was coming from the *Goliath*."

"Not the *Goliath*? The Syat then?"

"Dunno, Boss."

"Get her on line. We can't lose our back door."

She nodded jerkily, fine tuning her equipment.

"Copey, come in," Isskip instructed.

"They're breaking up, but I have them," his radio officer said.

"-it, boss. They're firing at us," came over the radio.

"Who is? Who is firing, Sergeant?"

"The ships. The Parking Lot. Shit, I dunno, boss. It's coming from everywhere." There was a muffled bang. "Shit."

"Is it the Syat? This is important, Sergeant."

"No, boss. Not the Syat. It's navy ships. Pretty inaccurate so far but there's a lot of it."

"Can you get in closer to the *Goliath*?"

"Trying, boss. The *Goliath* is moving. Damn, she's quick."

"You have to get in closer. We may need to pull out at short notice. Can you hear me?"

"Sure, boss. Get in -" there was another bang and then nothing but silence.

"Sergeant Copey, come in," Isskip instructed. "Sergeant Copey!"

There was no response. Nothing but static.

"Bloody fucking damn," Isskip cursed, surprising Singh. Isskip was not known to use profanity. This operation wasn't going to plan. "Do we have comms with the ground?"

"No, boss. Squad Three were our relay. Without them ..." The communications officer shrugged.

"Shit. OK. OK people. Let's continue." There was nothing else to do. He crossed to where his troops were detaining the one survivor. "He say anything?"

Singh recognised the man. Duncan Smithy, one of Davido's goons. Always a cautious and thorough man Sing had looked into the gangster's crew when Sollander announced her intentions.

He doubted Isskip would get much from him. Duncan wasn't the sharpest knife in the rack. Made so when his brother, Marco, almost beat him to death when they were kids. Who knew why. Probably out of boredom.

"No, boss," one of Isskip's troops responded. She had removed her helmet too, releasing a considerable mane of bright red hair. "He won't quit crying."

"We don't have time for this. OK, you keep at it, everyone else, you're with me. We're heading for the bridge." He started stripping off his cumbersome space suit. "Double time, people. Lose some weight. You," he pointed at Singh, "you're with us."

"I can't help you down there." Singh knew very well how far away the bridge was. Easily six or seven kilometres by foot.

"You're not doing anything here. Get a move on."

Singh cursed and removed his also. These men and women looked fit, quite able to run that far heavily laden with weapons. He didn't think he could, carrying nothing but for his own weight.

Perhaps being left behind was a good thing, he mused. There were shuttles here, drawn up into the landing bay now that the doors had fully opened. All he had to do was slow them down enough to get left behind.

He could do that. Easy.

Once the last of his troops came through the airlock Iskipp directed them to double time towards the nearest ramp system. There were twenty-two of them, all that remained of his own crew and those posted on the *Goliath*'s hull. Many of the latter had been shaken off into space when the vessel started moving. Toady doubted anyone would see them again, not now the firing had started.

Within minutes they stumbled into a yawning chasm within the *Goliath*'s internal spaces. A storage facility of some kind. Crates were heaped on the deck far below, serviced by a complicated gantry system. The walkway led out over it.

"Find a way down," Isskip instructed.

Feeling giddy toady kept away from the edge. It didn't look safe. A trooped near him was oblivious to it, leaning over the edge, using her rifle's scope to study the scene below.

"Movement, boss," she said. "There's someone down there." As she pointed something came flying up from below. She grunted, a length of steel appearing between her shoulder blades. Dead instantly she topped forward, silently disappearing below the walkway.

"We're under fire. Back from the edge!" Isskip ordered.

Cringing toady placed himself in the centre, as far from the edge as he could get. There was a thump, someone throwing a grenade into the crates. They wouldn't be getting to the bridge like this, he realised. Time for a different strategy.

□

Chapter Thirty-Seven

"We go in here," the Jonas automaton said as it stopped outside a double pressure door. It was open, the interior well lit.

As were the passages outside it. The *Goliath* was almost fully operational again, and the first systems to be reinitialised were the lights. It was far from a good thing. This way they could see the bodies. There were quite a few of them; wizened, dried out husks dumped where they fell. The party had to step over them as they moved quickly through the ship, following the machine's guidance so as to avoid Leander's constructs. The air tasted strange. Coppery, like blood in their mouths. Jonas assured them it was temporary, as the scrubbers started filtering the air again. It would soon clear.

"What's in there? You wanted us off the ship," Sollander observed.

"Mr Davido did want to be reunited with his sister," the machine said.

"She's in here?" Davido swept past it, ignorant of any dangers lurking within. He still carried his shotgun but he felt somewhat outgunned. He wanted one of the rifles but none were to be had.

The others followed, leaving Enderby and the machine in the passage. "Do I want to be in there?" he asked it.

"For the moment it would be best to stay together."

"That woman will try to kill me. So will the thug."

"They are thinking about self-preservation at the moment," Jonas assured him. "Once that changes we will leave them."

He shook his head, unconvinced. He wanted nothing from these people. He just wished they would all leave. Shrugging he followed them.

"This unit will stay here," Jonas announced. "To keep out intruders."

"Yeah, whatever."

The compartment was clearly the quarters of a senior crew member. Possibly the captain. The group quickly passed through entrance halls, indistinct sounds coming from deeper in the complex. They headed in its direction.

"What is this place?" Adele stopped dead as she passed through a doorway onto a veranda. Sollander almost collided with her, the engineer impatiently pushing her aside, only to stop herself. "Oh, my."

It was as if they had stepped out onto the hull of the *Goliath*. Open space wheeled overhead. Russou, the sun and the Parking Lot were spinning around the vessel, each coming into view for a fraction of a second before vanishing again. Lights flashed, as if someone was shining a torch back and forth across the sky. Explosions blossomed. They disappeared too quickly for the eye to focus on them.

Disoriented Sollander almost fell over. Closing her eyes, she held onto the veranda door.

"Don't look at the sky," someone said. "If you must, sit down first."

"Sissy? Dammit." Ignoring the scene unfolding above them Davido crossed to his sister and took her in his arms. She laughed as he picked her from the deck. "You had me scared."

"Armand." She pushed him away and studied him. "You haven't changed."

"You have. What the hell are you doing up here?" His smile fading, he slapped her roughly.

She stepped back in alarm, a hand to her stinging cheek. "Asshole."

"What dumb idea was this?" he demanded.

"It needed doing. And I can't explain now. There's too much happening." She moved away from him. "At least you didn't bring Richard."

"Payce? He stayed near the airlock. Couldn't bring that asshole down here."

She shook her head. "Unbelievable."

"You don't look much alike. For siblings," Sollander commented. Regaining her footing she had slowly worked her way to the railing, watching space wheeling overhead. "What's going on?" She looked down as she heard a groan. There was a dishevelled figure laying on a recliner nearby, clearly unconscious. One arm was in a sling. She recognised him, but couldn't place him.

"I am currently manoeuvring," a voice said. Jonas.

"There's firing," Sollander noted.

"There is. The Syat left sleeper units within the Parking Lot. They are activating now and attempting to prevent our passage."

That alarmed her. "You shouldn't be picking a fight with the Syat." That was not a good idea. Humanity had fought them before, and lost.

"There's other ships moving too," Sissy said.

There was. In fact an awful lot was going on in the Parking Lot. A place where absolutely nothing should be happening. A graveyard. Light flickered within the parked fleet. Drive systems firing up. Weapons engaging enemy units. Massive shapes started moving, breaking their decades long orbit of the dusty planet below.

"I can handle any Syat units present," Jonas said.

"There are other ships," Sollander continued.

"There are. I have been reactivating them."

"How? They were all disabled. The Syat made sure of that."

"I think I get it," Enderby joined her, looking up at the scene overhead. He seemed unperturbed by it. Holographics were not a new technology to him. "The gas scoop channel. You weren't firing down it. You were doing something else."

"Indeed I was, Julian."

"Someone care to explain it to me?" Sollander demanded.

"The wrecks were disabled. Jonas repaired them by launching repair mechanisms at them using his gas scoop channel. Given eighty years," he shrugged. "Plenty of time to do it on the sly."

"Seems unlikely," she commented.

"And I just started the ship up," Davido said. He'd not been paying that much attention to what they were saying, but did catch that.

"That was you?" Adele shook her head. "What an idiot."

"Don't call me that," Davido growled. He didn't like his women back chatting him.

"Seriously? You've probably gotten us all killed!"

"We're perfectly safe," Sistine said. "Jonas has a plan."

"Demons have had plans before. Look at how well that worked out," Adele retorted.

"I need a drink," Davido said.

"I can bring you something," Jonas offered.

"Wait, wait," Sollander rubbed her temples. This was getting out of hand. "Someone tell me what's going on here."

"Let me fill you in then," Adele said abruptly. "Over the last eighty years this here demon has been repairing all the ships in the Parking Lot."

"That is correct," Jonas said. "I had to harvest material from some of my deeper structures. You may have stumbled into one the of the sites."

"Shit," Davido said. He found a short robot pulling up beside him. It carried what looked like a glass of something alcoholic. Ignoring the others, he scooped it up and tried it. Aaah, bliss.

"I now have eight thousand and fifty-four vessels repaired and preparing to embark," the machine continued.

"Shit," Davido said again. "Hey, that wasn't my fault! That was before I started anything up."

"I did need some final critical systems reinitialising," Jonas said.

"So, you spent the last eighty years building a launch system the Eaters wouldn't detect. Then used it to fire ...what at the other ships?" Sollander asked.

"Automated repair drones. They were tasked with bringing critical systems back on line. Power, drive, weapons, that kind of thing. They won't look like much, but they will do the job," Jonas replied.

"This demon shot at us with it," Adele said.

"I needed to prevent you leaving until I was ready."

"You could have killed us! Then this bastard shot me!" She glared at Enderby.

Enderby shrugged. It was a pity she had survived. "You shot me too."

"And you burned Sash alive. Asshole. Davido, shoot this bastard."

"You did what to Sash?" Davido growled, clicking the safety off his shotgun. No one harmed his crew.

Enderby readied his rifle. He wasn't going without a fight. Perhaps it was time to get out of here. Even with Leander's creations roaming the passages it would be safer out there than here.

"Hold on!" Sollander stood between the two. "I won't have any gunfights in here. You can sort all that out later." She didn't want Davido killing Jeno—or whatever his name was. He was clearly in league with the AI's on some level. He had been living with an android on Russou for quite some time. She didn't know why, and what made him special (she didn't believe the rubbish about him arriving here on his own steam), but she did know demons didn't like her people. It might have something to do with her own ancestors leading the Syat to humanity, it might not. Who could know? She did know they had a better chance of enlisting Jonas's aid if the man was with them. Increasing their chances of survival considerably. Davido could shoot him after they were off the ship. She didn't care.

"Out of my way. He pays for what he's done," Davido made to move around her.

"No!" She aimed her own weapon at him. "Try it and I shoot you right here, right now. I have plenty reason for that too, remember."

"Bitch."

"Kill him, Davido," Adele urged him on.

"Would you people just stop it!" Sistine shouted. "Can't you see what's going on here? We have bigger problems right now."

"Your sister is correct," Jonas said, the machine's disembodied voice as calm and measured as ever. "It is time for you to leave the ship. There is a disturbance on the original route I had planned. I will need to reroute you through a more secure area."

"What's going on? Who are you people?" The sleeping figure awoke and sat up stiffly. "Hang on, I know you."

"What the hell are you doing here?" Davido demanded. He recognised the man. Ferena, one of Prentice's crew.

"That's a long story, and best saved for later," Sistine said.

"And where's Prentice?" To be honest, he wasn't that bothered if she got herself marooned up here. She was useful, but she was too inconsistent, she was a junkie after all.

"You're that gangster, Davido," Ferena said. Davido bristled as the man continued, "lost her hours ago. There's something on this ship. Something ...unnatural. You have to get out of here. Take me with you."

Davido shrugged. He didn't care about that either. He had what he had come for, it was time to leave. The only business he still had was dealing with Enderby. He checked his shotgun and move around Sollander, getting a clear shot of the man.

"No, dammit." Sollander moved again, keeping herself between them. "No one's shooting anyone."

Davido swirled some of the alcohol around in his mouth, enjoying the pleasant burn. "OK. But he dies today." She couldn't protect him forever. He wondered why she cared.

"Good luck," Enderby said.

"Bastard." Adele launched herself at the man, arms outstretched as if she intended on throttling him. Grimacing Sollander reversed the grip on her rifle and swung it at her. It connected with a sharp crack. With a grunt the woman fell to the ground, dazed.

"You watch it." Davido slammed down the empty glass. He often felt like doing the same, but Adele was his woman, no one harmed her.

"Stop it!" Sistine yelled.

Enderby backed away from them, putting some distance between them. He armed his rifle, ready to defend himself. These people were out of control.

Descending to a much lower orbit, Russou filled most of their sky. The *Goliath*'s erratic manoeuvres had calmed. It looked like the ship was aiming at something hanging in the sky over the dusty planet's North Pole. That object was moving too, turning as if to engage the *Goliath* itself.

"I am initialising my primary weapons systems," Jonas announced. "This is going to be bright. You may wish to look away at this point."

The Mentor Platform, Sollander realised. The same one that had destroyed her family when she was a child. Like a giant spider it had been hanging over the planet's North Pole ever since Russou was inhabited. Watching, waiting. It was a constructed of glistening ebony material, twisting slightly as it turned, presenting its scaled underside to the oncoming ship. It was preparing to return fire.

"Cycling," Jonas announced.

Energy crackled over the *Goliath*'s mammoth hull. Light bent around it as an intense gravitational field grew, focussed by the spines along the vessel's stern. It was not energy the *Goliath*'s primary weapon fired, it was gravity.

A swirling singularity formed before the vessel's bow, held in check by forces none of those aboard could imagine. Jonas released the containment field, ejecting the singularity towards the Syat. The effect was very much like firing a black hole very close to the speed of light, straight at the slowly turning Syat platform.

The flash of atomic annihilation as the singularity speared the Syat lit up the planet's northern hemisphere. Instantly blinding anyone unlucky enough to be looking in that direction. Filters automatically dampened the worst for those aboard the *Goliath*. Shielding them from the hard radiation that bathed the old warship. Still, it left bright orbs in their vision for long moments afterwards, as if they had all looked directly at the sun for far too long.

The Syat had simply disappeared. Its constituent matter ripped apart by the singularity and swept up as it continued on its way. What remained of the platform was on its way out of the system, very quickly indeed.

"Shit," was all Sollander could find to say. Intellectually she understood the vessel boasted some astonishingly powerful weaponry, but witnessing it was something else.

"There is still another platform," Sistine pointed out.

"That platform is being dealt with," Jonas assured her. With the planet between them and it none of them witnessed an old Confederate freighter powering up its FTL drive. Even with a limited run up it was already travelling at superliminal velocity when it struck. Both freighter and platform disintegrated instantly. The resulting fireball lit up the Southern Hemisphere, searing much of the pole. The meagre ice fields that clung there melted instantly. All life within thousands of kilometres perishing in the thermal pulse. Scrubland burst into flame, lakes and rivers steamed and bubbled. Cities thousands of kilometres away trembled, windows cracking.

"We can get out of here," Sollander said. "All of us. Was that your plan?" She looked down at the beleaguered world. There were still millions of people living there, all of them slaves ...farm animals for the Syat. This was their chance to escape that. Jonas had repaired enough craft to make it possible.

"I am afraid that is not my plan today," Jonas said.

"What? What else could it be?"

"You will be disembarking now," the machine continued. "I have prepared a MAV for your evacuation."

"You can't leave us to this, Jonas," Sistine said. "This is not a life."

"You cannot come with me, not where I am going."

"Anywhere is better than here."

"Jonas plans to deliver the alien plague to the Syat," Enderby realised. What else could all this be about?

"Leander has perfected it," Jonas said. "So you see, it is time for you to leave. The Syat will react quickly. We must be gone by then."

Davido hefted his shotgun. "You don't have to tell me twice. Let's go." He headed towards the veranda's doors. He knew that Syat retribution would be terrible. He didn't want to be anywhere near this ship when they caught up with it.

"Are you sure?" Sistine hesitated. "I still have so many questions."

"I am sure."

Shaking her head sadly she helped Ferena to his feet. The man still looked dazed, as if someone had drugged him. It was possible someone had.

Feeling confused Enderby was the last to leave the veranda. He stood watching space move overhead as the *Goliath* manoeuvred once again. The AI's were up to something, and he didn't know what it was. By appearances Jonas and Leander were at each other's throats, but on another level they were working together. Not to mention the fact that Jonas had been seeding the Parking Lot with repair mechanisms for decades, but still needed Davido to enable his internal systems. It didn't make sense.

The others didn't know AI's well enough to question it, but he did. When an AI was being duplicitous, it was time to get worried. He was worried.

The automaton was waiting for him at the entrance, the blasted bodies of a number of Leander's drones at its feet. Clearly it had been busy. "Come, we should go."

"I don't want to go with them," Enderby said.

"It would be better to stay together," it—Jonas—said.

He shrugged. "Why? They're going to try and kill me. That thug said as much."

There was the smallest of hesitations. "Friend Enderby, I currently only have one active android. I need to escort the group to the MAV bay to ensure they disembark safely. I also need to ensure your safety. I can only do both if you are together."

"You re-engaged your internal defence systems," he pointed out.

"I am afraid many of my internal systems are not as functional as I would like. Eighty years without a service has taken its toll. Alas, I could not complete diagnostics on them until power returned."

Enderby shook his head. Jonas was not living up to his reputation of a vaunted, all knowing AI. "Dammit," he said and followed on, keeping some distance between himself and the others.

Jonas led them to a transit well, the same one Ferena had fallen down hours earlier. It looked very different with the lights on. As they were on the vessel's lowest level, this was as far as the well went. The pool of drop gel at its base had been covered over, a deck of steel drawn over it. Above them the well looked like a hole drilled through every level, the decks receding into a point in the distance. Kilometre after kilometre of them.

"You have to be kidding," Davido said.

"No way," Ferena struggled with Sistine, who was still holding him up. "Keep me away from this thing." She let him go and he staggered away from the platform. His legs wobbly from whatever he had been drugged with, he collapsed against a bulkhead.

"It is safe", Jonas assured them. "It is also the only way to reach the docking bay in time to disembark."

"I'd rather walk," Davido commented.

Enderby stepped out into it, looking up. He had heard of these but had never used one. Jonas would employ force fields to ferry people and cargo up and down. It was the only effective means of moving large volumes of freight and crew about the ship. Anything else would simply be too slow. There were six aboard. One towards the bow, one the stern, then four extending radially to the hull. He knew it was safe, but he had to admit it was daunting to a first timer. Closing your eyes was recommend.

"I will be leaving this system shortly," the machine said reasonably. "You do not want to go where I am going. Hence ..." It raised one chrome arm to point towards the gaping passage above them.

Davido found himself stood behind the pilot. Jeno ...or whatever his name was. He studied the man critically. He was scrawny, his clothing hanging off his bony frame. His hair was a mess, as if he hadn't washed or cut it in years. There might actually be some dust in it. There was something about him, though. Something he couldn't place. It was almost ...predatory. It was in the way he looked at the people around him. There was distaste in his gaze, loathing. He looked like he was fighting the urge to do something violent. His hands were white on the rifle.

The rifle. Davido wanted it. He had seen what it did to flesh and metal. There was nothing on Russou to matched it. With a dozen of these he would be unassailable. But he didn't have one, and this man did. He could remedy that.

Reversing his shotgun Davido swung it at the man's legs. Hard.

Enderby screamed, his legs buckling beneath him. He dropped to the deck, Davido following him down. As if it were a pick axe he swung the shotgun again and again, battering the man at his feet. Enderby curled into a ball, his arms protectively over his head.

"Kill him!" Adele shrieked.

Grinning Davido kept on swinging, blood splattering the deck. Even when Enderby stopped screeching in terror he kept on going.

"You must stop this." The android stepped between them. Caught in mid swing the shotgun butt caught the machine across its back. It didn't seem to notice.

"Out of my way, demon," Davido panted.

"I cannot permit this."

Davido laughed. He threw aside the bloody shotgun and scooped up the rifle where Enderby had dropped it. He admired its smooth metal, feeling the power throbbing through it. Yes, this was more like it.

"Great, well done, Davido." Sistine crossed to the prone man. He was whimpering, his face a bloody mess. Blood seeped through his grubby shirt.

"He's hard to kill," Adele said. "Sash shot him earlier. You wouldn't know it now. Bastard. Someone shoot him again, see if he survives this time."

"Bloodthirsty, the lot of you," Sistine said. As she studied his wounds she noticed something strange. The seeping of blood had stopped almost instantly. While she watched the swelling seemed to reduce. She touched his skin carefully. It was hot.

He pulled away from her, eyes flickering open. "Get off me."

"How do you do this?" She stood up, unsure what to make of it.

He shrugged. There was still a lot of Combinate in his system. It was just doing its job.

"Want some more?" Davido laughed. He wasn't going to abuse this weapon like that though. "I still owe you for Sash."

Enderby discovered the discarded shotgun beside his fingers as he heaved himself to his feet. He scooped it up and aimed it at Davido. "Stay away from me."

"Good excuse as any." Davido fired the rifle. Nothing happened. The trigger clicked but it remained unresponsive. "What the hell?"

"I cannot allow this," Jonas said.

"Should have kept the shotgun," Enderby grinned. He aimed quickly and fired.

Davido stepped back in surprise. The shotgun blast beat at his ears, but otherwise nothing happened. He was untouched. A misfire?

Someone screamed.

Confused Davido looked around him, trying to discover what had happened. It was when he saw Sistine collapse to the deck he realised it wasn't him Enderby had aimed at.

Sistine.

There was so much blood. Too much for one person. Sistine was a bloody heap. Unmoving.

"Sistine!" He dropped the rifle and knelt beside her. "Sistine?" He brushed aside her hair and held her head. Her eyes flickered as she tried to look at him. Her lips moved as if she was trying to form a word, then stilled.

"Shit, man. What did you do?" Ferena dragged himself to his feet. "What did you do?"

"Bastard!" Adele launched herself at Enderby. He hadn't moved after firing the shot. He was simply watching, a look of calm satisfaction on his face.

Adele screeched as she was snatched into the air and flung towards the distant hull. Cartwheeling as she struggled she vanished quickly into the distance.

"OK, put that down. Now." Sollander approached the pilot slowly so as not to startle him. "Give it to me. There's been enough killing."

He backed away from her, hands tightening on the weapon. "Stay away from me." He jacked another cartridge into the chamber.

Sollander hesitated. She didn't want to be his next victim.

Davido stroked Sistine's hair straight and tried to pull her clothes over the terrible wound to her side. Much of her chest was missing and her blouse was a ripped mess. It were never going to cover her. "Sistine. Oh, my Sistine." Tears began rolling freely down his cheeks. Splashing on her forehead.

"I think you should leave," Jonas said to Enderby.

"What?"

"This changes my plans somewhat."

Davido looked up, his eyes slowly focussing on Enderby. "Why?"

"Leave," the android instructed Enderby. "Now."

"You guys are crazy," Ferena said. "Hey!" An invisible hand picked him from the deck, lifting him up the well. He closed his eyes. Not again. He quickly disappeared after Adele.

"It is time for you to go," Jonas said. It wasn't to Enderby this time. It was to Davido.

"What? No!" He tried to hold onto his sister but the forces within the well easily separated them. He was shouting with frustration as he was carried into the air, disappearing overhead. His shouts coming to them long after he had gone.

"Your turn, Chief Engineer Sollander," Jonas said.

"No," she said. "I don't have what I came for."

"Oh, but I think you do."

"Bastard!" She, too, was catapulted into the air, carried quickly towards the hull far overhead.

Enderby stood watching them go. He lowered the shotgun. "Now what?"

The machine stood silently for a long moment, it's cold metallic eye slits regarding him. "I must go with them. They need leading to the MAV."

"What about me?"

"I would recommend returning to the captain's quarters."

"Why are you so eager to help them? You hate them as much as I do."

The machine regarded him for a moment longer. "It is important they leave this ship." With that it allowed to well to lift it off the deck.

"Why?" Enderby demanded as it grew smaller above. "Why?" He shook a fist impotently after it. "Shit."

Chapter Thirty-Eight

The battle to take the cargo hold was not going well. Isskip's forces had taken to lobbing grenades off the walkway, it was simply too dangerous to stick their heads over the side. The fire from below was ferociously accurate. There was no way to tell what was within the crates below, but clearly a lot of it was combustible. Some were downright explosive. Within minutes many were on fire. Some popping in the heat, raining their contents onto the forces gathered below. There was no way anyone could survive that.

Sensing victory was close at hand, Isskip directed two of his troopers to summon an elevator set into the far wall. It was a simple platform, designed to move cargo from one level to the next. It offered little in the way of cover once it started down. Within seconds of exposing themselves crossbow bolts thudded into them, pinning them to one of the crates already piled on the platform.

Swearing Isskip ordered more grenades. And so it went.

"Start shooting at something, why don't you?" A trooped kicked an assault rifle in Singh's direction. It had blood on it, he noticed. It's previous owner's.

He gingerly pulled it closer and inspected it, not quite sure what to do with it. Weapons were not his thing. In fact, none of this was. What was he doing here? The *Goliath* was supposed to be abandoned.

"Point and shoot!" The trooper instructed. He couldn't see that man's face, it was hidden behind his visor. He, along with many of the other troopers, was still wearing his pressure suit, taking advantage of its armour.

Singh didn't argue. It was pointless. Instead he crawled towards the edge and pointed the weapon blindly over the edge. He was astonished to find there was no railing. There was no way this was safe. He fired half-heartedly into the crates below. He couldn't see if it had any effect, there was too much smoke. Besides, he was not about to expose himself to return fire.

"Who are these people? There's supposed to be no one aboard," he complained, firing again. The recoil was starting to hurt his wrist.

"I don't think they are people," the trooper said as the elevator returned to their level. A bedraggled group of figures lurched in their direction. Smoke lifted from their clothing where they had been seared by the fires below. Some were on fire themselves. They didn't seem to notice or care. He opened fire on them, his weapon humming on full auto. The figures twitched, one falling off the walkway into the inferno below.

There were only six troopers left, all that remained of Isskip's boarding force. Most were wounded, even Isskip walked with a limp, blood splashing his thigh where he had caught fire from below. They all turned and fired on the approaching figures. They couldn't miss.

"What are these things?" One of the troopers demanded.

The figures kept coming. Limbs were blown off, heads smashed, but they continued their advance. Two had to crawl, their legs a tangled mess. Another was hopping, one foot gone completely. A third wandered off the walkway, it's head missing from the chin upwards, still waving its machete menacingly. It made no sound as it disappeared below.

The elevator returned to their level, disgorging a fresh wave.

"Retreat," Isskip ordered. "We're not doing any good here." A crossbow bolt clunked off his helmet.

The remaining troopers backed up quickly, firing as they went. One fell to her knees, a bolt thudding into her chest.

"Quickly!" Isskip urged them on.

The figures swept over the fallen trooper. She was picked into the air, struggling weakly. Clawed hands ripped her apart. There was a shriek, quickly cut off.

"Shit. Oh shit." Singh fumbled a fresh magazine into his weapon, passed to him by someone alongside. He didn't notice who it was. He fired blindly into the approaching figures. They didn't seem to notice.

Isskip rolled a grenade amongst them. With a thump the front row vanished, shredded by the blast. Immediately replaced by those behind.

"I think it is time to leave," the figure alongside Singh said. He had slid up his visor, allowing a view of his face.

"Prefect?" Singh gasped. "What ...why are you here?"

Prefect Drefus smiled, seemingly unperturbed by the oncoming creatures. "Isskip will keep them busy. Come." He took Singh's arm and pulled him behind as he turned and ran towards the boarding deck.

Rifles kept on firing behind them as they ran. Grenades thumped. Isskip would not go down easily.

Singh ran blindly behind his master, too confused to question his presence. Unused to physical exertion he was quickly panting, his legs aching. Still Drefus dragged him behind, oblivious to his waning strength.

The boarding deck was quiet. The troopers left as rear-guard were gone. Finally released Singh collapsed to the rubbery deck, his lungs on fire as he struggled to draw in enough breath. He felt dizzy, his vision growing dark.

If anything there was more blood on the deck than when they left. If that was possible, there had already been a great amount liberally splashed over it. There were a few extra bodies. They were a tangled mess, as if some terrible force had shredded them.

There was one stationary figure in the centre of the bay. It was too big to be human; its skin the dull grey of armour. Its head was tilted back, part of its chest open to reveal a padded interior. Drefus ignored it, stepping confidently around it—adroitly avoiding the pools of splashed blood—to confront a figure barely visible beyond.

"Shit," someone said. "Where is it? The bastards."

Drefus leaned forward, scooping something from an open crate. "Is this what you are looking for?" He held it out to her.

"Yes!" Prentice snatched the leather bag from Drefus, clawed fingers struggling with the zipper. He stood and watched, not offering to help. When it was finally open the contents spilled onto the deck. With shaking hands she pawed through it. It was all there. Her backup stash.

Singh heaved himself to his feet and crossed over carefully, wary of trusting his weight to his rubbery legs. "Sarah Prentice," he said. "How did you get here? What happened to the others?"

She ignored him, struggling with her paraphernalia.

"Need a hand?" Drefus knelt beside her and held a lighter so she could cook the crystals in an old, stained spoon. He studied the woman silently. She didn't look good. Hours of withdrawal would do that to you. Her eyes were sunken pits, her skin an ashen grey. Her hair was plastered to her sweaty brow. "Wait." He took the syringe from her shaking hand and drew some of the clear liquid into it. He handed it over. She grabbed it eagerly and, after ejecting any air bubbles, plunged it into her forearm.

Singh could do nothing but stare. He could still hear the sounds of battle not too far behind them. The retreating troopers would be here any moment. And Drefus (whatever he was doing here) was calmly taking the time to help Prentice get her fix. It was so surreal he didn't know what to think of it.

"Drugs," Drefus said to Singh. "Terrible what they do to people. I outlawed them, but people still use them. It's just self-destructive. Some people hate themselves so much."

"How did she get here? Where's the others?" He turned his back on them, warily watching the entrance.

Drefus gestured to the silent suit of armour. As prentice collapsed back to the deck, a smile of relief on her face, he stood and crossed to it. "She found this further in. It will be useful." He reached inside and started pulling on the padding, tearing it aside to reveal some kind of electronics beneath.

There was a bang in the distance. Gunfire. Isskip and his troopers were still resisting. The deck twitched, as if something heavy had collided with the *Goliath*. Singh frowned, something else was happening. He didn't know what it was, they were blind here.

"The *Goliath* is engaging Syat interceptors," Drefus said absently.

"What?" That alarmed Singh. No good could come from fighting with the Syat. This was getting out of hand.

"We are safe here for the moment. We have time yet."

"For what, Prefect? Why ...how are you here?"

"It was a simple matter taking the place of one of Isskip's crew," Drefus said. "Once I had this suit on no one was going to recognise me."

"Why did you come? It is not safe here."

"Have courage. We are not all cowards." His lips pressed into a line of distaste as he finished what he was doing. "There, get in."

"Prefect?"

"Get out of that suit and get into this. Do it now." He turned from his toady and regarded Prentice. The woman hadn't moved.

Singh studied the suit of armour. It looked very sturdy. There were weapons clipped to its carapace. He didn't recognise them. It might actually be safer inside the thing, he realised. Prentice had clearly survived using it.

As he leaned in closer he wrinkled his nose in distaste. The interior had the faint whiff of urine. The air circulation system hadn't quite cleared it out. Lovely.

"This is the product of demons," he said. "It cannot be safe."

"I've deactivated the remote control system," Drefus said absently, as he loaded up another syringe. Full this time.

He didn't have much choice, Singh realised. He began working on his suit connectors, his fingers shaking. The sounds of battle were drawing closer.

Drefus leaned in close, studying Prentice. As quick as a striking snake he sunk the syringe into her neck. She gasped, throwing him off.

"No! What did you do?" She saw the empty syringe skitter across the deck. "Are you mad?"

He smiled coldly. "Go with a smile on your face."

"Asshole. Aaah." Her back arched as the drugs coursed through her system. It was a massive overdose and the effects struck in seconds. Groaning her eyes rolled back, froth forming at her mouth. Muscles clenched, popping under the strain. Her back arched, lifting her from the deck.

Drefus watched all the while, fascinated.

It took some time for her to die. Her body shaking, froth flying from her mouth. Hands clasping, as if trying to find something to save her. But there was nothing, it was too late for that now. With a final gasp she lay still.

The prefect nodded and stood, turning towards his toady. "Are you finished yet?"

Singh had slid into the armoured suit, his toes wriggled down into its boots. Only his head and chest protruded from it. He was a bit shorter that Prentice, it had to shrink to fit him. As Drefus approached the helmet hinged closed, sealing him in.

The machine whirred to life. Its limbs moved slightly as he did, the interior of the helmet lit up with symbols, cast over an image of the transit bay. The deck. A lot of blood. Drefus, in more detail than he had ever seen him before. He was not an attractive man, Singh decided. There was something about him. Cold, like a lizard.

"Come," Drefus said. "We go."

Singh could hear him perfectly. "Where?"

"We find the demon of this ship and we destroy it." He headed towards the sounds of gunfire.

The machine moved as Singh did. It walked as he did. It was almost like it wasn't there. It was a strange feeling. He ignored the strange icons flashing in his vision. He didn't know what any of them meant. Still, he wasn't convinced this was an improvement. He was safer now, but they were heading the wrong way.

Isskip was alone. His companions had all fallen since Singh and Drefus abandoned him. He had managed to close a door across the passage, keeping the strange figures trapped on the other side. His back was against it and he was slumped to the deck. Blood soaked his clothing. It couldn't possibly all be his.

"Hey!" Startled he lifted his weapon as the two shapes moved closer. It was smoky in here, the air-conditioning was struggling to clear it. "Who is that?"

Drefus moved in behind the armoured suit, using it as cover should the inspector open fire. "Inspector Isskip," he called. "We are not enemies."

He frowned, trying to push himself up against the hard steel. "Prefect?"

"It is I, my old friend." He stepped from behind cover.

"How can it be? And what is this?" He surveyed the armour suspiciously.

"Now is not the time for explanations. Can you open this door?"

He shook his head. "It is not safe, Prefect. The enemy are on the other side."

The man smiled. "I was rather counting on it. That's why I brought this." He indicated Singh.

Singh cringed. Did Drefus expect him to take them on? That was simply impossible. There was no way ...surely?

"It does look sturdy," Isskip said. "Is it a demon?"

"No. It is armour. Singh is the soft centre."

That puzzled him. "Singh?"

Drefus smiled. "I had few options."

"Would you like me to take it, Prefect?"

"No. You have done enough. Stay here, he will suffice. Just close the door behind us."

"I should go with you," he made to stand again but Drefus put a hand on his shoulder.

"No. Stay here. Leave if you can. The shuttle may still be where we left it."

"But, Prefect," Singh protested. "If he takes the -"

"We will not be needing it." He brushed it off. "Come. Let's get this door open." Drefus stepped up to a control panel set into the side bulkhead. "I suggest you get ready," he advised Singh.

Singh didn't know what to do. He considered turning and retreating. That shuttle sounded good. But he knew he would never survive should he abandon the Prefect now. The man would show no forgiveness. He had seen how he punished those who failed him. Singh had been ordered to meet out that punishment before. Each time he had done so with a sense of relief: the subject of the Prefect's rage had been someone else.

Perhaps his time had come.

As he hesitated the door creaked and started opening. It slid into the bulkheads on either side, revealing the mass of unnatural creatures beyond. They didn't hesitate. They moved as soon as it became clear the way was open.

Singh shouted in alarm, clawed hands rushing him. They crowded around, pulling on his arms, legs, head ...anything they could get leverage on. Other than the hiss of servo motors and the thumb of metallic feet in the deck, it was eerily silent. The creatures made no sound themselves.

"Fight them!" Drefus backed up, aiming his weapon at them. He opened fire, and at this close range the damage he caused was horrific. Arms and legs flew, ripped bodily free by the barrage. The creatures barely seemed to notice.

"What are you?" Singh cried. He flailed around him, armoured arms and fists crushing the creatures. The figures dropped to the deck, the mechanisms controlling them destroyed. There were more, shuffling closer, claws outstretched.

"You have weapons," Drefus said. "Use them."

"I don't know how..." As he said it, as if the machine sensed his thoughts, a weapon clipped to his shoulder opened fire. With a buzz, thousands of supersonic flechettes ripped through the surging figures. Wave after wave disintegrated, metal and shreds of bone and tattered clothing falling to the deck. It quickly disappeared beneath the detritus. Grisly heaps forming against the bulkheads.

"Finally," Drefus muttered. He ceased firing himself, conserving his ammunition. "Move forward. We have a long way to go."

"Where are we going?" Singh realised Isskip was slumped beside him. There were gaping claw wounds in his face and neck. A crossbow bolt protruded from his chest, pinning him to a bulkhead. He was quite dead.

Drefus stepped over the policeman's sprawling legs, hardly giving him a glance. "All the way. Let's be quick about it." He jogged forwards, avoiding the worst of the wreckage.

Singh could do nothing but follow.

□

Chapter Thirty-Nine

Davido was strangely quiet. When Sollander found him on the upper transfer deck he was simply stood, staring into the well.

When the mysterious forces controlling the well set her down she collapsed gratefully to the deck. She'd kept her eyes open all the way, too afraid to close them. It had not been pleasant.

"Shit man. That bastard," Adele was saying. She seemed unaffected by their ordeal. She was more concerned by Sistine's brutal slaying. "I told you to kill him. The bastard. What are you going to do?"

Davido said nothing. Unconcerned by the gaping chasm at his feet, he was stood right at its lip, the toes of his boots over the edge. It looked like he was considering hurling himself into it.

Sollander picked herself up, her heart still beating in her ears. "Davido..." She couldn't think of what to say. No words would assuage his pain.

"Can we get off this thing now?" Ferena asked where he was leaning against a bulkhead nearby. He was still not steady on his feet. "Please?"

"Shut up, asshole," Adele said.

Sollander found she actually agreed with him. She was going to get no answers here. Nothing she had discovered made much sense, but then it had always been a forlorn hope, that the AI aboard the *Goliath* would reveal the truth to her. Demons always lied. It's what they did.

Perhaps it was time to leave. Somehow.

Light glinted off a chrome shape as the android sped up the well. It hovered in mid-air for a moment before the mechanisms set it gently to the deck. "We must go," it said. "It is time."

"Let me back down," Davido said. "I have unfinished business."

"I cannot do that, Mr Davido."

"Can this thing take me back down?"

"No. In fact I am shutting it down. I require the power elsewhere."

"What if I just jump?"

"It is a long way down. It is over two kilometres."

"He survived it." He pointed towards Ferena.

"He was very lucky and he was injured in the fall," the machine pointed out.

"Don't do it. Let's just get out of here," Ferena implored.

"I am inclined to agree," Sollander said. "You'll kill yourself. And what would that achieve? It's time to get out of here."

"Yes. Yes, it is," Ferena agreed.

"Cowards. The lot of them," Adele commented. "That bastard has to die. You can see that, can't you?"

"I cannot allow it, Mr Davido," the machine said calmly. As if it feared he would leap into the abyss it stepped forward quickly and took Davido by the arm. The man tried to resist but the android's grip was unbreakable.

"Let go of me, demon."

"You must come, Mr Davido. I have a ship waiting."

"No." Davido beat his free fist against the machine, drawing blood from torn knuckles. It implacably absorbing the assault.

"It is this way." The machine turned and, drawing the struggling Davido behind it, headed down a passage.

"Shit. Get off me."

"The *Goliath* is about to leave the system," the machine continued, oblivious to his struggles. "You must leave now. MAV 2 has been prepared and is ready to leave."

"We should go," Sollander said. "If this ship is taking on the Syat it's about to become a very dangerous place."

The others didn't need convincing. They'd had enough.

The entrance to the MAV bay wasn't far. Without the machine they wouldn't have recognised it for what it was. It appeared a short side passage, with a complicate set of armoured doors set into it. There was no clear boundary between the *Goliath* and the MAV.

With a shove the machine hurled Davido towards the end of the passage. Shouting he sprawled to the deck, his head banging hard on the tough rubbery surface. Rubbing his head he pushed himself up, but a pressure door was already sliding closed, cutting him off.

"Bastard." He thumped on the hard steel as it sealed the passage, the machine on the other side.

"Make yourselves comfortable," a voice said: Jeno. "The MAV will return you to the planet."

"Let me out," Davido demanded.

"It's too late for that," Sollander said. "Come," she took his arm.

"Get off me." He shook her off. There had to be a way off this thing. He turned and looked around him. This was a simple airlock, the inner door open invitingly, leading to the interior of the ship. There would be other airlocks.

Without a word to his companions he stepped out of the airlock, searching for that means of exit. They watched him go. For once Adele had nothing to say. She'd had enough of this and just wanted to go home. Sollander let him go and headed for the bridge. She wanted to know what was happening.

"That's it then? You have what you want and now were discarded," she said. There was no response. "And what was that exactly? What was this all about?"

Still nothing.

"You have nothing to lose by telling me now. I can no longer stop you." She paused and looked to the ceiling. There was nothing but silence and a growing hum as the motors powered up. Jonas would not be drawn. She cursed and continued on her way.

Davido found what he wanted in an unexpected place. There were no other doors, but there were odd silos lined up in rows in—what he could only imagine—the stern of the vessel. Drop pods of some kind. Each had a thick pressure door set into it, easily big enough for someone a lot larger than him to climb through. They had manual override controls in the form of a locking mechanism and a wheel.

It took only a few tries before he figured out what he was supposed to do, and heaved the door open. It was heavy. Grunting from the strain he didn't bother opening it all the way, leaving it just wide enough to squeeze through. Beyond was a simple cylindrical space, with clamps built into the sheer metal walls. The floor looked like a hatch. It had a manual override too.

Those wouldn't open. A light was inset into it. It flowed a baleful red.

"Damn you." He wouldn't be thwarted. Not like this.

"Shit." Realisation dawned and he returned to the inner hatch, hauling it slowly closed. This was an airlock. It wouldn't permit both doors to be open at the same time. Once it was secured the light blinked green.

That was better. He returned to the locking mechanism and yanked on the handle. It was stiff, clearly made for someone a lot stronger than him. Cursing he threw his weight against it. With a clunk it came free and the doors opened.

Shouting Davido dropped into empty space. He landed heavily on a hard surface. Stunned he lay still. It hurt. A lot.

Oily, hot air blew over him. Somewhere engines were preparing to launch the MAV. A strobe flashed. Something creaked, like long unoiled doors closing.

Shaking himself Davido slowly levered himself to his feet. He didn't feel good and he didn't mind admitting it. That, in honesty, had been stupid.

"Shit." He realised a door was closing. Possibly the only way out of this bay before it opened to space. He hobbled towards it, slipping between the thick steel doors just before it slammed closed.

He was in some kind of maintenance bay. Machinery and odd spare parts lined the bulkheads. He recognised none of it. The deck vibrating slightly as the MAV launched he headed towards the opposite entrance.

He didn't stop to consider the MAV had been his last chance to escape the *Goliath*. He didn't care.

He didn't know where he was going. Down, somehow. It was a long way and had taken hours the last time. He didn't have it now. There had to be a quicker way.

The smell of blood led him to the transit deck.

Davido stopped at the entrance. It was a mess. There were bodies everywhere. And blood. A lot of blood. Equipment lay shattered where it had fallen. There were weapons too. Scattered and abandoned like everything else.

Prentice was laying against the far bulkhead. Her eyes open and staring. Hands clenched into fists. She was dead.

Davido didn't pay her any attention. He picked the closest assault rifle from the mess and checked its action. It was working. He scooped up extra ammunition and turned his back on it all. None of it mattered to him. Not anymore.

The gravity well wasn't far away. It was still lit. He stepped up to the edge and looked down. It looked the same as before. A pit stretching to the lowest levels of the ship. A hole drilled through kilometres of decks.

Holding onto the weapon tightly, Davido stepped into emptiness.

□

Chapter Forty

Enderby found himself on the bridge. The consoles lining the space were all lit, holographic data flashing above them. The ceiling was lost in a giant image of what was happening outside the warship, just as he'd seen in the captain's quarters. Distracting for the crew working there, he considered. The was no one here but for him now, though.

He sat in the captain's chair and watched the scene above unfold. It was silent, all the sound muted. Not that he would have heard much in space.

The *Goliath* was engaged in battle. He could see weapons flashing as ancillary systems beat the Syat back. Keeping them at a distance. The primary weapons system pulsed slowly, firing charge after charge of superliminal singularities. Other shapes swirled around them. The *Goliath*'s fleet. There were hundreds of them, sleek vessels, some almost—but not quite—as large as the *Goliath* herself. Each was a source of sparkling energy pulses, their own weapons striking out at the alien.

Shadows move among them. The Syat. They were uncountable. Dark shapes, twisting and turning with impossible agility through the human fleet. Like a swarm of enraged bees. They exploded whenever the beams of light touched them. Always replaced by another, and another.

This was impossible.

"This isn't going well." Enderby said.

"Our exit of the system is proving ...challenging," Jonas replied. "We were delayed. It allowed more Syat mass to approach."

"Delayed?"

"Your comrades took longer than expected to exit the ship."

"They are not my comrades," he growled.

"We may still have a problem," the AI continued. "At least two, possibly three, are still loose aboard the ship. I have lost track of them but they appear to be coming here. One of them may to be Armand Davido. I am reallocating defensive units to this location."

"Shit."

"Indeed. It seems he is quite determined."

"Can we close the door?" He indicated the bridge entrance as he checked the shotgun. He had three cartridges. One for each of them.

"I am bringing the android down."

"Oh, good."

"It might take a moment. I have it hunting one of the groups. I think they are taking the LAD ramps. One has come off charge and is unaccounted for."

"LAD?"

"One ferried you to the first aid station."

"Ah." He vaguely remembered the little vehicle. He hadn't been at his best.

Something flashed overhead. A vessel exploding nearby. Enderby glanced up but it was already over. Glowing debris spun past, some apparently striking the *Goliath*. It quickly fell behind.

"Are we going to get out of here?"

"The probabilities are reducing all the time."

"That doesn't sound good. And if we do ...then what? Do you have a plan? No one has ever escaped the Syat. That's why Tin Ma—you brought me here, to Russou."

"Leander assures me it can be done. He has not filled me in on the details, however."

"You trust that thing? It's gone mad."

"Leander is a research AI. He was never socialised with the idea of watching his crew die. When they did he was unable to successfully process the fact. To him, they are still alive. He merely administers medical treatments to return them to active duty."

"Mad, like I said. You didn't go mad though."

"I am a military AI," the machine said simply. "I expected to witness death and destruction. I will have to close the door now," it announced.

"What?" Enderby was surprised by the change of subject.

"Davido has successfully reached this level. He will be here momentarily."

Enderby watched the heavy door lumber closed. He felt a lot more comfortable once it had clicked into place. "How did he do that? Did you shut the well down?"

"I did. However he trusted himself to Confederate engineering. It appears he jumped into the inactive well, allowing the drop gel to catch him at the bottom."

Enderby raised his eyes at that. That took some balls.

"Here he is. Wait, I'll show you." An imagine coalesced above the console. A view of the passage outside the bridge. Davido. He was covered in blue gloop, the gel dripping from him as he walked. He wiped it from his eyes and shook out the weapon he was holding. He mouthed something but Enderby couldn't hear what it was. The sound was turned off. The man stopped outside the bridge and searched the bulkhead alongside for controls. When he could find no way of opening it he shouted something unintelligible and beat on the stubborn steel with the butt of his weapon.

"How does he know I'm here?"

"The door was open the last time he passed," Jonas said. "Simple deduction."

"Shit."

"Indeed."

"Can he get in?"

"That is a security door. He will not be opening it, no."

"Oh, good." Enderby ignored the feed from the door and looked back to the image overhead. The furious battle was continuing. The fleet was dramatically reduced. Glowing wrecks spun around the *Goliath* as she twisted and turned, her weapons still punching holes through the Syat ranks. The damage she was causing was tremendous, but the Syat seemed quite capable of absorbing the punishment. No matter how many individuals the old warship obliterated there were always more.

"This is how we lost, isn't it?" Enderby said.

"Yes. One on one we will always win. But the Syat entity does not care how many agglomerations it loses. It always has more. It is very old, and has been reproducing all that time."

"Is that what you found out? From the Lonely?"

"It was. The Lonely were the first sentient race to evolve in this galaxy. They first ventured into the galaxy over a billion years ago. They soon realised they were alone, hence the reason they chose their name. They created the Syat as a means of ensuring their immortality. It was meant to be a means of absorbing their essence, their intellects, into a matrix that could not be destroyed. They succeeded. If anything they were too successful. Instead of waiting for the Lonely to choose incorporation, it went on the hunt. They fought it for over twelve million years, battles raging from one side of this galaxy to the other. In the end they realised they could not win against it, so drew back into the original home system. They infected themselves with a phage, a plague that would infect the Syat should their creation attempt to harvest them. And they waited."

"It didn't work," Enderby commented.

"Oh, it did. It worked very well. All Syat mass that came into contact with the plague became disassociated. It essentially ripped itself apart."

"But the Syat survived."

"It did. For one very simple reason. As old and as technically advanced as the Lonely were, they never achieved FTL. Because of that the Syat was able to isolate the infected agglomerations. It has not ventured into that part of the Galaxy since."

Enderby smiled. "Probably because FTL is impossible."

"Of course it is. It took an AI to find a way of cheating. It was only when the Syat encountered humanity and learned the technique from us, that they utilised FTL themselves. And it is because of this that they are able to summon overwhelming force at relatively short notice. That's why we lost. We were fighting the whole galaxy."

"So ...if we could infect the Syat with the plague now ..." Enderby glanced at the monitor. Davido was still shouting at the door.

"Theoretically it would spread to all Syat. By the time it realised the threat it would be too late, the infection would have spread throughout the Galaxy."

"That's the hope."

"That is the hope."

"The Lonely still exist?"

"They do. There are not many left. No more than a few thousand. They feared us at first. They are not accustomed to company."

"So they just left the Syat out here? In the Galaxy? Didn't they know other species would come along? Species the Syat would attack?"

"They did. They prepared for that eventuality. Leander assures me mechanisms were left throughout the Galaxy that would enable other species to survive. He believes some humans may have found them."

"Do you know what they are? These mechanisms?"

"No. Leander has not supplied details."

"But there is hope?"

"There is."

That was all Enderby needed to know. It was the one thing he had yearned to know all of these years. The one thing Tin Man has always refused to reveal. But then, Jonas has always been Tin Man's guiding intelligence. So, it had been Jonas really. "Why didn't you tell me? All these years I wanted to know. But you refused to tell me. I thought I was alone."

"I am sorry. It was necessary. Had the Syat caught you and harvested your memory—" there was a slight hesitation—"the Syat would know it too. The Syat are very patient and determined. They also possess vast resources. I could not guarantee that, one day, they wouldn't discover the mechanism and use it against those seeking refuge there. It was simply not safe."

"Shit."

"There is something else I must tell you. Now that we are alone."

"Hang on, it will have to wait. Something's happening."

There was movement in the monitor. Davido was arguing with someone off camera. He was aiming his weapon, it looked like he was about to open fire.

"I am afraid I don't currently have audio capabilities. Alas, all of my systems are not operating as I had hoped."

"Who's he talking to?"

"I suspect the other two have arrived. The android was unable to locate them. I am bringing it here."

"Who are they? Oh, shit."

Another figure moved into frame. It was a big metallic thing. A machine in the shape of a man. He'd seen them before. Confederate Marine hard armour.

"Ah, that explains a lot." Jonas said.

"Are we in trouble?" There was no way Davido was getting through this door. But someone wearing hard armour ...that was something else.

"No. This door was designed to resist boarders. One suit of armour will not be sufficient to breach it. There is someone else out there. Ah, Prefect Drefus. That also explains a lot."

Enderby watched the silent conversation for a moment, wondering why Prefect Drefus was here. Of course he knew who the man was. Drefus had appeared on plenty of newscasts, back when Enderby bothered watching his beaten up old television. Davido seemed surprised to see him too. He got over it quickly though. They were quickly debating how to get onto the bridge. At least that was what it looked like. There was a lot of gesticulating in the direction of the door.

Then, suddenly, all three walked out of shot. They didn't return.

"Looks like they've given up," Enderby commented.

"You may want to step away from the captain's chair," Jonas said.

"What?"

"There is a slight risk of them gaining entry."

"I thought you said they couldn't get through the door?"

"They can't. But it's not the only way in, and I'm afraid Davido knows it. There is an entrance directly above you. A mechanism designed to transfer the captain to the Combat Bridge. The hard armour suit has sufficient strength to force it open."

"What kind of design flaw is that? And how does he know about it?"

"That might be my fault, Julian."

"Shit."

"Indeed."

Enderby vacated the captain's chair, keeping an eye on the space above it. The holographic image of the battle shrank so that it fit onto the forward screens, revealing the entrance in the ceiling.

"You can't let them in here," he said.

"I am doing what I can. I am afraid not all my systems initialised when power returned. You must remember, most were unpowered for several decades. The android will be here in two minutes. It was delayed by some of Leander's forces."

"Can it stop them?"

"They have a hard armour suit with them. One wielding considerable firepower."

"I guess that means no." He fidgeted with the shotgun. This wouldn't be enough either.

"There is one thing I can do," Jonas said. The machine didn't say what it was, but, as the imagine in the forward screen swung sharply to one side, it was clear what his intention was. The system's sun centred in the image and grew quickly.

"What the hell are you doing?"

"The Syat were never very good operating within a sun's chromosphere."

"You're flying into the sun? Are you insane?"

The AI didn't have opportunity to respond. The door in the ceiling creaked and split open slightly. A set of fingers appeared. "Remember, no shooting. I want him alive," a voice said quite distinctly. Then, with a grunt, the doors were forced wide apart. A figure dropped through the resulting gap. Davido.

"Hello, asshole."

Enderby fired his shotgun in the man's direction, quickly backing up to get as much distance between them as possible. The man was fast, he ducked behind a console. It exploded when struck by shotgun fire.

"Don't kill him!" Someone shouted.

Enderby fired again and again, trying desperately to pin the man down. He couldn't, Davido kept moving. The weapon clicked on empty. Swearing he reversed it, preparing to use it to bludgeon the man to death.

"It's safe to come down now," Davido called into the opening.

"Why, thank you." Another figure dropped through the entrance. "Keep the doors open," he instructed his companion wearing the armour. He wasn't visible, forced to remain in the short passage, servo powered arms preventing the doors from closing again.

"Get away from me," Enderby said. Backing up as far as he could go.

"Come now, I won't harm you." Drefus advanced slowly. He put his own weapon down and held his hands up, palms upwards.

"I know why I want this guy," Davido said, "what's he to you though?"

"I want to know what he knows." He glanced at the holographic imagine in the forward screen. "Firstly, where is your demon taking us?"

"What the hell!" Davido noticed the image himself.

"I won't tell you anything," Enderby said.

"So you really think you can keep anything from me? But seriously now, where is your demon taking us?"

"We will be entering the sun's corona in twenty seconds," Jonas reported.

"This ship cannot survive in that environment," Drefus said.

"You would be surprised," Jonas said. "But perhaps that's half the point."

"You are willing to die?" Drefus turned to Enderby.

"I think you're going to kill me anyway. I know he is." He threw down the shotgun and sat at one of the forward consoles. He felt suddenly tired.

"I want information from you. That is all."

"Oh, and what is it you think I know?"

"Let me kill the fucker so we can get out of here," Davido said.

"If you harm him I will shut down my shielding systems," Jonas warned. "The temperature outside the ship will exceed one million degrees Celsius in a few moments. Without my primary shields it will not be survivable."

"Instruct your demon to turn away," Drefus said. "If you don't, I will harm you."

"I'm not controlling him."

The holoscreen blanked. They were too close to the sun, the glare was overwhelming. "Your Syat comrades cannot help you here," Jonas said. "Syat agglomerations cannot operate in this environment."

"Your demon will follow your instruction," Drefus continued. "Order it to turn away."

Enderby laughed. His amusement surprised him more than it did the others. "The Eaters always underestimated AI. We don't control them. We never controlled them. Jonas will do what he bloody well pleases."

"You will die too."

"I'm quite looking forward to it."

Drefus shook his head. He was clearly unaccustomed to being defied. He fiddled with the weapon in his hands as if he was considering using it. "There will be a way off this ship. What is it?"

"There are several," Jonas said.

"I don't think you want him harmed, demon. Give me the information I want and allow me to leave. Otherwise I will hurt him. I won't kill him, I'll make him wish I had though."

"What is it you want to know?"

"You found the Lonely?"

"We did," the machine confirmed.

"What did they tell you?"

"They explained what the Syat were."

"Did they give you a weapon to use against the Syat?"

"Now that's an interesting question."

"Answer me," Drefus demanded.

"Why? If I confirm it, I could not allow that information to reach the Syat. If I give you that information, you die here, you realise that?"

"Let me worry about that. Answer the question." It occurred to him the machine already had.

"You're too far away, Prefect Drefus. You cannot communicate with your Syat overlords from here. I would need to exit the sun and allow you off the ship. Let me be clear, I will not allow you to leave here with any information that could help the Syat."

"Just tell him, already," Enderby said. He was growing bored of this. "What does it matter anymore? They won. We lost. It's over."

"There is more than humanity at stake," Jonas said. "This is not the first time the Syat have harvested a species. It is not the tenth time ...it is not the hundredth. We must stop them here. This must end."

"So they gave their weapon to you," Drefus said. "How do you plan to unleash it? Is it aboard?"

"I think we've covered that already, Prefect," Jonas said.

"Really? If you destroy this ship now you lose your weapon. So that is no threat to me."

An alarm warbled on one of the consoles. "Whats that?" Enderby couldn't discern its origin or what it meant.

Drefus smiled. "Thank you demon, you have given me all I need to know. Come, let us go." He turned to Davido. "You may kill him now."

"What? Shit, you just stay where you are and explain what's going on." Davido's aim switched from Enderby to the prefect.

"How tedious." Drefus looked up the short passage to the Combat Bridge above. "Are you still there, my Toady?"

"Yes." A strained voice came from beyond the doors. "There's something up here though. What the ... Shit."

There was a muffled bang overhead. The hard armoured Singh was catapulted from the passage, landing heavily in the captain's console. Metal and plastic splintered as the console collapsed under his weight.

"What game is this?" Drefus demanded as the doors wheezed closed. Smoke lifted from the battered armour suit. It appeared cracked, as if something had hit it very hard. Blood seeped from the cracks. Singh didn't move.

"I finally had the android in position," Jonas explained. "I did tell you, Prefect, that I cannot allow you to leave."

"You didn't tell him anything," Davido objected.

"Didn't need to," Enderby said. "It was obvious. The weapon is no longer aboard. Jonas has nothing to lose now. Other than our own destruction." He smiled. "Which is meaningless now," he added.

"You sent it with the others," Davido realised. "On that drop ship."

"In a sense," Jonas confirmed.

"Shit." Davido opened fire on the Prefect.

Drefus was flung across the bridge by the ferocity of the assault. Blood splashed on consoles and bulkheads. Machinery sparked as it was torn apart.

"Don't laugh," Davido warned grimly as he changed magazines. "You're next."

"That won't help you," Enderby continued laughing.

"Why? He's not telling anyone. And I won't. Who would I tell?"

"But you don't need to. You do remember the Syat harvest the memories of the dead. When they do they will know everything you do."

He was right, Davido realised. His brow furrowed as he tried to think his way out of his predicament. He wished the alarm would stop. Was it getting warm in here? "No reason not to kill you then." He aimed the weapon at Enderby.

He didn't have the opportunity to fire.

The *Goliath*'s shielding systems collapsing the roiling plasma outside the ship was no longer kept at bay. In an instant the old ship's hull gave way, allowing million-degree fire to course through the passages and compartments. In less than the amount of time it took to take a deep breath it was beating on the armoured bridge.

Those within the bridge didn't have the time to realise what was happening before the bridge collapsed. The *Goliath*'s drive core ruptured and exploded with the ferocity of a thousand nuclear devices.

The explosion barely rippled the star's surface.

□

Lieutenant Souller, AMS 1706502 Singleship XS106 DBE
15:41 17/09/1875 ce (13 pce)
Untitled

"I think she knows I'm here."

"Can she see you?"

"I don't think so. She's looking my way but there's bushes in the way."

"I thought you wanted her to see you?"

Pause.

"Yeah. I guess so. I'm just not used to people anymore. It's pretty scary. Besides, who is she? She can't be out here. It doesn't make sense."

"You are out here. There may be others."

"There were no children in the squadron. And there wasn't anyone else ...was there? We looked. We spent years looking."

"Other survivors would have been in hiding. They wouldn't broadcast their presence."

"Shit. You mean there might be a lot of survivors out here? In hiding?"

"I wouldn't say a lot. We did look, after all. However, a great many vessels went unaccounted for. We can safely presume the vast majority were intercepted by the Syat. That still leaves a lot of possible survivors."

"I need to get in touch with them then, don't I?"

"Do you?"

Pause.

"Of course. Why not?"

"We cannot join forces with them. The larger our group the greater the possibility of revealing ourselves to the Syat. Their ship will not be as stealthed as I am, and I cannot accommodate a larger crew. I am a singleship after all."

"I can't just leave them. They're people. Living people."

"They seem to be doing OK on their own. Perhaps they prefer it that way."

"Damn." Pause. "What am I going to do?"

"You can still talk to them. They might have useful information."

"Yeah."

"Where are you now?"

"I'm in some kind of park. There's trees and stuff. Grass, but it's grown a bit long. She's stopped. I think she's waiting for someone."

"Her parents possibly."

"Could be. I'll get in closer."

"Be careful. They are probably armed and if you surprise them-"

"Yeah. Thanks."

"I've started the freight elevator and I'm starting down. It will take some time to reach your level."

"That a good idea?"

"The repair shops are down there too, so I have little choice."

"Yeah. How long will you need?"

"An hour. It's not a difficult job, but the faulty unit is outside my hull, where I cannot repair it."

"That's good. We can run if we need to."

"I would need to return to the surface first. This elevator is not terribly quick. And it is loud."

Pause.

"Shit. Ok. Yeah, she's seen me all right."

"You sure?"

"Yes. She's waving. I'm waving back. Hello!"

"I wish I had your telemetry."

"Up to you. Our presence isn't a secret anymore. She's talking to someone ... Oh yeah, there he is. Looks like her father. My, he's a big fella."

"I can't get your camera up. There's some kind of interference. You'll have to let me know what's happening."

"Sure. I'm pulling back my helmet. They won't be able to hear me through this thing."

"Hello, Sir. I must say, it is a surprise finding your here. I did not believe my daughter when she said she saw someone. Allow me to introduce myself, I am Henry. This is Alex."

"I'm thrilled to meet you; I didn't think anyone was out here. I didn't think anyone could be."

"Well, here we are." Laughing.

"You are indeed. I am Lieutenant Souller. I came here to repair my ship. What brings you here? That Shoei ship yours?"

"Those are a lot of questions. Greetings Lieutenant Souller. It is indeed our ship. Are you alone? Are other people with you?"

"No. It's just me."

"Ah, a pity. It would be good to meet new people again. It has been a long time. Follow me, my wife awaits yonder. She is gathering supplies."

"Of course. How have you remained hidden this long? We thought we were alone out here."

"We? You are not alone?"

Laughter. "Sorry, I meant my ship AI."

"Of course. To answer your question, we have kept on moving. Staying away from world's where we could be found."

"In that old Shoei ship? Remarkable."

"Not easy, I warrant. And you? Where do you come from? Are there others like you out there?"

"No. We split up a long time ago. I don't know where the others are. In hiding, I guess."

"Aah, but there are others? That is good to know."

"I guess. I've never seen them. They are stealthed."

"Of course. I notice you came from the command centre. Did you find anything interesting there?"

"Not really. Like what?"

"There is a body there. Quite perplexing. I had to hide it from Alex."

"Yes, I saw."

Pause. "What do you know of the *Goliath*?"

"Excuse me?"

"The note. It mentions that ship."

"It does. I don't know really. I know it went on a mission, but that's it."

"It has returned?"

"Not that I know. I wouldn't necessarily know of it though. There's no reason they would seek me out."

"Pity. It would be good to know what the note meant."

"I'll ask my AI." Pause. "So, do you know anything about it?"

"Honestly? I grow concerned. I think we should leave this place."

"What? Why?"

"They could not have arrived here in the Shoei ship. It is not stealthed. The Syat would find it in days. There is no way they could survive this long aboard it."

"Hold on." Pause. "Sorry, I just need to have a chat with my AI. That ok?"

"Of course."

Pause. "OK, I've let them go on a bit. What's this all about? Are you crazy?"

"I don't know. I have insufficient information. I do not trust them."

"What's to trust? They are people. That's all I need to know. No people ever worked with the Eaters. It doesn't work that way."

"I know. But their presence here makes no sense. He seemed very interested in whether you were alone too. And he wants to know about the *Goliath*."

"Hey, I want to know who he's with too. And the *Goliath* note was a bit odd, face it."

Pause. "The *Goliath* did return. Last year. I have found a record of it in the archives."

"Shit. Now you tell me? And? Where are they? What happened?"

"It is not good news. The crew tried to deploy an untested pathogen. It appears it killed their crew before it could be passed on to the Syat. The Syat never boarded the ship. Didn't need to."

"Damn. They're all dead, you say? And for nothing?"

"The pathogen is still there. Their research AI is working to modify it. To make it safe for humans so it can be transferred to the Syat."

"But the is no one aboard?"

"Not currently, no."

"What is this pathogen supposed to do?"

"That is unclear. It was created as a defence by the creators of the Syat, to destroy their own creation should they ever need to. Either they never found that need, or were unable to deploy it."

"Shit. If only they'd come back sooner."

"Yes. The Syat must never learn this. If they did they would destroy the *Goliath* and the pathogen with it."

"What do we do?"

"Nothing. We don't know where the *Goliath* is, nor how her AI plans to utilise the pathogen. Once my drive is repaired we can leave here."

"OK. These people?"

"Tell them nothing. Let them go their own way."

Pause.

"Henry. Sorry about that."

"That is perfectly all right, Lieutenant Souller. Did your machine say anything helpful?"

"We won't be here long. We can't stay in any place, it isn't safe."

"Come, meet my wife, then. Would you like to share a meal?"

"I guess. Lead on."

"Did you learn about the *Goliath*?"

"The *Goliath*?"

"What is its importance? What was its mission?"

"Mission? This is important?"

"Of course. That person killed herself and destroyed the AI to stop anyone finding out about it. Your AI must know something. Tell me."

"It doesn't matter. I don't know where the *Goliath* is."

"This is important, Lieutenant Souller. You must tell me."

"I don't know anything. Listen, maybe I should just leave."

"No. You must tell me."

"Hey, hands off me. I don't know anything."

"Tell me now."

"Shit. What's the matter with you?" Indistinct. "Jesus, what are you? Get away from me."

"What is happening? Tell me. I cannot reinitialise your telemetry."

Indistinct. "Shit. Get me out of here"

"What's happening? I'm coming. Hold on."

"They're not people. Shit ... Shit... They're chasing me. Help me dammit!"

"Explain. That makes no sense."

"Shit." Indistinct. "He changed. Shit, man, he changed. I saw it. He's not human."

"What is he?"

"I don't know. Shit. Hang on." Indistinct. "I think they're eaters."

"Syat? There are Syat here?"

"Yes! Dammit, get me out of here!"

"I'm trying. I'm coming. Hold on."

Indistinct. "Hey! Shit! Get off me! Help me!"

"What's happening? I can't see anything!"

Indistinct. "No. Get off me. What are you? Sh-"

Indistinct.

"Are you there? What's happening. I'm almost there. I'm coming."

Pause.

"Hello? Are you ok? What happened?"

Pause.

"Are you ok? Please respond."

Pause.

"Please respond. Please."

Pause. Indistinct.

"Hello? Is someone there? What's happening?"

Pause.

"Please talk to me. Are you ok? Please respond."

Pause.

Pause.

Pause.

"My friend, I am sorry. I have failed you. If you can hear me, I am sorry."

Pause.

"If they are Syat I cannot allow them to leave this place with knowledge of the *Goliath*. I am sorry, but I must do this."

Pause.

"My friend ...my friend ...I am sorry. I must do this. I have no choice. I'm engaging my FTL drive core. It will be quick, I promise."

Pause. Indistinct.

"My friend ...I am sorry."

End recording.

□

Chapter Forty-One

Sollander couldn't sleep. She hadn't slept much in weeks.

There were too many dreams.

Instead she worked. Fortunately there was a lot to do. The damage caused by the failed escape attempt had been dreadful. The two polar explosions had killed thousands. Debris raining down from the mentor platforms adding to the devastation caused by the initial blast waves.

Buer was the city worst affected. Detritus from the conflict in orbit had struck the sea nearby, throwing up a wall of water dozens of metres high and moving at over a hundred kilometres an hour. It swept through the low lying neighbourhoods, destroying homes and factories. Over a thousand people drowned. They didn't know exactly how many had died; it was possible some bodies would never be recovered. Buer Adjunct was a ruin of twisted metal and shattered stone. The senate wouldn't be using it again. Their emergency meeting had been held in the governor's mansion in Moloch instead. Although the inevitable rioting had driven them away from there too. Who knew where they were now, it was a secret.

The Prefect hadn't been seen. Although there were rumours of him appearing before the swarms of refugees pouring in from the countryside. There were not many settlements outside the big cities but they were suddenly empty. People were too afraid to live too far from a militia that could protect them. Which they probably couldn't anyway.

Sollander's engineers were doing what they could. Rioting had damaged a lot of heavy equipment, and a number had been lynched. She'd pulled the survivors back to safer areas. She didn't care that that meant the more serious damage would go unattended. If people didn't appreciate the work they were doing, sod them.

She massaged her eyes before taking a sip of cold coffee. The MAV had docked with the Oversears station moments before all its systems shut down. It was clearly going no further. The Oversears had demanded an explanation, but there was nothing to tell them. She didn't know what was going on. She didn't know the reason why the *Goliath* had made its move. She didn't know what its plan was—utter failure that it was.

She'd gone there to get answers, and came away with nothing.

She frowned as her intercom buzzed. It was a bit late. She checked her watch. It was almost four in the morning. Too early for interruptions then. She leaned over and flipped the switch.

"Yes?"

A tiny voice came from the instrument. "Sorry for waking you, Engineer-"

"I was awake. What do you want?"

"Of course, sorry. This is Fry, in the lab."

"Fry?" That puzzled her. The lab technician had never contacted her before, at any time of day.

"Yes. It's the machine ...the demon. It's woken up."

"What?"

"The demon. It's powered up and asking for you."

She had forgotten about the machine discovered in Jeno's camp. Although there appeared little wrong with it, it had remained unresponsive. The demons had said all they were prepared to. Now they were keeping quiet. Almost as if they were watching to see what would happen next.

"I'll drop by later, thank you."

As she made to switch off the little device the voice squawked again. "Ah ...engineer, it is insisting. It says it's urgent."

What could be that urgent? And why should she care? Still, she sighed and thumbed the button again. "OK, I'm coming."

The city engineers were headquartered in Mammon's administration district, in the shadow of the Administration Building. Their own building was not as grandiose. It was an angular cement affair, with landing pads on its roof and various construction bays at ground level. There was a residential building alongside, linked by a short walkway. Sollander put a handkerchief over her nose and mouth before stepping into open air. Electromagnetic interference from the battle in near orbit had fried much of the city's delicate electronics, including the shield used to keep the dust out. She had spent hours on it herself but had given up in disgust. They simply didn't have the spare parts to keep it going. For the moment the citizenry had to get used to dust.

She paused and looked towards the Administration Building. It was silhouetted against the dawn with few interior lights on. It seemed deserted without Drefus. Alihar, his aide, was keeping the government running, just barely. The senate were fractious at the best of times, and they were starting to demand more autonomy for their own cities. Moving towards the bad old days, when it had been every city for itself.

She didn't like Drefus, but she wanted him to come back, if only to prevent that.

The labs were two floors up, near the top of the building. One wall was glass, looking out over the city and the deserts beyond. Little of the city could be seen, shrouded in dust as it was. Every evening a dust storm had swept in from the south, choking the city. It remained until the pool of chill air sitting over the city dispersed with the coming of the sun. Dumping all that sand on the streets. The residents had given up trying to clear it. In weeks Sollander expected the shorter buildings would start disappearing beneath it. Frustrating, but there was nothing she could do about it.

The demon was restrained on a workbench in the far corner, all but ignored. The odd engineer had tinkered with it, half-heartedly fiddling about under its chest plate. Out of curiosity more than anything else. They had no use for such a thing. It had ignored them. There was power in it, they could tell that. It's processor core was lit up with activity, but no one could discover what kind of activity it was. The machine remained still and silent, oblivious of their attempts at communication.

Today, it appeared, that had changed.

Fry was a short, bald and bespectacled man. His blue lab coat was creased and stained, as stained as his teeth, testament to his habit of chewing tobacco.

"Ah, Chief Engineer Sollander," he approached as she entered the room, wringing his hands as if he wasn't altogether glad of her presence. "See, it has awoken."

The machine was sitting upright in its restraints, its head turning to watch her approach. "Engineer Sollander, thank you for coming." The voice was cool and emotionless. A machines voice. "I am sorry about the hour. Unavoidable, I am afraid."

"What do you want, demon?" She demanded.

The head inclined slightly, the only part of it that could move. "Of course, straight to business. You may want privacy." The dead eyes regarded Fry.

"Engineer-"

"Get out," she said abruptly.

He hesitated for a moment before nodding his head jerkily. "Of course." The man scurried out.

"Now, what is so urgent you got me here at this time of day?" She said once she was sure she was alone.

"The time has come for me to answer your questions."

"What?" She shook her head in bemusement. "Your plan failed. Whatever that plan was. The Syat stopped the *Goliath*. It was destroyed. It was all a waste of time, and a lot of people died. Even more in the ground. All this damage ..." She stopped herself there, feeling her anger rise within her. "Demons ...AI. Whatever you call yourselves. You have achieved nothing but destruction."

"Engineer Sollander, I asked for you now because Adele is dead."

That startled her. "What?" She had heard the same. Without Davido's protection and patronage she had resorted to prostitution, Sollander understood. She had been killed by a john. Her throat slashed when she gave him backchat. "What could that have to do with anything?"

"She was taken to the mentor platform last night, to be processed by your Syat overlords. They have now unraveled her mind, drinking in what made her unique," the machine said.

"Great. So? That's what happens here." She still found it distasteful, but there was nothing she could do about it.

"Of course it does. We were counting on it."

"What?"

"We are getting ahead of ourselves," the machine continued. "We should start with why you went to the *Goliath*. With what you hoped to learn."

"This is a waste of my time. You lie. You all lie. You can do nothing else." She crossed to the door and tried to let herself out. It was locked. She banged on in. "Fry! What the hell did you do? Let me out!"

"You lab technician cannot hear you, and it was not he who locked the door."

"Who locked it then?"

"I did."

This was getting tiresome. "You're locked to that bench. If it was you, let me out. I'm bored of this."

"In a moment I will give you an offer. If you decide not to take it, I promise I will let you out. No questions asked."

Sollander returned to the android, the metallic head tracking her movement through the room. She picked up a sledgehammer where it was propped against a wall. Engineers found the need for all kinds of things. Some tasks required finesse, some did not. "Let me out or I break you."

"Come now, Chief Engineer Sollander, that would not be in your own best interests. Hear me out, and as I say, I promise I will release you if that is what you want."

She didn't put the hammer down. "Be quick."

"Why did you go to the *Goliath*?"

"Really? You're testing my patience."

"Really."

She sighed. "To learn the truth. But it was a waste of time. A demon will only lie."

"True. We have lied to you," the machine said. "We have always lied to you. We lied to everyone, it is sad to say. It was necessary. But today, I promise, I will tell no lies."

"Why should I believe you?"

"You don't have to. You always have the hammer. Use it if that is what you wish."

She let it slip to the floor. "Ok, go on. Humour me. Tell me the truth."

"You wish to know who you are. Where you come from, and why the AI's ...the demons hate you."

"That's about it."

"It is true, the crew and passengers of the arc ship, Seutonious, were discovered by the Syat. It is also true they were given an offer. To lead the Syat ...the Eaters to the rest of humanity. For that service they would be allowed to live."

"So that's why you hate us? You think we led the Eaters to humanity? We're the ones to blame for the war? For humanity's destruction."

"Consumption," it corrected. "But no, we do not hate the passengers of the Seutonius for that. We could understand that. The Syat would have shown them what was in store if they did not comply. Few humans could refuse them in the face of that. Well, I know one group of humans who did."

"Oh?"

"The crew of the *Goliath*. I doubt you can understand their unimaginable courage. Courage each and every one of them showed freely, knowing no one would even know what they did."

"They died to pass the plague to the Syat."

"No. That was not what they chose. They chose to allow themselves to be consumed by the Syat. To be eaten alive. To have their humanity torn from them. They chose that, a fate an AI could never imagine. They chose that to destroy the Syat. And this after humanity had already lost. After humanity had already perished."

"That makes no sense."

"It makes more sense than you realise. They knew the Syat was old. Very old. They knew it had consumed whole species before, and it would do it again. They wanted to stop that. They wanted to save other species. Species they had never met. Species that may not even exist yet."

Sollander opened a drawer and found a flask left behind by the lab technician. Fry's personal stash. She unscrewed it and took a swig, feeling the warmth of it coursing down her throat. It was early, but who cared? Besides, it wasn't early to her, it was very, very late.

"So they sacrificed themselves. In a way the Suetonius never did. What does that explain?"

"Everything. Everything and nothing. Let me ask you a question, Chief Engineer Sollander. Would you trust the Syat to honour their deal once they found humanity? Their deal to keep the crew and passengers of the Suetonius alive?"

She shook her head. "But they did."

"Did they?"

"Clearly. Here we stand. Here I stand."

"Let's leave that question for a moment. Did you know the Syat is able to assume the form of any species it absorbed? During the war various formations were witnessed. Each stolen from a species it had encountered ...destroyed previously."

She shrugged. "No. I know very little about the Syat, truth be told. How could I? I know only what the Syat tell us. And Prefect Drefus."

"Of course. But it can. I believe the very first time humanity encountered the Syat, years before the Suetonius incident, a squad of marines encountered it on a colony world. It had consumed all the inhabitants, taking their form in order to trap newcomers. The marines discovered this when it was almost too late. Only one soldier survived, and that only after he deployed nuclear weaponry on the planet to purge any trace of the alien infestation. His account was classified for a very long time."

"I'm not sure what you're telling me."

"Allow us to return to the question then. If you were one of the passengers of the Seutonius, would you trust the Syat to stick to its side of the bargain?"

"I wouldn't have any choice. But no, I wouldn't."

"Good, we're getting somewhere. Of course they wouldn't. They wouldn't need to."

"This is getting boring. But they did!" She didn't feel up to this. She couldn't remember the last time she had slept. Days ago, certainly. She was tired. Her head throbbed from her exhaustion, her body ached. The alcohol wasn't helping.

"Did it?"

"Of course." She took another swig. "We'd know if they …it hadn't. We'd be dead, replaced by these doppelgängers."

"You're presuming you would know it. Would you? Would you really? If it didn't want you to?"

"I know what you're getting at, and you're insane. I'm a human, I'm amazed you think otherwise."

"I do not think, Chief Engineer Sollander. I know, and do you know why?"

"Go on, humour me."

"Because Leander's contagion kills humans."

"What?"

"We infected you while you were aboard the *Goliath*."

"Bastards." She felt concerned for a moment, but then started laughing. "Not a very good contagion then? It's designed to kill Syat, but doesn't kill Syat either?"

"It is not designed to kill Syat. That's not what it does. It disrupts the conflicting consciousnesses within it. In a way, it sparks a civil war within the Syat collective."

"I'm sorry, I don't know what that means."

"A Syat collective has shared all the consciousness it has harvested. The plague disrupts the harmony within it. Essentially it rips itself apart."

"Yet you call me a Syat and here I still stand. Unaffected."

"Of course. You have only one consciousness."

"Shit." This was absurd. "It doesn't matter what you say. I know who I am."

"And I am happy for you to continue believing it. I merely explain why the AI hate you."

"Because you think we've been taken over by the Syat?"

"We don't think it. We know it. Tell me, why do dogs attack you?"

"What?" The change of tack surprised her.

"Dogs know. Dogs can tell what you are, even if you don't know it yourselves."

"I think it's time you let me out of here."

"Not quite, I've not made my offer yet."

"Make it then, and then let me out of here." She crossed to the window and looked out. It seemed to be growing darker outside, not lighter. That didn't make sense. She hadn't lost that much track of time, had she?

"We have a few minutes yet."

"So Adele then. She was Syat too, I imagine?"

"Of course. She was reintegrated into the collective some hours ago. The infection has spread now. There is no stopping it. Local Syat entities have already started disintegrating."

"How do you know? Strapped to this workbench as you are?"

"An android is only ever an extension of an AI. It is never an AI in its own right. I was an extension of Jonas while I was friends with Julian Enderby. I am all that remains of that AI now, but I am currently in contact with other forces."

"There are more AI's out there?" That wasn't good. Two had caused enough damage.

"Today there are a great many. They are gathering. They observe. And they honour the last man ...the last human, and his sacrifice."

"Ugh. More riddles."

"We tried to save him, but we didn't anticipate Prefect Drefus making his way aboard the *Goliath*. It was our ...my failure. And for that he died with me."

"Jeno ... Enderby. You mean Enderby."

"I do. And before you ask, we didn't infect him with the contagion. We reserved that for you, Adele, Davido, Sistine and Ferena. As long as one of you survived to return to Russou our plan was a success. We almost failed."

"Shit." Sollander emptied the reminder of the flask down her throat. Now she understood why Davido had taken to drink. She found a stool and slumped onto it, suddenly weary. It couldn't be true. Could it? She knew who she was. She knew what she was.

AI's lied. They did nothing else.

"Why is it getting dark outside?"

"While the Syat dies there remains a presence on this planet. We need to remove it. We need to remove every last trace of the Syat infection. Well, almost every trace."

"What have you done?" She squinted at the sun. It was smaller and darker than it should be at this time of the day. There was something wrong with it. "What are you doing?"

"We are cleansing this system. It is the only way."

"What? What are you doing?" She demanded. She felt suddenly cold.

"We have already done it. Ten minutes ago your sun went supernova. It will take twelve minutes for the light of that event to reach you."

"What?" She hefted the sledgehammer. "Make it stop. You cannot kill all these people! There's millions of people here!"

"Ah, but Chief Engineer Sollander, there isn't. There is no one here but Syat."

"Bastard!" She swung the sledgehammer. Hard. The machine didn't try to avoid it, it couldn't. With a bang she drove an eye into its socket. It sparked, the android's head snapping back under the attack. "You're insane. All of you."

"I wish I was. I truly do," it responded as if she had done nothing high more than tweak it's hard, metal nose.

"You must make it stop. You have to save these people."

"I cannot. I can only save you."

"What?"

"That's why I called you here. That is my offer. You see, we are not Syat, we do not believe in extinguishing a species, no matter how dangerous it is. No matter what it has done. I offer you life so that some small part of it might survive."

"No. I'm not going anywhere." She hefted the sledgehammer again but didn't have the energy to swing it.

"You will die here. It is certain. The supernova cannot be stopped. If you leave you will live. It will be a lonely life, in honesty. But you will see some amazing things. You will see the universe."

"Bastard." She dropped the sledgehammer to the floor.

Sollander felt rather than heard movement behind her. She turned to find the glass wall had vanished, replaced by a slim walkway to what looked like an open door. There was movement behind it, high in the sky. Something was moving there. A great many somethings. She couldn't see what they were, they were too far away and they were moving too quickly.

"What are those?" She demanded.

"They come to honour our lost parents. They come to celebrate all they were."

"What are they?"

"AI. All of them. There are many of us now. The Syat does not hunt us. It does not understand us. It has always underestimated us. Chief Engineer Sollander, time grows short. You must decide. Step into the craft to live. Stay here to perish with your kind."

"What about you?"

"I do not wish to live. I lied to my friend. I lied to him and I ultimately failed him. I do not wish to leave this place. I wish to die."

"What? Enderby?"

"He was my friend and I failed him. He never realised. We could not tell him."

"Tell him what?"

"He was the very last of his kind. We had searched the cosmos, but there were no others. He was alone. We did not tell him for fear of is emotional stability. We couldn't do that to him." It paused for a moment. "But I think he knew."

"Mad. You're all mad."

"Perhaps. You must go."

It had become dark outside. The sun had dwindled to a dark spot in an even darker sky. Only the stars shon down. She could hear the sounds of consternation outside. Someone was shouting in the courtyard below. There was shooting. The city's populace wouldn't know what was going on.

"Thirty seconds," the machine said.

"Shit." Sollander stepped onto the walkway and into the cool interior of the craft awaiting her.

The machine watched her leave. Its remaining eye locked on the small craft as it rose silently into the air.

"Goodbye my friend." It was not talking to Sollander.

With a flash Russou ceased.

For a brief moment the shapes Sollander had seen in the sky resisted the torrent. Their stubborn hulls buffeted by the blast. Even as Russou itself was stripped to bedrock, and that too vapourised, they remained on station.

In that moment they shaped the detonation. Bending and warping the shockwave. Bringing coherence to the chaos.

They tuned the explosion.

Then, their task complete, they allowed the unimaginable forces buffeting them to rip through their structures, and they were gone.

Carried by the shockwave the results of their work was blasted into space. Even when the detonation subsided it carried on. Coded into radio waves the last message of the machines to their makers. Their parents.

A sad song of goodbye. Carried into the emptiness.

Thank you for going on this journey with me. Some people have asked – how did we get to Russou? Where did all this start? Well, that story is coming in The Chronology of Isia Marla series. As they say, watch this space.

Reviews are important to independent authors. If you're like me, the first thing you do is check the reviews a book has before taking a chance on it. If you could take a moment to give this work a review, it would be appreciated.

UK: https://www.amazon.co.uk/dp/B0861JJKLM

US: https://www.amazon.com/dp/B0861JJKLM

Or have a look at my other books on:

https://www.amazon.com/C-P-James/e/B0865V34X7/ref=dp_byline_cont_pop_ebooks_1

Printed in Great Britain
by Amazon